D1367629

Thou hast multiplied thy merchants
above the stars of heaven...
Nahum 3:16 KJV

Also by Keith Clemons:

If I Should Die

When Glory Rises

ABOVE THE STARS

by Keith Clemons

For information write:
George Colton Publishing, Inc.
PO Box 375, Orangeville,
ON. Canada L9W 2Z7

Churches, schools, charities, and other not for profit organizations may acquire George Colton books by writing to the above attn: Ministerial Markets Department.

This book is a work of fiction. The characters, incidents, and dialogues are products of the author's imagination and are not to be construed as real. Any resemblance to actual events or persons, living or dead, is entirely coincidental.

National Library of Canada Cataloging in Publication

Clemons, Keith, 1949-
Above the Stars / Keith Clemons.

ISBN 0-9731048-1-3

I. Title.

PS3603.L44A63 2004 813'.6 C2003-906413-1

Printed and bound in Canada

First Edition

04 05 06 07 08 09 10 - 10 9 8 7 6 5 4 3 2 1

Dedication

To my Mother and Father, Walter and Norma Clemons, who raised me on Biblical principles and sound advice, and then faithfully prayed for my safe passage through those tempestuous and rebellious teenage years, until I found my way back to God's throne of grace.

And to Kathryn, my wife, who, with patience, encouragement and love, has enabled me to achieve more than I ever dreamed possible.

Acknowledgements

I am grateful for men like Michael Medved and Ted Baehr, who, through their individual ministries, have taken a stand against the decline of virtue in the television and film industry. If the ideas they espouse have crept into this manuscript, I consider myself in their debt, for I know their efforts make the airwaves safe for children of all ages.

An unedited book is like a gem in the rough, it may have intrinsic value, but it doesn't truly shine until it's cut and polished. Thus, I want to acknowledge my editor, Anne Severance, who is good not only at spotting technical flaws, but also has a sensitive ear for the way words sound, and an eye for the visual images they create.

Similarly, you may not be able to tell a book by its cover, but without a good cover, few will drawn to the book to evaluate what's inside. Thus, I want to express my thanks to Laurie Smith of AA Graphic Design for her many hours at creating this book's cover, as well as the professional design of the layout and text.

Last, but certainly not least, is my friend Rod Hembree, pastor of Good Friends Fellowship and host of Television's "Quick Study" Bible broadcast, whose all-consuming love of Christ is a constant source of inspiration. Thank you, Rod, for providing me with an example of what it's like to live, day-by-day, through faith in God alone.

Soli Deo Gloria

ONE

The sun looks like the yolk of an egg sizzling sunny side up on the white hot pan of the sky.

THIS IS the sun of Posada—a time-forgotten village nestled deep in the mountains of Mexico like an undiscovered emerald resting in folds of velvet green. Here, in the Sierra Madre del Sur, the jungle is so dense mountain lion and puma prowl within thirty feet of the village without being seen. Only sound escapes: the cry of the scarlet macaw, the whoosh of water tumbling over white waterfalls, and the rumbling of the wind in the trees. Outcrops of granite rise up to form a basin in which the town sits, but to the west, where the village stands at the edge of a vertical drop, Posada is open. Through this portal the Pacific can be seen shimmering thousands of feet below, and evening shades of orange and magenta, violet, rose and blue, offer a view of the sunset rivaling any to be seen in the western world.

Lonnie stands at the cliff's jagged edge observing the town's ebb and flow. This is his place, the one plot of land on the whole of planet earth uniquely designed for him. He likes to think the heavens opened and dropped him here, in the present, erasing the enigma of his past. He is part of Posada, the soil his flesh, the rock his bone, and the vines his sinew and muscle. His soul and the soul of the village are inseparably intertwined.

He breathes deeply, not to relax, but to squeeze air from the thick humidity, the curious habit of a white man. He wears the muslin of a village peasant, dripping with sweat, but his sandy blond hair and blue eyes stand out in stark contrast to the indigenous people around him. Lonnie's own skin is tan as leather, but it will never be as brown as the natives. God has blessed the Indians with a special covering that shields them from the burning sun. Lonnie breathes the heavy air, like molasses in his lungs, and scratches under his beard where moisture is causing an itch. The heat and humidity are unbearable, but he loves the heat.

More, he loves the consistency, the predictability, the security of knowing that as surely as the sun rises, one breath will lead to the next and his life, every facet of it, will continue unchanged. Today is like yesterday. Tomorrow will be the same. The sun beats down on the hot cobblestones of the town's only road, just as it has for centuries, just as it will for centuries to come.

The natives don't seem to notice how isolated they are from the rest of the world—Posada is a village of four thousand souls and one telephone—nor do they seem to notice the intensity of the beauty that surrounds them. They go about their business, growing and harvesting coffee beans for the local plantation, while their half-naked children run around chasing chickens, playing catch me if you can. And this, too, Lonnie loves.

A narrow lane divides the village into equal halves, except in the center where the road widens into a broad circular plaza with a fountain, known as the market. A man moves slowly across the plaza, taking languid, patient strides. He wears the vestments of a Franciscan monk. His brown robe is girded about his waist with a short piece of braided hemp. He is tall and lean, and were it not for his clerical garb, he would blend with the Indian population unnoticed. Lonnie raises his hand in greeting, jumps down from his rocky perch, and runs to join his friend, his sandals flapping against the hard-packed earth, lifting clouds of dust.

"Hola, Padre," he says. They turn and wander through the market together, skirting the baked adobe huts, watching the brown backs of the children at play.

Father Ceylon places his hands behind his back as he walks. "It is a marvelous thing you do for the people, Señor," he says.

"Thank you, Father. By the way, I was speaking with the foreman this morning. He thinks we're about a month away from moving in."

The father smiles, his white teeth bright against his swarthy complexion. "We must declare a holiday," he ventures. "We must have a fiesta. People from all over will come to see the opening. You will be the guest of honor, Señor Lonnie."

"I'll be here, I promise you that, but I won't be the guest of honor. This is a work of God."

Out across the open circular plaza, the two men see the hospital nearing completion. Bare-chested men in Levis and steel-toed boots, with wide belts that dangle hammers and screwdrivers, carry flats of drywall across the dusty ground. Already much of the medical equipment has begun to arrive. They've had to store it under large plastic sheets in the rough unfinished quarters of the main floor. Lonnie pauses, taking it all in. This is his third and most ambitious project to date. An orphanage and a homeless shelter already stand on either side of the new construction.

Two churches preside over opposite ends of the plaza. St. Christopher's is a large, white adobe structure, with porticoes and arches and walkways made of brick. Inside, an altar of gold leaf is surrounded by paintings depicting Christ's birth, death, and ascension into heaven. The sanctuary glows in the soft, playful light of seventy candles that continually burn with the prayers of the saints—a sweet smelling savor unto God. The building could be a hundred years old but, under fresh coats of whitewash, looks as good as the day it was built. It is a Catholic cathedral and is under the administration of Father Paulo Ceylon.

Lonnie's own church, a boxlike structure made of cinder blocks painted white, is modest by comparison, but sufficient to meet the needs of the small Protestant community. The building's peaked roof supports a crude wooden cross. Lonnie used his own money to build the church. He'd used his own money to build the orphanage and the homeless shelter too. And he's funding the hospital project. But it's a cooperative effort; the Sisters of Mercy have volunteered to provide the nursing staff. The money is the easy part. Lonnie often wonders why God has blessed him with such great wealth, when money is something he cares so little about.

Behind them the men hear the rumble of an approaching vehicle. They turn to see wheels sweeping up a cloud of grit from the cobblestones. The Jeep squeals to a stop. Lonnie recognizes the driver as a courier from Pochutla, a city twenty miles down the mountain. The man earns his living making deliveries between the dozens of remote mountain villages nestled in the Sierra Madre del Sur and the larger cities down along the coast. The driver climbs out over a door that seems permanently rusted shut.

"Hola, Eduardo," Lonnie says, greeting the man.

"Hola, Señor Lonnie, I have something for you. Important, I think. They pay me double extra to get it here muy pronto." The man hands Lonnie an envelope. It is stamped with red letters reading: "High Priority—Rush."

Lonnie feels the prickly sweat at the back of his neck. His heart begins to race, and his fingers to tremble. A premonition looms large, like an omen of evil to come. The envelope is addressed by hand, with a U.S. courier's stamp affixed. The stamp indicates that the letter originated in Malibu, California. His apprehension tightens like a fist inside his stomach. Nothing good ever comes out of Malibu. As his fingers play along the edge of the envelope, he has the unsettling feeling that his life is about to change.

Father Ceylon looks at Lonnie, observing his deeply tanned face turning white. His forehead furrows with concern. "What is it, Señor?"

"I'm not sure." Lonnie uses his fingernail to lift the flap. In the humid weather, the glue separates easily. He slips the letter out and shakes it open. One quick glance confirms his suspicions. It's worse than he thought.

The message is short and to the point. It reads: "Lonnie, you must come home. Your brother is dying. He wants you here. Please, let bygones be bygones. It's urgent you come home—now."

The letter is signed: Trudy Striker.

TWO

LONNIE PASSED the letter to Father Ceylon, who took it and held it out at arm's length, the big sleeves of his brown frock sagging around his elbows. He tromboned it back and forth until he was able to focus. Lonnie could see the thin veil of moisture on the man's forehead, shining and slick in the noonday light. It was no small sacrifice to wear that robe under such a warm sun. Lonnie was glad his denomination did not require a sacramental garment. But the good father never complained, nor did he ever appear without the vestment. It was part of his calling, a sacrifice of comfort made unto Christ. When Paulo finished reading, he paused and looked into Lonnie's eyes. "I did not know you had a brother, Señor," he said.

Lonnie shifted uneasily, scratching under his beard. "I don't," he answered. "Not really. I mean I do, but not in the real sense of the word. I hardly know the man. Harlan was raised by Buddy, and I was raised by Mom. At least until Mom died. Then I went to live with Buddy, too, but only for a year."

Father Ceylon raised an eyebrow.

"Sorry. Buddy was my father. He insisted we use his name. He said calling him Dad made him feel old. Anyway, after high school, I came down here to work among the Indians."

The priest nodded. "So you ran away."

Lonnie grimaced. "No. I wanted to be a missionary before I went to live with Harlan and Buddy. Mom was a devout Christian. She raised me right. Besides, Buddy's dead and Harlan and I have nothing in common. I've never had a reason to go back. That's the first I've heard of him in twenty years."

Father Ceylon turned, placing his hands behind his back as he took a step forward, Lonnie at his side. His fingers flicked the letter in his hand. Swallows darted in and out, collecting mosquitoes on the fly. He drew in a slow breath. The air was filled with the sweet smell of jungle humus. Several of the children had stopped playing and were now surrounding the town fountain, pumping the long iron handle to get a drink. The priest's eyes narrowed meditatively. He pursed his lips. They took three more measured steps before Father Ceylon finally spoke: "What do you intend to do?"

Lonnie glanced at the hospital, saw the shirtless brown-skinned workers and the children splashing in the water to cool themselves. They were his responsibility. "I can't leave. I'm needed here. What's the point of going home just to watch Harlan die. We haven't spoken in twenty years. I don't know. What do you think?"

"I think you are a servant of God. I think you should do what God wants you to do."

Ouch! Father Ceylon wasn't known for pulling punches. What *did* God want? It would seem He usually asked his servants to take the more difficult path, to suffer for Christ, to *forgive and forget.* Lonnie could forgive but he would never forget. Sometimes God asked too much. "Then you think I should go?"

"I only said you should do as God wills. If you feel this is what He would have you do, then yes, you should go." Father Ceylon handed the letter back to Lonnie. "Don't worry about the hospital or about your flock. If God wants you to go, He'll manage your affairs while you're away."

The children went squealing off across the plaza. Eduardo was sitting in his rusty Jeep with the engine running. He only made two trips a week, and there was no other way down the mountain. It was now or never. Lonnie had little to pack. Whatever he needed could be tossed into a duffel bag in minutes.

"Then let it be as God wills," Lonnie said. "I think I see my ride. Adios, my friend." He embraced Father Ceylon. "I'll call and let Don Alexandro know when I've arrived." He turned and raced off in the direction of Eduardo, who was grinding metal as he tried to get the jeep in gear. He caught him just as he was beginning to pull away.

LONNIE STEPPED out of the cab and paid the driver, hefting his duffel bag over his shoulder. He had caught a five A.M. flight out of Huatulco International Airport so, except for those few uncomfortable moments he'd been able to doze while waiting, he'd been awake all night. His long hair was matted and oily. He tried to comb it with his fingers but it was like trying to untangle a clump of wet grass. He'd changed out of his white muslin pants into Levis, just to look more civilized, but they were soiled from the dusty ride down the mountain, and itchy, and his collarless muslin shirt stuck to his chest. He stood in front of his brother's swank, ocean-view residence in his sandaled feet, feeling like a village vagrant. His eyes were wino red, and blurry from lack of sleep.

Judging from the house, Harlan had done well, though Lonnie would never say so publicly. It would be tantamount to admitting his brother was right. Besides, money couldn't buy taste. The building was a massive monstrosity painted champagne-pink with white trim, almost as big as the hospital Lonnie was trying to build—only this was a monument to vanity and waste. The roof was covered with half moon Spanish tiles and the front was graced with rows of tall, vertical windows. The house was set a fair distance back on the property. An iron gate blocked access. Looking through the bars, Lonnie could see the driveway circled a fountain before returning to the street.

Well, they had a fountain in Posada, too, didn't they? Only not like this. The fountain in Posada was used by the villagers to fill wood buckets and clay jars with the water they would need for the day. An iron-handled pump drew the water up. The overflow fell back into a huge bowl at the fountain's base where the water collected and turned green with algae, providing a cistern from which dogs and burros drank.

This fountain was designed with sculpted flutes and vases and marble fish that spewed smooth arcs of crystal blue water from their mouths. *Pure unadulterated waste.* Bordering the driveway on both sides were palm trees, their fronds waving in the turquoise morning sky. The entire estate was surrounded by a brick and iron fence. Shrubbery planted in front of the bars preserved the resident's privacy. The lawn was freshly manicured. Cotton clouds billowing overhead enhanced the flight of a dozen white seagulls playing on the breeze. Lonnie could hear the surf pounding somewhere in the distance.

He tried the gate but it was locked. He walked to the edge of the driveway where an intercom was mounted on a steel post at car window height, but before pushing the button he spotted another iron gate, this one smaller and covered with ivy, off to the left. It appeared to be slightly ajar. There was a small sign wired to the fence and another intercom. He pushed, and the gate gave way with the creak of iron hinges to reveal a paving stone path that meandered down toward the house. Lonnie closed the gate behind him with a loud *clang* and heard it snap shut. When he tried it again, it wouldn't budge. *Shouldn't have been open in the first place.* He pulled his bag over his shoulder and walked past the glorious fountain to the front door.

He drew in a calming breath as he mounted the wide porch bordered by rails of twisted black iron. Each footstep felt heaver than the one before. He set his duffel bag down. The air held the briny smell of the ocean. He rolled his shoulders and shook his head. His stomach filled with gaseous bubbles. His heart thudded against the walls of his chest. The doors were huge, at least half again as tall as he was. They appeared to be solid oak. He searched for a doorbell, but didn't see one, which he thought odd until he realized people were expected to announce themselves at the gate. Too late for that. He gave a loud rap on the wood and waited. No one answered. He tried again. *And again.* Yanking his duffel bag up over his shoulder, he took a step back, assuming everyone had gone to the hospital, and wondering how he could find out where that was, when the door opened.

And there stood Trudy—just the way he remembered her. Smooth, almost creamy skin, with those dark green eyes and that wavy auburn hair, thick and luxurious, worn collar length with a slight flip at the end. She was tall of stature, thin, and poised. He tried to speak, but his heart melted in his throat, blocking his words.

The green eyes turned cold, and the creamy face flushed pink. "How did you get in?" she demanded. "Didn't you read the sign? Please, go, before I call the police." She tried to slam the door, but Lonnie put out his hand.

"Trudy! It's me, Lonnie."

The woman froze, her fingers locked on the doorknob. Her mouth opened, then closed. Her eyes narrowed. "Lonnie?"

Lonnie set his bag down and slipped his hand into his pocket, retrieving the letter. He held it out. "You asked me to come. I know how it looks, but if you let me in, I can explain. I left the minute I got your note. I didn't have time to change."

Trudy continued to stare, but her face began to relax and she stood back, opening the door. "Lonnie. I'm so sorry. Please come in."

Lonnie stepped over the threshold. The foyer was magnificent, a circular room with a resplendent crystal chandelier overhead. On the left and right, paintings, bigger than life, adorned the walls. One was the portrait of a man, the other of a woman. The dark-haired man wore an English riding outfit, with a coiled whip at his side. His handsome chiseled features dominated the pastoral background exuding an air of intimidating strength. The woman was a green-eyed, auburn-haired maiden wearing a gown of white lace. In her hands was a bouquet of spring flowers tied with a ribbon. It puzzled Lonnie that Harlan and Trudy would want such narcissistic likenesses of themselves on display.

Beyond the anteroom, Lonnie could see a parlor with another crystal chandelier. Two broad staircases, one on either side, swept up to a balcony with a railing that circled the entire space. Through a vaulted archway the second room flowed into a third that was furnished with chairs and couches covered in white linen. The back of the room was a wall of glass panels that overlooked the ocean. If the wealth of this world counted for anything, his brother had it all, just as he'd predicted. Lonnie turned to address Trudy again. "How's Harlan doing? Your letter made it sound like he was in pretty bad shape."

"Why don't you come in and sit down," she said. She turned and led the way into the parlor. Music played brightly in the background. "Can I fix you a drink? Name your poison; we've got just about everything."

"Never touch the stuff," Lonnie responded, his smile coy, as he gave his shoulders a shrug.

Trudy raised an eyebrow. She went to the bar, an ebony black polished cabinet with a black marble top, and reached below the counter to lower the volume of the stereo. She fetched a long-stemmed glass, one that appeared, from the red lipstick on the rim, to have already been used. She reached for the bottle of vodka sitting on the counter, poured, and then eyed Lonnie. "Sit down. Make yourself comfortable." She added a jigger of vermouth, stirred, tossed her swizzle stick into the trash, and stabbed a green olive with a toothpick, placing it in her glass.

But Lonnie continued to stand. "Actually, I apologize if this seems rude, but I was wondering if I could freshen up somewhere, and then maybe lie down for a few minutes. I couldn't get a plane out until five A.M. I've been up all night. I need a little shut-eye before I visit Harlan—only about an hour. I'd like to see him as soon as possible. I assume he's in the hospital."

"You're too late, Lonnie. Harlan's already gone. He died Saturday. The doctor thought he might hang on another few days, but he went just like that. The funeral's at three o'clock today, with the viewing at two."

Lonnie folded his arms, slowly shaking his head. He'd wasted a pile of money on an airline ticket—*for what?* His lips puckered. Oddly, he now found himself feeling disappointed. *Why?* It wasn't as if he expected some kind of warm family reunion. No, what he'd expected was confrontation. He should be feeling relieved. After all, now he could avoid further resentment. But he knew the answer. He felt let down. He'd actually dared to hope that Harlan, with his dying breath, would beg his forgiveness.

"I...ah, well, I have a favor to ask," Trudy continued. "I know you just got here, but I promised Harlan, if you made it on time, I'd ask you to conduct the service. I know I'm putting you on the spot, and if you refuse, I'll understand. But Harlan said it was important to him."

Conduct the service...pontificate on Harlan's benevolence, his kindness, his charity, his brotherly love? Not in this life...not for him...but for Trudy? She stood there waiting for his answer, drowning in her sorrow, *poor, miserable, wretched, dumb, and blind...*not for him, but for her. "Of course," Lonnie said, "don't give it another thought. I assume you have people lined up to give eulogies."

Trudy nodded and took a sip of her martini. Now he understood why she was drinking so early in the day. She was trying to dull her grief. *Poor kid.* "I'm sorry I missed him. It seems kind of a waste to come all this way and not get to say even a parting word. But I guess there's nothing to do about it now. Could you show me to my room? I think I should rest for a few minutes. I'll need my strength to get through the afternoon."

"Certainly," Trudy said. She took another hurried sip and set her martini glass down on the black marble bar with a dull *clink.* "Follow me."

LONNIE STOOD looking at himself in the full-length mirror. No wonder she had taken him for a vagrant. It suddenly dawned on him that he had to buy a suit, and that he needed time to have it tailored. He couldn't take a nap. He barely had time for a shower. He slipped out of his shirt and tossed it on the bed. Harlan had done it again. He'd somehow managed the last hurrah. He'd slipped into eternity without having to explain himself, leaving Lonnie to forever wonder what might have been.

But into which eternity had he gone? Had Harlan followed the path of destruction? And if so, would the loss of his soul be held to Lonnie's account? Was Abel responsible for the sins of Cain? Nonsense! Harlan had made his own choices. Let the dead bury the dead. Lonnie's ministry was to the living. *Trudy?* Had he been sent to rescue her soul from the pit? Didn't God require a surviving brother to take his deceased brother's wife as his own? *STOP IT! That which is born of the flesh is flesh. Hold fast to the things of the spirit.* This wasn't going to work. He hadn't been there a half-hour, and already he was plotting to steal his brother's wife.

THREE

LONNIE TOWELED off in a bathroom filled with steam. The hot shower felt incredibly good. He could easily succumb to the luxury of running water. In his tiny village, people bathed with hot wet rags boiled in an iron pot. He cleared a circle on the surface of the mirror so he could see himself. Such a bright image. He'd never seen so many lights in a bathroom. He'd never seen so many mirrors. The spot he'd cleared began to fog. He wiped it again, and took a good look. The beard and hair would have to go. He rummaged through the drawers of the pristine-white, marble-topped vanity. No scissors or razor, but he did find a comb.

He wandered back to the bedroom, rubbing his head with the towel. The suite in which he was staying, presumably a guest room, was bigger than his whole house in Posada—heck, the *bed* was bigger than his whole house! He picked up his denims and pulled them on, then leaned over and scooped his shirt off the bed. It was the same shirt he'd worn yesterday, and all night on the plane, and was now forced to wear again. He lifted the arm and sniffed. *Wheeew!* He didn't want to put it back on, but he had no choice. Everything in his duffel bag was dirty. He needed more than a new suit, he needed a whole new wardrobe, or at least another pair of pants and a shirt. He wouldn't be around long enough to need more than that.

He slipped the shirt over his head and walked to the window, lifting his arm one more time to check for odor. He'd have to keep a few feet between himself and Trudy until he found something clean to wear. He stood next to a door that led onto a private balcony, but he didn't want to step outside barefoot. The rolling green carpet could be seen stretching for miles, leaving the impression that his brother's property included the entire Pacific ocean. Down below, beyond the rounded, rust-colored, ceramic roof tiles, the layout of the estate presented itself, no doubt designed by a professional. It had all the right shrubbery, a bush here and flowers there, each precisely pruned. Brick patios and walkways provided access to various playgrounds. Off to his right, an aqua-blue swimming pool shimmered with splashy strokes of light. *Of course,* Harlan wouldn't be without one. And there was the high dive, Harlan's own personal stage. He did like to show off. To the left was a giant chain link fence surrounding a green-surfaced tennis court. And at the back of the property a staircase led down to the beach. Once again Lonnie considered the extravagance. How many crippled children could receive corrective surgery or an artificial limb with what it cost to heat that pool? How many mouths might be fed? Perhaps with Harlan gone, Trudy would come to her senses. The injunction was clear: *Store not up for yourselves treasures on earth...go sell what you have and give to the poor.*

He walked back to his bed and fell to his knees. He needed wisdom—and he needed it now!

LONNIE LAID his hand on the balustrade, and began his slow descent of the broad sweeping staircase. A second set of stairs rose along the opposite wall. Both were curved, like opposite halves of a circle split down the middle. One was completely unnecessary because they both started and ended at the same place. *Maybe one's for going up and the other's for going down.* How ridiculous. Another example of excess. He turned left at the bottom of the stairs and made his way to the living room to find Trudy.

As he approached the high vaulted entry, he could hear her chatting with someone on the phone. She let out a cheerful laugh, as though the other person had said something funny. *Laughter? Gaiety?* Odd for someone in mourning. He entered the room just as Trudy was saying good-bye.

"That was a quick nap," she said, cradling the phone. She picked up her glass. Her words carried a slight slur, though she tried to mask it. Lonnie doubted she was still nursing the same drink she'd poured before he went upstairs.

"I decided I didn't have time to take one," he said. "I have to do some shopping. I can't show up at the funeral looking like this. You think I could use your phone to call a cab?"

"You needn't do that. You can use my car."

Lonnie rubbed his neck. "I appreciate the offer," he said, "but the truth is, I don't drive. Where I live, hardly anybody does. I never bothered to get a license."

Trudy tapped a scarlet fingernail on the marble counter top, her mouth pursed in thought, but if she considered what Lonnie said strange, she refrained from saying so. She turned the phone in his direction. "I'd let you use the limo, but we need it for the funeral. I guess you're on your own."

"Thanks. Ah, one more thing...I need to let the folks in my village know I've arrived safely. I told them I'd call. It's long distance, but I don't mind paying."

"For heaven's sake, Lonnie, you're our guest. You don't have to ask to use the phone, and you certainly don't have to pay."

Lonnie picked up the receiver and asked for an operator, and Trudy left the room to give him privacy. She returned holding a tall glass of iced tea. "Here," she said, offering it to him. "Non-alcoholic." Lonnie noticed she'd refreshed her own drink as well.

The glass felt cool and wet in his hand. He took a sip, pushing the phone aside. "The man said he'll have a cab here in twenty minutes."

Trudy sat on the white linen couch with her martini in one hand, and patted the smooth, silky cushion with the other. "Good," she said. "We have a lot of catching up to do. Sit down. Tell me all about yourself. What have you been doing for the last twenty years?"

Lonnie did as told, but stayed at the far end of the couch so Trudy couldn't get a whiff of his shirt. The seductive gloss of her red lips and the way her long manicured red nails scratched the smooth fabric of the sofa, made him regret the distance. He cleared his throat. "I'm a missionary. I minister to the native Indians of the Sierra Madre del Sur, in Mexico."

Trudy gulped and accidentally sloshed her drink. She slipped a finger under her lip to catch a drip. "A missionary? No kidding. Harlan was right. I guess I didn't believe him. But it does make sense. You always were religious, weren't you?" She set her glass on the cherry-wood table to her right and pulled a facial tissue from her pocket to wipe her mouth.

Lonnie noticed how her silk blouse slipped tightly around the firm line of her waist as she turned, emphasizing her trim figure. She rescued her drink and leaned toward him again. "Why didn't you keep in touch? We didn't know where you were until recently. It's like you fell off the map. I mean, we knew you were alive—we kept sending checks to your lawyer and they were always cashed—but if you'd told us where you were, we could have sent them direct."

Lonnie nodded, but didn't say anything.

"So why *did* you stay away so long? What are you trying to hide?"

"I wasn't hiding," he said. "You didn't have trouble finding me when you needed to, did you?"

"Yes, but actually, that was a fluke. Harlan read an article about an American philanthropist building a hospital in Mexico. Since not many people would want to do a thing like that, and since we figured you had to be down there somewhere, Harlan played a hunch and hired a private investigator. Turned out he was right. It *was* you."

Lonnie finished his iced tea and set the glass down. "Yes, I saw that piece," he said. "I'm glad they left my name out of it. I wouldn't want anything upsetting the life I've made for myself. Speaking of which, I should probably let you know, I'll be leaving tomorrow. The hospital we're building is almost finished. I have to get back in case they need me for anything."

"Hold on. Tomorrow's Tuesday. That's the reading of Harlan's will. You have to stick around for that. You're family."

Lonnie flinched. He'd missed the reading of Buddy's will, and Buddy had left him fifty percent of the company. Not that his father had a choice; it was part of the divorce settlement. Lonnie's mother had stipulated that no portion of Buddy's estate was to be given to either son until after his death, and subsequently, both her sons were to receive an equal share. She'd done it to protect Lonnie; otherwise Harlan would have got it all. Lonnie was sure Harlan begrudged him for it, so there wasn't much chance he'd leave him something now. Unless...unless God had prompted him to make amends. "I'll have to play it by ear," he said. "We'll see how it goes. So...you know all about my life. Tell me about yours."

Trudy set her empty glass down, by Lonnie's count, her third. *Must be finding it hard to carry on a conversation.*

"Not much to tell," she said. "Harlan turned your dad's film company into a huge success. He stopped doing nature films. Now we're into action and adventure. As for me, I haven't done much of anything. I guess it's all been done for me. Not that I'm complaining, but I kinda envy you...know what I mean? You're out there making a difference. Me, I just exist. Maybe when this is all over, I'll pop down and pay you a visit. Who knows, maybe I can help. Though I do have Quentin to consider."

Lonnie looked up.

"Oh, I'm sorry. Silly of me. You don't know Quentin. How could you? You have a nephew, Lonnie, though he's not a child. He'll be twenty in a few months. My goodness, I just realized I haven't seen him yet this morning. He doesn't even know you're here. It's about time you two met. Come on, I'll introduce you." She tried to stand, teetered for a moment, but quickly regained her balance.

Lonnie followed Trudy down a long, wide hallway, her light perfume, smelling of roses, trailing in the air. He could tell she was bracing herself by sliding one hand along the wall. How was she going to manage the funeral if she couldn't navigate her own home?

When they reached the end of the corridor, Trudy stopped. The wall on this side of the house seemed to vibrate with sound. Trudy turned the knob, put her hand against the oak door, and gave it a push. As they stepped inside, Lonnie felt his senses being assaulted. The music, if that's what it was, was deafening. *Thump, dada-thump, dada-thump.* The room glared with chrome stands, bright lights, and mirrors, and the air held the fragrance of a gym locker. At least he could stop worrying about his own body odor. Judging by the number of chrome devices, Lonnie guessed the room rivaled most professional fitness clubs.

Behind one row of polished machines, a young man was lying on a bench, holding a chrome bar attached to a cable and a stack of metal weights. He was grunting, his face red from exertion, sweat pouring off his forehead, and the veins of his neck engorged and distended. Quentin pulled down, straining himself, but was unable to bring the bar to his chest. He struggled, gritting his teeth, eyes bulging. Finally, he eased up, letting his arms fall to the side. A sigh wheezed from his lungs.

Owing to the volume of the stereo, which was loud enough to send sound waves thudding against the wall, Lonnie and Trudy had entered unnoticed. Trudy leaned toward Lonnie to be heard above the din. "My son's very concerned about keeping his body in shape."

The young man took hold of a trapeze and used it to hoist himself up. With his arms, he slid his body forward and swung himself to the right, grabbing a wheelchair that had been camouflaged behind all the chrome poles, pulleys, and rails. Lonnie hadn't noticed it before. He watched as Quentin lowered himself onto the leather seat and gripped the rubber tires with both hands. Trudy reached over her shoulder toward the wall where the amplifier was resting on a shelf. She gave the knob a twist, turning down the volume. Quentin looked up, glaring darkly.

"Quentin, your uncle's arrived. Come here, sweetheart. I want to introduce you."

Quentin took a white towel from the bench and buried his face in it. His sleeveless sweatshirt revealed the hard mounds of his biceps. There were half melons of perspiration under each arm, with a pie-shaped wedge soaked into the front of his shirt. He flipped the towel around the back of his neck.

"Quentin was in a mountain biking accident a year ago. He damaged his spinal cord and lost the use of his legs," Trudy explained.

"But look at how well he gets along. He has his father's fighting spirit."

Quentin rolled his wheelchair over to where his mother and uncle stood.

"Quentin, this is your Uncle Lonnie—the one I told you about."

The young man's eyes were blue, his sandy hair short and wavy, and his face unblemished. His handsome, squared-off features were those of a young corporate manager with executive potential. He dropped his hands into his lap and pushed his shoulders back into his chair. His gaze was distant and unfocused, his lips pinched tight. There was a long sustained pause. Lonnie started to say something to fill the void, but Quentin spoke first. "So, you're my long lost uncle."

"You can call me Lonnie." Lonnie extended his arm, palm out, expecting a cordial handshake. But Quentin ignored the gesture. He deliberately drew his hands back and placed them on the wheels of his chair. He pushed and pulled, pulled and pushed, causing the chair to swing back and forth. Lonnie stepped back to get out of the way.

"What are you, some kind of hippie? I thought all you flower-power types died of drug overdoses back in the sixties. Know what's..."

"Quentin! Don't be rude."

"...know what's funny? My dad never mentioned you. I have an uncle I never knew about until my dad was dead. How do you explain that, Mr. Uncle?"

"Quentin!"

"Sorry, Mother. How do you account for that, Uncle, Sir?" But he didn't wait for an answer. He spun his chair to the right, then swung left again and started for the door.

Lonnie tried to get out of his way but wasn't quick enough and the boy clipped his shin with the chair. He grimaced and shot a questioning glance at Trudy. She had held her emotions in check so far, but now her face flushed red. She looked like she'd just been slapped.

FOUR

THE WINDS raced down the street in currents, picking up dust and debris and tossing them into the hair of people passing by. Gusty winds were normal in Posada, too. It's just that Lonnie wasn't used to having them in his face. Posada was hemmed in behind the protective walls of the jungle. He was familiar with a wind you could see, one that played in the branches as it rippled through the trees, but not one you could feel. Even when the clouds backed against the mountains and the rain fell in torrents, winds of any consequence were seldom felt. The bush was just too thick.

Lonnie got out of the cab with his suit lapels flapping and reached for his wallet. As he released his grip on the car door, it was ripped from his hand and slammed shut. He leaned through the passenger side window and paid the driver, and then stood back, holding his tie against his shirt. The sign in front of the building read, "Wilcox and Blears, Funeral Home." He wondered why his brother hadn't had the foresight to request that his funeral be held in a church. But that would be presumptuous, wouldn't it? From what he remembered of Harlan, a secular funeral was probably best.

The wind tossed Lonnie's hair, lifting tufts of the new short cut around his clean-shaven face. He felt naked with the air touching his skin. He hoped no one would notice that the flesh around his jaw was a shade lighter than the tanned skin around his forehead and cheeks.

He entered the doors at the front, pushing on the wood frame. The names—Wilcox and Blears—were etched into the glass in frosted, scrolling letters. In the foyer he found a signboard standing on an easel: "Funeral service, Harlan Striker, room 103, viewing room 102." He swallowed and tried clearing his throat. He looked at the watch Trudy had loaned him. He didn't own a watch himself—where he lived a timepiece wasn't needed—but Trudy had insisted he take one of Harlan's so he wouldn't be late. It was a Rolex. Lonnie didn't know a Rolex from a Timex, and frankly, as long as it kept time, didn't care. The watch did seem a bit heavy, though, and was certainly more ostentatious than any he'd previously owned. The time was 1:40. He was early. The official viewing wouldn't begin for another twenty minutes.

Trudy had apologized for her son's rude behavior. She'd asked that Lonnie be patient. She'd wiped her nose on a tissue, and without attempting to disguise how proud she was, explained that Quentin had formerly been a varsity letterman on his high school track team. The loss of his legs was akin to clipping the wings of a bird. To make matters worse, he'd been forced to go through rehabilitation while watching his father die. Quentin had survived two great losses: the loss of his legs and the loss of his father, both within the space of a year, so it was understandable that this once energetic and outgoing young man had become sullen and bitter.

Lonnie did understand. Caring for the sick and dying was part of his calling. He knew what it was to watch a child, burned beyond recognition, die while screaming in pain, or to watch an otherwise healthy man have his arm amputated to stop the spread of poison from the bite of a venomous snake. He knew what it was to be angry at God. It might be that such trials were meant to build character, but trying to explain God's purpose to the person going through it...well, that was another matter. He wished there was something he could do for the boy.

He and Trudy had continued sharing tidbits about their lives while she downed another drink. She described her dream of taking a trip around the world, and Lonnie explained how he, though he'd only been gone a few hours, already missed his simple life among the Indians. When the cab finally showed up, Lonnie found himself wishing he didn't have to leave.

As he stood in the lobby of the funeral home, Lonnie wondered what kind of shape Trudy would be in when she arrived. For all her controlled emotions, she wasn't handling the situation well. She'd had at least four drinks before he left. He couldn't begin to guess how many she might have had since.

He wandered down the corridor until he came to a men's room. Might as well use the facilities. He pushed back the door and went inside. He loved American bathrooms, so clean and white, no comparison to the latrines of Posada. He washed his hands and toweled off, then stood in front of the mirror straightening his tie. A new Lonnie stared back, quite different from the Lonnie he'd seen in the mirror earlier. He smoothed the lapels of his suit and removed a piece of lint. Trudy had given him the name of Harlan's tailor, but Lonnie needed something off the rack. The cab driver had smiled when, while standing in front of Harlan's glorious mansion looking like a wino-eyed bum, Lonnie had asked to be taken to the nearest Salvation Army Thrift Store.

Fortunately, the store was in a strip mall that also had a barbershop. He'd sat through the ordeal of having his locks removed while nondescript music played in the background helping him to relax. At least the barber had offered him a newspaper. He loved to read. The mail was only delivered to Posada twice a week but Lonnie received two different newspapers, the *El Excelsior* from Mexico City, and *The LA Times*, though they were always days late. He also subscribed to a dozen or more monthly publications, mostly Christian, and conservative in their stance. The tiny hovel he called home had four filing cabinets filled with news clippings he'd collected on a variety of topics, but he was particularly keen on saving those that dealt with the way the world was changing. He knew when the courts ruled against prayer in schools, or removed the ten commandments from public buildings, or approved condom distribution under the guise of sex education. The world might end up going to hell in a handbasket, but Lonnie was determined not to let it take him by surprise.

Standing in the bathroom of the funeral parlor he was able to see, for the first time, the fruit of his labor. His shoes felt tight, the pants were at least a half-inch too short, and the jacket was frumpy and held a faint musty odor, but all in all, he was passable. He combed his fingers through his short wavy hair. It felt light on top of his head. Like his nephew, Lonnie's sandy curl was natural. Without the weight of the longer hair to pull it down, it sprang back into shape with a quick combing of his hand. He felt his jaw, smooth and angular, his cheeks high and flat. His eyes were as blue as the afternoon sky, a color strange to the Indians of Posada. They said his eyes were magic, that he could see right into their souls, though he'd explained over and over again how it wasn't true. He turned his face from side to side. He looked pretty good for his thirty-seven years. He just wished he felt as good as he looked. He pushed his knuckles into the small of his back and stretched. His body ached from lack of sleep. He splashed cold water on his face and dried himself with a paper towel.

Another glance at his watch told him he still had fifteen minutes before the viewing, but Trudy was likely to arrive early. And besides, it didn't mean he couldn't go ahead and take a look for himself. He left the men's room and wandered down the hall, searching for room 102. It was the second door on his right. He paused before going in, his heart *rap-tap-tapping* to the rush of adrenalin. He placed his hand against the door and took a deep breath, feeling light-headed and critical of himself for being nervous. The man was dead, for Pete's sake.

He forced himself around the corner. The room was arranged in rows of chairs with an aisle down the middle. The coffin was at the front with the lid open. He wasn't able to see inside from where he stood. He took a step forward, glad no one else was there, now coveting a moment alone with his brother. He had to hurry. Trudy would arrive at any minute to receive those who came to pay their condolences. Lonnie inched his way down the aisle, trying to muster courage. His heart was *thud, thud, thudding* in his chest. *The Lord is my strength and my salvation.* The walk seemed to take forever, *one step, and then another, and another,* but finally, he was able to see Harlan, lying in cold estate, an empty shell without the fire of life.

Lonnie sipped in air and held his breath. Harlan didn't look so big and threatening now. He looked almost puny, certainly not the mountain of a man Lonnie remembered—he was too slack-jawed, too thin-boned, too pasty white. He was dead, and death was the great equalizer. Lonnie glanced around making sure he was still alone, then reached in to touch the body just to be sure. His hand was trembling. He inched up, *closer, closer, almost there, and...*Harlan's eyes popped open! Lonnie jumped back three feet, his heart kicking the walls of his chest, his legs wobbling. *What? No, not possible.* He was hyperventilating, trying to catch his breath. He chanced another peek at the body in the casket...but Harlan's eyes were closed.

Lonnie's head snapped up. Three people had entered the room. Trudy, pushing Quentin's wheelchair, and a man dressed in a professional shroud. The man had a black leather notebook wrapped in his arms.

"This room is reserved for private viewing," the man said. "If you're not with the family, I'll have to ask you to leave."

Lonnie tried to answer, but the words wouldn't come. Trudy came to his aid. "It's all right, Burton. This is my brother-in-law."

"Very good, ma'am. I'll be outside directing the guests as they come in, if you need me." The man turned and walked away.

"Well, you gave me a bit of a start," Trudy said. "That's the second time today I didn't recognize you. I must say I approve the change."

Quentin's eyes wandered about the room, staring off into space, refusing to acknowledge his uncle.

People were beginning to file in. A portly man shuffled through the door, followed by his family. A young couple came next, arm in arm, looking suitably somber. A gray-haired woman stepped in a few seconds later, knotting a handkerchief with her fingers.

Lonnie was doing what he could to keep from passing out. His head was pounding like an anvil. He couldn't stay. He stumbled forward. Trudy began hugging the gray-haired lady, patting her on the back as if she were consoling the woman, instead of the other way around. Lonnie tried to squeeze by, but they were blocking the aisle. Trudy caught him by the sleeve. "Lonnie, this is Mrs. Warner, Harlan's nurse. She helped him through his last months. They became quite close."

Lonnie took the woman's hand. She dabbed her eyes with the tissue. "He was a good man," she said. "A real good man."

Lonnie offered a weak smile in reply. He excused himself, saying he needed to get some fresh air. He left Trudy shaking her head, watching his retreat. He couldn't help it. He'd been defeated by the ghost in the box. Retreat was his only option.

OUTSIDE, the news vans of several network affiliates and a local cable channel had taken up positions in the parking lot. On-camera reporters were testing video and sound, preparing to comment on Hollywood's tragic loss.

The wind was sweeping up the dust and swirling it around. Lonnie held onto his coat and dodged the media circus, seeking shelter. He found it in the narrow space between the funeral home and the building next door, where the wind was partially blocked. He had to get a grip. *Those eyes could not have opened.* He watched the curious climbing out of their cars, doing their best to anchor their dresses and ties as they scurried toward the entrance. A car circled the lot and, finding no empty spaces, pulled into the street to park. A line formed, of those waiting to get inside, and the news cameras rolled, recording the crowd. Lonnie wandered along the sidewalk, barely registering the throng that had showed up to honor his brother. He was spent. His body ached, and his eyes felt gritty. He wanted to lie down. He looked at his watch again. He'd been awake almost thirty hours.

More and more people flowed into the lobby. Why were so many coming to pay their respects to someone who viewed others with such contempt? The answer was obvious. They didn't know the Harlan he knew. *"Right, genius, it is an odd shape, but you don't throw a football like a baseball. You have to grab it like this, and throw it with a spin."* That was the real Harlan. *"Look, don't worry about it. It's not your fault. Your mother named you Loony, for cripes sake. How can you expect to be normal with a name like that?"*

Lonnie couldn't reconcile his past with the present, though he knew the past was as dead as the body in that box and the future still alive with possibilities. But the lines were indistinct, and one had such bearing on the other they seemed inseparable—one and the same. How do you forgive and forget? Answer: you don't! *Thanks for the memories, Harlan.* He was glad they were few and far between.

A sudden gust kicked grains of sand into Lonnie's face. He closed his eyes, blocking the assault, but when he opened them, he was back in Mexico staring up into the sun. He was momentarily blinded. As he began seeing shadows and shapes again he realized he wasn't in the Sierra Madre del Sur; he was in the dry Mexican desert of his youth. He could feel sweat squeezing from his pores like warm lemon oil. Back with Buddy and Harlan again in the dusty, yellow badlands of Coahuila, where they'd come to document the ecosystem surrounding the dry wadi. Not Mother—she was off visiting her sister—just Buddy and the boys. Buddy had been commissioned to capture on film the delicate balance of the cycle of life—coyote eats badger, badger eats owl, owl eats snake, snake eats mouse, ad infinitum. There was something to be learned from that.

Buddy had guaranteed them a real man's trip, with Coleman stove and lantern, sleeping around a campfire beneath a billion stars blinking in a cobalt blue sky, roughing it all the way. Then, at the last minute, he'd decided to bring his assistant. It was only a slight change of plans. She wouldn't be in the way. She had her own tent. The men would bunk outside in the open air, taking in the grandeur of the starry hosts as they drifted off to sleep. But when the yellow light of morning broke across the hard pan of the desert, Buddy crawled out of the tent, followed by the young lady. It was a routine that was to repeat itself every night. Lonnie kept his mouth shut, too young to understand, but not too young to know it made him feel queasy.

What wasn't known at the time was that his mother, while staying with her sister, was consulting a lawyer. The marriage dissolved shortly after that. Lonnie remained in the custody of his mother while Harlan stayed with Buddy, which seemed best for all concerned. Until, that is, Lonnie's final year of high school when his mother, after fighting it for more than a year, surrendered to the cancer that had consumed her cervix, and Lonnie found himself living with Harlan and Buddy again.

Lonnie had moved into Buddy's house with a chip as big as a brick on his shoulder. He half suspected, but couldn't prove, Buddy had caused his mother's cancer so, as with everything else, he and Harlan saw the breakdown of the marriage through different eyes. The whole thing came to a head the night Lonnie debuted in his high school play. Buddy, though he'd promised to attend, failed to show, and Lonnie had come home sulking. He had withdrawn to his room, locked the door, and refused to come out. Harlan couldn't stand to see Lonnie acting snooty. He broke the lock with a screwdriver, busted in, and then proceeded to berate Lonnie for being such a pansy. *"Look here Spud, if I were you, I'd be more concerned about how folks saw me every day than I would about Buddy not seeing me one night! All the world's a stage, Spud. You gotta get your act together if you want to play a part."*

But Harlan had missed the point. Lonnie didn't care what anyone else thought. At that moment, Buddy was all that mattered. The yelling had escalated. *"Buddy's too busy tickling every girl's fancy to have time for anyone else,"* Lonnie screeched. *"He's only doing what a man has to do,"* Harlan bellowed back. *"He has needs. If Mom had been there for him, they wouldn't have got divorced!"* Lonnie, unable to express his fury in words, scrunched his knuckles and took a swing, but Harlan stepped aside and used Lonnie's thrust to yank him forward while stuffing a closed fist into his stomach. Lonnie crumpled to the floor retching, and Harlan stomped out.

The swirling memories, so vivid, and yet so blurred—from burning sun, to arid desert, to the badlands back home—almost caused Lonnie to faint. He pressed the flat of his palms against the wall and leaned back, propping himself up until the dizziness passed. And he was supposed to grieve over Harlan's death?

Lonnie turned, peeking around the corner of the building. The news crews were still sitting there, looking bored. Someone flicked the butt of a cigarette into the parking lot. A last-minute straggler, ducking his head against the wind, looked at his watch and hurried toward the door. Lonnie could hear the sound of organ music. It was time to go inside. He was about to lead a service in memory of his dearly departed brother, and he couldn't think of a single thing to say.

There was a crowd standing outside room 103 waiting to get inside. Lonnie slipped his hand between their shoulders and excused himself as he squeezed through. The room must have seated two hundred, but it was packed. He made his way to the center aisle at the back of the room. Everyone was in elegant dress. He'd never seen so many shiny black gowns and feathered hats in one place, more fashion show than funeral. He scanned the front, searching for Trudy. She was there, easy to spot because Quentin's wheelchair was parked in the aisle next to her pew, but she didn't look the part of a grieving widow. She wore a strapless dress with a lacy black shawl wrapped loosely around her creamy shoulders. Her auburn hair was smooth and shiny, turning in under her chin, and, oddly, her carefully applied makeup was perfect, and showed no sign of being tracked by tears.

A man rose from his seat, walked through the aisle of flowers, and stepped up to the podium with every hair of his head sprayed neatly in place. His voice was clear as it resonated across the room. He smiled at the audience like an emcee on Oscar night. He ran through his monologue, his polished teeth gleaming in the light. Lonnie caught Trudy's eye looking back over her shoulder. She lifted her hand to signal him, her forearm covered with a long black glove. Her gesture betrayed her impatience as she urged him to make his way down to the family section.

Lonnie worked his way over to the side aisle and slipped as unobtrusively as he could to the front, though he was aware of being watched. What had he gotten himself into? They would wonder who he was. Now he imagined everyone staring at him, the geek in the Sally Ann suit with pants too short and a silly candy-striped tie. And he was expected to get up there in front of everyone?

A second man had taken the podium and was telling stories about the good times he and Harlan had shared. Harlan was with the Big Guy upstairs, the man said. He went on to suggest that God probably called Harlan home because he wanted to produce a movie about heaven. A polite chuckle rippled through the audience. Lonnie sat down. It was sad, really, that all these people could be gathered to honor a man's life and not be concerned about the kind of account he would have to give his Creator.

Lonnie took a seat at the end of the pew with a whole row of people between himself and Trudy. He didn't recognize the others. They were seated in the section reserved for relatives. Had to be from Trudy's side of the family. She leaned forward and motioned for him, indicating she expected him to squeeze around the people's knees and come sit beside her, but he wasn't about to do that. He shook his head and waved her off. She turned away, looking peeved. The second man sat down and was followed by a third, who took his place on the platform. He, too, rambled on about Harlan's magnanimous personality. Either they were all a bunch of really great actors, or they were talking about someone Lonnie didn't know.

Forgiveness, forgiveness, forgiveness. He had to practice—forgiveness!

Lonnie tried concentrating on what he was going to say. He felt his heart picking up speed again. So many people. It should be a powerful message, full of the gospel. He would tell them how Jesus, Lord of the universe, had died so that they, by believing in Him, could pass from death unto life. In this crowd, that kind of message would be a show-stopper. He could almost see their jaws drop. *You can't say that! You have to respect the beliefs of others.*

Lonnie ventured a clandestine look over his shoulder. The man across the aisle to his right was wearing a turban. He was probably from India, which would make him either Hindu or Muslim. *We have to esteem all religions as equal. There are many ways to God.* He'd heard it all before. The problem was, Christ said: "I am the way, the truth, and the life, no man comes to the Father but by *Me!*" If Buddha or Mohammed or Confucius, or anyone else could provide another way, then Jesus was a liar. That's just what Lonnie would tell them. They needed to know the truth. His heart was pounding so loud, he feared it could be heard. He tried to steady himself. He didn't want to hyperventilate, perish the thought.

Just then he heard his name, "...the brother of Harlan Striker, Lonnie, will lead us in a brief homily." His legs felt weak as he stood. Perhaps it was just his lack of sleep. He walked to the podium, but he could feel himself fading in and out. He still didn't know what he was going to say. He took hold of the sides of the pulpit for support and looked out over the sea of faces. His heart began to fibrillate. Beads of sweat prickled on his forehead. He started to open his mouth. He heard a loud droning sound in his ears and felt a *whoosh* inside his skull. Suddenly his knees buckled, and everything went black.

FIVE

LONNIE OPENED his eyes. It took a second to realize he was flat on his back behind the pulpit. His head was buzzing and...*what's that awful smell?* He could feel someone's sweaty palms touching his face, trying to lift his head. *Ohhh, that stinks!* The funeral director was shoving something putrid under his nose—*smelling salts*? Lonnie shook his head and pushed the swab away. He tried to sit up. Two men stepped forward, one on either side, and hoisted him to his feet. He felt an arm around his waist as he was guided to a seat in the front row. His head was still spinning. He fought off the dizziness, struggling to get his bearings. The room began to settle. A man in a black suit took the pulpit, cleared his throat, said a few words about continuing, and then read a prayer from a book to conclude the service.

Lonnie propped his elbows on his knees and buried his face in his hands, trying to make sense of what had just happened. Was he *that* tired? No, of course not, but unless he blamed it on fatigue, it didn't make sense. He felt a river of sweat rolling down his chest. Nothing about it made *sense*. God should have given him strength. If he could have hung on another few minutes, hundreds of people would have heard the gospel, people who might not get another chance. *Why?* It wasn't lack of sleep. He was exhausted, but not so spent as to fall apart in public. Nor could he claim he was overcome by grief because he felt no grief at all. Deep inside, as the truth began to emerge, a shiver ran down his spine. *Fear!* That's what it was. The crowd had intimidated him. His brother would have boldly taken charge. He, on the other hand, had caved in under pressure.

The man finished his prayer and closed the book. Organ music began to play as six pallbearers stood and made their way to the front. The scrolled oak coffin was resting on a wheeled cart draped with a floor-length burgundy curtain. The casket had brass handles and a lacquered finish that reflected the light. Another example of grotesque waste. What did a dead man need? If Harlan had died in Posada, he would have been laid to rest in a pine box.

Someone removed the wreath of flowers, and the casket was turned and presented to the audience. Lonnie dreaded what was coming next. He was expected to follow the procession out and take his place in the reception line. Whatever made him think this was a good idea? He'd failed God and made a fool of himself besides. Harlan would be busting a gut inside that box. *He who laughs last, laughs best.* And the worst was yet to come. Everyone would be asking him what happened. He would have to lie, well, maybe not lie so much as bend the truth. *Yes, I'm overcome by grief and yes, I'm in desperate need of sleep?* He *had* to say something.

The congregation stood. The cart bearing the casket was rolled down the aisle. Those who had been seated in the first pew fell in behind. Lonnie followed the others, marching in somber silence as the procession made its way to the back of the room. The funeral director helped by placing a supportive hand under Lonnie's arm. Lonnie felt sure he wouldn't faint again, but he didn't resist the man's assistance. Better to look as if he were struggling with grief.

Trudy stepped into the aisle beside him, taking his hand. She leaned in to ask if he was all right.

Lonnie nodded. "Sorry. I don't know what came over me."

"Don't worry about it," Trudy said, patting his arm. "It went just fine." She continued speaking softly in his ear. "Now, when we get to the back, unless you feel you have to sit down, I want you to stand beside me. Don't go wandering off. We have to greet those who came. After that, the funeral procession will be going back to our house for a little get-together. You know, relatives and friends. I want you to ride in the limo with us."

"What about the interment service?"

"There isn't one. Harlan asked to be cremated."

Lonnie felt a stab at his heels—*ouch*—and glanced over his shoulder. It was Quentin. The young man backed his wheelchair up with an apologetic shrug, but Lonnie was sure he saw an ill-concealed smirk on the boy's face.

A YELLOW DUSK was filtering through the blinds as the evening began to settle in. The house was filled with people, meandering in and out with drinks in their hands. Some feigned long faces in Trudy's presence, but most seemed oblivious as to why they were there. It seemed Harlan's funeral was just another excuse for a cocktail party.

The room caroled with background music, punctuated with bright conversation. Guests occupied themselves by flitting from one group to the next, catching the latest tidbits of gossip and warming themselves with flattering words and polite laughter. Some lounged on sofas and chairs, the men with their Italian leather shoes propped up over their knees, and the ladies with their polished lips and nails, chatting it up. Those craving a cigarette respected the house no-smoking rule and braved the winds outside, the women pushing back their hair and the men holding down their flapping ties.

Lonnie felt beached, a useless castaway tossed up on shore, the proverbial fish out of water. He didn't know a soul. He looked around. Even his sister-in-law was avoiding him. Quentin had disappeared, probably to his room. Lonnie envied the escape. Trudy had asked if he would stay and help entertain, but no one seemed anxious to engage him in conversation, so what was the point? He stayed only because he felt obliged to be there in case Trudy needed him, but she appeared to be doing fine on her own. She was busy circulating through the crowd in her strapless dress, talking to one group, flirting with another, a drink ever in hand. As the evening drew on, her voice grew loud and shrill, while her speech slowed and her words became increasingly slurred.

Lonnie stood off by himself leaning against the wall for support. Even with all the coffee he'd been drinking, he was fading fast. It was all he could do to respond to the occasional word of condolence. For the most part, people left him alone, which suited him fine.

He caught his eyes drifting closed and forced himself upright, standing straight, clearing his head with a brisk shake. B*etter get moving or I'll fall asleep on my feet*, he thought. Without looking, he turned jostling the elbow of the woman standing behind him.

"Oh, excuse me! Sorry about that," he said, taking her arm to steady her drink.

"Quite all right. No harm done," the woman responded with a smile. Lonnie guessed her to be in her twenties, an attractive brunette with her hair swept up into a chignon. "You're the brother, aren't you?"

Lonnie felt flattered. At least someone recognized him, and a very pretty someone at that. "Yes, I'm Lonnie. Harlan was my brother, older by nearly three years."

The woman nodded. "I'm Deborah Nations. I was in one of your brother's pictures once. You probably don't recognize me; it was just a small part. Anyway, that's how I got my start. I owe Harley for that." With her free hand she grabbed the arm of the man standing to her left. "This is Jim Mendelson, he directed several of Harley's films, and Connie Doyle. Connie this is Lonnie. Connie and Lonnie, I like that. Hey, you two make a cute couple. Connie used to be in wardrobe, but was recently discovered by Bob Donah and is now an actress, isn't that right, Connie? What do *you* do, Lonnie?"

Lonnie caught Trudy's eye. Her lips, full and red, held a seductive gloss, but she quickly looked away. He couldn't recall Trudy ever calling Harlan—*Harley*. Fact, he couldn't recall anyone ever calling his brother that. Lonnie turned his attention back to Deborah. "I'm a missionary. I work with the indigenous Indians of southern Mexico."

The group gave a polite chuckle, and Connie said, "Right, and Debbie here is Mother Teresa." She reached out and straightened Lonnie's tie, trailing her long, plum-colored fingernails lightly across his chest. "Okay, I'll bite. What do you *really* do?"

For a second, Lonnie was caught off guard, but he recovered

quickly. "I *really* am a missionary—you know, one of those guys that goes to another country to tell people about Jesus, saving souls and all that. Fact is, kind of a male version of Mother Teresa, now that you mention it. Only, I work down in Mexico—not on the streets of Calcutta."

All three stood silent. Lonnie could see they were embarrassed. Finally Jim spoke up. "Well, isn't that interesting? I don't think Harlan ever mentioned that, at least not to me." He looked at his empty glass and gave it a flick of his wrist, clattering the ice cubes. "I think it's time to refresh my drink. Nice meeting you, Lonnie."

Connie removed her hand from Lonnie's chest. "Well, I hate to say it, but I have to use the powder room."

Deborah set her glass on a nearby table. "Hold on. I'll come with you," she said. "Perhaps we'll get a chance to talk later, Lonnie." And with that, all three turned away.

Maybe I should have said I own half of Striker Films, Lonnie thought. But that would have been a cop-out. *"Ye shall be hated of all men for My name's sake,"* Jesus had said.

Succumbing to his fatigue, Lonnie staggered to the center of the room and found a place on the sofa. *Alone again.* It was the story of his life. He felt like going back to his room, calling the airport, and booking the first available flight home. The people of Mexico might be simple, but at least they had manners.

A shrill bark of laughter brought Lonnie from his thoughts.

"Sounds like Trudy's having a good time."

The voice came from somewhere behind the couch.

"Wouldn't *you* if you'd just inherited Harlan's estate? I like Trudy. It's about time she got a break."

"How do you mean?"

"Come on. You knew Harlan. The guy had a bed in his office. Used if for auditions, if you get my drift. I don't fault her for being happy."

"That's easy for you to say. If Harlan left her the company, she's my new boss. Not that I mind answering to a woman, I can handle that, but I can't imagine reporting to a drunk."

Lonnie tried peeking over his shoulder, curious to see who was talking, but couldn't manage it without showing his face. He didn't want them knowing he was eavesdropping, so he cocked his ear to listen hoping they'd continue.

"I wouldn't worry about it. She may assume control, but she won't try and run the company. She'll hire someone for that. Now about the IPO coming out on Parapharm. The initial offering is limited to five million shares. My broker can get us in on the ground floor, but we have to act fast..."

The two men moved out of Lonnie's hearing. That was interesting. *Poor Trudy.* Well, as the man said, it was payoff time. Trudy was about to receive her just reward. Lonnie had already deduced that his stake in the company was a well kept secret, but that was okay; the important thing was, Trudy would be getting the other half. They would own it together, a team. He was happy to remain a silent partner, as long as the checks kept coming so he could continue his work south of the border.

THE CLOCK in Harlan's study had chimed ten by the time the last lingering guests shuffled off to other parties. Lonnie found the stereo and turned it off. The sound of silence, echoing in the emptiness, fell heavily on the room. Trudy was slouched on the white linen couch. She used the toe of one foot to pop the shoe off the other. Lonnie was beyond sleep now, too tired to close his eyes. He walked into the room and held out a cup of coffee. "Here," he said, "it'll help sober you up."

But Trudy waved him off. "I don't need cohffee," she said. "What I need is a...a...a nightcap. Lon, be a doll and fixish me one?"

"I think you've had enough. It's time for bed." Lonnie set the cup down and reached out to take Trudy's hand. "Come on." He pulled her up and put an arm around her waist, holding her till she found her balance. "Atta girl. I'll help you to your room."

She started to take a step forward but at the last second turned and reached for the table, nearly falling over. Lonnie quickly grabbed her hips to keep her from crashing to the floor. She stood for a moment bowed double, with her hands on the coffee table. Then she took the glass, balanced herself on one hand while tipping her head back to pour the last of her drink down her throat. "Okay, all gone. Now I'm ready," she said, standing again.

Lonnie helped her to the stairs. She paused, took hold of the railing and put a tentative foot on the first step, but then removed it. She raised a finger and waggled it in front of Lonnie's nose. "I'm not going up that way, un uh. Ssshake me to the elevator."

"What elevator?" It didn't surprise Lonnie they would have one. Quentin had to get upstairs somehow. "Where is it?"

Trudy took Lonnie's arm for support. "Come on, I'll sh...show you."

They made their way slowly through the parlor into the living room and turned down the hall heading toward the gym. Halfway down, Trudy stopped. She held out her hand, suspended in air for a moment with her finger pointed at the wall as she tried to zero in on the elevator button, but she missed and poked the chrome switch-plate instead. Lonnie pushed the button for her. In appearance the door looked just like any other but, instead of opening out, it moved sideways. The opening revealed a roomy carpeted box. Lonnie helped Trudy over the threshold. Inside he found another button and gave it a push. The door closed and the elevator began to rise. When they came to a stop, Lonnie found they were just down the hall from the twin staircases. His bedroom was past those stairs on the right, but Trudy steered him away from his room.

"My room is thish way," she said. "Quentin's on the right. I'm on the left. Quentin on the right, Trudy on the left. Remember that, so you don't get confushed, casesh you need me. I wouldn't want you to fall in bed with Quentin," she said, giggling.

Lonnie ignored the remark.

As they entered the room, Trudy turned and bumped the door with her shoulder, trying to nudge it shut. But the attempt was awkward and the door bounced off the heel of Lonnie's shoe, closing only slightly.

"Lonnie, Lonnie, Lonnie, I'd forgotten how handshome you are."

Trudy flung her arms around Lonnie's neck and kissed him full on the mouth.

At first Lonnie didn't resist. He swooned at the fragrance of her hair. But Trudy wasn't in her right mind. He pulled free and walked her backward, holding her shoulders until her legs bumped the bed. She fell back, off balance, but she managed to capture his neck and drag him down with her. The bed bounced as they landed with Lonnie on top, using his arms to keep his full weight from crushing Trudy. She placed her hands on the sides of his face, staring into his eyes. "Oh Lonnie, I've misshed you. We had such good times, you and me, remember?" She let go and began unbuttoning his shirt, but he took hold of her wrist.

"Lonnie...?"

QUENTIN HAD been in his room all evening, working at his computer. He'd heard his Mother's loud voice all the way down the hall. She was with a man, that much was obvious, but he didn't know who. He rolled to the entry, turned off his light, and quietly opened his door a crack to listen.

"Come on Lonnie, don't play shy..."

Quentin closed his eyes. His hands gripped the wheels of his chair until his knuckles turned white. Then he let go, took a deep breath, closed his door and sat in the darkness, trying not to think about what was going on in his mother's bedroom.

He did not see his uncle roll off the bed. He did not see him pull the silk sheets over his mother's bare shoulders, though she was fully clothed. He did not see Lonnie stoop to kiss her cheek, or hear him whisper, "Good-night, Trudy, pleasant dreams." Nor did he hear his mother crying. She turned her face to the pillow to mute her sobs as Lonnie left the room, closing the door behind him.

SIX

It wasn't a nightmare, it was more like a dream with a troubling end—Lonnie and Trudy were getting married...

LONNIE HAD planned on beginning his day as usual, spending time in his room in prayer, but the cry of the gulls had called him to the window. As he'd gazed out over the ocean, with the yellow morning sun sitting like broken shards of glass on the surface of the water, he'd decided to slip down to the beach to have his quiet time with the Lord. It was early. Quentin and Trudy were still asleep.

He shuffled along, kicking wet sand, listening to the pounding waves and looking for a place on the rocks where he could sit and meditate. A thought was wedged in the back of his mind, but it eluded his grasp. He shook his head trying to remember. He knew he'd slept fitfully, but several things could account for that: travel fatigue, a strange bed, bad dreams?

The ocean surged, its raw power, measureless expanse, and unfailing constancy proclaiming the attributes of its Creator—*the heavens declare the glory of God, and the firmament showeth his handiwork*—but after reading a few Psalms, and watching the morning sun paint the waters in ever-changing shades of blue and green, Lonnie began to be concerned that he might have stayed too long. He didn't want to come traipsing back into the house, trailing sand, and stumble upon Trudy and Quentin eating breakfast. He wanted a chance to change first. He was glad he'd worn his unwashed travel clothes down to the beach. The wet shoreline would have made a mess of his new suit.

His morning reflections had given him time to think. He'd considered his options, prayed, and made his decision. He would go back to his room, shower and dress, and then attend the reading of Harlan's will. Harlan had known about the hospital. It was possible he, in some desperate attempt to make amends, had left part of his estate to the mission. Trying to buy favor with God would be just the kind of thing Harlan would do. After the reading, Lonnie would grab a taxi and scoot directly to the airport, where he would hop the next flight back to Huatulco. He wasn't sure how he'd get to Posada from there, but he'd find a way.

The surf slammed against the shore with a vengeance, whooshing in and out. Gulls screeched overhead. The sand crunched beneath his feet. He swallowed the lump in his throat. That left only Trudy, and how to break the news. *Nuts.* He and Trudy were from two different worlds. He'd watched her last night, the consummate socialite. She'd hate the kind of life he'd carved out for himself. She would want him here. She'd insist on his running the mission from a distance, making visits to Mexico only when necessary. The idea was tempting, but it was a temptation he wanted to avoid.

Lonnie paused to look out over the ocean again. He picked up a stone and hurled it as far as he could into the surf. *Thwuunk.* Waking up each morning to such a day as this, rising from silk sheets knowing all your needs were taken care of, breathing the salty air and feeling the wind tossing your hair, lounging by the pool, playing a morning game of tennis, or walking along the sandy beach—that was the good life. But it was her life—*not his.*

Lonnie turned, continuing his climb, step by step. Going down had been easy but he could feel the tiredness in his bones going up. He watched the pale pink mansion looming larger and larger with each upward stride as he neared the top of the stairs. He could fit half the population of Posada inside that house. He wandered back through the gardens, enjoying the morning sun the way he imagined Harlan might have done, probably dressed in a Polo shirt and white shorts with a tennis racquet in his hand. He looked again at the watch

Trudy had loaned him, the one she said Harlan used to wear. He questioned whether it was waterproof, and then realized it had to be if Harlan had worn it. It was about nine in the morning. He wondered what time they would be reading the will. Trudy hadn't said.

The sun burst over the house, its blinding glare causing him to squint—must be seventy degrees already. He could feel himself perspiring and was thankful, once again, that he'd decided not to wear the suit. Now he had something clean to change into after his shower.

Lonnie heard a splash. Someone was in the pool—that would be Trudy. He walked over to say hi, but was surprised to find it was Quentin. The young man pushed off and headed toward the deep end, wearing a flotation device that kept his legs suspended as he swam. His feet were useless for kicking; all his forward movement came from his powerful arms. Lonnie watched the machine-like precision of the boy's muscles as his body cut a smooth swath through the aqua blue water. Like father, like son except—Lonnie eyed the three-meter platform towering over the deep end of the pool—there was no possible way he could dive. No more ribbons for this family. That must have been hard for Harlan to take.

Quentin tagged the far end and turned. His face was buried in the water, coming up only long enough to receive breath. He appeared not to notice Lonnie until he came to a stop at the shallow end. He crawled up on the steps and rolled over to remove the swimming apparatus. He looked at his uncle but didn't say anything as he pushed the aluminum and Styrofoam contraption onto the pool's deck.

"Oh, there you are. I've been looking for you." Lonnie turned at the unexpected sound of Trudy's voice. "Actually, I wanted to see both of you. I have to take the car into town and run a few errands. The limo will bring the two of you to the lawyer's office. The reading of Harlan's will is scheduled for eleven in the offices of Gladdon, Vickers and Cox. Quentin, you know where it is, don't you? I want you to bring your uncle along and make sure he doesn't get lost. Lonnie, are you okay with that?"

Lonnie nodded. Trudy was wearing a white summer dress

complete with a large-brimmed white hat that covered her face on one side. She held a white patent purse under her arm. Day after the funeral, and it appeared mourning was over. Now it was down to business. The white ensemble made a striking contrast to the strawberry blond highlights of her hair. Her eyes were as green as the ocean, and her lips their signature crimson red.

"All right then. Quentin, you'd better start getting ready. You only have an hour. The limo will pick you up at ten. You too, Lon. I'll see you both there." And with that she turned on the toe of her white pumps, her spiked heels clicking on the wet pavement as she walked away.

Quentin was sitting on the steps of the pool leaning back on his elbows, his legs still submerged in the shimmering aqua water. He pushed himself up and back with his hands, scaling one step at a time until he reached the top. "You heading out any time soon?" he asked.

"Matter of fact, I plan to leave after the reading of the will."

Quentin nodded, then hoisted himself onto a lift that had been installed at the edge of the pool, adjusting his position until he was centered. "Can I be straight with you?"

Lonnie shrugged. "Of course. What's on your mind?"

"I think you want Dad's company. I think you're sucking up to Mom so she'll proxy her shares to you, so you can take control." He narrowed his gaze, making an observation. "Nice haircut. I'm sure she likes it, but you'll have to do better than that." Quentin toweled off and, using the lift device, raised himself to the height of his wheelchair. He set the brake, removed one of the arms from the chair, and scooted to the side until he was comfortably seated. Then he replaced the arm and took hold of the rubber tires, releasing the brake again. He rocked the wheels a few times, swiveling the chair back and forth. "You're wasting your time," he said. "Mom knows Dad wanted me in charge. She'll let me run the company. The point I'm making is, you're not needed. Go back to wherever it is you came from and leave me and my mother alone. She doesn't need your help, and neither do I."

For the life of him, Lonnie couldn't understand the boy's hostility. He hadn't done anything to deserve it. Maybe it was genetic, a character flaw handed down from Striker to Striker—Buddy to Harlan to Quentin. Didn't matter, Quentin was only asking him to do exactly what he planned to do anyway. "Sounds fine to me," Lonnie said. And with that, he turned and walked back to the house.

THEY WERE somewhere in the jungles of downtown Los Angeles. Huge cement, metal alloy, and glass towers loomed up on both sides of the road, dwarfing the cars as they skittered about like tiny ants on hot asphalt. The wind was gusting, tearing at clothes and hair, making sure no one arrived anywhere without looking mussed. With the breeze blowing, and the temperature so warm, it was like walking around inside a blast furnace.

The windows were reflecting the city-scape as the limo pulled to the curb. Lonnie stared out at the dizzying tall black-glass skyscraper, wondering if this was where the law firm had its office. If so, their services didn't come cheap. Quentin gave an affirming nod, answering his question. Surprisingly, his nephew had been civil on the ride over. He'd asked about Lonnie's work in Mexico, his marital status, or whether or not he was seeing someone, to which Lonnie bashfully answered, "No," but defended himself by saying he was still waiting for the right girl to come along. It seemed as though, now that Quentin had said what he felt needed saying, things between them were more relaxed. Quentin had mistakenly thought Lonnie was after the family business, but they'd straightened that out. Lonnie had his duffel bag in the car to prove he was ready to leave. Maybe now they could be friends.

The driver helped Quentin out of the limo and into his chair. Lonnie hesitated before climbing out. He reached for his wallet, wondering if he should offer to pay. He stood at the curb fishing for bills, while Quentin pulled his chair around to the side of the car. With all their money, you'd think the boy would have a motorized scooter, but he seemed to like going places under his own steam. Probably had something to do with self-reliance. Lonnie would have offered to push, but he sensed Quentin would take it wrong. Quentin patted the limo with the flat of his hand, and the car pulled away. Neither of them had paid. *Must have an account with the limo service*, Lonnie surmised.

Entry to the ebony building was through a wide revolving door. Lonnie stood aside so Quentin could maneuver his chair through first, then picked up his duffel bag and followed. Quentin rolled effortlessly across the smooth marble tiles. The lobby was teeming with men and women in fashionable business dress, their hard-soled shoes clapping on the shiny floor. Lonnie felt conspicuous in his second-hand suit with the soiled bag under his arm. Suddenly self-conscious, he pinched the legs of his trousers and tugged them down so they would appear longer. No one seemed to pay them any mind as Quentin weaved his wheelchair in and out of traffic, with Lonnie trailing a few feet behind.

The sun poured through the tinted glass providing light to the dozens of full-size palms growing inside the lobby. Three banks of elevators rose from the center of the building with six elevators in each bank. Small brass plaques at the end of the aisle showed the numbers of the floors serviced by each of the elevators. Lonnie was tempted to stop and ask the man at the security desk which floor Gladdon, Vickers, and Cox was on, but he had to keep up with Quentin, and Quentin refused to wait.

"It's down at the end," Quentin called over his shoulder as though reading Lonnie's thoughts. "Gladdon's in the tower suite, up on floor forty-two."

Lonnie finally caught up as Quentin pulled to a stop in front of the last row of elevators. They endured the wait in the middle of a growing crowd until they heard a bell, *ding,* and watched the doors open. As the car began filling with people, Quentin spun his chair around backwards, and when there was barely room, wheeled himself inside, letting the door slide shut in Lonnie's face. Lonnie heard him cry out, "Race you to the top, Unk."

Whether Quentin was playing games or being rude, Lonnie didn't know, but all of a sudden he found himself standing alone. A few seconds passed and another elevator opened. People were getting on and off. Lonnie squeezed in and pushed the button. The race was on. He grew impatient as the elevator stopped and started at various floors, taking on new passengers and spewing out others. By the time he reached the penthouse, he was out of breath, but there was Quentin, waiting, with a triumphant grin on his face. "You lose," he said. He spun around and rolled his chair into the reception area of Gladdon, Vickers, and Cox. Must have been some kind of game. Lonnie decided to leave it at that.

A receptionist sitting behind a circular walnut desk picked up a phone, "They're here sir...uh huh...all right," she said. She let Quentin and Lonnie know it would be a few minutes, and suggested they make themselves comfortable. But before Lonnie had a chance to sit down, a door opened behind them. A well dressed woman holding a clipboard beckoned them to follow. Lonnie wondered how they looked—one in an ill-fitting business suit with a duffel bag under his arm and the other in a wheelchair—certainly not your typical corporate clients. She led them down the hall to a boardroom. Lonnie checked the time again, wondering how he could have gone for so many years without wearing a watch. He had to remember to give it back.

They were ushered inside. It appeared everyone was awaiting their arrival. Two men in slick lawyer suits, a woman with a legal pad ready to take notes, and Trudy in her summer white, were seated around a long boardroom table. Lonnie laid his duffel bag by the door. He turned and found Trudy glaring at him. Her face was flushed. *The duffel bag!* He hadn't had a chance to tell her, but there was nothing he could do about it now.

Lonnie avoided eye contact, choosing to fix his gaze on the scenery outside the window. The winds had carried off most of the smog, leaving a spectacular view. From where he stood, he could see across the entire L.A. basin, the heart of the planet, with a network of veins and arteries that carried people to the ends of the earth. A chair was removed so Quentin could roll up to the table, and Lonnie took a seat opposite.

Barry Gladdon introduced himself, and Lonnie stood to shake his hand across the table. The man was lean and tan, with a breezy look that suggested he favored yachting. He was impeccably dressed in a midnight-blue suit made of a silk fabric that shimmered as he turned in the light. His hair was burnished silver swept back in waves, and his chin was thrust forward as though spoiling for a fight. But this was a statesman. His battles were fought with words. He released Lonnie's hand, and Lonnie slumped back into his chair.

The man seated next to Barry was introduced as Carl Monahan, a junior with the firm. The legal assistant who would be taking minutes was Bette Williams. The woman who had escorted Lonnie and Quentin into the room put her clipboard down and asked if they would like coffee. Quentin was the only one to decline the offer.

Mr. Gladdon removed a document from a binder, and placed it on the table before him. "With respect to the last will and testament of Harlan Striker, since all concerned parties are either present or otherwise accounted for, I suggest we get the proceedings underway."

He ran through a few pages of legal jargon, pacing back and forth as he stipulated definitions and affirmed that Harlan, being of sound mind, had recently revised the will. Lonnie began to see how this might be a more complicated process than he'd originally thought. He hoped it wouldn't take too long. He still wanted to catch a plane. He risked a glance at Trudy. Her face was turned, hidden behind the curved brim of her hat, but she appeared stoic. Would she understand his decision?

After pages of reading, it was established that all fixed assets, cash, securities, and other investments, spelled out in tedious detail, were left to Trudy, while certain specific items, defined as heirlooms, were willed to Quentin. Lonnie was doing his best to stay awake, but the reading was monotonous, and Barry's droning voice proved hypnotic. The fact that Lonnie hadn't caught up on his sleep was beginning to show. He rubbed his eyes and took another sip of coffee. The thing about American coffee was, it didn't taste like coffee. Mexican coffee was thick and black, more like espresso. It had a real jolt to it, enough to jump-start the most sluggish metabolism. Its American cousin tasted more like watered-down broth with a mild coffee flavor.

Except for the action of bringing the cup to his lips, the brew did little to keep him awake. Lonnie kept wondering why he was there. So far he hadn't heard his name even once.

"...As to Striker Films, I hereby bequeath my fifty percent of the company to be divided as follows: To my wife, Trudy Ann Striker, twenty-five percent; to my son, George Quentin Striker, twenty percent; and to my brother, Lonnie Allen Striker, five percent." Lonnie had coffee in his mouth and was about to swallow, but upon hearing the pronouncement sputtered and pulled his cup back so abruptly, he almost spilled its entire contents. He wiped a drip off his chin and caught Quentin's glare. The boy obviously felt betrayed. That five percent should have been his. By passing it to Lonnie, Harlan had effectively given Lonnie control. *Why?* All he wanted was a cash donation—not a company! It didn't make sense. They hadn't even liked each other. He shifted his gaze back to Trudy. The expression on her face was flat, and her bright lips were set in a tight line. He knew he was in trouble.

Barry Gladdon folded the document and set it on the table. "And that concludes the Last Will and Testament of Harlan Striker." He reached into his coat and removed an envelope, handing it to Lonnie. "This is for you also, Mr. Striker. Your brother has asked that you read it before leaving the building. If you'll just step this way, we'll show you to a room where you can have some privacy."

LONNIE WAS led to a room with tables and chairs and leather-bound volumes occupying shelves around the walls. Had to be the firm's law library, or at least a place where staff members could do legal research. He settled into a chair and opened the letter.

> Hey there, Spud.
>
> I guess if you're reading this, then I'm already dead. I don't want to waste time arguing about who was right and who was wrong, but I think running off to Mexico was a cowardly act. You should have been

man enough to own up to your actions. And don't pretend you don't know what I mean.

Well it's time you grew up, Lonnie boy. I've been working my tail off for the past twenty years while you've been watching the moss grow on rocks down in Mexico, living on money I had to earn. I've turned Buddy's little company into a full blown studio. Ask anyone. We've produced some of the best. Until just recently, we were making money hand over fist, but now it seems we've run into a bit of bad luck. After a long string of successes we've gone and made a few pictures that, for whatever reason, haven't done so well at the box office, which means we sank more into their making than we were able to recoup. In other words, our last three consecutive films lost money. You'll have to talk to Brent Crowley, our VP of Finance, to get the actuals, but in round numbers we're about thirty million in the hole.

Don't panic, it's not as bad as it sounds. As you read this letter, the company should be a few weeks away from releasing a real blockbuster. I need you to stick around long enough to make sure the movie gets to market. In this business, thirty million is nothing. We'll get it back within a week of the film's release. I have people in place to carry the project forward. Your job is to make sure everyone else does their job and make sure everything gets finished on time. This is extremely important. I used the company as collateral. If the film isn't released on schedule, we'll default on our loans and our creditors will step in and seize our assets. In other words, my wife and son will be left penniless, and you'll have to quit playing lord of the Mexicans.

I suppose you're asking—why me? Truth is, there isn't anyone else. I can't leave the company to

Quentin. I would if I could, but I don't think he's up to the job. Not right now. Not with all he's been through. As for Trudy, she just doesn't understand the business well enough to make it fly. Not that you do, but at least you have Striker blood and that ought to count for something. It's about time you earned your money. And there's another reason: I don't want Trudy or Quentin to know the company's in trouble. It's important they believe I'm continuing to provide for them, even after I'm dead.

I know you don't want to do it, but I'm afraid you don't have a choice. You're not doing it for me, you're doing it for Trudy and Quentin, and for yourself because if Striker Films goes under, you'll own fifty-five percent of nothing.

I'm not asking all that much. Just sit at my desk until the film is finished and see that it gets released on time. And do it without letting Quentin or Trudy know there was ever a problem. That's all. Once our debts are paid, and we're in the black again, you can find yourself a replacement, someone you trust so your own future, as well as Trudy's and Quentin's, will be secure. Then you can run off to your little hiding place in Mexico and be mosquito bait for the rest of your natural life, if that's what you want. You know what? I'm betting you won't. I'm betting you'll like it at the top. I think you'll stick around awhile. The perks are great for the man in the seat of power, Spud. The perks are great.

The letter was signed: Harlan Lloyd Striker.

SEVEN

LONNIE STARED at the building, his eyes scrolling from street level into the clouds. It was the same building he'd been in the day before. He was sure of it. The same black, shiny monolith stood before him, mounting up to heaven like the Tower of Babel. Gladdon, Vickers and Cox had their office in this building. It was where they'd had their meeting. He asked the driver to confirm the address. The man read it out loud. It was the right place.

Lonnie pulled himself from the cab and stretched. The wind had finally subsided, leaving an unbearable heat. He grabbed the knot of his tie, putting a finger under his collar to relieve the pressure—*a pox on the man who invented ties.* He couldn't get used to having a rope around his neck. And this was his third day in the same clothes. *Such a miserable suit! Harlan was buried in a better suit than this.* Lonnie had only planned on wearing it once. The temperature was already in the nineties. At this rate, his shirt would soon reek.

He put his thumbs in his pockets and tried hitching down the pants. Maybe he should buy himself another outfit, something more in fashion, or at least something that fit. Here he was, ready to march in and assume the role of president and Chief Executive Officer of the great Striker Films, and he looked like a country bumpkin in hand-me-downs. He was sure he'd be met with gawks and stares. It wouldn't take them five minutes to figure out he didn't know a thing about making movies, let alone running a business. He straightened his tie. Well, too bad. It wasn't his decision; there wasn't a thing anyone could do about it. They'd just have to suffer through it together.

His real goal was to gain the support of Trudy and Quentin. They were the ones who mattered. After reading Harlan's confidential letter, he had made his way back to the boardroom only to find them already gone. They'd left a message saying they'd decided to get some lunch and would meet him back at the house. The note had included a key, and the code for disarming the security system. Fortunately, they'd also arranged for the limo to give him a ride home. He'd called the Inn in Posada and had them locate Father Ceylon so he could explain his predicament. The good father assured him everything would be fine while he was away. The project was on schedule, and they could always call if they needed him.

Paulo's reassurance helped, but Lonnie still felt deserted as he meandered through Harlan's grapefruit-pink mausoleum all alone. *Such a big house—big and empty!* His mind was burdened by the weight of what he was being asked to do. He decided to change his clothes and walk down to the beach to seek divine counsel.

It was late afternoon by the time he reached the ocean. He sat on weathered stone like a grain of sand, small and insignificant, with the force of wind and water whipping his hair and spraying his face. He stayed and prayed, and watched the sun lower itself on the pink horizon till the translucent waves were yellow-green and the sky at his back had faded to a purple dusk.

He began making his way back to the house on a sandy path subdued by twilight. When he reached the front door, he had to flick on the lights to see. The life-sized portraits jumped out at him giving him a start—Sir Harlan and his lady fair—ghosts of his past and present. He caught his breath and continued into the house, surprised to find it still empty. He couldn't fathom what was taking Trudy and Quentin so long. His body ached. He decided to pass the time by taking a nap.

He slept until dawn, dead to the world until he heard the morning cry of seagulls. He stirred, waking to a cool offshore breeze seeping through an open window. They closed that window every day to preserve the air conditioning, but he couldn't stand not breathing fresh air, so he opened it every night before going to bed. Slipping downstairs, he found evidence that Trudy and Quentin had made it home. It was too early for them to be up, so he decided to return to the beach to seek God's advice once more. It wasn't that he didn't know what he had to do; he knew, but he didn't *want* to do it, and he questioned why God was requiring it of him. *"Father, let this cup pass from me,"* he prayed. The seagull's lament voiced his emotions. Breathing deeply, he imbibed the musty smell of seaweed and wet sand, which provided momentary relief. But the morning sun soon created an uncomfortable itch, and his stomach doubled in knots, and his mouth became dry—and he knew his calm had given way to fear. His heart was pounding with the beat of the waves as he knelt to pray. He stayed until the water soaked into his knees and finally God said: "*Not 'thy' will but 'Mine' be done.*"

He'd do it. That's why he was standing at the curb now, dreading going inside because he knew the minute he passed through those doors, his life would change—forever. The enormity of what he was being asked to do bore down on his shoulders. Saving Striker Films was one thing. If it weren't for the personal issues involved, he might even enjoy the challenge. But being forced to run the company put him at odds with his nephew, just when they'd been on the verge of reconciliation. They were about to part as friends—*it was nice meeting you, drop by the next time you're in town*—and *wham*, they'd been broadsided by Harlan's will. Now the boy had a reason to hate him. Quentin would consider him a thief. And for all he knew, so might Trudy. He suspected she and Quentin had ditched him so they could be alone to console each other. They'd probably gone off to drown their troubles in a drink and had ended up closing the bar. What happened wasn't fair. They would have expected to receive it all—and they should have. He didn't want it; it had been foisted on him, but he couldn't share that simple fact without disclosing Harlan's secret.

What was he supposed to say? Trudy was probably okay, Harlan's decision didn't affect her share—but Quentin deserved an explanation. So far they had missed each other. Lonnie had slipped out while Quentin was still in the gym, but their paths were bound to cross sooner or later. His nephew would think he'd lied when he'd said he wanted no part of running the company. But his brother's last request had to be honored. He would just have to ignore the criticism until they were out of debt. A few weeks at best. He didn't agree with Harlan's assessment of Quentin. The boy was hurt, and those who are hurt, often hurt others, but there was good beneath that brusque exterior. Lonnie could feel it. The boy was strong. Lonnie needed to find a way to crack through the facade, but first he had to get the company out of debt. Then, maybe he could install Quentin as its new president. All would be forgiven once he stepped aside and let the boy assume his rightful place.

Lonnie pushed through the revolving door, stopping at the security desk to ask which elevator he should take. He rode up in silence. The people around him seemed self-absorbed, staring at the walls. A *ding* sounded, the door opened, and Lonnie got off on the thirty-second floor, facing another set of elevators.

He stood looking to his right and left. One way emptied into a corridor. The other stopped at two glass doors. The words Striker Films were spelled out in large brass letters mounted on the wall behind a reception desk. He entered the office, clearing his throat to get the receptionist's attention. She looked up and smiled, and when he said his name, picked up the phone and dialed. "Someone will be with you in a minute, Mr. Striker," she said. "Why don't you have a seat."

Evidently, she didn't know he owned the place. Lonnie adjusted his tie and smoothed his hair as he sat down, hoping he was presentable. He looked around for a newspaper but didn't see one. He pulled the sleeves of his coat over his shirt cuffs and picked up a magazine, "The Cinematic Review," obviously an industry rag. He began flipping through the pages until the door opened. He looked up to see a young woman standing there, perhaps in her late twenties, with blond hair pulled back and tied with a ribbon, quite good-looking really—and shapely. She introduced herself as Nicole, Harlan's assistant, and invited Lonnie in. He followed her trim figure as she swished her way down the hall. *Like father, like son,* Lonnie thought. *Some things never change.*

Nicole walked him past dozens of cubicles. He felt the eyes of the occupants staring at his too-small business suit—*hey bro, get a load of this!* Well, too bad. He wasn't there to impress anyone. They weren't doing much to impress him either. He didn't see anyone else wearing a coat and tie as he and Nicole zigzagged through the maze of fabric work-stations, but he did see computer screens, popping with the mind-blowing graphics of games and dot.com sites and shop-on-line stores. More than enough trivia to occupy the mind and limit productivity. Why weren't these people making movies? He wasn't sure what he'd expected but whatever it was, this wasn't it. There should be cameras and actors in costumes rehearsing their lines. Why would anyone put a film company in a high-rise anyway? They should be in an industrial complex with a back lot full of Quonset huts and disassembled sets, surrounded by a chain link fence.

The woman stopped at two huge oak doors, and Lonnie was shown inside. "This is your office," she announced.

Lonnie scanned the room quickly. It was a brightly lit suite with huge floor-to-ceiling windows. The view was as grand as the one he'd seen from the law office of Gladdon, Vickers and Cox. There was a desk, big as a car, and behind it a tall, cushy, brown leather chair. Two guest chairs faced the desk and a long couch occupied the wall. "*My* office?" Lonnie questioned.

"Yes, well it was your brother's. I mean, Harlan's. Sorry, I mean Mr. Striker's. We've been told it now belongs to you."

"Told? By whom?"

"Mrs. Striker called to say you were on your way over. She said her husband left you in charge of the company, and that we should treat you just the way we would treat him."

Lonnie nodded. The man at the wake had said Trudy would hire someone to manage the business. Maybe she was okay with the transition. It only made sense. She got the house, the car, the investments, and a guaranteed income for life. Of course, she probably thought she owned twenty-five percent of a healthy corporation, not twenty-five percent of a thirty-million-dollar debt.

"Nice," Lonnie said, referring to the room.

"Well, have a seat. Can I get you anything—coffee, tea, a soft drink?"

"Nothing, thanks. I'll tell you what I'd really like. I'd like you to take me around and introduce me. I'd like to meet the people I'll be working with."

"Uh huh, okay. Your three vice presidents are expecting you. I can call them to the boardroom, but it will take a few minutes. You might as well make yourself comfortable while you wait."

"Thanks, I'll do that. And could you come back soon as you're done? There's something we need to discuss."

Nicole nodded. "Sure...uh...you okay?"

"Okay? I'm fine. Why?"

"You took quite a fall at the funeral the other day. I was just wondering."

Lonnie brought his hand up to his head and felt for a knot. "No. I wasn't hurt. I'm fine. Really."

Nicole tilted her head back and smiled with a wink that suggested she really understood him to say: *Yes, it hurts, but boys don't cry.* She turned and went back to her station. Lonnie glanced at the computer screen sitting on his desk. It was as worthless to him as the car parked in Trudy's garage. *A vehicle's no good when you don't know how to drive.* He busied himself rummaging through the desk drawers, not looking for anything in particular, just curious.

A few minutes later Nicole returned and stood at the door.

Lonnie looked up and waved her in. "Please, have a seat," and as an afterthought added, "Oh, ah, would you mind closing the door."

"If it's all right with you, I'd prefer to leave the door open." She entered cautiously and took a seat in front of the desk. "What can I do for you, Mr. Striker?"

"First off, you can drop the Mister and call me Lonnie, like everyone else does."

She nodded.

Lonnie looked her over. It didn't surprise him that Harlan would hire someone so attractive, but he could only imagine how it must have made Trudy feel. His brother always did have a way with the ladies. He glanced at the soft leather couch. At least it wasn't a bed. He didn't want nasty rumors following him around. Nicole's refusal to close the door suggested she had a reputation to protect. Good for her. "You were Harlan's executive assistant," he said. "Would I be correct in assuming that from time to time he had to share information with you he didn't want others to know—confidential memos and things like that?"

Again Nicole nodded.

"Good. Look, I'm going to be straight with you. My dad may have started this company, and I'm sure my brother deserves credit for building it up, but now it's been passed on to me, and truth is, I don't know the first thing about making movies." Lonnie leaned back and picked up a pencil, drumming the eraser on the desk while trying to gauge Nicole's reaction. She didn't appear overly surprised. "What I'm about to say, I'd like kept just between the two of us, okay? I find myself in a awkward position. On the one hand, I don't know a thing about this business, and on the other, I'm supposed to run it. If everyone finds out how ignorant I am, I'll lose their respect and it will diminish my authority. So I walk a pretty fine line between ignorance and trying not to let it show. I need someone I can trust to explain things to me, especially when I get into trouble. I was hoping that someone would be you. Of course it means you'll have to sit in on most of my meetings, like the one we're about to have. I don't know if my brother had you attend his meetings or not, but I'd like you there to take notes. Then, later, if I need clarification on a point, you can help me out. Is that all right with you?"

So far Nicole hadn't said a word. Her expression remained flat as she dipped her head in agreement.

"All right, then. Perhaps you can begin by spending a few minutes explaining how this business works."

Nicole's eyes widened as she leaned forward. "That's a pretty tall order," she said.

"But it's information I'm going to need. How about just giving me the highlights. We can save the details for later."

Nicole laced her fingers together and locked them around

her knees. "Well, the first thing you need is a script," she said. "Sometimes the idea comes from a book someone has read and thinks would make a good movie. We buy the rights and hire a screenwriter to adapt the book to film. Or sometimes a writer comes to us with an original script and tries to sell it to us. We've even had producers hire us to make movies from scripts they own, but producers usually want to make creative decisions and Harlan liked to reserve those for himself, so he avoided working with them whenever possible."

At this, Lonnie had to smile, though he tried keeping it to himself, but the idea of Harlan letting anyone else make any kind of decision was laughable. He crossed his arms and brought a hand up to cover his mouth as though contemplating the significance of what Nicole had said.

"Of course, you can't make a movie without money, and a producer usually brings money to the table. More often than not, that would force Harlan to relinquish control. I mean no disrespect, but personally I think we made some of our best films that way, though I'm sure Harlan would have disagreed. Anyway, if we don't get money from a producer, we usually have to go out and find independent financing. Most of our films have been paid for by financiers and private backers willing to invest in our success. We went through a brief period where we had enough money to do everything ourselves, but then we made a few bad pictures and I guess the money ran out. You'll have to ask our VP of finance, Brent Crowley, about that. He's the one in charge of the budget."

"Will Mr. Crowley be in the meeting we're about to have." Lonnie interjected.

Nicole nodded. "Yes, of course. He's part of our executive management team. Anyway, the next step is handled by our casting director, Jeremy Jones. I'll take you around and introduce you a little later, if you'd like. Jeremy reads the script, figures out who's right for what part, and then holds auditions and screen tests. He's limited somewhat because he has to work within the budget set by Brent. Agents always want more than you're willing to offer, that's a given, but Jeremy's real talent is getting the actors excited about the project.

Good actors get dozens of scripts to read and they pick and choose very carefully which ones they'll accept. If they like what you're doing, the money can be negotiated.

"Jeremy is usually asked to hire the director as well. It isn't always done that way; some companies hire the director separately, but Harlan liked having Jeremy negotiate the entire package. Just like with actors, good directors have to be convinced that the film you're doing is worth their involvement. A good film can further their career, and a bad one can ruin it. And certain actors work well with certain directors, which is another reason Harlan had the casting director hire both. Jeremy is paid to know who works well with who."

Lonnie leaned back in his chair. According to Harlan's letter, the film they were working on was almost done. He probably wouldn't have a chance to meet the actors. He certainly didn't want to. To his way of thinking, the homage paid to stars by adoring fans was silly. In fact, it was downright offensive.

"Everything after that falls under the umbrella of Les Miller, our VP of Production," Nicole went on. "He oversees the making of the film from story-boarding to the actual filming, to post-production editing, sound engineering, and special effects—the list goes on. You've got a lot to learn, Mr...ah, Lonnie, and I'm not sure I know enough to be your teacher."

Lonnie looked at his watch and stood, placing his hands flat on his desk. "Are you kidding? You've already been a big help. I feel much better about this meeting. Speaking of which, we'd better be going. But remember to keep this conversation under your hat, at least until I gain some confidence, okay?"

LONNIE FOUND the vice presidents were ready and waiting when he and Nicole entered the boardroom. At his insistence Nicole introduced him by his first name. He shook each of their hands, in turn. First was Michael Sugarman, who handed Lonnie a card with tiny letters behind his name indicating he had a degree in law. He was introduced as the Executive VP, which Nicole explained was another way of saying he had been Harlan's second-in-command. He was a tall man with a firm handshake and manicured fingernails. He looked down on Lonnie from his impressive height with a gaze both cool and dark. He didn't say anything, nor did he smile. *Second-in-command?* It begged the question as to why Harlan hadn't left *him* in charge.

Next was Les Miller, VP of Production, a short, bald man in a wild Hawaiian print shirt that barely covered his overhanging gut. The man's clothes reeked of cigarette smoke and Old Spice. Finally came the woolly-headed Brent Crowley, the company's VP of Finance. None of the men wore suits. Casual attire appeared to be in order even at the executive level. Lonnie fingered the knot of his tie, considering whether he should pull it loose, but that would be too obvious. He let go and tugged on the sleeves of his coat.

Nicole closed the door while Lonnie explained that he had asked her to stay so she could take notes. The three men took their seats. Lonnie chose a spot at the side rather than the head of the table, though he figured the head of the table was where his brother would have sat. Les lit a cigarette and snapped his chrome-topped lighter shut, sliding it back into his pocket. He looped a finger into an ashtray and dragged it toward himself.

Lonnie cleared his throat. "Well, I guess we're here to get to know each other," he said. "Let me start by saying I'd appreciate your cooperation." He cleared his throat again, and continued. "My father started this company and, as you know, Harlan took over from him. I haven't been involved for a number of years, so I'll need you to bring me up to speed. Harlan said we're about finished with a new movie. I believe he said it was due for release in a few weeks. Let's start with that."

There was silence in the room. Les blew a stream of smoke out the side of his mouth and leaned in to knock the ash off the end of his cigarette. Lonnie waited but no one seemed anxious to speak. "I'm not asking for a complete history, just an update."

The three men looked around the table at each other, obviously reluctant to say anything, but their eyes finally settled on Brent, prompting him to break the silence. "Nicole, I expect you already know this, but please keep it confidential," he said. He turned his attention back to Lonnie. "I don't know how much you were told about our financial picture, but it's pretty bleak. We've sunk about thirty million of borrowed money into this new film and that, along with about twenty million in accumulated debt, puts us in a pretty tight spot. The problem is, you can't make much of a film for thirty million, and unless this new release is good enough to rake in the cash, we could be out of business. Our vendors have been good so far but several are refusing to extend our credit any further. Truth is, we may not have enough money to finish the film, and we need to finish to get out of debt, so," he shrugged, spreading his hands, "it's a catch 22."

Lonnie drummed his fingers on the table. "So you're saying I'm wasting my time, is that it?"

Brent looked at Les, and then at Michael. "No, I wouldn't go that far. I just want you to know our situation."

Lonnie was leaving fingerprints on the highly polished wood. He stopped his tapping and pulled his cuffs down. "Harlan mentioned the thirty million, and how not paying it back means we lose the company, which isn't good news. He didn't say anything about the other twenty million, but I'm sure he knew about it, and he didn't seem worried. He claimed a good film could gross thirty million in a week. Do you agree?"

"Sure, providing it *is* a good film, and there's enough pre-publicity."

"And is it? A good film, I mean."

The three men exchanged glances across the table, their expressions revealing an awkwardness that bordered on discomfort. Michael spoke first. "Harlan thought it would be a box office smash."

"But what do you think?"

"I think we'd prefer to have you make up your own mind. We have our first assembly cued up. It's a long way from a final cut but you'll be able to get the gist of it. It's about a two hour running time. If you want to know what we've got, the screening room is just through that door." Michael tipped his head indicating a door at the far end of the room.

"Well, I guess I should see it then." Lonnie pressed his fingers against the table and stood, and the others followed his lead.

The adjoining room was arranged like a small theater with two dozen comfortable theater chairs mounted on three carpeted risers, eight seats to a row with an aisle down the middle. Through a door at the rear, a projection booth was situated on an elevated platform. Lonnie could see the projectionist sitting behind a glass window. The men seated themselves. On cue the lights went out and for a moment all was dark. Then a beam pierced the darkness, throwing images onto the screen. Les had taken the seat in front of Lonnie, so Lonnie had to view the images through a veil of cigarette smoke.

Lonnie watched the titles roll, and saw the Striker Films logo and a roster of actors whose names he didn't recognize. That wasn't surprising considering where he lived and how often he went to the theater. Finally the movie title appeared on screen. "LOST CAUSE." *Lost cause???*

The plot developed slowly at first, a typical boy-meets-girl love story. Lonnie found himself enjoying it until they came to a scene where the clothes came off and the screen was filled with a few minutes of steamy grunting and panting, and pulsating limb-locked bodies. He slouched in his chair and glanced around the room. Was he the only one embarrassed? The girl on the screen was naked! But even Nicole seemed unfazed. *That will have to come out,* he decided. Otherwise, the story seemed innocent enough, almost sweet.

Another scene revealed that the parents couldn't understand their daughter, Lisa, and didn't trust her boyfriend, Kirk, but failed at trying to communicate what they felt. The daughter claimed the boyfriend was her, "astral soul mate." The parents confronted the boyfriend, but their growing frustration erupted in anger with both mother and father screaming, leaving the audience to conclude they were card-carrying members of the lunatic fringe. Lisa and Kirk decided it was time to run away.

Lonnie shook his head. There was no reason to portray the parents that way. It didn't add to the plot, it only made fools of two people who had their daughter's best interests at heart. It was one more thing he'd have to change.

On their own now, the young couple faced mounting pressure. Kirk lost his job, and Lisa started having repeated headaches. A series of tests revealed an abnormal growth on her cerebrum—*cancer!*—malignant and inoperable. She was living on borrowed time. Complicating the situation, the physician also let her know she was pregnant. It was her choice, he said, but as long as they didn't use chemo, which, at best, would only extend her life a few months, they might be able to save the child. Lisa told Kirk she planned to refuse the treatment. They couldn't afford radiation therapy, she argued. But she didn't tell him about the baby. With all the problems they already had, she didn't know how he would respond.

Up to this point, the drama was building. Lonnie felt his emotions being charged. He liked Lisa's choice to give her baby life. He could empathize with the girl, though he forced his expression to remain impassive. He wondered if Harlan's selection of this particular script had anything to do with his own cancer. He would have felt the young woman's hopelessness as he lay awake at night, thinking about the certainty of death. Or maybe Harlan meant it as a tribute to their mother. Cancer had taken her as well. If so, Harlan had a sentimental side Lonnie was unaware of.

The film rolled along as a dozen scenarios played out, some of which Lonnie agreed with, but most of which he didn't. Lisa's surgeon, probably the most compassionate person in the story, turned out to be gay. Lonnie cringed. It was political correctness at its worst, the gay doctor being presented as more Christlike than the girl's religious parents, who condemned Kirk for dragging their daughter into sin. Lonnie kept hoping to find some moral, some hint that righteousness would prevail, but things just went from bad to worse.

Lisa was fading fast, growing weaker each day, and Kirk continued to grow more and more despondent. One day Lisa passed out in his arms, alive but hanging on by a thread. A team of nurses bolted in and, spinning her bed around, rushed her down the hall. In the flurry of confusion, Kirk was left standing alone. Tears gushed down his cheeks as he raised his arm and shook his fist in the face of God, screaming: "It isn't fair," It isn't...*fair*!" He stumbled from the hospital, cursing the doctors for not doing enough and vowing to get even.

He was hiding behind a hedge in the yard of a sleeping house, cloaked in the black of night. His eyes were dead in their sockets, his movements robotic. He broke a window, slipped inside, and quietly made his way to the gun cabinet. He tucked two pistols into his belt and removed a shotgun, which he cocked over his arm. He returned to the hospital, slinking down back streets and alleys, dark as a shadow at midnight. He began in the lobby and went striding down the hall yelling, "THIS IS FOR LISA!" as he shot doctors, nurses, and innocent bystanders alike. "LIFE ISN'T FAIR, IS IT?" he bellowed. Smoke was streaming from the barrel of his gun, his eyes were narrow and malevolent, the sound deafening as blood splattered across the screen. The assault of sound and images was horrifying.

Sirens began to wail and red lights to flash as Kirk worked his way back to Lisa's room. He shot a nurse and stepped over her body. "Life's not fair," he said. He took his girlfriend, cradled her in his arms and began stroking her hair. They were Romeo and Juliet, he whispered. In life, everyone and everything had tried to keep them apart, but in death they would be together forever. He kissed Lisa and vowed to see her on the other side, but she was too sedated to understand. A police tactical squad surrounded the room. One tried to peek around the door and Kirk responded by shooting him in the face. Chaos broke out. He dropped Lisa's hand and backed away from her bed, putting himself in front of a blank wall as the officers opened fire. His body danced in slow motion as it was riddled with bullets. He never noticed the bassinet in the corner, but as he lay bleeding to death on the floor, he could hear his newborn baby cry.

Lonnie stood. "I've seen enough. Can we have the lights, please?" He turned and walked back into the boardroom. The three executives were caught off guard, but followed.

Lonnie sat down and closed his eyes for a moment, tapping his fingers on the table as he took a deep breath. Harlan would have loved that ending—everyone dies! In a perverted way it *did* seem fair. But he wasn't Harlan. He couldn't put that kind of movie into theaters where it might be seen by innocent children, or for that matter, by anyone else. Then again, how could he avoid it? Not releasing the film meant insolvency. Only a fool would sabotage a critical project for the sake of moral integrity. *No! Only a fool would try to peddle garbage.* He opened his eyes. "Gentlemen, we have a bigger problem than the money. That film can't go out. I won't release it. Not that way."

Les, the man in charge of production, raised an eyebrow. He pulled an ashtray in to snuff his cigarette. "Won't release it. What do you mean?"

"I mean I won't let that kind of film bear the Striker name, not while I'm head of the company. I don't have kids, but if I did, I wouldn't let them see a movie like that. I won't be guilty of foisting that kind of material on young, impressionable minds."

"Oh. Well, then, no problem. The rating system will keep juveniles from seeing it. The audience will have to be eighteen or older."

Lonnie searched for an answer but none came. He was talking about trashing a thirty-million-dollar project. No more hospital and all the good it would bring. What about the investors? They probably had a contract that guaranteed the film's release. He could be sued! Didn't anyone understand? If you sell poison to kids, you have to take responsibility for the death it brings. Didn't they have an obligation to produce films with some kind of social value? From the incredulous looks he was getting, the answer was—*No!* For them the only thing that mattered was the money. How could he make them understand? He could not with a clear conscience show young people fornicating and call it love. It contravened God's laws, and breaking God's laws meant broken lives—teen pregnancies, sexually transmitted diseases—*hello, does anybody see the connection?* And parents struggling to communicate truth to their children didn't need to be pictured as narrow-minded Neanderthals.

Of course, the boy did end up getting the girl pregnant. At least the movie showed the result of their actions, but what were the repercussions? When he saw his dreams being shattered, instead of admitting his mistake and facing his problem with courage, this guy went on a killing spree. What kind of message was there in that? The film was teaching kids that the way to deal with their problems was to blow innocent people away. And with impunity because, in the end, the boy got exactly what he wanted—the fulfillment of his death wish. He'd gone out in a blaze of glory. One bad message after another. Didn't anyone else see it?

The faces around the table remained blank, but the eyes betrayed questions, Lonnie knew behind the masks were comic grins. His executives thought they were dealing with some kind of nut. *What do you mean you won't release it?* Nicole was biting a fingernail. Even *she* looked nervous. What right did he have to force his morals on the rest of the world—the edict of God? *Well, yes, God was pretty clear about some things.* "It's not about the rating," he said. "That film can't be released the way it is."

The three sat dumbfounded. "Look, I agree with you to a point," Brent said. "Maybe not about the effect the film might have on teenagers—kids see worse every day—but I agree it's not much in the way of good cinema. And while I hope I'm wrong, I doubt it will make the money we need." He shook his head. "But it has to go out as is. Les will tell you, we're in the final stages of sound and edit. We don't have time for changes, and we couldn't afford them even if we did."

Lonnie shook his head. His mouth was dry, his stomach in knots, but he was determined to stand his ground. "I'm sorry, gentlemen, but that film cannot be released." He pushed himself to his feet, indicating the meeting was over. "If it means folding the company, then so be it, but I'd like time to consider my options, if there are any. Les, I know you're on a tight schedule, but I ask that you hold off for the moment. I'll get back to you after I've had a chance to think this through."

LONNIE WANDERED back to his office without stopping to speak to anyone along the way. He knew the workers were curious about the new boss. He didn't want to seem aloof, but there was little point in getting to know people he might have to fire in a few days.

And that's just what he'd have to do if the company had to be shut down. How could he explain to Paulo that he wouldn't be able to finish the hospital? Desperate for a few minutes of privacy, he closed his office door, placed his elbows on his desk, and bowed his head. His stomach tightened. It felt like his prayers hit the ceiling and bounced back, or at least no voice thundered from the halls of heaven to bring him an answer. He raised his head. Someone was rapping on the door.

Nicole stepped in with a cup of coffee and set it on his desk. "Here," she said, "you look like you could use one."

Lonnie nodded. "I really don't know what to do," he said, rubbing his face with his hands. "If I kill the film, we're out of business. You won't have a job, my sister-in-law and nephew will be broke, and I myself will be unable to keep the commitments I've made. But if I release it, I'll be contradicting everything I believe."

Nicole hesitated, shifting her weight from one foot to the other. She crossed her arms, then tapped a red nail on her lips. "As you already pointed out, I was Harlan's confidential assistant. He told me something...ah, something I don't think anyone else knows about..."

Lonnie jerked his head up from his hands, instantly intrigued.

"...but, if the reins of power have been handed over to you, and if I'm now going to be your assistant, maybe I should tell you."

"Go on," he said, leaning back in his chair.

"The thing is, that movie isn't what it was intended to be. Harlan didn't follow the script."

"In what way? How do you mean?"

Nicole hesitated. "I don't know how much I should say. There's a rumor going around that you used to be some kind of missionary. Is that true?"

Lonnie nodded, wondering what his vocation had to do with anything. It was only his first day on the job. News traveled fast.

"Because Harlan swore me to secrecy, but if you can't trust a missionary with a secret, who can you trust?"

"Look, if Harlan told you something personal, I don't want to hear it, but if it concerns the company, then I'm all ears."

"No, it's nothing personal. It's about the company, or at least about the script."

"Okay, I'm listening."

"Well, the thing is, the original script was good. Harlan bought it years ago, but he never did anything with it. He just kept it on file. Then, when we started having financial problems and he was looking for ways to cut corners, he pulled it out again. Since it was already paid for, I guess he figured it would save us money, but he rewrote several of the scenes and changed the ending. I know because I was the one who typed the revisions. In my opinion, his changes didn't help. In fact, I didn't like the way the new script turned out. But he didn't want Quentin to know what he was doing, so he made me promise not to say anything."

"Quentin? What's Quentin got to do with it?"

"He wrote it. At least he wrote the first draft, the one I liked, before his father took it apart."

Lonnie felt his pulse quicken. *Quentin had written a better script?* "Where's the script Quentin wrote? Do you have a copy?"

"Yes."

"Can I see it?"

"I...suppose so..."

LONNIE ARRIVED home late that evening—long after normal business hours. He'd stayed until he'd read the entire original script written by his nephew. Nicole had been right—it *was* good. The boy had written a touching love story (*Quentin a closet romantic, go figure*) that ended in tragedy, not bloodshed, and clearly showed the difference between right and wrong. That's what Lonnie wanted to see—some redeeming social value. The story line was pretty much the same, so most of the film could be salvaged. All they had to do was cut out the nudity, revamp the conflict with Lisa's parents, edit one scene with her doctor, and change the ending. Now he had something to work with—he had hope!

EIGHT

LONNIE WOKE at dawn—*again*—though with each passing day he found it more difficult to free himself from the freshly laundered smell of those wonderful sheets. He tugged the cool white linens up under his chin, snuggled in, wasted a few more minutes enjoying the luxury, then pushed them aside. Wouldn't do to become too soft.

He forced himself to roll out of bed, stretched and yawned. He reached down and pulled the covers up over his pillow, tucking them in, though he wondered why he bothered. Someone, probably the same someone that insisted on closing his window, changed the bedding every day. How different this dream castle from his tiny bed back home—a cot with spring webbing and a mattress stuffed with cotton wadding. But that was then; he had to live in the present. He rubbed his cheeks, felt the stubble of his beard, and trundled off to the bathroom to enjoy another luxury—a hot shower and a shave!

A half-hour later he was standing in front of a huge walk-in closet that contained only four items: a shirt, jacket, pants, and tie. Trudy had left a note on his pillow advising him not to bother looking for his other clothes because she had "burned" them. He hoped it wasn't true. He slid the pants from a wooden hanger, leaving it rocking back and forth on the rod. The shirt needed to be washed, but it would have to do for now. He slipped it on, buttoned it up, and tucked it in. That left the coat and tie.

Through his bedroom window he could see a faint crimson light spreading across the inky spill of the ocean, not a cloud in the sky.

It would be another warm day. He shook his head and closed the closet door. He would have to sneak out of the office as soon as stores opened. He hated spending money, but he had no choice, dealing with Harlan's request would take a few weeks, and he needed something comfortable to wear.

In the meantime, he buckled his belt and debated whether to visit the beach or not. He had to get to the office and go over the script. Time on the beach would present a delay. He decided against it. The clock on the lamp table read 6:00 a.m. If true to form, Quentin and Trudy would be in bed another few hours. *Good.* He wanted to slip out while they were still asleep. His thoughts wandered as he began to visualize Trudy's thick auburn hair fanned across her pillow, shining in the morning sun with the richness of dark cherries, her lips full and lustrous, and her silky skin emitting the light fragrance of some seductive perfume; he could hear her sultry voice seducing him, pulling him onto the bed, her fingers on his chest unbuttoning his shirt as she whispered, *"Lonnie, Lonnie, Lonnie, I've missed you,"* and, *and*...Enough! He was getting worked up over nothing. It had been a drunken tryst, for heaven's sake, not a romance. It didn't mean anything. She'd lost her husband. In her emotionally unstable way, she'd been trying to cope. She needed someone to hold—he'd been there. She probably didn't even remember it; she hadn't mentioned it since.

The whole idea of becoming involved was absurd. He had to stay focused. His goal was to release Harlan's film and get the company back on track. He had to think about returning to Mexico. He was a missionary, called of God to minister to the needy. She was a socialite caught up in the cares and pleasures of this world—*eat, drink and be merry.* Different worlds, poles apart—and never the twain shall meet.

He turned to look at his reflection in the mirror. The misfit preacher in ill-fitting clothes. He rolled back the cuffs of his shirtsleeves, and combed his fingers through his hair. At least the years had been kind to him. If anything he'd filled out. He was no longer gangly and inept. *"I'd forgotten how handsome you are,"* she'd said. Okay, maybe there was some attraction. But even so, he was headed for Mexico, and she belonged here, and that was that.

He picked up his Bible, tucked it under his arm, and finished rolling his sleeves over his forearms as he exited the door to the balcony. The view overlooked the ocean. It was almost as good as being there. He inhaled a lung full of salty air, took his Bible and stretched his arms until his shoulders felt a tingling sensation. He shivered for a moment, then settled into a softly padded white wicker chair. He could hear the ocean *whooshing* and *thwacking* on the rocks below and the seagulls keening above. He watched the white birds circling in the skies overhead, their sharply pointed wings tipped with black, like writing quills dipped in ink. *Not one falls without the Father knowing.* He flipped his Bible open. Maybe God would provide him with a verse to give him strength, or better yet, wisdom.

Today he would ask his management team, men who knew the business far better than he, to support a decision he knew he couldn't defend, at least not with logic. His arguments would seem naive—*I'd rather bankrupt the company than show a little skin.* Of course, he didn't have to ask; he was the boss. He could insist his subordinates carry out his directive, but he would prefer to have their cooperation voluntarily. His eyes scanned the page, book of Galatians, fifth chapter, verse sixteen: "This I say then, walk in the spirit and you shall not fulfil the lust of the flesh." *Whoa.* He'd wanted to convince himself he was right in making changes to the film. Instead he was being admonished to flee temptation. He wondered if, from God's perspective, the real issue wasn't...Trudy.

LONNIE SAT at his desk shuffling through sheets of paper. The sleeves of his shirt were rolled up on his forearms and he had a pencil clamped between his teeth. He'd been the first one to arrive at the office, but the few minutes of quiet he'd enjoyed were over. The room outside was now buzzing with activity. He looked up, caught Nicole standing at his door, and waved her in.

"I'm going through the two scripts," he said, removing the pencil from his mouth. "I read Quentin's last night and I agree with you, the way he had it was better. What I need to do is find all of Harlan's changes and figure out what has to be done to put the story back the way it was."

"I can save you the trouble," she said.

"You can?"

"Sure. I have a copy of Quentin's script with Harlan's changes noted in the margins."

Lonnie wished he'd known that earlier. "Humm. Okay, listen, that's great. I'm going to need your help. Can you make two copies, one for each of us, and then go round up the projectionist and have him meet us in the screening room? As soon as you're ready, we'll review the scenes Harlan changed. I want to know what has to be done to restore the film to Quentin's original version. But try to be discreet. I don't want everyone knowing what we're up to, at least not until I'm sure what I'm going to do with all this." Lonnie looked at his watch. "It's eight-thirty. If we start now, think we can be done by lunch?"

Nicole thought for a moment. "Sure. I don't see why not."

HARLAN'S THREE executives and Nicole were sitting around the table, waiting, when Lonnie entered the room sporting an olive-green polo shirt and gray slacks. He noticed Nicole's lifted brow. The two of them had spent the morning rolling the film back and forth, going over one scene after the other to determine what changes needed to be made. They'd been able to maintain secrecy because they'd already been in the screening room, behind closed doors, when the other executives arrived at the office. Since none of the others knew when to expect Lonnie, they'd assumed he wasn't in yet. And they'd left for lunch, muttering about the hold on production, before Lonnie and Nicole emerged with the newly revised script. Nicole had volunteered to work through the noon hour. While she typed in the changes and made five copies, Lonnie had dashed out on an errand. Before leaving, he had asked Nicole to round up the three vice-presidents and have them meet him in the boardroom at two. At least now she could see what he'd been up to. He met her gaze, but she blushed and her eyes darted away.

"Sorry I'm late, gentlemen...Nicole," Lonnie began. With his hair neatly brushed, his slacks sharply pressed, and his snug shirt emphasizing his firm waist, he looked the part of a corporate yuppie—straight from the pages of "GQ." But had they been able to look beneath his skin, they would have seen his stomach fizzing like a carbonated drink. It was all he could do to keep the jitters out of his voice. "I hope you haven't been waiting long." Lonnie remained standing. He could feel their impatience. He glanced at his watch. He was only seven minutes late. In Mexico, showing up a few minutes late for a meeting was akin to arriving early, but judging from the stiffness in the room, he deduced that a few minutes in the busy world of corporate executives, was an eternity.

Lonnie nodded at Nicole, who stood and leaned over to retrieve several documents. She handed a copy to each of the men, and they in turn began leafing through the pages. Lonnie tried to maintain his composure. He wasn't cut out for this. He was a novice. They were professionals. Who was he to tell them what to do? He'd back off the minute they began raising objections. He could feel a bubbly effervescence in his stomach. *No*, he wouldn't! He was determined to see this through. He cleared his throat and proceeded. "What you have before you is a revised script. As you examine it, you'll see places where I'm recommending we reshoot the film to add substance and improve its moral content. You'll also see that the ending has been changed. What I need from you is an estimate of what it will cost in terms of time and money to make these changes. And I need your input by tomorrow morning. I know it's short notice, but I trust you can at least provide a good ballpark estimate in that amount of time."

The three looked around the table at each other. He could read the protest on their faces—*We can't make changes at the last minute! Who does this guy think he is?* It made him feel queasy, but he resolved to stand firm. He wasn't there to make friends. With any luck they'd release the film, pay off their debt, and he'd hop a flight to Mexico leaving Quentin in charge. Lonnie waited for a reaction, but no one spoke. "Any questions?" he probed.

Les refused to look at him. His bald head was bowed as he examined his nails. Brent's lips were clamped so tight they were turning white, and Michael's eyes were locked onto the script. "All right then, let's plan on meeting here tomorrow at nine to see what you've come up with."

"With all due respect, it can't be done," Michael finally said.

Lonnie knew the silence had been deceiving. "And why not?"

"We went through all this yesterday. The film has to be released as is. We don't have time to make changes. Les barely has time to do a final edit. He's already lost a day because you put a hold on production." Les stopped fiddling with his fingernails long enough to look up and nod. Michael continued, "And even if we had all the time in the world, we wouldn't have the money. We're over budget, and there's nothing in the bank. Film crews don't work for free, and neither do actors. The only option we have is to pour our energy into getting what we've got to market and hope for the best."

Lonnie listened patiently. Michael was the firm's Executive Vice President. He was paid to know his stuff and give good advice; he'd said exactly what Lonnie expected to hear. Still, Lonnie couldn't help wishing his idea had been given at least some consideration. *Nothing is impossible, boss. We'll make it happen!* Was that asking too much? Maybe Michael's blood type was B-negative. Maybe he was a glass-half-empty kind of guy. Maybe that was why Harlan had decided not to leave him in charge.

He looked around the table. It wasn't just Michael; the others were doubtful, too. Nicole was busily stacking papers. Even she seemed unsure. Well, too bad. It *was* possible—and they *had* to do it! He took a breath. "I apologize for interrupting your schedule, and for the delay, but I want you to indulge me in this. Please. I need to know the time and cost by tomorrow morning."

Michael rose from his seat, shaking his head. He shuffled a few papers, then lifted his chin, straightened himself and looked Lonnie squarely in the eye. Lonnie had to force himself to hold the gaze. "All right, you'll have it," Michael said, "but you're not going to like it. It's a waste of time. I want to go on record as saying this is a bad idea. If we miss our deadline and the company goes belly up, you'll have no one but yourself to blame."

Lonnie's clenched his jaw. His eyes narrowed ever so slightly, but he continued to stare Michael down. The man's self-confidence was to be admired, but he was bordering on insubordination. It was probably a calculated risk since the company was going bankrupt anyway. *When you ain't got nothin', you got nothin' to lose.* Lonnie's stomach churned and made a gurgling noise he hoped the others didn't hear. Right or wrong, he was risking other people's futures to promote his own moral agenda. *Blast you, Harlan. You dealt me a losing hand. You did it on purpose. Blast you...*

Lonnie tried to steady his faltering breath by taking time to swallow. He picked up his script so they wouldn't notice his trembling hands. "Anything else?" he asked. He was sure they could hear the tremor in his voice. He half expected them to rise up in revolt, but the room remained silent. "Okay, we'll meet here again tomorrow at nine. Please have your reports ready."

The three men gathered their papers and filed out. Lonnie waited for Nicole and escorted her down the hall. As soon as the others were out of earshot, he asked, "How do you think it went?"

Nicole hugged her script to her breast, her ponytail resting on her shoulder. "As well as could be expected, I suppose. I mean, you're asking a lot from them. I'm surprised they didn't give you more static than they did."

Lonnie noted she was wearing a dress, still tasteful, but more conservative than the bun-hugging skirt she'd worn the day before. "You think I'm being unreasonable?"

"No, not necessarily. You stood up for what you believe. That took guts. I wouldn't have wanted to be in your shoes."

"Believe me, I was nervous. I think my hands are still shaking."

She glanced over, eyeing Lonnie up and down. "Really? It didn't show."

Lonnie took it in stride, though he was at a loss to explain why her remark made him feel warm. Perhaps he'd done better than he thought. "As soon as you're back at your desk I need you to do two things. First, I want you to look up the guy who financed our film, the guy we borrowed the money from. Unfortunately, I can't give you his name. I don't even know who he is."

"It's Ben Lowen," Nicole offered.

"Ben Lowen. Okay, see if you can arrange a meeting with Mr. Lowen here in our office sometime tomorrow. Tell him I've inherited the company and that I want a chance to meet with him to review our commitment, just to make sure both parties are on the same track. Then I need you to find the one person in our company who knows more about films than anyone else. I need someone who can tell me what films won the most Oscars, made the most money, that kind of thing."

"That's easy. You're describing Rolly Buttes. He works in market research. He's a walking encyclopedia of film trivia."

"Perfect. Send him in as soon as you get the chance." They were back at Nicole's work station. As she turned to sit down, Lonnie said, "I really appreciate your working through lunch. After you set up the appointment with Mr. Lowen, go ahead and take off for an hour. Or, on second thought, you may want to wait and leave an hour early. Whichever you decide."

Nicole blushed as she smiled and settled in at her desk.

ROLLY BUTTES fit his name to a tee. He was a walking butterball, about as round as a man could get. Lonnie imagined he could have as easily rolled into the office, as shuffle in the way he did. He puffed and wheezed as he spoke, thoroughly nervous, with beads of sweat dotting his forehead. In a "misery loves company" sort of way, it made Lonnie feel good to know someone else felt as intimidated as he. He wondered if he made an imposing figure sitting there behind that huge desk with those floor-to-ceiling windows behind him and the kingdoms of the world at his feet. He could see how it might have made Harlan feel important, but to Lonnie's way of thinking, it wasn't nearly as nice as watching a sunset from the cliffs of Posada. The creations of man were never as inspiring as the creation of God.

Lonnie waited until Rolly was comfortably seated. The poor man probably wondered why he'd been called into the new boss's office so soon. Was he being let go? Lonnie did his best to put him at ease. "Thanks for coming by," he said. "Did Nicole happen to say why I wanted to see you?"

Rolly's chubby cheeks waddled as he shook his head. He had more hair than Les, but it was thin on top, and it curled around his ears and neck where it hung long and shaggy. His expression remained flat, but his eyes, tiny slits though they were, revealed his discomfort. Lonnie surmised from the moisture on the man's face that his palms were sweaty, too. "Relax, Mr. Buttes. You're not in trouble. Fact is, I need your help. They tell me you're an expert on film trivia."

Rolly feigned a smile, but his face was a mask, and behind it Lonnie could see his apprehension. He'd hoped the compliment would loosen him up. The man should be proud of his knowledge.

"I'm going to level with you," Lonnie said. "I don't like the film this company just made, too much focus on the negative, which is why I'm asking we change it. To be frank, I'm not a big fan of macho movies, especially those that use violence and sex to hold the attention of their audience instead of a good story. Personally, I think they pander to depraved minds, and since I'm not into that, we're going to stop making them. Our goal from here on in is to provide decent people with wholesome entertainment. At least, that's how I see it. I'm betting there's a market for good, clean films. In fact, I bet we can make just as much money producing family entertainment as we can making the kind of junk Striker Films seems to be known for. When I was a kid, all the really good movies were made by Disney. We stood in line to see *The Love Bug* and *Mary Poppins*, and they made Mr. Disney rich. I have a hunch we can do the same, but I can't prove it. That's where you come in, Mr. Buttes. I want to use you as a resource. I'm hoping you can provide me with a list of recent films that have made money without sacrificing moral content."

Now Rolly's head was bobbing enthusiastically. His face flushed. His eyes opened wider, and his grin was broad. "Oh, yes, yes! You're so right. Oh, yes!" Rolly's voice was pitched in contralto as he wheezed out his words. From the way he presented himself, Lonnie guessed he wasn't well received in management circles, but that didn't matter. What mattered was that he seemed to agree. "I've been saying that forever, but nobody listens. Family films are big money. Oh yes! Look at *Star Wars*. It was huge. It was good guys beating bad guys, and people loved it. Oh yes, you're so right!"

Rolly was a godsend. When their meeting was over, Nicole handed Lonnie a message saying Mr. Lowen would be there tomorrow at one-thirty. Rolly had given him exactly what he needed for that meeting. Lonnie would propose a plan that would make Mr. Lowen more money. All Lowen had to do was give him a little more time. It was a straightforward business proposition that benefitted both parties. As an astute businessman, Lowen would have to agree.

NINE

THE SANTA MONICA Mountains stood like kings with the ocean's royal robes gathered at their feet, a glassy sea upon which the sun's golden crown had been cast. In the serenity of such an environment, Lonnie should have been able to relax. He'd spent many an evening such as this perched on a bluff overlooking the Sierra Madre del Sur, freeing himself from the trials and tribulations of the day. Having instructed Frank to keep the stereo off, he was enjoying the tranquillity and comfort of his own private space. He was gliding along in a limousine, with tinted windows, and a super-quiet ride. A constant stream of frosty air swept across his arms, drying the light veil of moisture that had accumulated there. But though the long sleek vehicle rolled down the Coast Highway with a cushioned ride, and though the pastoral landscape racing by his window was as fine as any he'd ever seen, he felt only a throbbing behind his eyes and a growing ache in the hollow of his chest.

His stomach turned. He should have gained the support of his management team. He needed their cooperation. Their willingness to work with him, was based on fear—and fear was a terrible motivator. Would they stonewall his plan? He prayed they wouldn't. They might win a battle, but they would lose the war. He was determined the company would henceforth show some responsibility for the films it made, and the sooner they got used to the idea, the better.

At least he wasn't alone. Rolly had proved to be an asset, not only because of his vast knowledge, but because in principle he agreed with what Lonnie was trying to do. He even loaned Lonnie a few books he said would support his argument. *Good!* Lonnie was pretty well versed on the subject. The effect of movies on children was documented in a number of the publications he received, but they were filed away at home, not here. And he was always looking for something new to read.

Nicole, too, bless her heart, appeared to be on his side. She could have left early. Instead, she'd worked till six helping him put together a proposal to present to Mr. Lowen. Lonnie was proud of the finished product. Any reasonable person could see why the deadline for the film's release should be extended. They stood to make more money. But what if Mr. Lowen wasn't a reasonable person? What if he raised some unforeseen objection. As the limo rolled into the hot distance, Lonnie considered his future. His head rested on a soft cushion of leather. He could hear the humming of the tires on the road. The fleeting landscape, zooming by the window, melded into a long, uninterrupted blur.

How did he get dragged into this? He should be back in Mexico, building a hospital, caring for the meek and lowly, not cruising around Tinseltown in a limousine, imitating the rich and famous. But building a hospital took money. Without Striker Films the program would cease to exist. His stomach churned. He poked his tongue around his gums and teeth trying to find moisture, but his mouth was dry. He reached to open the walnut bar in front of him but was disappointed to find a lone bottle of cognac and a two small glasses. All that luxury and not a drop of water to drink.

He closed the door and settled back into the soft leather upholstery. Even the smell was rich. He ran his hand across the smooth surface of the seat. No one could accuse Harlan of not going in style: the big house, his own private limo, and yes—even Trudy. *Trudy, Trudy, Trudy*, what was he going to do about her? She brought such a mix of emotions to the table. Each time he saw her lips, his craving intensified, but it was like eating cotton candy—all fluff, without substance.

Lonnie drummed his fingers on the armrest and stared out the window. Mile after unsettled mile of rolling hills, endless ocean, plenty of time to think, but no forthcoming answers—only a continuous accumulation of questions. Why did Harlan live so far from the office? Traveling back and forth was a waste of time. Yesterday, Lonnie had taken a cab but he knew he wouldn't be able to afford it every day. He'd been thankful to find the limo waiting for him this morning. The driver apologized for missing him the day before but, as he explained, Harlan had never needed him before nine. From then on, he promised to be ready to go at six sharp.

The limo pulled slowly around the U-shaped drive to the front of the house and stood with its motor running while Lonnie collected his books and packages. At least, it didn't cost him anything. The chauffeur, who introduced himself as Frank, explained that the service was being billed to the company. *Good.* Tax-deductible that way. Lonnie assured the man he would not be needed for the rest of the evening and turned to go inside.

He entered the house by the front door, holding his breath as he pushed on the heavy oak wood, but it opened with a loud *crack*, as if it had been glued shut. So much for slipping in unnoticed. Trudy had to have heard that. *Oh well*, he had to face her sometime.

He hated coming in this way. Hated being subjected to Harlan's haughty look. Trudy should redecorate the vestibule now that Harlan was gone. Get rid of such vainglory. At the very least, the portrait of Harlan ought to go. He closed the door and turned, but...*too late*. Trudy stood in the far corner of the living room in her tight jeans and high-heeled sandals. Over a halter top, she wore a white shirt left unbuttoned with the tails tied in front to accentuate her slim waist.

"Well, hello, stranger," she said. "Long time no see." Through the window behind her, Lonnie could see the ocean, infinite and eternal. The sun, on its late afternoon descent, rested momentarily just above her shoulders, setting her hair ablaze with its glory. Trudy lifted her cocktail glass in salute. "Well, don't just stand there. Come on in."

Lonnie set his books and bags by the stairs and walked through the room. Music was playing over the intercom, and an electronic voice droned from the TV in the den.

Trudy took a sip and set her glass on the marble-topped bar.

"Been out shopping, I see. Well, don't be shy. Come on, let's get a look at you."

Lonnie did as asked. He stopped a few feet in front of Trudy and raised his hands, palms out. "So, what do you think?"

"Nice. Very nice. You have good taste."

Lonnie folded his arms and tried to relax, but he feared the pounding of his heart could be seen through the thin fabric of his shirt. "Sorry I haven't been around. There's a lot going on at the office."

Trudy approached, placed her hands on his shoulders, and for a fraction of a second, gazed directly into his eyes. Then she stood on tiptoes and brushed the side of his face with her lips. "Now you sound just like your brother," she said, stepping back to retrieve her drink.

The kiss was light, no more than a welcome-home peck on the cheek, but Lonnie felt himself melting. If she had stayed another second, he would have been powerless to resist taking her in his arms. He needed something to hang onto. Her breath held the faint odor of alcohol, but she wasn't slurring her words. She was nowhere near as far gone as she'd been the other night. He was determined not to take advantage. She was lonely, and still grieving her dead husband. "Don't accuse me of that," he said. "I'm just trying to acquaint myself with the business, not have a good time."

"Good. Make sure you keep it that way." She turned and went into the kitchen, her spiked shoes clicking on the tile floor. "Have you eaten yet?" she called over her shoulder. "I gave the cook the night off, but there's lasagna in the oven." Lonnie could hear an oven door being opened, and the sound of a cookie sheet sliding across a metal rack. The room filled with the aroma of tomato sauce, garlic, and melted cheese. Trudy raised her voice a notch. "I think there's also a loaf of French bread in here and a salad in the refrigerator. And if that doesn't tempt you, I have a fantastic merlot to wash it down. What do you say? Will you join me for dinner? I hate eating alone."

Lonnie heard a bell ringing in his head, a warning, but it wasn't as pronounced as the burn inside his chest. He thought about men with drinking problems he'd counseled to stay out of bars; he thought about those struggling with lust who just needed to close their eyes. Funny how a man could know something was wrong and do it anyway, even knowing he'd regret it later. He felt himself falling into the trap of believing he was stronger than the problem, that he could entertain a certain level of enjoyment without going *too* far. *I can have a drink, I just won't get drunk. I can flirt, I just won't touch.* Wisdom dictated he grab the evening paper and one of Rolly's books and retire to his room, alone. "What about Quentin?" he asked.

Trudy reappeared with a potholder glove on her hand. "He doesn't eat lasagna," she said. "He's on some kind of health diet. Besides, we rarely have dinner together. He spends his evenings in his room working on his computer. It's a social thing. He has a group of friends all across the country that talk to each other on a chat line. You know how it is." Trudy removed the glove and lowered her voice to just above a whisper. "I hate to say it, but Quentin has become a bit of a recluse since the accident. He can't believe anyone will accept him with his disability, so he makes friends by computer. What do you really know about someone three thousand miles away except what they tell you, huh? Anyway, I doubt we'll see hide nor hair of him tonight."

Lonnie stood there, admiring this fire-haired beauty and her strength. Trudy the domestic, Trudy the homemaker, Trudy with potholder gloves, if only...The lasagna did smell good, and Trudy even better, and he *did* have to eat..."Sure," he said. "Just let me take my things up to my room. How long do I have till the lasagna comes out?"

"Actually, I can take it out anytime. I'm just keeping it warm. You go ahead while I set the table. Give me about five minutes. It'll be ready when you get here."

Upstairs in his room, Lonnie laid each of the items he'd purchased on the bed. He'd spent far more time and money shopping than he'd planned, but now he had several outfits from which to choose—not to mention his accessories. And most of his new wardrobe was interchangeable, providing him with several mix-and-match options. He would probably regret the excess when he got back to Mexico, but for now, it felt good to look nice. He put the shirts and pants on hangers, making sure the creases were smooth before placing them in the walk-in closet. Then he folded his socks and underwear and put them in the drawer. He thought about changing for dinner, but decided against it. Trudy would notice. It might look like he was fishing for another compliment.

Lonnie went into the bathroom to wash his hands. As he worked the lather through his fingers, he considered what the evening might bring. He pondered what it would be like to hold Trudy, and feel the warmth of her body next to his. *"I'd forgotten how handsome you are."* That was what she'd said the *last* time they were alone. His breathing, accentuated by his unbridled imagination, felt heavy and labored. He brought his hands to his face. *Why are you shaking?* It was because she needed him. And now that Harlan was gone...*whoa, slow down!* It was his mind that needed washing, not his hands. *Why?* How could he have such conflicted emotions over someone he hadn't seen in twenty years?

When he'd hi-tailed it for Mexico, he'd closed the door on his past. Then, four days ago, he'd stood on her front porch and, *wham,* deja vu, it was like he'd never been away. Now he could hardly think of anything else. Twenty years! Must have something to do with his being unable to forgive and forget. Oh, he'd *forgiven* everyone involved, but there was no way to *forget.* So when he'd seen her again, *pow,* all those pent-up emotions had jumped up and smacked him in the face. Apparently, he was no further along than when he'd left. He found himself toying with the idea of trying to pick it up again—which was insane! He *did* need a shower—a cold one!

He dried his hands and walked out onto the balcony to clear his head. He rolled his shoulders in the sultry evening air and leaned forward, taking hold of the rail. The sun was finally setting, a grand and glorious orange ball bobbing on the rolling ocean. He could smell the wet sand and seaweed below, the home of starfish and crab, and hear the pounding of the waves on the rocks. *If men and women are meant to be together, why is getting together so darn difficult?* He thought about Buddy and his mother, and Harlan and Trudy—a legacy of infidelity handed down from father to son, generation to generation...

Lonnie looked up into the blistering sun, using the palm of his hand to shield his eyes. The Mexican sun was a monster, even first thing in the morning. He crawled out of his sleeping bag and rubbed the back of his neck. It felt hot and gritty. Where was Harlan? The tent was alive, the walls undulating with movement, but the sound escaping was not something Lonnie wanted to hear. He moved away. He did not want to see Buddy come crawling out followed by his young "assistant" displaying more than just a little cleavage. He didn't want to know what was going on. When Harlan tried to explain, because Harlan claimed to know about such things, Lonnie turned his head away, pretending to listen to a hawk screeching somewhere off in the distance.

"Look, Spud, do I gotta explain everything? I mean, it's obvious. Buddy doesn't get what he needs from Mom. Sometimes it's like that. Sometimes a man's wife won't put out, know what I mean? And sometimes they can't be together. Like now. It ain't Dad's fault he has to travel so much, it's part of the job, but where's Mom? She's with her sister, that's where. She ain't here, and Dad has needs, so this other lady has to fill in. That's all it is, Spud, the birds and bees, get it?" But Lonnie didn't, "get it." He only knew he didn't like the way it made him feel.

Lonnie searched the camp, but Harlan was nowhere in sight. He wandered off to explore the wadi—anything to get away from the tent. His shoulders were red, his unwashed feet clad in sandals with desert grime scraping his toes. He came to a channel in the earth where the water had once flowed. He hopped into the dry riverbed and picked up a small flat stone, which he skimmed across the hard-packed earth. A little cloud of yellow dust erupted with each bounce. When he heard voices, he ducked behind the ridge and saw the flap of the tent swing open, revealing Buddy's assistant. She was on her knees, her bosom exposed for all the world to see as she pushed her arms through the straps of her bra, but the shirtless man crawling out wasn't Buddy—it was Harlan!

Their parents separated shortly thereafter. Lonnie, raised by his mother, grew up observing the sacraments of the church; he embraced Christ, and was taught that sex outside of marriage was taboo. One thing he knew for certain—Harlan was wrong! Their mother was a saint. She'd remained faithful to her husband even after the divorce. And by all accounts she was a handsome woman, so it wasn't for lack of opportunity. No, sir! If anyone was at fault, it was Buddy. *Congratulations, Harlan, you always did want to be like Dad.*

LONNIE BOUNCED off the bottom step and looked around. The room was different somehow. Then he realized what it was. Most of the lights had been turned out. Only a few miscellaneous lamps were still glowing, and those seemed to be on their lowest setting. *Either she's trying to save money, or she's doing her best to create a mood.* Even the crystal chandelier had been dimmed. The music flowed smooth and easy from invisible speakers.

He stood in the middle of the atrium, a pair of doors on either side. One set of doors ran beneath the sweeping staircase on his left, providing entrance to the den; the other went under the staircase on his right, leading to the dining room. He could see into the living room, but Trudy wasn't there. She was probably in the kitchen, though she was being awfully quiet. Lonnie decided to check the den first. He didn't expect to find her; he just wanted to be sure. He stepped inside to look around. A series of ceiling lamps circled the walls, providing low-watt illumination. He had been there once before, on the evening of the reception. The place was designed for comfort, complete with a billiard table and a built-in home entertainment center with a fifty-two inch screen. Two reclining leather chairs and a thickly padded leather couch were positioned around a dense Persian rug in front of the TV, but other than that, the room was empty.

He turned and crossed the atrium to the other side of the house. The music seemed to surround him, echoing off the walls. He stuck his head into the dining room. The solid mahogany table was long enough to seat twenty or more. Lonnie wasn't surprised when he didn't see Trudy. He moved on into the kitchen, but she wasn't there either. At the far end, a glass sun-porch extended out from the house, creating a less formal dining area with a view that overlooked the pool and the ocean beyond. Inside, Lonnie found a smaller oak table surrounded by six chairs. It was a quaint little nook with ferns growing overhead and a floor of sand-colored Mexican tiles. This was clearly where Trudy intended for them to eat. The table was set for two with hand-painted china, crystal wine goblets, and burnished silver cutlery. The room glowed in the flickering light of two tall white candles, while low on the horizon, the fading rays of a bright orange sun poured through the panels of glass. It couldn't have been more romantic. Still, Trudy was nowhere to be seen.

Lonnie went back through the kitchen, the smell of tomato sauce and fresh garlic whetting his appetite, and on into the living room. No Trudy anywhere. *Must have gone up to her bedroom,* he thought. Or perhaps she was sitting out on the deck enjoying the sunset. He started to look outside, but heard her voice behind him.

"Oh, good. You're here. I was just about to call you. Come on, let's go sit down." Trudy closed the bathroom door and led the way. For once, Lonnie noticed she didn't have a drink in her hand. He followed her into the kitchen. The lasagna, baked in a heavy Tuscan casserole dish, was already on the counter. Trudy asked Lonnie to bring the dinner plates from the table, and quickly served up two thick slices of the cheese-covered pasta. A loaf of French bread, warm from the oven, and a crisp romaine salad rounded out the menu.

Lonnie took a seat at the table. Trudy stood beside him, filling their salad bowls. The leafy greens were smothered in a white Caesar dressing mixed lightly with anchovy and garlic and garnished with crusty croutons. She passed one bowl to Lonnie and set the other in front of her own plate, and then sat.

Surprisingly, Trudy seemed right at home in the kitchen. Again, he could not miss the radiance of her hair glistening with the last rays of sunset, her eyes green as the ocean depths. A delicate fragrance wafted through the air, reeling him in, and...*and*, stop it! He was playing the fool again. *Walk in the spirit and you shall not fulfil the lust of the flesh!*

"Could you pour the wine?" Trudy asked, interrupting his thoughts.

"Sure." Lonnie stood and leaned into the table to remove the bottle from a silver bucket of ice, the glass clinking against the metal. He drew it out slowly, relieved to see the cork had already been removed. It would have been embarrassing to ask for a corkscrew since he wasn't sure how to use one. He filled the glass in front of Trudy, set the bottle back into the bucket, and sat down.

"You're not having any?"

"You know I don't drink," he said. He picked up the rose-colored napkin lying beside his plate, wiped his hands, and laid it in his lap.

Trudy raised an eyebrow giving him a look that suggested she knew better.

"Really. I haven't had a drink since...well since...you know..."

Trudy smiled. Her rosy cheeks were emphasized by the flickering light of the candles. "You've become a teetotaler on me."

"Actually, I never did like the taste very much, couldn't get used to it. After I left for Mexico, I decided I didn't need it. Haven't had a drop since."

Trudy picked up her glass and took a sip. "To each his own." She gave a shrug and set the glass down again. "Well, let's eat." She was bringing a bite to her mouth, when she cut a glance at Lonnie who sat with his hands still folded in his lap. "Something wrong?"

"Would you mind if I said grace?"

Trudy quickly put her fork down. "Of course," she said. "How thoughtless of me."

Lonnie detected sarcasm in her tone, but chose to ignore it. He bowed his head. "Lord, for the food we are about to eat, we are truly thankful. Please bless it in the name of Jesus. Amen."

Lonnie took his fork and knife and sliced off a healthy bite. "Hey, that's really good," he said, savoring a mouthful. "I can't tell you how long it's been since I had a home-cooked meal, especially Italian."

"My cook is Italian. She can make just about anything, but her specialty is pasta."

THE SUN ended the day with a dip in the ocean and the sky outside mellowed into cooler shades of blue, but inside the evening was warm with music, candlelight, and laughter. Lonnie was drunk, but not on alcohol; he was tipsy with the smell of Trudy's perfume. He was trying to keep a rein on his heart, but it was becoming more difficult as the evening wore on. *Listen more, and think less,* he cautioned himself. He sought to recognize Trudy for who she really was, not as an unrequited love upon which time had somehow bestowed the rank of goddess, but as a mere mortal, with hurts and pains inflicted by Harlan, much like his own. Still, as the table conversation progressed, he had to admire her ability to overlook his brother's faults. Like his mother, she'd stayed true to her husband even after he'd begun having affairs.

"After all," she said, "Harlan never pretended to be someone he wasn't. I knew he was running around even before we were married. But you have to accept people for who they are without trying to change them," Her voice dropped an octave and became pensive. "Still, I might have had second thoughts if I hadn't become pregnant while we were still dating. Oh, well," she resumed her cheerful optimism, "I have no regrets. Quentin is worth every bit of it. Harlan was just being Harlan. I don't blame him. Any suffering I've done, I've brought upon myself."

Lonnie shook his head. Was she really that forgiving, or had her skin become so thick she could no longer feel pain?

"It wasn't so bad," she went on. "There were good times, too. Like our wedding..." She interrupted herself with a little-girl giggle, momentarily placing her fingers over her lips as though embarrassed. "A hundred white balloons were supposed to fall from the ceiling as Harlan and I left the church," she continued, "but guess what? Someone accidentally released them while we were still on the platform saying our vows. We had to try and look dignified while standing ankle deep in a sea of bouncing white. Harlan barely got the 'I do' out of his mouth when he backed up and stepped on one, and *pow!*"

Recalling the scene sent Trudy into peals of laughter. She began

to sputter uncontrollably, and paused to take a sip
putting a soft white hand to her throat, she said, "A
you had been there. You and I were such good frien
have to leave?"

Lonnie began shaking his head, wrestling w
memories he did not want to exhume. "You know
attempt to restore the light-heartedness, said, "Tell
your choice of doing anything you wanted to do, any
would it be?"

"Oh, that's easy," Trudy responded. "I'd take
faraway place where no one knows me, some place
haven't even heard of motion pictures, and I'd lie in th
all about...well, I'd just forget, that's all."

Lonnie realized that without meaning to, she
Posada—*time forgotten, no movie theaters, plenty of su*
hope? He came within seconds of sharing his thoug
off. It wasn't safe to speculate. "Would you take Qu
he manage on his own?" It was an innocent question,
quickly regretted asking.

Trudy's expression grew solemn as she focused i
becoming misty. She brought a hand up and twirle
hair with her finger. "Lonnie I...there's something..."
her lip starting to quiver.

"Trudy, what is it?"

"Did I tell you how it happened?" she asked. "Que
I mean."

"I believe you said he was on a bike, or something

"It was awful. He was racing downhill...going too
of his back brake came loose and the front brake wa
stop him...not with his weight and the steepness of th
was no way. He slammed into a retaining barrier an
into the bush. They found him unconscious. He'd la
back against the stump of a tree." Her voice broke. Sh
enough to take a fluttering breath, then continued. "
good. It happened in the Sierras, but Harlan got a helic

there and bring Quentin home. Quentin woke up in the hospital ·h spinal cord damage. He's had complete paralysis of both his ver limbs, ever since..."

Trudy's eyes had become moist in the telling and Lonnie, in spite the warning bells going off in his head, reached out to give her mfort. She welcomed his arms. Lonnie could smell the sweet scent her perfume as he held her in his embrace.

QUENTIN SIGNED off, telling his chat room buddies he s going off-line. He was thirsty. He rolled his wheelchair into e elevator and pressed the down button, exiting to the left at the ttom. He continued down the hall through the living room and to the kitchen, rolling to a stop in front of the refrigerator. He was out to open the door when he noticed that the light was on in the nroom. He sat in the dark recess of the kitchen looking across the unter with an unobstructed view into the glass dining area. They ere holding each other, his uncle, his mother...*he was stroking her ir...he was...they were...*

He cranked his chair around and pushed, his hands spinning e wheels as fast as he could manage. He reached the elevator d sat pounding the button with his thumb even though the door mediately began to open. His teeth were clamped shut, his jaw iff, his eyes burning. He rushed inside and spun his chair around as e door closed and the elevator began to rise.

When the door opened he exited to the left, in the opposite irection of his room. He didn't know why, or what purpose it might erve, but he raced into his uncle's suite. He sat alone in the dark tting his eyes adjust to the shadows. Light spilling through the oor was reflecting off something glittery and gold on the dresser—*a Bible—the hypocrite!* He tightened his grip on the wheels of his chair ill his knuckles turned white. *Unh, unh, uh. Bingo!* He spun the hair around and quickly fled. If he was right, his uncle wouldn't last week.

TEN

THE EMBRACE was like a breath, giving life, but swiftly gone. Lonnie gave Trudy one final squeeze, then gripped her shoulders and held her at arm's length. "You okay?" he asked. He dipped his head, trying to make eye contact, but she refused to look at him.

She nodded and brought the back of her hand up to wipe her cheek, the air in her lungs fluttering as she inhaled. "There are so many things you don't understand," she said. "Things I wish I could tell you, but I...I just can't."

Lonnie let her go and leaned back in his chair. He wasn't certain he wanted to hear Trudy's confession. Anything that involved Quentin would ultimately involve Harlan. Perhaps another day, another time. He crossed his arms, realizing his brother had once again succeeded in keeping them apart. He stood, gathered his plate, and began stacking the dishes.

"Leave that. The maid will get it in the morning." Trudy pushed herself up from the table, looking fragile, her eyes misty and red. She turned and went to the counter for a tissue. "It's warm in here. Can we go outside for a minute?" she said, daubing moisture from her face. "I need to cool off."

THEY STROLLED through the garden to the back of the property. Two brass lanterns were lit, one on each side of the stairs leading down to the beach. The sun had been down for an hour, leaving a deep purple sky. The moon hung low and orange over the sea. They stood for a moment with the warm offshore breeze lifting their hair and the sound of the pounding surf echoing in their ears. "Come on," Trudy said. "Follow me."

They discarded their shoes at the bottom of the stairs. Lonnie stuffed his socks into his pockets and rolled up his pants to walk barefoot along the breakwater. It was a reckless act. His expensive new slacks were sure to be ruined, but the moon was full and bright, and Trudy's melancholy mood seemed to lift as they walked. Dreams didn't come true every day. Trudy took Lonnie's hand to steady herself as she skipped from one rock to the next. She laughed when she lost her balance and gripped his hand tightly to keep her footing. It was a welcome transformation. Gone was the uptight socialite. The carefree Trudy of his youth had returned. The waves crashing against the shore blessed the air with a cooling mist.

Where the rock shelf ended, the beach opened into a sheltered cove. Lonnie hopped down. Tracy placed her hands on his shoulders, and he took her waist, lifting her gently onto the hard, wet sand. They drifted down the beach, arm in arm, squishing sand between their toes with each step. The waves were pounding the shore in a never ending sequence, leaving lacy white foam swirling around their feet. Trudy lay her head on Lonnie's shoulder. Neither one spoke. Words were unnecessary. They were sharing a form of communication as old as time. They reached a rock jetty, turned around, and saw the tracks of their feet glistening in the moonlight. Lonnie picked up a smooth stone and skimmed it along the surface of the water, one bounce...two...three.

Trudy laughed. "Not bad," she said. She picked up a stone and gave it a toss, but the rock hit the water, *plunk*, and sank beneath the waves. Her white blouse glowed bright in the moonlight, and her hair whipped about her face in the wind. A strand got caught in her mouth, but she used her finger to pull it free. Her lips were moist, her eyes a combination of the ocean's green and the twinkling stars. Lonnie struggled not to reach out and take her in his arms. Twenty years might have passed, but it seemed like only a moment. The moon had been bright on that night too, only the air was cold—and they'd had too much wine...

"It was nice of your dad to let you have the station wagon," Lonnie said.

"What else could he do? He wasn't going to let his little girl stay home and cry herself to sleep, not on prom night. Move over. Where's that bottle?" Trudy pushed the blankets aside, searching for the gallon jug. She looped her finger through the hole in the bottle's neck and let it rest on her forearm as she raised her elbow to take another deep swig.

"Better go easy on that. Your dad will have a fit if you end up puking in the back of his car."

"Shut up. Here," she said, shoving the bottle in his direction. "I think he'd understand given the circumstances."

They were parked on a bluff at the end of a dirt road on a cattle ranch in the hills of *Brea. They didn't know who owned the ranch. They only knew high school kids used the place to party. The moon was hiding behind the blades of an ancient windmill, looking fuzzy through the warm breath that clouded the windows—or was that just the wine? Lonnie could see the silhouettes of scrub oaks lining the ridge, and down in the city below, a blanket of lights that resembled fallen stars.*

"We can still go to the dance. It isn't too late. We're dressed for it."

"Not for long." Trudy sat up. She pulled off one high-heeled shoe and threw it across the car. It bounced off the dashboard and landed on the front seat. The second one hit the mirror, knocking it askew. Then she unwrapped her shawl, slid it from her neck, and tossed it over the seat, leaving her bare arms exposed. "I couldn't possibly. Can you imagine what everyone would say? 'Harlan ditched Trudy. Stood her up again. Why does she put up with it?' I'd be the laughing stock of the entire school."

"Why do you?"

"What?"

"Put up with it?"

Trudy shivered. "Now I'm cold." She crawled over and wrapped herself in Lonnie's arms. "Hold me," she said. Then she leaned over and reached for the bottle.

"You're too good for him, you know."
"Shut up and kiss me," she said.

Lonnie picked up another stone, avoiding the lure of Trudy's eyes. He tossed it over the water, not to see it skim, but to see how far he could throw. He heard it, *plop,* but didn't see where it landed. It was gone—*just like Trudy on that night.* He'd done what he had to do. He'd packed his bags and headed for Mexico. He signed on to build homes for the homeless, enlisting himself in the service of the church. Once the decision was made, there was no turning back.

The moon was shrinking in size and turning white as it rose over the water. Trudy held her hair against her neck. Their eyes found each other again. His heart burned in his chest, a fire so deep all the water of the ocean couldn't put it out. A rising swell came crashing down wrapping another foamy stream around their feet. He looked away breaking the spell. "I'd better be getting back," he said. "I have to get up early."

THE SUN was blazing through the window by the time Lonnie awoke Friday morning. He opened his eyes and immediately realized he'd overslept. The clock by his bed said seven. It was the most restful sleep he'd had since arriving in Malibu and he hated giving it up, but if he wanted to get out without confronting Quentin, he'd have to hurry. He kicked back the covers and made a dash for the shower.

He was out and ready to dress in record time. He slipped into a pair of cotton khaki slacks and a long-sleeved, light blue shirt with a button-down collar. He finished the ensemble off with brown belt and shoes. He looked at himself in the mirror. The creases felt sharp and crisp, and the color of the shirt flattered his eyes. He hardly recognized himself. He brushed his sandy blond hair, letting the waves snap into their natural place.

Then he went outside to spend a few minutes in meditation. This time his Bible fell open to Proverbs. "Trust in the Lord with all thine heart; and lean not unto thine own understanding. In all thy ways acknowledge him and he shall direct thy paths." That's the ticket. It was just what he needed to hear.

Lonnie checked his watch. He made his way downstairs, carrying the book he'd borrowed from Rolly. It was likely both Quentin and Trudy were still in bed. For once, he passed the portraits in the entry without a second thought. The driver, dressed in his usual blue blazer and dark tie, had the limo ready. He leaned over the car, polishing the hood with a soft cloth. Lonnie could see his face reflected in the paint. His cap was pushed back on his head revealing drops of sweat under his hairline. He looked up as Lonnie approached.

"Morning, Mr. Striker."

"Morning, Frank."

Lonnie reached for the door but Frank got there first. "Guess I get to serve the two Mister Strikers today." Lonnie looked puzzled. Then his eye caught movement behind the smoked glass. The door opened, and there sat Quentin. *Blam dada, boom boom blam.*

"Morning, Unk," he said, raising his voice to be heard above the din.

The music was *blam, blam, blamming* as they rolled down the driveway. Quentin asked Frank to crank up the volume and Lonnie, to keep the peace, did not object, but the racket was giving him a headache. Lonnie stared out the tinted window to divert his attention. The ocean was blue as indigo and speckled with gold flecks, and with a cloudless sky, resembled the front of a store-bought postcard. The temperature outside was rising. He was thankful for the air conditioning and tried to relax. The cushy seat provided ample comfort; still, he caught himself thumping his fingers on the armrest.

Quentin spoke into an intercom and asked Frank to turn down the stereo for a moment. "So, Unk, I figured I'd hitch a ride to the office and see if I could be of any help." Quentin wore a snug-fitting, yellow cotton golf shirt, the fruit of his weightlifting efforts clearly on display, and a pair of white slacks with white canvas deck shoes. Sitting there, he looked like a prime specimen of physical fitness. Lonnie found it hard to believe he couldn't walk.

Lonnie inclined his head toward his nephew. "Help? How? In

what way?"

"Don't know exactly. But I suspect you're in over your head. I mean, you haven't been around for the past twenty years, so you gotta be a little lost. Me, on the other hand, I grew up in that place. I know my way around. Maybe I can help you through the maze."

Lonnie nodded. "I'd appreciate that. Look, you know what happened wasn't my fault. I had no idea Harlan was going to do that. I was as surprised as you were."

"Forget it. We'll just have to make the best of it. Life goes on. You're talking to someone with no legs, remember. Life isn't always fair, but like my dad always said: 'You gotta play the cards you get, even when you're dealt a bad hand.' "

Lonnie smiled. *Perfect!* He knew the boy had it in him. He knew it! That rough exterior was only a facade, a mask to hide his pain. *Thank You, Lord!* He wanted to tell Quentin how, once they made it through the next few weeks, he'd turn over the reins and leave him in charge, but he couldn't. Not yet. The company had to be in good financial shape first. He'd wait to spring the news, not because he felt some misdirected loyalty to Harlan, but because Harlan was dead, and a dead man's last request had to be honored. Lonnie turned his head toward the window. Palm trees lined the road, their fronds waving in the gentle breeze; a couple meandered arm in arm down the boardwalk, not a care in the world; the sun blossomed in the sky overhead. *Perfect*!

THE ELEVATOR doors opened with a *ding*. Quentin rolled his wheelchair out and spun to the left, his strong hands driving the wheels up to the two glass doors leading into Striker Films. He reached for the handle, pulled it open with a powerful tug, and while it was still in outward motion, raced his wheelchair through. Then and then only did he pause to wait for Lonnie. Lonnie caught the door as it was closing and pressed in behind. The door thumped him on the rear, pushing him into the handles of Quentin's wheelchair as he tried to squeeze by.

Quentin shook his head. "Okay, Unk, I'm going to leave you

for a few minutes. I want to say hi to some people I haven't seen in awhile."

Lonnie straightened himself and glanced at his watch. "That's okay. I have a meeting to attend. Maybe we can get together for lunch. Why don't you stop by your dad's old office around noon?"

Quentin turned his head, looking back over his shoulder, and winked. "Sure, Unk. See you then," and with the powerful pistons of his machine-hardened arms, he crossed the lobby and sped through the door into the heart of Striker Films.

Lonnie smiled and gave the receptionist a nod, but didn't wait to be announced. He followed Quentin through the door and worked his way down the corridor, feeling as if every eye in the company was on him. He'd improved his image. His new outfit was from Hudsons, a men's store that catered to corporate yuppies, but something was missing. He held his book in one hand and tugged at his sleeve, pulling his cuff straight with the other. He should probably have spent money on a good briefcase.

He turned into his office, set his book on the desk, and stood in a patch of sunlight with his hands in his pockets, facing the floor-to-ceiling windows. Tall buildings of glistening concrete, steel, and glass rose before him. Was this what Satan promised Christ on the mount of temptation? *All this I will give you, if you bow down and worship me.* Lonnie slid his executive chair back and dropped into the luxury of its soft leather. If he were home, he'd be sitting on a hard rock aching with stiffness—but his thoughts would be on God, not the creations of man.

He found the script laid out for him. He picked it up and began to read. Quentin was bound to figure out they were using his script, sooner or later. He flipped to the back to see where the changes had been made. In a few minutes he would find out what those changes were going to cost and, after his meeting later that afternoon, whether or not he'd have the required time. He'd worry about the money later, but he had a few ideas about that, too. Quentin wasn't likely to stumble upon the script right away. As soon as everything was agreed to, he'd bring Quentin in on it. That could be as early as this afternoon.

Nicole appeared at his door with a cup of coffee. "Here. I thought you might need a morning eye-opener."

"Thank you. I didn't see you when I came in. How did you know I was here?"

"I asked reception to let me know when you arrived. Your meeting's in fifteen minutes."

Lonnie looked at his watch. Traffic had been heavy on the long drive in, the downside of leaving late, but he had little to do until the meeting anyway. There was nothing to prepare. The reports would be given by his management team.

"Could you get me a copy of the proposal we're making to Mr. Lowen?" he said.

"Certainly."

Lonnie took a sip of coffee and frowned. It was flavorless, like warm water, but this was California, what could he expect? He turned the mug to read the lettering. The Striker Films logo popped off the burgundy surface in bright gold letters: a lightning bolt blazing through the company name with the words, "Where Lightning Strikes Twice." *Kinda corny for a heavyweight like you, Harlan old man.* He set the cup down and brought his hand to his cheek, touching the place where Trudy had kissed him good-night. He smiled and shook his head to clear his thoughts. At least she was showing progress, and Quentin was here helping out; it did seem things were moving in the right direction.

Nicole slid a file in front of him, interrupting his thoughts. Lonnie picked it up and folded it back. "Tell me something. Have you ever met Ben Lowen?"

"Yes...not that I really know him. I've only said hi once or twice."

"What kind of man is he? I mean, what was your initial impression?"

"Seemed nice enough. He's backed us a few times, but never on a scale as big as this."

"You think he'll accept our proposal?"

"That's hard to say. If your numbers are accurate, and you can convince him he'll make more money, I don't see why not."

Lonnie glanced at the script. *Of course we'll make more money. If we leave it the way it is, we won't make any.*

SCRIPT IN HAND, Lonnie made his way down the hall to the boardroom. Heads turned his way. He resisted the impulse to introduce himself. They had to wonder about the new boss, but he was determined to be on time for the meeting. He passed Les Miller's office and saw Quentin in what appeared to be a serious discussion. Les stood, crushing a cigarette in his ashtray. He looked up and caught Lonnie's eye.

Brent Crowley and Michael Sugarman were waiting in the boardroom, though neither were seated, suggesting they hadn't been there long. Nicole was pouring coffee. Brent and Michael curtailed their conversation and turned as Lonnie entered the room.

The boardroom was on an outside wall offering another magnificent view of the city. There were Ficus trees in the corners and a series of gold plaques hanging on wallpaper made of woven straw. The adjoining screening room had been on an inside wall without windows so when the lights were out the room was dark. "Morning," Lonnie said. He laid his copy of the script on the table, took a seat, and tried to appear relaxed. He leaned back in his chair, crossed one leg over the other, and fingered the cuff of his new beige slacks.

Les walked in. "Sorry I'm late," he said as he sat down.

Michael looked at his watch and frowned, shaking his head.

Harlan must have been a stickler for promptness. That was a surprise. Lonnie leaned forward, elbows on the table, and laced his fingers. "Well, we're all here. Now that you've had time to review the changes, I assume you're ready to give me cost and time estimates. Who wants to go first?"

He was met with the same cool silence he'd experienced the day before. He looked around the room. Les tapped a cigarette from his pack and coughed into his hand, then put the cigarette to his lips and snapped open his lighter. Brent began fumbling with the papers in front of him. He scratched his woolly head. The reports would come from these two. The issues were time and money, and Michael, as a lawyer, wasn't involved with either.

"Alright." Lonnie hoped his tone was firm, yet friendly. "Brent, you look like you've got some numbers there. How 'bout we start with you?"

Brent scratched his chest. His open collar revealed a tuft of curly body hair. "I don't mind," he said, "but my figures relate directly to how much time it will take to make the changes and how much the actors will have to be paid, so we should probably begin with Les."

Les glanced up, cutting Brent an acrid look. He picked up the script, flipping to the back, and squinted through the smoke rising from the cigarette between his lips. He put the cigarette in the ashtray and exhaled a blue cloud into the air. "Well, I have good news and bad news. The good news is, some of what you're asking just requires we take stuff out. That's easy. Providing we can get the lab to extend our credit, we can probably get it done on time." His voice sounded like gravel, but he cleared his throat and continued. "The problem is you're also asking for a bunch of retakes. The whole ending has been rewritten. I don't see how we can possibly do it without another two months of shooting. And that's assuming we can get our actors back. They may have already moved on to other projects."

Lonnie withheld comment. *Two months?* He reflected over the changes he was requesting. There weren't that many. Yes, they had to edit out the gratuitous sex but, as Les admitted, that wouldn't impact their schedule. And yes, the whole ending had to change, but that was only the last fifteen minutes of the movie. Lonnie didn't know how things were done in Hollywood, but he couldn't imagine those kinds of changes taking more than a few weeks. "And what about the cost?" he asked.

Brent's eyes darted from Les to Michael. He picked up a piece of paper and held it in front of him like a shield, his fingers visibly shaking. "Over a million dollars."

"A million *what?*" This time Lonnie didn't let it pass. There was no way so few changes could cost so much. "We're not going to get a million dollars," he said, "nor do we have that much time."

The men around the table seemed to relax. They began to gather their papers. Les put his cigarette in his mouth and reached for the script, turning it sideways to pound it back into shape. "Sorry about that, chief, but that's just the way it is. If you'll give the go-ahead, we'll get back to work so we can finish what we've got."

"Slow down. I believe you're forgetting something. I said I wouldn't release the picture as it is. That's not an option. Now we have two choices: We can trash the film, in which case we're all out of a job, or you can go back and sharpen your pencils. Here's what I propose. I'm going to see Ben Lowen this afternoon. I'm going to ask for three weeks, and not a minute longer. And I'll see if he'll front us more money, but no more than half the amount you just quoted. Either we work with that, or we forget it."

Lonnie paused waiting for his words to sink in. They had to follow his directive. He was the boss. Harlan had said he'd like being on top—*The perks are great Spud!* He smiled, feeling a surge of adrenalin. Power was a potent elixir.

Les and Brent were fidgeting, either unready, unable, or unwilling to give him an answer. Les was snapping his lighter open and closed, *click, click, click,* and Brent was hiding behind his sheaf of papers. Michael just sat there with a sardonic smile, shaking his head. Lonnie's resolve faded. It wasn't about power. That was vanity. *My strength cometh from the Lord!*

He tapped the script in front of him and continued. "There's something else you may want to consider. I had a chance to look at some of what we've done in the past. You may be surprised to learn that every time we released a decent movie, something rated PG or lower, we made money. In fact, every time we've lost money, it's been on films like this." He tossed the unedited version of *Lost Cause* on the table. "I'm absolutely convinced that if we make the changes, the film will do so much better we'll not only be able to pay our debt, we'll make a healthy profit. Help me with this, and I'll see you each receives a generous bonus. Otherwise, well, let's just say we've run out of options. We either move ahead on a tighter budget, or we trash the film and call it quits."

"And what if Lowen doesn't agree?"

"That's *my* problem."

ELEVEN

HIDING BEHIND the blue gray walls of an empty cubicle, Quentin waited for the boardroom to empty. He heard the quiet shuffle of shoes on the carpet. He heard the muffled voices of the management team passing by, though he couldn't discern what was being said. He waited until all was quiet, and then waited a moment longer. When he was sure his uncle had turned the corner and was out of sight, he launched himself across the hall. The sign on the door read, Les Miller - Vice President - Production. Les himself had only just entered the office. The unexpected intrusion startled him causing him to jerk his head up, tweaking a nerve.

Quentin reached over his shoulder to close the door. "How did it go?" he asked.

Les began rubbing his neck. His shirt, a shiny blue polyester with white Hawaiian orchids, gaped open at the middle where the buttons strained to contain his bulging gut. He fingered the last cigarette from his pack, tossed the crumpled cellophane and foil wrapper into the trash, and grabbed his chair to take a seat. "Pretty much like you said," he answered. He brought the cigarette to his lips, snapped his lighter open, and inhaled as he leaned back. Then he coughed a cloud of smoke into the air, and wheezed, clearing his throat. "Once your uncle saw what it was going to cost, we thought he'd be reasonable; instead, he's put our backs to the wall. He's still insisting on the same bunch of changes. And we're still saying we don't have the money or the time." Les leaned forward, his cigarette sandwiched between his knuckles. He fidgeted with his thumb, rubbing his cuticle. "You need to tell the others what you told me. I think it will sound better coming from you."

Quentin glanced sharply to the right making sure the door was closed, then turned back to Les. "Agreed, but we can't do it here. You think you can get Brent and Michael to meet us somewhere for lunch?"

Les slid an ashtray over. It was a shallow marble dish with a stainless steel Oscar standing proudly in the center. "Name the place. I'll get them there," He opened his palms, knocking the ash from his cigarette onto his desk. "What choice do we have? We gotta do something, or the company goes belly up."

Quentin rested his elbows on the arms of his chair and laced his fingers over his firm stomach. "How about we say noon at The Farm. You know the one I'm talking about? Down the street, main floor of Bancorp Towers, just a hop, skip and a jump from here." Quentin looked at his legs, and then back at Les. "Unless you have wheel-trans, like I do. Arrange it with the others. I have to duck out to avoid being cornered by the uncle. If I leave now, I can have a table waiting."

Les leaned back in his chair. "Sounds good. See you in a few minutes."

AT HIGH NOON, the pavement was hot. The sun overhead bore down mercilessly, leaving no shadow in which to hide. Quentin could feel his tires heating up as he rolled down the sidewalk, dodging pedestrian traffic. He turned into the air-conditioned oasis of the restaurant, feeling the heat throbbing in his temples. Tiny beads of perspiration were rolling down his chest.

The Farm stood at street level in the mall of a major downtown high-rise. It took a few moments for Quentin's eyes to adjust to the dark. In the middle of a modern glass and brushed-aluminum building was a room that resembled the interior of a barn. Several square posts supported beams that ran the length of the ceiling. The tables were in small booths that looked like stalls, and rusty antique tillers and hoes and harrows were mounted on the wide plank walls.

At one end of the room was a loft that held bales of hay. The floor was covered with sawdust and peanut shells. Quentin could hear the shells crunching under his wheels as he followed the hostess to his table.

"Could we get something in the back," he asked.

The girl, dressed like a farmhand with work boots, bib overalls, a T-shirt, and straw hat, led him to a table along the back wall. He waited while she removed one of the chairs, then he scooted the remaining chairs around on the sawdust, positioning them so he could sit facing the front door. A grizzly woodsman's axe was mounted on the wall behind him, and there was a stack of wooden egg crates along with a half dozen milk tins in the corner. Quentin picked up the menu. The restaurant was known for its "farm fresh" food, with an emphasis on organically grown greens and beef raised on organic fodder—no chemicals or pesticides allowed. Quentin glanced at the pictures and set the menu down. He knew what he wanted: tuna smothered in melted mozzarella on an open-faced onion bun, and a side of chowder.

A voluptuous waitress with shapely legs and blond hair stopped by the table. In her tight, ragged-edge mini-skirt, and white blouse with red polka dots, she was a parody of Daisy Mae. She set a glass of water down and seeing the unopened menu asked if Quentin was ready to order. He pointed at the three empty chairs and explained he was waiting for friends.

Quentin took a sip of the cool, natural spring water and nibbled on a bread stick. He glanced up and saw three men standing in the open door, but with the light at their backs, their features were hidden. One was notably taller than the others. He waited till the door closed and his own eyes readjusted to the light. The three men were walking in his direction.

"Hey there, Quentin," Les said, patting him on the shoulder. He struggled to maneuver his stomach around the table. The Hawaiian print shirt had wet wedges under the arms. He curled his knuckles around his lighter and reached into his pocket for a cigarette.

Brent pulled a napkin into his lap.

Michael nodded at Quentin.

Les exhaled a cloud of gray smoke. The waitress came back with an armful of menus which she passed around the table. Then she leaned over with her hands on her knees bringing her shiny red lips to Les's ear. "I'm sorry, sir, the restaurant has a no-smoking policy." She pointed at a wanted poster nailed to a nearby post, but Les ignored her. His eyes were busy traveling down her blouse.

She stood, bringing his peep show to an end. He took his cigarette, squashed it on a saucer, and handed it to the girl. "Don't have ashtrays either." Then, looking at Quentin, "Is there somewhere else we can go?"

"Relax, we're already here. You can handle it for an hour." Michael said, looking peeved. Then, turning to Quentin. "Have you already ordered?"

Quentin shook his head. "No, I thought I'd wait."

Michael picked up his menu, scanned the various selections and put it down again, folding his hands in front of him on the table. "Les says you wanted to talk to us."

Quentin leaned back in his chair placing his elbows on the armrests. He started to answer but the waitress interrupted. She raised her pad with her pen poised. "Can I get you gentlemen something from the bar?" she said.

Quentin shook his head no.

Les looked up but rolled his eyes. "Beer, on tap," he said.

"Make it two," Brent said, "and I'm ready to order."

"And I'll have a Tom Collins," Michael said. "I'm ready too. How 'bout you Les."

Les nodded. "I'll have your Bull Burger with the works, and a house salad with Thousand Island." He laid his menu down, forcing the waitress to reach across the table so he could admire her cleavage again.

"Quentin ordered his tuna and Michael a clubhouse. Brent said, "I'll have the chicken sandwich without the fries."

LONNIE LAID the proposal on his desk. He'd read it three times. One more review wouldn't make a difference. It was a simple proposition. A slight delay to make a few changes meant the film would earn more money. Lonnie planned to give Mr. Lowen an additional five percent. He should be delighted. Lonnie looked at his watch wondering where Quentin was. It was half past noon. They were supposed to meet for lunch. Lonnie had to eat now or risk being late for his meeting.

He went to the door to ask Nicole if she'd seen his nephew, but she wasn't at her desk. *Probably stepped out for a bite.* He wandered down the corridor, glancing left and right. The building seemed deserted. He stopped at Les's office, but it was empty. Same for Michael and Brent. Everyone was gone. Lonnie felt abandoned. He stuck his head into the lobby. At least the receptionist was there. "You're not taking lunch?" he asked.

She looked up from her magazine. "No, sir, I go after everyone else gets back. Someone from the secretarial pool has to relieve me."

"Ah, right. You didn't happen to see my nephew, Quentin, did you? I thought we were meeting for lunch but I don't see him around."

The receptionist picked up the magazine and turned a page. "I think he left about an hour ago."

Lonnie looked at his watch. "That would have been eleven thirty. It's twelve thirty now." *Odd. He must have forgotten.* "I guess I'm on my own. Know anywhere I can grab a quick sandwich?"

"Sure. Basement level. There's a sandwich counter. Makes great pastrami."

Lonnie nodded, but he wasn't in a pastrami kind of mood. "Thanks," he said.

LONNIE MADE his way outside and was blasted by a wave of rolling heat. He tried to shake it off. It was no worse than Posada, except in Posada there weren't any air-conditioned buildings so you didn't have the shock of going from cold to hot. He looked up and down the street. Neon and flat painted signs were hanging from buildings in cluttered disarray. The downtown traffic surged like a herd of stampeding cattle, the bulls in front being prodded by the horns of those behind. The fumes made him nauseous. On second thought, it was a lot worse than Posada.

A line of taxis idling at the curb partially blocked his view, but it looked like the building on the corner was a restaurant. A green and yellow palm tree glowed in bright neon colors with the words "Banana Splits" scrolled in red letters across the bottom. He squeezed through the crowd and stood at the corner, waiting for the light to change. A street musician played a fiddle while a white-faced mime tried to escape from an invisible box. The light turned green. Lonnie crossed the street and turned toward the café passing by the window of a giant electronics warehouse. It was a window full of televisions. He stopped for a moment at the door. There were more TVs than he'd ever seen before, more plasma screen faces and rolling scenes of paradise, more computers flashing high-res, dot-matrix, color-graphic displays, more home entertainment stereos and portable jukeboxes, more wall-to-wall cell phones chirping and warbling with dozens of musical ringer tones, and pile upon pile of videos, CDs and DVDs. How could anyone think through all the clutter? How could they ponder questions like, "who am I, and why am I here?" when Satan jammed the God signal with *thump dada* music, cell phone chatter, surf-the-web mania, and non-stop news, weather and sports.

Lonnie turned away, shaking his head. Two doors down, he found the entrance to Banana Splits and went inside. It took a few moments for his eyes to adjust. He was standing in a 1950s soda fountain. There was a counter with a row of tall chairs. The chairs swiveled back and forth as customers came and went. The floor was made of black and white tiles in a checkerboard pattern. The tables in the middle of the room were topped with white Formica and the chairs were chrome with white Naugahyde seats.

Lonnie chose an empty booth by the window and sat down. There was a small jukebox at the end of the table advertising selections from the fifties that could be played for a quarter, but Lonnie didn't need a stroll down memory lane. Besides, music was already playing...*devil or angel—girl, will you be my-ine*, the singer crooned. Lonnie's eyes did a quick tour of the room to see if he recognized anyone. It was noisy and crowded, but the faces were all unfamiliar. The sun streaming in the window was warm, though the room was air conditioned. He wanted more than dessert, but at least ice cream would help him cool off. His short hike down the sidewalk had made his underarms moist.

A girl came over and set a glass of water on the table. Her hair was long and roped in a thick braid, tied with a ribbon. She was wearing a fifties-style blue pleated skirt with a small fringed apron and a white puffed-sleeve blouse with the Banana Splits palm tree logo embroidered on the pocket.

"Hi, my name is Allison and I'll be your waitress. Our luncheon special is the Burger Basket which comes with fries and a soft drink for $5.99, or we have a great BLT topped with a thick slice of Canadian bacon for the same price, and of course our regular menu. Do you already know what you want, or would you like a few minutes to decide?" Her smile held dimples at the corners, and her lips were full and naturally pink. She handed a menu to Lonnie and wiped her hands on her tiny apron while she waited.

"And my name's Lonnie Striker," he said, returning her smile. "So, tell me Allison, what do you recommend, one of the specials—or should I take time to read the menu?"

"Well, to tell the truth, I like the chili. It's our speciality, and it's homemade. Or, if you really want something good, try one of our chili and cheese dogs. An inch-thick Polish sausage on a bun smothered in our world-famous chili and topped with a pile of cheddar cheese. And our fries are made from real potatoes cut right here on the premises."

Lonnie held out the menu. "Say no more. You've sold me."

"One chili and cheese dog coming right up. And what can I get you to drink?"

Lonnie glanced around at the other tables. Some were eating hot fudge sundaes from glass vases shaped like flowers. Others were drinking malts from tall stainless steel carafes straight from the blender. A woman reached for a napkin to wipe her chocolate brown moustache. *When in Rome.* "I'll have a chocolate malt."

"Good choice. Back in a dash."

Lonnie toyed with his spoon. The titter of conversation and the rake and rattle of glass against silverware created enough confusion to keep him from feeling the full weight of the snub, but deep inside he knew he'd been ditched—*again!* Things seemed so good. Quentin even volunteered to help. But where was he now? Lonnie stared out the window watching the traffic in the street, tapping the bowl of the spoon against the Formica-topped table.

THE ANSWER Lonnie sought was two blocks down the street in another restaurant. The room buzzed, electric with conversation, bankers, brokers and bond salesmen on cell phones, all hustling to close the day's hottest deal.

Michael passed the saltshaker to his left. "You still haven't explained why you wanted to see us," he said.

Quentin put his fork down and took a sip of water. "I understand my uncle is making it hard for you to get your latest project finished. I was telling Les that I might be able to shed some light on the matter."

Les chomped on his burger and chewed as he eyed the room. He set the burger down and swallowed, using his napkin to wipe his mouth. "He's not making it hard. He's making it impossible," he said. "We're on a tight budget with this one, and it's crucial we finish on time. For a lot of reasons. But just when we're in the final stages, your uncle walks in and pulls the plug. He's got us changing everything."

Quentin took a sip of water and leaned back in his chair. "What kind of changes?"

"He wants us to clean it up. He says it's too freaking naughty just because we show a little breast. Can you imagine? I mean, come on. That's what we hired Laurna for. People want to see her breasts. It's what they pay for."

Quentin looked around the table gauging the reaction of the others.

"But it's not just that," Les continued. "He also thinks it's too violent. He's worried kids will go home and have nightmares. I told him little kids won't even be able to see it. It'll have an R rating, but that's not good enough. He's about to throw the whole freaking project out the window, and that's something the company can't afford."

Quentin interlocked his fingers and twiddled his thumbs for a minute, sucking in his cheeks. "*Ummm*, I thought as much. You've heard about his being a missionary, haven't you? I don't want to get down on religious people—some of them do a lot of good—but there are some who just sit around and complain, especially when they see other people having fun. It's like they think enjoying life is some kind of sin, know what I mean? That's what we're dealing with here. I've only known my uncle for a few days but it's pretty obvious. He's one of the Bible-thumping kind. Repent or burn. I get the feeling he thinks Hollywood is a euphemism for Sodom and Gomorrah."

"You hit the nail on the head, kid. And I'll tell you what really bothers me. It's knowing Harlan's the one who called the play. He wouldn't have agreed with your uncle. I know that. Heck, he never even told us he had a brother. Then he up and dies and leaves a majority share to the little nerd, and leaves us to clean up the mess. So what are we supposed to do?"

Quentin grabbed the wheels of his chair and rocked back and forth. "I don't know. I wish Dad were here to ask, but he's not. Your deadline is Friday, one week from today, is that right?" Quentin paused and leaned forward, weaving his fingers in his lap. His eyes met the others as each man gave an affirming nod. "And I'm also given to understand that there's no way you can do what my uncle's asking in that amount of time." The nods continued. "Then what I would suggest is that you simply don't do it."

Brent held his beer at his mouth looking over the top with the foam splashing up the sides of the mug. "Easy for you to say, but your job isn't on the line."

"No? Maybe not, but my future is. I own twenty percent of the company, don't forget. Look, we can't have a religious nut running things. Say, for example, he gets away with it. Are you guys going to be happy doing remakes of *Pollyanna*? A lot of kids may love you, but you'll lose the respect of your peers. To survive in this town, you've got to be winning Oscars. That's what my dad was striving for. If my uncle has his way, we might as well change the name of the company because, as far as the industry's concerned, the great Striker Films will be dead."

Quentin picked up a pepper shaker and sprinkled his chowder. "The thing is, it doesn't have to be that way." His eyes darted from one man to the next, ensuring he had their attention. "Suppose you tell my uncle you're doing what he's asked, and even make a pretense of doing it. Then, at the same time, you finish the film as is, without the changes. Come next Friday, you send the film to the distributor and meet our contractual obligations. The film is released, the company makes money and..."

"And we'll all be fired. The three of us will be looking for new jobs."

"No, I'm not going to let that happen. Remember, my mother and I still own forty-five percent. I'll tell her it was my idea, that we had to do it to save the company's reputation. I know she'll side with me. And my uncle won't buck her. He wouldn't dare. In the meantime, I'm going to find a way to buy back what should have been mine in the first place. I only need another six percent, the five my uncle was given, plus one extra so my mom and I can control the vote. Once my uncle sees he's alone, he'll step aside. I doubt he'll even stick around. Nobody wants to be where they're not wanted. I'll offer to buy six percent of his shares, and he'll accept because it's best for everyone. It will be just like it was before. He'll continue to get his share of the money, and he can go back and play good Samaritan to his heart's content. It's really the only solution..."

LONNIE WIPED chili from his chin. The waitress had been right. It was *gooood*! He hadn't had good old-fashioned American junk food in as long as he could remember. Allison returned to his table and handed him another napkin.

"Thank you. You're right, it was tasty, but it was also sloppy," Lonnie said, licking his fingers.

"That's why we have a big stock of *napkins*." She stood at the end of the booth with a dishtowel in her hand. "I don't think I've seen you in here before. Is this your first visit?"

"Yes. I just got into town a few days ago."

"Where from?"

"Mexico."

"Mexico? Never would have guessed. On vacation?"

"No, I live there. I'm a missionary."

The girl raised her eyebrows. "A missionary?" She reached for Lonnie's empty plate. "Let me get that for you." Her arm was tan and freckled, as was the bridge of her small nose. "That's interesting," she said. "So what brings you here?"

"I had to come back for my brother's funeral, but when I went to the reading of the will, I found I'd inherited his company. Here, let me get out of your way." Lonnie scooted off the bench.

Allison set the plate aside and began wiping the table, but she appeared distracted. Suddenly, she stopped and with one hand on her hip, turned to face Lonnie. "Wait a minute. You said your last name was Striker. I thought that sounded familiar. Your brother, was he president of Striker Films?"

"Yes. Why? You knew him?"

Allison's gazed strayed to the tall, ebony building outside the window. "Uh huh. I auditioned there once." She leaned over to wipe the table again.

Lonnie reached for his wallet. "Are you an actress?"

"Everyone's an actress in this town, mister," she said, but the smile had gone out of her voice.

TWELVE

"Ben? I have an update. I just had lunch with Harlan's son."

"Yes, and..?"

"He suggested we ignore his uncle. Said we should try to finish the film on time."

"The uncle, yes. This disturbs me. Someone must have known. Why wasn't I told?"

"We've already been over this. None of us knew about him. Harlan kept it from everyone. I couldn't tell you what I didn't know."

"All right, that's one problem. You say Harlan's boy is encouraging you to meet the deadline?"

"Yes. We just had a meeting. He wants his uncle out of the way so he can have the company for himself."

"Uh huh, and how did the others react?"

"I think they bought it."

"That's not good. All right, leave it with me. I appreciate the call."

"No problem, and ah, good luck."

"Luck has nothing to do with it. These things happen because we make them happen."

"Of course, Mr. Lowen. Good-bye."

LONNIE STARED at the city beyond the panes of glass. There was a certain symmetry to it, the way the angles and planes caught the light, some absorbing, some reflecting, interconnected mirrors and walls as far as the eye could see. The city-scape represented decades of ingenuity and labor: the concrete of the old, with its molded arches, spiked spires and gargoyles, contrasting with towers made of aluminum, glass and steel, soaring into the clouds. Lonnie didn't mean to belittle the achievements of man, but he understood the source of man's creativity, so he gave credit where it was due. He glanced at his watch. Mr. Lowen would be arriving any minute.

Lonnie turned his attention to the tallest building—a communication tower pointing to God. The sun behind the spire flashed directly into his eyes, blinding him. For a moment, everything went black...

He was walking with his mother up a winding trail to the crest of a hill. They had been driving north on the Coast Highway, sagebrush and ocean view whisking by hour upon hour while Lonnie considered what life would be like living with his mother. They were on their own now, putting miles between themselves and the insults of Harlan and Buddy. As far as he was concerned, the farther they got, the better.

The sun was just beginning to set over the Pacific when his mother had suddenly pulled the car off the road and parked. He could remember the gravel crunching beneath the tires and the tang of saltwater greeting his nostrils as they stepped out into the open air. His mother hadn't explained, she'd simply said: "We've got to pray." Then she'd taken his hand and pulled him along, huffing and puffing and breathing the dusty air, until they'd reached the crown of the hill. The vista from the peak was spectacular. The sun sent out a fan of radiant colors—oranges and yellows and purples and blues—spanning the great vastness of the deep green sea.

"Lonnie," his mother said, "I want you to know we're not alone. We'll never be alone. God's out there Lonnie." She pointed toward the setting sun, which momentarily blinded him. "Whenever you need help, remember, Jesus loves you. He wants what's best for you. We had to get away, you understand, we had to. But it's not the way it's supposed to be. Pray, Lonnie. Pray like you've never prayed before. Petition your real father, the Father of Light, in Jesus' name, and He'll answer. That's a promise, Lonnie. You can count on it. That's a promise!"

The words were stamped indelibly on his mind. He'd heard them again and again. Every time he stood watching the sunset from the cliffs of Posada, he was reminded how, in the darkness of that moment, God had spoken to him. And now, as he stood blinded again, the message was the same. *"The world cannot see for the brightness of the Son."*

Lonnie heard a buzzing sound behind him. He murmured a quick prayer, "You know better than I, what needs to be done, Lord," then spoke into the intercom. "Yes, Nicole...all right, show him in."

Lonnie's stomach tightened. Goosebumps prickled his arms. He heard the hum of the air conditioner and suddenly felt cold. He rubbed his shirtsleeves, pulling his shoulders back to stretch and release the tension.

Nicole opened the door and held it for the gentleman standing behind her. Over his shoulder she looped her thumb and index finger into an OK sign. She winked at Lonnie and silently mouthed the words, "Good luck," before stepping back and closing the door again.

Mr. Lowen was bigger than Lonnie expected, taller by several inches and carried more weight. His light gray business suit made Lonnie feel underdressed, even though the suit was frumpy and made of fabric from another era. A tie, shorter than it should have been, rolled over the curve of his tummy. He wasn't fat, but his once firm body was now soft and fleshy. His hairline was receding. What remained was wiry and gray, bushing out at the sides. Thick black glasses rested on the bridge of a bulbous nose, and his jowls sagged like a pair of hams on either side of his face.

The man extended a large, meaty hand and Lonnie received it in kind.

"Ben Lowen," the man said. His handshake was firm, and there was power in the grip. According to Nicole, Lowen owned two newspapers and three magazines. A publishing magnate. This was a man used to having his way.

"Lonnie Striker," Lonnie returned. He gestured toward the couch. "Please, have a seat."

The cushions wheezed as the two men settled onto the soft leather. Mr. Lowen crossed one leg over the other, tugging the crease of his slacks to make himself comfortable.

Lonnie tried to look nonchalant, but a bevy of butterflies had taken up residence in his stomach. "Thank you for coming," he said. "I know you must be busy, but I felt we needed to talk."

Lowen grunted and gave an affirming nod.

Lonnie shifted uneasily, waiting for Ben to speak, but the man held his peace. Lonnie rubbed his hands together, feeling moisture in his palms. "I don't want to waste your time, so let me get right to the point," he said. "I gather our company, Striker Films, has borrowed against our assets and—correct me if I'm wrong—the film, due for release next Friday, must be completed, or we face foreclosure."

Again Lonnie paused. He slipped his hand up and down the arm of his ice-blue shirt. *Why doesn't he say something? Anything!* The silence was awkward.

"Not that there's a problem," Lonnie went on. "My staff tells me we can get the project done on time. We have a week to do what amounts to a final edit, which should be easy. As for the loan repayment, I'm sure once we hit the street, the film will make money. At least that's what I'm told. The problem is, I don't like the storyline. I think we can do better. Right now, it's a grade B shoot 'em up action film. I'm proposing we turn it into a love story."

That should have evoked a response, but the silence continued. Was the man dead? Was he practicing the art of intimidation? Lonnie raised his hand. "Now before you say anything, hear me out. I have two good reasons for making such a suggestion. The first is, I think we should try to improve the film's moral content. I believe we have a responsibility to show young people how the world should be, not necessarily how it is. And second, we stand to make a lot more money."

Lonnie reached down, picked up a folder, and passed it to Mr. Lowen, "I've drafted a proposal, which I think you'll find of interest." He leaned forward with his elbows on his knees, cupping his palms in front of him. "Everyone loves a good love story, especially one with an emotional ending. You'll see it all outlined here. Love stories are big at the box office. I think with the few changes I propose, we can make twice, even three times the money we originally thought. But we need about three more weeks. I'm asking that you grant us an extension, and perhaps even allow us to increase our loan, in return for which we'll give you an additional five percent of our net profits. That's five percent over and above the loan and interest repayment."

Mr. Lowen's eyebrows feathered as he squinted, and when he shook his head, his jowls jiggled like Jell-O. Without bothering to open it, he tossed the file back on the table. Loose papers came sliding out. "And why would I want to do that?"

Lonnie thought he'd made himself clear—*improve the moral content, make more money.* The full explanation, including an estimated return on investment, was in the file. *He didn't even glance at it.* Lonnie stared at his unread proposal, unable to look the man in the eye. "I, ah, as I said, you'll make more money. You'll get the money we owe you, with interest, plus five percent of our net profits. It's a much better deal than you had before."

Lonnie heard a grunt. He looked up to see Lowen slowly shaking his head, his bottom lip protruding.

"Young man, let me make myself clear," he said. "I'm not after more money. I want your *company.* If I wait until next Friday, I'll have it—lock, stock, and barrel. My sources tell me you've put a hold on production. There's not much chance you'll finish the film by Friday, but even if you do, it will die at the box office. You'll be lucky to keep it in circulation two months—which suits me fine. The only reason I loaned Harlan the money was because I read the script and I knew it would be a flop. I never expected him to repay the loan. And I have no intention of granting you additional time. By the end of next week, or a few months at most, I plan to be sitting in that chair over there." Mr. Lowen extended his hand toward Lonnie's desk. "Then I can rework the film myself. I know what it needs far better than you. And when I'm done, I'll re-release it and make enough to pay myself back."

Lonnie could feel the color draining from his cheeks.

Lowen stood. "I hope I haven't upset your day too much," he said, putting his hand out to shake Lonnie's. It was a polite gesture, but not the handshake of a friend. Lowen's grip was that of a general preparing for a battle in which the victory was assured. "I know I've given you a lot to think about. Don't bother with formalities. I'll show myself out." And with that he turned and walked to the door. The last thing Lonnie saw was a small bald spot on the back of his head, shining in the light.

Lonnie was in a stupor, his mind still reeling from the blow. He gave his head a shake. Was it really Lowen's intent to wrest control of the company? Why would Harlan agree to such a thing? Why hadn't his lawyers advised against it?

Lonnie went to the door to find Nicole. She wasn't at her desk. He looked out across the maze of cubicles. Copper, silver, and brass plaques—awards of merit bestowed by industry peers—decorated the wall outside the boardroom. Other walls held framed advertising posters displaying the company's previous films. Not all of them were losers. Harlan must have done some things right. At the very least he'd made Buddy's small company a target for takeover. Would it all belong to Lowen in a week? Had he, Lonnie, unwittingly put that possibility within his grasp? He'd been warned, but he'd gone ahead and stopped production. It was like he was handing the business over without a fight. He should have listened—but to whom? It suddenly occurred to him he had a Judas in his camp. Someone was feeding Lowen information. Which one? Perhaps all three.

Nicole turned the corner. She appeared carefree as she strolled to her desk, a little smile playing on her lips. *Nicole?* Lonnie tried to gauge her expression. Was she wearing a mask to cover her duplicity? If so, she was in the wrong business. What was it the waitress said? "Everyone's an actress in this town, mister." Did that include Nicole?

"How did it go?" she asked.

Lonnie held his office door open. "Let's talk about it inside," he said, feeling tension in his voice.

Nicole took a seat in front of the desk. Lonnie walked around and dropped into his chair, his elbow planted on the table and his palm supporting his chin. His blue eyes probed Nicole for answers. He waited, allowing her the opportunity to be first to speak. He could see she was growing uncomfortable.

"Uh...I take it things didn't go well," she finally offered.

"No, they didn't. Actually, our Mr. Lowen seems to know everything that's going on around here, right down to the fact that I've stopped work on the final edit. He as much as said he has a spy in the ranks. That wouldn't be you, would it?"

Nicole's head snapped back as if she'd been slapped. "Me? Hardly. I barely know the man."

Lonnie couldn't tell if the rush of blood to her face revealed anger over being accused, or embarrassment over being caught. He wanted to believe her; she was one of the few people he'd brought into his confidence, but until he knew more, he'd have to watch what he said. "Okay, I'll take your word for it, but if this company has a pipeline to Mr. Lowen, I intend to see it gets plugged. In the meantime I need to see a copy of the agreement Harlan signed."

Nicole shook her head slightly, a glassy film washing her eyes. "I...I'm sorry, but I don't have a copy. The original is held by our legal counsel, Barry Gladdon, upstairs."

Lonnie pushed back from the desk. "Fine. Get me an appointment with Mr. Gladdon, and the sooner the better."

"Certainly, Mr. Striker." Nicole went back to her desk. The tone of her voice was icy, but whether she felt hurt or outrage, he couldn't tell. He did note that, as she sat down, she removed a tissue from her drawer.

A few moments later the phone rang in Lonnie's office. He picked it up. "Mr. Gladdon has a few minutes if you can see him right now," Nicole said. "Otherwise, it will have to wait until Monday."

"Tell him I'm on the way."

Lonnie rode the elevator in silence. The car stopped at various floors as, one by one, other passengers got off. He was all alone when the elevator doors opened into the vestibule of Gladdon, Vickers and Cox. He was welcomed by the receptionist who escorted him down the hall to a corner office, twice the size of Lonnie's own.

Barry Gladdon rose from his desk, the fabric of his dark blue suit shining in the light. The cut of his perfectly tailored jacket was in sharp contrast to the rumpled look of Mr. Lowen.

The sun streaming through the two glass walls illuminated the rich cherry paneling. Most of the furnishings were made of the same gleaming red wood. The surface of the desk was immaculate. Nothing—not even a loose paper clip—was out of place. There was nothing to suggest work was being done. The wall to Lonnie's right held photographs of Gladdon shaking hands with movie stars, politicians, and other persona grata. One showed a younger, brown-haired version of the man kneeling with his arms around three little girls. Lonnie assumed they where his daughters. His law degrees were central to the display. "HARVARD" was spelled out in an outline typeface on the largest of the three framed documents.

"Hello, Lonnie. Welcome, welcome," he said, walking around to the other side of his desk. "What can I do for you?" He put his hand against Lonnie's back, steering him to an alcove at the rear of the office. Here the walls were lined with shelves of neatly organized law books. In the center was a table surrounded by six chairs.

"I understand you have the original contract between my brother and Ben Lowen," Lonnie said. I need to get a copy so I can review it."

"Yes, of course. Here, sit down, sit down." While Lonnie took a seat, Barry went back to his desk and picked up the phone. "Maureen, I need you to make a copy of the Striker/Lowen agreement and bring it here," he said. Then he returned to the table, his look of distinction accented by his lustrous gray hair. He folded his hands in front of him. "Are you looking for anything in particular?"

The man was smooth, Lonnie had to grant that, but so were snakes. "I'm not sure. I just had a meeting with Mr. Lowen. He's under the impression he'll own Striker Films in less than a month. He's convinced we'll default on our contract. I guess I'm hoping I'll find some kind of loophole."

Barry blinked slowly, and with a curt nod, lifted his chin in a manner that suggested Lonnie had stated a foregone conclusion. It wasn't what Lonnie expected to see. Where was the emotional outburst? *Shouldn't he be pounding the table, insisting no such thing will ever happen.* Instead, Lonnie heard him say: "Oh, I doubt you'll find that. We wouldn't be very good at what we do if we drew up contracts with loopholes."

Lonnie was incredulous. "Are you saying it's over, that we should give up without a fight? What about the fact that my brother was dying? Isn't there some kind of death provision? A man can't be expected to fulfill his obligations from the grave. The courts must understand that."

"Unfortunately, your brother was aware of his impending death. When he signed the contract, he waived any recourse resulting from his premature demise."

Why would Harlan do such a thing? "What about Mr. Lowen? Maybe we can show undue coercion. Harlan was in a weakened state; maybe we can prove he wasn't thinking clearly."

"No. That, too, was considered. Mr. Lowen was careful to eliminate the possibility of a later court challenge. And your brother was willing to do anything to get the money. Apparently, he felt he had a dynamite script and that the risk was worth taking. We were legal counsel for both parties, so we were right in the middle of it. We drew up a contract that satisfied the needs of both your brother and Ben Lowen. Although, it should be pointed out that the contract is really between Striker Films Incorporated, and Lowen Enterprises, those being the legal names of the firms involved."

Whose side is this guy on? Harlan had retained Gladdon, Vickers and Cox as legal counsel. Why weren't they defending the company? Lonnie narrowed his gaze. "You represented both parties? Doesn't that suggest a conflict of interest?"

"Not when both parties agree to it in advance."

A woman stepped into the room but paused at the door until she had Mr. Gladdon's attention. She held a folio of paper against her purple business suit. Her silver hair was swept into a stylish French twist at the back.

"Yes, Maureen?"

She handed him the document. "The copy of the Striker/Lowen contract you requested."

"Ah, here it is. You can take it and read it for yourself." Gladdon handed the thick sheaf of paper to Lonnie. His white cuff, extending from the sleeve of his suit, was buttoned with a mother of pearl cufflink. "However, I'm afraid your only hope is to release the film on time and use the proceeds to repay Mr. Lowen. But please, call me if there's anything you don't understand. That's what I'm here for."

Lonnie could see he was being dismissed.

Lonnie left Gladdon's office and walked down the hall, aching all over. His back was sore. He applied pressure to his lumbar region with the palm of his hand, massaging the muscle as he stepped into the elevator. Less than one week to remake an entire film, or lose the company. Maybe he should just release the picture. After all, if Lowen took over, he'd probably make the same kind of films. What did one more matter? Maybe it was necessary to let this one slip by and wait until the company was in the black before making changes. It certainly seemed easy to justify. But that was the problem. How could he justify something he knew was wrong? If even one such film went out with his name on it, he would be as guilty as Harlan.

The elevator was filling with people again, stopping at every floor on the way down, but the more crowded it became, the more alone Lonnie felt. How could one law firm represent the interests of two opposing clients and treat them both fairly? There had to be favoritism on one side or the other. And since Harlan was dying, it would make sense to favor Lowen and thereby secure his future business. Lonnie held up the document and flipped the cover sheet aside. His eyes scanned the first page...*a corporation existing under the laws of the state of California...hereinafter called...subject to the terms of this agreement either party shall...read with all changes of number and gender as required by the context...*it was gibberish. Lonnie needed a second opinion. When the elevator bell chimed, it came to him...

He was standing in three inches of stagnant water, trying to wedge a piece of re-bar under the spring to release it from the pump's handle. The sun was yellow and thick in the sky, beating down on his white muslin shirt. He could feel the river of sweat trickling down his chest. Most of the men and women of the village were away. They'd been picked up by the plantation bus and taxied into the jungle where they pruned shrubs, trimmed overgrowth, and harvested coffee beans for Señor Ramirez. Lonnie was one of the few people with enough time on his hands to fix the pump when it broke, so he'd volunteered.

A fender-bent, lime-green Volkswagen came clanking up the road, stirring up a dirty brown cloud. After a long stretch without rain, the hard-packed earth was dry. Two men got out fanning dust from their faces. The passenger walked around to the driver's side of the car to ask a question, and the driver pointed at Lonnie. Lonnie stopped his work and climbed out of the basin, wiping his hands. The man approached, carrying an old leather briefcase, with his jacket draped over one arm and his tie hanging loose around his neck.

"You Mr. Lonnie Striker?" he inquired. He stooped, setting his briefcase on the hot ground.

"I am," Lonnie said, reaching out to receive the man's handshake.

"I'm Don Maniux." He dipped two fingers into his shirt pocket to retrieve a soiled business card, which he held out to Lonnie. "I'm an attorney. That's my firm there—Maniux and Associates—though to be honest, the associates are mostly students doing paralegal work. I'm the only full-time lawyer we got. Anyway, I've been retained by your deceased father's law firm, Wemble and Briggs, to locate you and release your inheritance."

Maniux and Associates, that's who he needed to call. Lonnie couldn't remember much about the man—but he did remember his first impression. Instead of pretending to be larger than life, the lawyer had confessed to being a one-man band. That spoke volumes about his character. They'd gone into the Inn because there were no chairs in Lonnie's tiny hut for visitors. Don had explained how the terms of Lonnie's parents' divorce stipulated that upon Buddy's demise, both brothers were to receive an equal share of Striker films. Lonnie, who up to that time had existed on a small stipend from his mother's church, was about to start receiving an income.

Lonnie wanted no part of running a film company, but that had been anticipated. Mr. Maniux had papers in his briefcase that would allow Lonnie to have his share of the company's profits deposited wherever he chose. The only thing required was his signature on a letter of direction. Pursuant to Lonnie's agreement, Harlan would continue in the role of company president.

They arranged for Maniux and Associates to receive Lonnie's checks and forward them to him. Sending Lonnie's share to a law firm would keep Harlan honest, since he'd know any ambiguities in the payments would be investigated. And having an intermediary meant Lonnie would have a resource he could turn to if a problem ever arose, but it never had.

Lonnie recalled that Maniux and Associates had an office somewhere in Orange County—*but where?*

Lonnie hurried through the lobby and made his way to his office. On his desk he found a slip of pink paper torn from a message pad. It was from Quentin saying he was sorry to have missed lunch, but something had come up. He'd taken the limo home but would send it back for Lonnie. Lonnie crumpled the note and tossed it into the trash. Then he picked up the phone and dialed information. The operator informed him that Maniux and Associates had an Anaheim address.

Lonnie punched in the number and turned to stare out the window while waiting for the phone to ring. The late afternoon sun had painted the high rise towers a bright pink. To the uninitiated, those who had never seen the sun setting on the Sierra Madre del Sur, he could understand how a view such as this might seem beautiful, but they had nothing to compare to. He, on the other hand, knew better, and he was anxious to return.

A woman's voice answered the phone. "Maniux and Associates."

"Could I speak with Don Maniux, please?"

"Just one second. May I say who's calling?"

Don came on the line almost instantly. "I wondered if I'd be hearing from you. I read about the passing of your brother. Please accept my condolences."

Lonnie didn't need consoling, but murmured a polite reply. He tried to explain, without going into detail, the situation the company was in. He asked if Don could read the contract over the weekend and advise him of his options, and also keep an eye out for any escape clauses Barry might have missed.

"Sorry I can't come down and meet with you in person," he said, "but this is urgent. If you'll give me your fax number, I'll have my secretary send a copy of the contract right away."

Lonnie didn't bother telling Nicole who he was faxing the contract to, or why. He just gave her the number, turned and went back into his office, closing the door so he could make a few calls in private.

LONNIE FOUND Les Miller sitting at his desk reading the gossip column of a movie tabloid. He stood looking around, waiting to be acknowledged. It was four square walls of clutter. There were piles of paper on the floor, printouts of scripts and stacks of magazines. The surface of the desk was stained with brown coffee rings and covered with news clippings, courier packs, staples, and rubber bands. The ashtray with the chrome Oscar sprouting from its center was full to overflowing. The nicotine smell was rancid. Lonnie finally pulled a chair back and sat down, uninvited. Les didn't look up till he finished underlining and making a note on the section he'd been reading.

Lonnie crossed his legs, folding his hands in his lap. "Have any luck getting our actors back?" he began.

Les looked around his desk, searching for something. His fingers, yellow with tobacco stains, riffled under the newspaper until they located his pack of cigarettes. He tried shaking one out, but Lonnie held up his hand.

"I'd appreciate it if you could hold off. I'll only be a minute."

Les put the cigarette down. "Nope. Not at all," he said. He cleared his throat with a guttural cough. "I called Jim Mifflin—he represents Laurna Dove, our leading lady—but he said she was vacationing in Europe. She isn't scheduled to return for a month."

Lonnie brought his hand up to rub the back of his neck. Another setback. Was Les telling the truth or deliberately putting him off? Out the corner of his eye, Lonnie caught Michael walking by and flagged him down. "Could you join us for a moment?"

Michael stepped into the office but didn't take a seat. He stood by a credenza piled high with paper and crossed his arms, looking down on Lonnie. Lonnie chose to ignore it. "I want you both to hear this. Les, you do whatever it takes to get our actors back. I want them here by Monday—no excuses. I have to leave. I'm booked on a four o'clock flight. I have some unfinished business to take care of and I won't be back until Tuesday, but when I return, I want to hear that filming has begun."

Michael raised an eyebrow. "Did Ben agree to extend the deadline?"

"Don't worry about Ben. He's *my* problem."

THIRTEEN

LONNIE WATCHED the long skirt of the coastline appear as the plane arched to the left and swooped in toward Huatulco International Airport. From a distance the earth looked like a giant carpet—blues, browns, and greens—with the jungles and ocean separated by a narrow strip of sand. But as they drew nearer the scene took on life. On the surface of the blue, Lonnie could see the white triangular fins of a school of porpoise undulating over the foam-capped waves. And the green spaces were filled with bug-like vehicles scurrying around cities that blossomed in the jungle like flowers. He was almost home, feeling like a child returning from camp with stories to tell.

He felt the bounce now, the tires bruising the pavement, the smoke rising off the wheels with a screech. A second bounce and they were down. Outside the window the tarmac rose up in waves of corrugated heat. Lonnie slipped his book into the seat pocket. At least the flight had given him a chance to read. He waited till the light in the cabin turned green. Then he released his seatbelt and pulled himself up, ducking to avoid the overhead baggage compartment. The aisle was suddenly filled with people scrambling to disembark.

Lonnie had one advantage. He didn't have any luggage. His decision to return had been made impulsively. He'd been sitting at his desk, weary of hearing loan officers say no, holding his head in his hands, trying to figure out what to do and wishing there was someone he could talk to, when it dawned on him—it was Friday! He couldn't go back to the house. He couldn't be alone with Trudy. A whole weekend of temptation would be too much. He needed a listening ear, not seducing eyes. He needed to talk to Paulo.

And he also needed the money that American banks didn't seem willing to lend. He was about to take the biggest gamble of his life. He was going ahead with the changes when, as yet, he didn't have the wherewithal to make them, or any guarantee he'd own the company long enough to see them made.

Trudy would likely view his duck-and-run routine as weakness, but he knew better. *"Flee temptation"*—it was a biblical injunction. He'd called to explain but she wasn't home. Good thing. He didn't need a lecture, or a teary-eyed plea, to weaken his defenses. A simple message on the answering machine was safer.

Lonnie waited in line as the passengers exited down the ramp. They walked en masse through a maze of passageways and then waited in line again to clear customs. All the waiting was putting a damper on his excitement, but he knew the drill. His tenure with the International Missionary Alliance required he make occasional trips to the States to attend conferences and give reports on his mission's progress. Every time he entered and left the country, the government needed to see proof of his citizenship. He stood, shifting his weight from one foot to the other. He had nothing to hide, but he still felt nervous. Why did they always make these rooms so bright? It was like standing in a police lineup.

The overweight, mustachioed man checking passports had a dark complexion and dark eyes that narrowed as he scanned travel documents, but it was unfair to say he looked mean. He was probably a family man. Probably loved his children. Wouldn't harm a fly. Maybe it was the badge that made Lonnie feel like he was about to be strip-searched and thrown into a cell. His heart was thumping as he realized he was next. It was the stereotype, that's what it was. Even though every Mexican he knew was as nice a person as he'd ever want to meet, there was an image in his mind that all Latinos were somehow ruthless cutthroats—a bunch of gun-totin', bandolier-wearin' desperados. It was an image painted by Hollywood, and an excellent example of the point he'd been trying to make. Motion pictures influenced people's ideas about the way things were—for good or for bad. The customs officer eyed Lonnie and nodded. Lonnie stepped forward and handed the man his passport. With no luggage to inspect or purchases to declare, he was processed quickly.

He made his way to the gate. There were no stereotypes, not a single bandolier. The hoards of travelers wore a variety of styles, everything from peasant muslin, sandals and straw hats, to designer dresses and worsted business suits. It never ceased to amaze Lonnie how a small backwater town like Huatulco had become a bustling metropolis overnight. When he'd first arrived the city was unassuming and quiet, a reminder of a bygone era of Spanish rule. Now, twenty years later, it had become an international vacation resort offering sport fishing, scuba diving, hang gliding and jungle tours. Suntans were guaranteed. Lonnie pressed through the masses, hoping to hire a taxi, but as soon as he was outside he heard a familiar voice.

"Hola! Señor Lonnie. Over here."

He turned and saw the smiling face of Father Ceylon with his hooded brown robe roped around his waist and sandals on his feet, just like the priests of old.

Lonnie squeezed through the tangle of people, and the two men embraced. "Paulo, I didn't expect to see you here."

"Nor did I expect to be here, my friend. I was summoned to the cantina to take your call and when I turned around, I bumped into Señor Ramirez. I told him you had returned, and he insisted I take his car to meet you. Our driver is waiting outside. Come, come. Let's not waste time. We can speak in the car."

They found the black Mercedes at the curb and climbed in back. It was an older model vehicle, driven more for its dependability than its status. Paulo and Lonnie made themselves comfortable as the driver pulled away. Paulo turned in his seat and raised his arm, allowing the loose sleeve of his robe to fall down around his elbow. "So, what brings you back so soon? I thought you were going to stay and make a movie."

"I was. I mean, I am, but things have become complicated. Paulo, I gotta tell you, you're a sight for sore eyes. There's so much going on right now, I feel like I'm about to explode. Did I ever tell you about my sister-in-law? No, no, of course not. I never said anything because she was married to my brother, only now he's dead, and I...I just don't know...should I...It's a real mess. So many things have happened, I don't know where to begin."

Lonnie looked into the dark eyes of Father Ceylon. There were soft wrinkles at the corners, but the eyes were smiling. "It is a long ride back to Posada, my friend. I would suggest you begin at the beginning."

"Yes, I suppose I should."

THE JUNGLE was teeming with life. Macaws and toucans could be heard screeching in the trees. The car bumped over potholes and washboards in the road, the dust foaming up from the tires. The driver was much slower than Eduardo had been on the drive down. The old Jeep had bounced so high Lonnie at times thought he'd lose his seat, but the Mercedes had a smooth ride and held its ground even through the tight hairpin turns. They made their way up the mountain under a canopy of figus mecianos and cazara bushes that grew in the gallery woods. The jungle was so green, and the vegetation so thick, you couldn't see ten feet beyond the track of the road.

Lonnie stared out the window, feeling better with home just around the corner and the security of his jungle covering him like a blanket. The birds of the bush were conversing loudly. Their raucous *ka-ka-kaaa, ka-ka-kaaaing* was loud even with the windows rolled up. Lonnie bared his soul and felt the release of a sinner taking confession. Father Ceylon was as much a mentor as a friend. There were differences, yes. Lonnie's own missionary board had cautioned him about getting too close to "Mary-worshiping" Catholics, though he'd never seen Paulo worship anyone but Jesus. Lonnie opposed the kind of ecumenicalism that brought all faiths under one umbrella, and he didn't understand or accept all the rituals of the Catholic Church, but none of that mattered because he knew Father Ceylon was, above all else, a Christian.

When Lonnie had first arrived in the village, fully expecting to be shunned by the Catholic community, Paulo had welcomed him. Paulo embraced him as a friend and sought opportunity to share their mutual love for Christ. Over the years, in conversations too numerous to mention, Lonnie had come to realize that he and Paulo had more in common than not. The essentials of their faith were the same: one God in three persons, Father, Son and Holy Spirit. The Son, born of a virgin, was wholly God and wholly man. He was sinless, but He allowed His innocent blood to be offered up as a sacrifice to pay for the sins of men. His life was given so that men, who could not approach God in their sin, could by accepting His atonement, be brought back to God. Buried, He rose again after three days to demonstrate His power over death, and now waited at the right hand of the Father to take His rightful place as King of kings and Lord of lords, which would come at the end of the age.

Over time, Lonnie finally summoned enough courage to explain that salvation was a free gift available to anyone, and that believing in Christ alone provided access to the Father, but Paulo just nodded and said: "Si, this I also believe." Then he'd placed his hand on a huge leather Bible. "I have read this book many times, my friend. The message is clear." Paulo was even willing to acknowledge that some of the practices of his church were done more for the sake of tradition than to uphold biblical command, but he revered them nonetheless.

THEY WERE coming to a clearing. Lonnie could see the village ahead—the brown backs of children splashing in the well; the old women weaving baskets and blankets, just as they'd done for centuries; a burro being led through the plaza burdened with a load of sticks, the boiling pots, the women washing clothes. They pulled in front of the Inn and got out.

Lonnie didn't wait; he headed straight for the construction site, eager to inspect the progress of his hospital. The rooms were beginning to take shape, with more drywall applied to the studs, but they were a long way from completion. Paulo joined him and they walked through the building together, the residue of white drywall sand sticking to Lonnie's new shoes. Lonnie was concerned that more should have been done in his absence, but Paulo assured him that they were right on schedule. Finally Paulo pointed to a bucket of drywall compound and suggested if Lonnie was so anxious, he could do it himself.

What was most noticeable, however, was the way people reacted to him. Women in the marketplace paused to stare as if they knew him from somewhere, but had forgotten his name. He would catch their eye and they would bury their cheeks in their brightly colored blankets and turn away. He felt compelled to introduce himself at almost every turn. In his new tan slacks and blue shirt without his hair and beard, he was just another American turista, a gringo on summer vacation. Was the change that dramatic?

Paulo suggested they have dinner at the Inn. It was Friday evening. The workers would soon be returning from the plantation and the men would be stopping by the cantina to relax and unwind while the women cooked their meals. Word of Lonnie's return would spread as the men returned to their families. Saturday morning the plaza would be filled with street vendors selling corn tortillas and green peppers, slabs of salted pork, and sacks of flour, coffee beans, and grains. The women wouldn't be startled to see a white-faced gringo hovering around their stalls if they heard about it from their husbands first.

But it was Sunday Lonnie was looking forward to. He needed to be surrounded by the people of God, to be somewhere he felt like he belonged. Except he brooded over what he should, and should not, say. On Saturday, he paced the floor of his tiny cabana, working on his sermon. In his heart he knew Father Ceylon was right, that God was in control and that all would go according to His divine plan, but that didn't stop negative thoughts from creeping in.

He walked by his file cabinets for the umpteenth time. They were mismatched—two greens, a brown, and a grey—with slightly different heights, different handles, and dents along the bottom, but they did the job. The drawers creaked when he opened them to remove the files he'd kept on the film industry, particularly those dealing with the effect movies had on children. He also had a pretty extensive collection of articles reviewing the films made by his brother, most of which he didn't like. He began laying the clippings on the table so he could sort through them. He tried to calm himself, but his hands were shaky.

Late that afternoon, he walked through the skeletal frame of the hospital again. The construction site was deserted. The workers had retired for the weekend. He felt the weight of not being able to complete what he had started. *What man goeth to build a building without first counting the cost*? He'd made the mistake of thinking the money would always be there. But God had given him that money—he hadn't earned it—even Harlan pointed that out. It was a gift from God, and God could take it back if He wanted. But why would He? That was the question. Even Job struggled with that one. If he'd done something to displease God, Lonnie would repent, but like Job, he could think of no sin that required repentance—well maybe his recent bout with lust, but that was under control, wasn't it? Wasn't his decision to return to Posada based partly on the fact that he'd sensed danger in being alone with Trudy? He was working on keeping his feelings in check. *What more do You want me to do, Lord? What more do You want me to do?*

He kicked a piece of drywall with his foot. Saturday was a desolate place. His flock was busy tending to all the chores they couldn't get done during the workweek, and Father Ceylon was hearing confessions. By the end of the day, Lonnie found himself where he always found himself when he had more questions than answers—on the cliffs of Posada overlooking the Pacific ocean. He paused, listening to the sounds of creation: wind and water in a never-ending flow, and birds and animals *tittering* and *rat-tat-tattering* in conversation with God. He breathed in the primal healing smells: the humus of the earth, the brine of the sea, the moisture-laden air, but while he was able to purge his mind of the noise he'd assimilated the previous week, he still did not find the rest he sought. Tomorrow he would face his congregation. He would either carefully avoid sharing the trial he was going through, or he'd come clean—but that would show a lack of faith, wouldn't it? He was inclined to let it go, but he wasn't sure. Maybe it was better to tell. He rubbed his scalp to ward off a latent headache.

He turned to embrace the sun, but it was subdued. No bright light beamed over the horizon; he was not blinded, nor did he see a vision. He spread his arms like Christ on the cross reaching out, abandoned and alone. *My God, my God, why hast thou forsaken me?*

BY SUNDAY, Lonnie's return was old news. Hundreds filed into the little cinder block church. The doors were held back by people pressing in, their bodies flaking green paint from the wood as they squeezed by. When the room was full, they spilled onto the grass at the front and piled up against the windows on both sides. The day had begun with a tropical rain and now the sun pierced through the clouds roiling up steam, moist and hot. The chapel held fewer than a hundred folding chairs, and more than twice that many had come. Everyone wanted to hear about Lonnie's adventures in Hollywood. They stood shoulder to shoulder down the aisles and filled the foyer in the back. The windows along both sides of the building were open, but bodies packed along the wall prevented the air from circulating. The little congregation fanned their faces as they raised their hands to sing:

What a friend we have in Jesus.
Oh, qué amigo nos es Cristo!
All our sins and griefs to bear.

But the burden Lonnie felt was too great, and God's presence seemed elusive. He preached, pacing back and forth on the podium, wiping the sweat from his brow and thumping the Bible in his hand. The sun plowing in through the open doors made his shadow appear to be hovering around the cross on the back wall. He preached God's healing power and the miracles of Christ, attempting to tie it all in with the hospital. He wanted his message to communicate that the hospital shouldn't be important to those who believed in God. Should he ever have to tell them it wouldn't be completed, he wanted them to know they didn't need it anyway. God was there to heal them.

But toward the end of his delivery, his enthusiasm waned. He felt drained, incapable of putting on the good face he knew was expected of him. He'd always preached victory in Jesus, but right now he didn't feel the anointing or the power. By the end of the service, he was trembling. He paused, standing in front of his congregation with his shoulders stooped, and his Bible hanging limp at his side. Hundreds of dark eyes stared back at him, waiting for him to go on, but he turned away, walking to a stool behind the pulpit. He pulled it out, dreading the thought of sharing his burden with so many, but there was no turning back. He sat down. His forehead was a river. He used his arm to blot the perspiration. His ministry, if it survived, would never be the same. But it was too late to worry about that now. Everything had already changed.

When he was through, all was quiet. A baby began to cry, but the mother hushed him quickly. Someone else coughed. Suddenly from the back, an old woman, her head covered by a shawl, began to sing.

Por toda la noche, muchas veces él oraba.
Quería socorro Cristo el Señor.
Hermano, ya pide, ora por su fortaleza.
El nunca pecó. No, nunca, nunca pecó.

And the rest joined in.

He stayed up all night to pray for strength.
He stayed up all night, the holy Son of God.
My brother please pray. Please pray to be like Jesus.
He never gave in. My Jesus never gave in.

Lonnie bowed his head, his shoulders heaving. He heard a sound like the whisper of birds in flight and felt the hair rising on the back of his neck. He looked up to see hundreds of hands with their palms turned in his direction. The people were praying. They were praying for him.

LONNIE HAD not forgotten the prayers of the saints, but by the time Monday rolled around, he couldn't honestly say he still felt their effect. He awoke with the same ache in his shoulders he now felt almost every morning, an ache he was becoming accustomed to. He began the day like every day, spending time seeking a word from his Creator. He was hoping for another blessing, but it seemed the moment had passed. The Word opened up and he found himself staring at the book of Nehemiah. The siege of Jerusalem by Nebuchadnezzar had left the city in ruins. After seventy years in Babylon, a remnant of the people was released and allowed to go home, but the rubble they found offered no protection from invading armies. God commissioned Ezra and Nehemiah to assist with the rebuilding of the wall, a task so formidable, the idea seemed a joke—even to their enemies. Lonnie knew why he was drawn to this particular passage. Building that wall, with all the opposition it entailed, could not have seemed any more formidable to the children of Israel, than facing those who opposed the restructuring of Striker Films, seemed to him.

He met Father Ceylon for breakfast at the Inn. The father had imposed upon Señor Ramirez once again, commandeering a ride back down the mountain for Lonnie. Lonnie's bank was in a suburb of Huatulco known as Santa Cruz Bay. He needed to visit the bank to see if he could arrange a loan. He rode in the back seat, lost in his thoughts, unable to shake the feeling that he was wasting his time.

Santa Cruz was one of nine bays in Huatulco, but it was the main tourist area because of its access to the marina. Sightseers in shorts and sunglasses were milling about the market where street vendors sold original paintings, tooled leather, and hand-crafted jewelry. Lonnie's casual dress suited the environment, but he'd been wearing the same shirt for three days and needed a change. Living in Malibu did have its advantages, not the least of which were hot water and washing machines. He made a note to boil water as soon as he got back to the village. He'd have to wash his shirt before going into the office tomorrow.

The day was radiant. Seagulls clamored overhead, and wisps of the salty main filled the air. Lonnie assumed he'd need an appointment.

He went through the door and spoke with the girl at the desk. She excused herself and returned a few minutes later saying the manager of the bank, Juan Esperanza, was with someone but would try to squeeze Lonnie in if he could come back in a half-hour.

Lonnie stepped outside into the bright light, shielding his eyes with his hand. An old man was ripping chunks of stale bread from a loaf and throwing them into a throng of squealing seagulls. Lonnie wandered down the walkway, passing stores and restaurants. One vendor stand displayed hand-tooled leather goods—belts, wallets, and saddles. He picked up a briefcase and held it, snapping the locks. The lid opened smoothly, obviously well crafted. Inside were file pockets, pen, calculator and cell phone compartments, and ample space for documents. If he intended to take his newspaper clippings back with him, he'd need something to carry them in. This would do nicely. And it would give him more credibility at the bank. It would look like he was there on business, bearing important documents. They wouldn't know it was empty. He checked the tag. In spite of the fact that pesos were the national currency, the cost was listed in U.S. dollars, and was more than he wanted to pay. He could barter with the man to get the price down, but he made a habit of not doing that. He had so much, and the people here had so little. He opened his wallet and paid the man.

The briefcase felt good in his hand as he walked away. He was looking for another way of killing time when he picked up the scent of something familiar. He stopped, set his new briefcase by the wheel of the cart, and ordered Pescado a la Entrega, which was handed to him on a paper plate. It was a favorite of the area—fresh chopped seafood mixed with onions and parsley marinated in a mild garlic, wrapped in tortilla, and roasted slowly over hot coals. Lonnie ate with relish. When he was done, he wiped his hands and decided to try the bank again just in case the manager finished early. He assumed they'd bend over backwards to help him. At least they should—they'd been handling his account for almost twenty years. But he also knew he might be asking the impossible.

The manager freed himself and welcomed Lonnie as soon as he

stepped in. He was effusive in receiving him, making a grand gesture with a sweep of his hand. "Señor Striker, welcome, welcome. To what do I owe the pleasure of this unexpected visit?"

The tall, distinguished banker was dressed in a dark suit with a bright yellow tie that suggested he was just as much a yuppie as his American counterparts. He led Lonnie to a corner office and Lonnie took a seat, holding the briefcase in his lap. Juan had a clerk bring in two cups of espresso and then launched into a discussion about the weather—but what could you say about a place where it only rained fifty days a year and the average temperature was eighty-five degrees? It seemed to Lonnie that Juan was going out of his way to make small talk. He probably assumed Lonnie was there to move his account, but when Lonnie assured him otherwise, and explained the purpose of his visit, Jaun's expression registered real concern.

"Oh Señor Striker, you do not know what you ask. Our bank is not able to loan that kind of money. Five hundred thousand American dollars? You might as well ask a million. We make loans to farmers and businessmen—ten, twenty, maybe fifty thousand. But half a million? Where would you get the collateral to cover such an amount? It is not done. You say this problem is in the States. Why not borrow the money there?"

Lonnie explained how the mortgage on the company was held by a third party, which meant the company couldn't be used as a guarantee against the loan. He'd already made several inquiries at American banks and was told the loan would not go through, especially since the money would be used to make a movie. Banks shied away from loaning money to filmmakers. Too much risk. He knew it was a long shot, but he had hoped his own bank would help in consideration of the business he'd given them over the years. He wasn't surprised to be turned down; he understood the bank's position. Actually, he was relieved. He didn't feel right about borrowing money when he knew the company might not even be his by the end of the week. Lonnie thanked Juan again and stepped outside into the blazing sun.

HE RODE back to the village in silence. In the space of one short week, his entire world had spun out of orbit. He'd gone from the security of knowing who he was and what God expected of him, to a place where his every thought was brought into question. He didn't know if he'd wake up tomorrow and be Lonnie the missionary, Lonnie the corporate executive, or Lonnie the street beggar. What was the lesson in all this? *Trust in the Lord with all your heart and lean not on your own understanding. In all your ways acknowledge Him and He will direct your paths.* Okay, he could buy that. Rich or poor, he was God's to do with as he pleased, but was it fair to involve everyone else? He didn't mind that God wanted to test him. He was just sorry his test had to affect so many others. If he were the only one involved, then he would be the only one hurt. But failing this test meant the hospital would not be built, and that would hurt everyone.

Nuts! They didn't have a hospital before and the village had survived for hundreds of years. What made him think he was so crucial to the town's well being? He began to see how egotistical his thoughts were. They didn't need a hospital. They didn't need *him*. Maybe he was doing all this for the wrong reason. Maybe he was secretly guilty of wanting the praise. He knew there was at least some truth to that. He tried his best to be humble. He confessed he wanted no credit or thanks, but truth be known, every time someone said, "There goes the man who's building us a hospital," he reveled in it. Maybe that was the problem. Maybe God was removing him from the picture because of his own penchant for praise. He'd failed the test. Now there would be no hospital, and unless he could convince the missionary alliance to pick up his support again, he wouldn't be able to continue the mission. Trudy would be lost. If the company failed, she'd never speak to him again. Nor would Quentin. He was losing the battle. He could feel the enemy closing in. Was it time to fall on his sword? He sure didn't have the strength to stand and fight.

Lonnie sensed they were nearing the village. He looked up—*what in the*?—there was a commotion in the plaza, a rally of some sort; it looked like the whole town was having a parade. The driver tapped his horn several times as the car approached, trying to clear the way, but the multitude turned and surrounded the vehicle. Lonnie barely got the door open when the first hands were thrust through the crack, holding paper bills. They were waving them in the air, passing them up to Lonnie, pesos of every denomination were falling at his feet. Pesos from heaven.

The Sisters of Mercy with their wide-brimmed hats formed a wedge helping Paulo squeeze through the crowd. "I could not stop them!" he apologized, raising his voice so he could be heard above the clamor. "I called the bank to see how everything went, and when I told the people what happened, it was like a tidal wave. All of a sudden they started pouring in with their money. I told them it was futile, that we'd never collect enough. Every peso in the village would not be sufficient to meet your need, but they did not listen. So be it. Gracias a Dios!"

FOURTEEN

THE TAXI pulled up in front of Broadman Towers. The day was gray and overcast, accentuating Lonnie's mood. The image of the clouds reflecting off the black mirrored glass of the building created a cold dank mural in the sky. He reached for his briefcase, now full and weighted with the files he'd collected, and the money—just over three thousand dollars—donated by the people of Posada. It wouldn't help with the remaking of the film—he'd need a half million for that—but it was a love offering, and they couldn't be persuaded to take it back. They were determined to help in whatever way they could—*bless their hearts.* The sky was dark and heavy with moisture. A sudden gust lifted his hair, sending a chill down his spine. If he failed at bringing Striker Films back to life—and with only four days left, failure was looking imminent—at least he'd have something with which to continue his ministry in Mexico.

Lonnie paid the driver and climbed out, his eyes journeying up the side of the huge building—forty-two stories looming into space—and how small his mortal soul. A drop of rain hit his eye, causing him to blink as it rolled down his cheek. He wasn't ready to face his management team. He hadn't raised the money. They had a film to release by Friday, and no money or time to do it. His brother's words came back to haunt him. *Way to go, Spud. Looks like you stepped in it waist deep.*

He pushed through the revolving door and forced himself toward the elevators, rubbing his neck as he walked. His shoulders ached. His employees would gawk at him again; they still didn't know who he was. He made a mental note to introduce himself. He'd do it too, just as soon as he was apprized of everything that had happened while he was away. He might be the boss only until the end of the week, but at least he was the boss until then.

He passed a kiosk in the lobby and stopped to buy a paper, fishing in his pocket for some loose change. The headline stared back at him. "KILLING SPREE AT WEST VALLEY HIGH." *Not again.* Schools, once the bastion of rule and discipline, were becoming killing fields. He folded the paper under his arm, picked up his briefcase, and headed for the elevator.

The business day crowd bustled around him with cell phones dangling like ornamental jewelry from their ears. The drone of murmured conversation fused with the beat of shoe leather and spiked heels slapping and popping on the sparkling black marble tiles. He watched the lights descending and heard the elevator *ding,* but when the doors opened, the small space filled quickly, and the doors closed in his face, leaving him to wait for another car to arrive. Even then, he was barely able to jam himself in with the shoulder-to-shoulder mob.

When the elevator stopped at his floor, he went left instead of right, avoiding his destiny at Striker Films. He turned the corner heading down the hall to the public washroom. He needed a moment alone to collect his thoughts. The mirror over the vanity revealed what he already knew. His eyes were puffy and underlined with shadows. The fluorescent lights flickered. He leaned forward, gripping the sink. He didn't want to leave the bathroom. He didn't want to face—*them!* He couldn't keep up the charade. What was the point? According to Ben Lowen, he'd be gone by the end of the week. The film would not be done by then. And even if by some miracle he found a way to forestall the inevitable, he didn't have the money to make the necessary changes. All he could do was go in there and fake it. He straightened his back, feeling the ache. He was David against Goliath. It wasn't important that he win or lose, only that he be willing to die trying. God would expect no less. He stood straight, squaring his shoulders. His light blue shirt was freshly scrubbed—*thank heaven for permanent press.* He ran his hand through his wavy hair brushing it back. He had work to do. The people of Posada were counting on him. He rolled his newspaper and smacked it against his open palm. He'd swat them like a fly! He picked up his briefcase and went outside to face the giant.

LONNIE PAUSED at Nicole's desk on his way in. "Morning, Nicole. How was your weekend?

She scrambled to get her screen-saver up, as though hiding what she'd been typing, and stuffed a newspaper into her drawer. Then she moved a vase of daffodils out of the way, their fragrance filling the air. *Ummm.* She held her hands in her lap and smiled, her blond hair as soft and yellow as the flowers. "All right, I suppose. Uneventful. How was your trip?"

"Fine. Also uneventful. Could I see you in my office for a minute?" He turned and walked toward the floor-to-ceiling windows, laying his briefcase and newspaper on the polished surface of his desk as he passed by. The newspaper rolled open.

Nicole walked in with a cup of coffee. She set the burgundy mug in front of him, steam dancing in lazy wisps around the rim, and moved the paper to the side. "Terrible, isn't it?" she said, her blue eyes falling on the lead story.

"I haven't read it yet, but yes, any shooting in a school is awful. Did I receive any calls while I was away?"

Nicole's ponytail swayed as she shook her head. "No, not a one."

"Good. How's my schedule? Does anyone need to see me?"

"Les said to tell you he got Laurna back. It cost him a round-trip ticket and guaranteed payment of all her expenses while she's here, no matter how long it takes, and from what I understand, she has expensive tastes. She's staying in a suite at the Peninsula in Beverly Hills. She'll probably spend a couple thousand a day. Her room alone costs half that much. Les wanted me to let you know that. He also said she read the new script and wasn't happy. She wants to make changes to your changes. Les told her you wouldn't approve it. She's refusing to start until she can talk to you. She'll be in at two this afternoon."

Lonnie felt the ache in his shoulders deepen. "Why wait? I'm here now. See if you can get her in this morning. We might as well get it over with."

"I suggested that, but Les says she considers herself still officially on vacation. She says until you come to an agreement, she's not getting out of bed before noon."

Lonnie shook his head. "This is ridiculous. What about our male lead? Is he ready to go?"

"I think so. Les rounded up a film crew. They showed up for work yesterday, including Lance, but since Laurna wasn't there, the director couldn't start shooting so he sent everyone home. He says they're on the clock, which means he expects everyone will get paid."

"Right." Lonnie leaned in to open his desk drawer. He moved a few things around as though searching for something, and then closed it again. "Could you bring me the copy of the Striker/Lowen agreement I had you fax last Friday?"

Nicole spun on her heel and went out the door, her ponytail bouncing as she walked. She returned a few seconds later to place the document on Lonnie's desk. "Will you be needing me for anything else? I have some personal things to attend to. If it's all right with you, I'd like to take a few hours off. I'll be back before your appointment with Laurna."

"Sure, no problem. I don't suppose I need to call a management meeting. Les will just say, I told you so. I better get this mess with Miss Dove straightened out so we can get going." Lonnie looked at his watch. "I'll see you after lunch. Ah, could you close the door on your way out?"

Lonnie reached into his desk and removed the slip of paper on which he had written Maniux and Associates' number. He turned to the window, looking out at the gray city. A foreboding accumulation of clouds circled the spheres of power. He picked up the phone, dialed, and was put right through.

"Well, I'm glad to see you made it back."

"Hello, Don. Thank you. It's good to be back, I think. I guess you know why I'm calling. Did you happen to look at the contract I faxed over?"

"Yes, as a matter of fact I did, and I noticed something interesting."

"What's that?"

"I noticed you didn't sign it."

"So? I never signed anything. You know that. I agreed to let Harlan have signing authority. You were the one who set it up."

"Yes, indeed. If memory serves, you said you didn't care what your brother did with the company. You wanted nothing to do with it. You had me proxy your vote to him."

"So, what's your point?"

"My point is, I'm pretty sure that applied only to the everyday operations. You didn't give him the right to sell the company on your behalf. I don't think he could even sell the part he owned. I'm still a little fuzzy on this, but as I recall, your father didn't give you fifty percent of the company out of the kindness of his heart. It was a condition of his divorce settlement. I had access to the documents back when Wemble and Briggs hired me to find you, but that was a long time ago. Still, I seem to remember something in there that prohibited either of you from selling your stake in the company without the other's agreement. It was a stipulation your father made to protect your brother. He feared you'd want to cash out and stiff Harlan by selling to someone he couldn't stand. If I'm right about this, Harlan couldn't mortgage the company without your consent. Using the company as collateral assumes the property will change ownership if the debt isn't paid, and he didn't have the legal right to do that. He couldn't transfer title of his own half to someone else unless you agreed to it, let alone transfer yours. Your parents' divorce agreement precludes it."

Lonnie realized he was holding his breath. He felt his pulse pounding in his temples. The phone felt slippery in his hand. *Get a grip!* Even if what Don said was true, he still owed Lowen thirty million, money he couldn't get without first acquiring a half million to make changes to the film, and at the moment, that didn't seem very likely. And if he couldn't make the changes, he wouldn't release the film, and then the only way he could pay Lowen back would be to give him the company. So in fact, he was right back where he started. But one step at a time. He exhaled, raking his fingers through his hair.

"The only problem I'm having," Don continued, "is in trying to figure out why Gladdon, Vickers and Cox wouldn't have known this. They're pretty sharp. You'd think they wouldn't miss such an important detail. Anyway, don't get your hopes up. I'm trying to get my hands on a copy of the original settlement. I requested it from the county records office, but I haven't seen it yet. There may be something that permits liens and mortgages or some such thing. I should have it this afternoon. I'll try to read it tonight and get back to you. You going to be around for the next few days?"

Lonnie wiped his hand on his shirt. His heart was skidding off the wall of his chest, *thud, thud, thud*. "I'll be here," he said. "Please let me know as soon as you find out...anything! And ah, hey, nice work. I really appreciate it. You may have just saved the company." Lonnie cradled the receiver. He placed his palms together. "Man, oh man, oh man," he said, pacing the floor. Then he paused, turned and looked out the window. Maybe he couldn't see it, but beyond those clouds the sun was shining. "Gracias a Dios! Thank You, Lord!"

LONNIE STEPPED out into the sultry air and glanced up and down the street. It niggled him that he'd let Nicole go without thinking. He'd wanted her to introduce him to the rest of the staff—another missed opportunity. While she was away running errands, he stayed cloistered in his office reading the Striker/Lowen agreement, wondering what Les and Brent and Michael were up to, but unable to muster the courage to go find out. So basically he'd wasted the morning.

The sky was a sheet of dull tin sprayed with water. A young bongo player with long, stringy hair and a sparse goatee sat at the curb beating out a tribal rhythm. His wet black beret was overturned on the sidewalk to catch coins. His clothes were soaked, but he seemed determined not to give up his spot lest someone else come along and take it. The city flowed by in a river of cars. Buildings blocked the horizon, but Posada also had places where the light of day could only be seen by looking up. The city was indeed an asphalt jungle.

Lonnie stepped around a puddle from an earlier shower. Overhead, the sky was dark and smelled of more rain to come. A cluster of screeching seagulls circled on the wind while pigeons darted from one rooftop crevice to another. Lonnie headed to the corner. He could walk a block in either direction and probably find someplace new to eat, but something drew him back to Banana Splits.

He took a booth by the window and looked around for Allison, but she wasn't there. Lonnie shrugged. He was alone in a town where every face was a stranger. He would have welcomed a smile of recognition. Instead, he was waited on by a redhead who kept her eyes focused on her order pad. The black and white checkered floor seemed friendlier.

"Okay, what can I getcha? Right, one chili cheese dog comin' right up."

While waiting for his order, Lonnie watched the other patrons devouring their malts with long-handled spoons. He listened to the golden oldies and random bits of conversation from the surrounding tables. Outside the fingerprint-smudged window, he saw fat drops of water begin to dot the sidewalk. Pedestrians picked up the pace, using their purses and briefcases as umbrellas.

When he'd finished eating, Lonnie wiped his fingers, not quite as satisfied with his lunch as he'd been before. He went to the register to pay. He was counting his change when Allison came rushing in, her hair a wild tangle of damp curls. He paused for a moment thinking she might recognize him, but she didn't glance his way. She was occupied with tying her apron, her hands behind her back.

As he turned to leave, Lonnie heard her say to the girl at the register, "I think I've got an audition tomorrow. Is there any chance we can switch shifts?"

Lonnie went outside and held his hand over his head to protect him from the drizzle. He skipped across the street against the light, zig-zagging through the snarl of traffic, trying in vain to avoid getting wet.

NICOLE WAS already back at her desk when Lonnie entered the suite, shaking the rain from his arms. She was typing something, but clicked on the screen-saver as he approached. "Is there anything you need for your meeting?" she asked.

Lonnie shrugged and shook his head. "Not that I know of. I don't even know what the meeting is about. I don't want to see Miss Dove. I just want her back to work." He started to walk away, but stopped to admire the vase of tall, yellow flowers. "Umm, nice," he said. "Ah, there is one thing you can do for me. After I finish with Laurna, I'd appreciate your taking me around and introducing me to the rest of the staff."

Nicole smiled. "Sure, just let me know when." She turned and began stacking the papers on her desk into a neat pile.

Lonnie went into his office and sat down swiveling back and forth in his soft leather chair. He brought an elbow to rest on its arm, and massaged his nails with his thumb. *Now, what do I do?* He wanted to call Don for an update, but it was too soon. Nicole entered with a cup of coffee and set it on his desk. Harlan's words rang in his ear—*You'll love the perks, Spud!*—but Lonnie knew Harlan hadn't meant the coffee. He took a sip and pulled the newspaper in closer. He'd already read the front-page story. He turned to the editorial page and found an article by syndicated columnist, William Best.

> The findings of the Josephson Institute of Ethics should have been a clarion call. Perhaps if we'd listened and taken action, West Valley Senior High wouldn't have become the latest in a series of school shootings that seem epidemic in our nation. Instead, we chose to ignore, or perhaps rationalize away, the disturbing facts that came to light in their interview of 15,000 students. We chose to disregard that 60% of

all high school students have easy access to guns; and that 43% say it's perfectly alright to hit or threaten a person if they make you angry, and that 14% admit to already having brought a gun to school.

Faced with statistics like these, we shouldn't be surprised to learn it has happened again, but West Valley, being typically middle income and suburban, is perhaps the last place we'd expect such an incident to occur. Students had just returned from lunch and were heading back to their classrooms when a young tenth-grade student, Malcolm Maynard, slipped an automatic assault rifle from beneath his long tan overcoat and began firing into the crowd. His first victim was his sociology teacher, Brian Kempt, who had reportedly sent Malcolm home earlier that morning for failing to turn in an assignment. Mr. Kempt, a family man, leaves behind a wife and two daughters. He was killed instantly.

Malcolm, now calling himself Malcolm X, then allegedly turned and began spraying the crowd, fanning the weapon right and left as terrified students dove for cover. When the gun was empty, Malcolm reached into his coat for a second gun, a 22 caliber revolver, and began firing point blank at people's heads. According to witnesses he got off four or five rounds, shooting his victims one at a time until he came to Mary Bethmore, a young girl for whom he'd bought a valentine earlier in the year. Witnesses say Mary was kneeling beside another student who was already down with a bullet in his leg. Malcolm allegedly pointed the gun straight at Mary's head and screamed: "Do you love me?" but she was too terrified to answer. She raised her hand and whimpered, "Malcolm, please..." Then he turned the gun to his own temple and fired one bullet into his head, dropping dead on the spot.

A fellow student said Malcolm was a quiet person, and that he preferred keeping to himself. Friends say he was frequently teased for being introversive, but no one thought him capable of...

Lonnie understood. The boy was a reject, unloved and ridiculed. To a mentally tortured mind, that alone was reason enough to contemplate revenge. Lonnie had felt that way about himself until his mother won the custody battle. And even after that. He'd felt isolated and alone throughout his high school years, and felt the pain of it in even greater measure when forced to live with Harlan again. Lonnie shuddered at the thought.

Something had changed. Exactly what the change was and when the change had taken place were subjects for debate, but one thing was certain: Kids of Lonnie's generation would never have considered bringing a gun to school—and it wasn't because they weren't abused. Kids of every generation suffered abuse, but this generation responded differently. The violence in movies had something to do with it, of that he was sure, but it was more than that. You couldn't pin it on any one reason. Part of it had to do with a general disregard for the sanctity of life. Programs for abortion and euthanasia carried a veiled message that life was arbitrary and should be terminated when it became too inconvenient or caused too much pain. Then there was the notion that evolution was scientific fact. Instead of kids being taught they were created with worth and purpose, they were being told they were accidents of nature, bits of protoplasm with the good fortune of not being aborted by their mothers. Mere animals, no better than marmots and moles.

Lonnie could relate to Malcolm because, in effect, he *was* Malcolm, or any one of thousands like him, the underlings of Everyman's High. The world was full of them, the invisible ones, those who learned to survive by fading quietly into the background to avoid being seen, those terrified to wake each morning because it meant the beginning of another day over which they had no control.

The bullies were out there, boys who would search out and destroy anyone possessing the smell of fear. The underlings were their prey, these subhuman creatures. The mission was to expose their weakness to the world by challenging them to fight, knowing full well the underlings had no fight in them. *Why?* What special status did the bullies gain by making victims of the defenseless? What gift of power was bestowed on those who held sway over the weak?

How many times, *how many, many times,* had he, in the uttermost depravity of his soul, sought to understand the agony of his youth. It wasn't just about Harlan. Harlan was only part of the problem—yet that in itself was the problem because Harlan should have stood up for him—brothers to the end. But Harlan was three years older, and supposedly wiser, and would only impart words that, instead of helping, spelled a formula for disaster: "Don't get mad, Spud, get even."

Who could know the pain of a tormented soul, the deep, deep, anguish that makes a person want to lash out and hurt everyone who hurts him. He thought about Buddy's guns and the pain he would have inflicted upon his tormentors if only his actions could have been celebrated in the newspapers. Lonnie too, had considered suicide. Perhaps if he could have died some heroic death, he might have devised a plan to take others with him. Then he would have been seen as strong, holding the power of life and death in his hands. He had certainly harbored the evil in his heart, and in Christ's view, to think it was the same as doing it. So he'd repented. He'd allowed Christ's love to constrain him, trying to *forgive and forget,* while fighting to hold back his tears and keep his pain inside. He'd knelt before the cross, and the vision of an innocent Man crucified for the crimes of others. He knew that forgiveness was demanded of him, even when it wasn't deserved. That's where he and Malcolm differed. He had the cross to cling to. All Malcolm had was a gun.

Lonnie stared at the paper, drumming the top of the desk with his fingers. The media gave kids who were already suicidal, kids with a desperate need for recognition, a means by which they could become famous overnight. All they had to do was have enough guts to go out in a blaze of glory. It was the same tripe Harlan was trying to sell, only he'd used the big screen—*murder and mayhem*—coming soon to a theater near you. Anyone who argued that kids were able to digest what they read in the papers, saw in the theaters, and learned in their schools, without it rubbing off on them, was either blind or a fool.

The intercom buzzed. "Ms. Laurna Dove is here to see..." but before Nicole could finish her sentence the door flew open and a buxom blonde was standing there with her hand on her hip. She had the reddest lips Lonnie had ever seen.

"Hi, I'm Laurna Dove," she said, slipping her cell phone into her purse. She closed the door and walked forward with the back of her hand extended in a manner that suggested she expected Lonnie to kiss her fingers. "I'm sorry my agent couldn't be here, but he's tied up with someone. Figuratively, of course." She wore a low-cut, red T-shirt with three-quarter length sleeves. Her tight white slacks were split up the sides and stitched with red lacing through which you could see the skin of her thighs. The pants hung low on her hips exposing her navel, and her brief T-shirt revealed a good three inches of her waist. To avoid staring at her cleavage, or at her belly button, Lonnie had to focus on her feet. Her white shoes were straps of crisscrossed leather with open toes and four-inch heels.

Lonnie stood and came around from behind his desk, taking her fingers in his own and giving them a cordial squeeze. "Lonnie Striker," he said. "It's nice meeting you, Miss Dove. I understand you have questions about some of the changes I've made to the film."

"No, not questions, concerns. And its Ms, not Miss," she corrected him. "The problem is, I liked the film the way it was. As an actress, I'm careful about the parts I take. I have to make sure that what I do reflects the right kind of image."

Lonnie leaned against his desk, his arms folded. "That's understandable, but why would you be opposed to what I've done? Please, have a seat."

"You've taken the drama out of it," she said. Laurna set her purse on the desk and dropped into one of the chairs facing Lonnie. "Harlan had me cast as a tragic heroine. I read through the new script, and I can't figure out who I'm supposed to be anymore."

Lonnie raised an eyebrow. "Did you see the papers today—that story about the shooting in the school?"

Laurna nodded and crossed one slim leg over the other, leaning forward to remove a copy of the script from her purse.

Lonnie sat down in the chair opposite her. "And you don't see the problem? The movie you made glorifies that kind of behavior. The hero goes down the hall shooting everybody, just like that kid Malcolm did. That's why I want to clean it up. I don't want kids thinking that's a cool thing to do."

Laurna dropped the script into her lap and crossed her arms, her red fingernails digging into her flesh. Then her eyes narrowed and her lips twisted in a pout. "I think you got it backwards. We're not telling kids what to do. They're already doing it. You said it yourself—a kid shot up his school just yesterday. That's the way the world is. We're just a mirror. If society doesn't like what it sees when it looks at itself, it's not our fault. We just tell it like it is."

"I'm not so sure. Have you ever considered that maybe your mirror is really a paintbrush? You paint a picture, and kids imitate the art."

Laurna stood, letting the script slide into the chair as she leaned forward with her hand on the desk. "So you have a chicken and an egg. It's anybody's guess as to which came first." She reached for her purse and dug inside to find a cigarette and lighter. "Frankly, I couldn't care less," she said. "I'm not here to solve the world's problems. The world's a pretty screwed-up place. It's not my job to fix it." She put the cigarette between her lips, letting it bounce as she spoke. "My job is to give people what they want." She clicked the lighter and brought the flame to her mouth, cupping it in her hands.

"Please, could I ask you not to smoke in here?"

She stared at Lonnie, batting her artificially long lashes, but relaxed her thumb on the lighter. She pinched the cigarette and tipped it up, the butt now stained with red lipstick, and dropped both the cigarette and lighter back into her purse with an overly dramatic flair.

"You really don't get it, do you?" Laurna plopped her purse on the desk and crossed her arms, grabbing her shirt. In one quick motion, she pulled it over her head. She stood there fluffing her hair, naked from the waist up, except for a tiny red bra.

Lonnie jumped to his feet. "What are you...? Please, put it back on. What are you doing?"

"I'm showing you what people want." Laurna reached around and started to unhook the strap, but Lonnie screamed, "Don't!"

She stopped, leaving the bra in place. A slow smile spread over her face. "Why, I do believe you're blushing, Mr. Striker, but I think you get the point." She arched her back, accentuating her cleavage. "This is what people come to see. If you take this out of the picture, you might as well get rid of the rest of me."

Lonnie wasn't just blushing, his head felt light, and he was beginning to feel dizzy. He lifted his hand to object. "I'm sure that's not true. Please, put your top back on. You're an actress, people come to see you act. And, yes, you're attractive. I'm sure they appreciate that—too. But I doubt people stand in line and say, 'I hope I get to see Laurna's breasts today.' "

"Wanna bet? They may not say it, but that's what they're thinking. Look, I didn't build my career on being a good actress. My drama coach told me to keep my day job, but I was determined and I was willing to do whatever it took. Sometimes you gotta make a few concessions, give the people what they want, if you know what I mean. You know how I got this part? On my back, that's how. Lying right there," she said, pointing to the couch.

There was a long silence, a vacuum in the air waiting to be filled. Lonnie shuffled his feet. His face felt hot, and he was having trouble breathing. He tried to avoid staring at the half-naked actress. "I...I'm sorry. I really am," he finally said. "Look, I hate to say it, I'm sure you're a very nice person, but I don't think you're right for this part..."

He was interrupted by a knock at the door. "Who is it?"

"It's me, Les."

Lonnie swallowed. "Just a second, Les. Please, Miss Dove, put your shirt back on."

"Don't mind Lester. It's nothing he hasn't seen before." Laurna picked up her purse and moved to the door. "I'm sorry you feel that way, but it's probably best for both of us. I've already been paid. Lance and I insisted on getting our money up front, so you can go ahead and ruin the film, if that's what you're bent on doing, but not at my expense." She was still holding her shirt in her hand. She reached for the doorknob. "I think we're finished here. Come on in, Les, I was just leaving." She stood to the side while she wiggled back into her shirt. Then she grabbed her purse and walked out of the room.

If Les was surprised to find an undressed woman in Lonnie's office, it didn't show. He ogled Laurna's curves until she was gone, leaned back on his heels with a chuckle, and gave Lonnie a wink. "Well, I guess she passed the audition, eh, boss?"

FIFTEEN

LONNIE'S WORDS were stuck in his throat. He heard a familiar droning in his ears, a sound that increased like wood through a buzz saw. He was hyperventilating, the way he'd done at the funeral. He grabbed the desk for support, fearful he'd pass out. He held on, teetering, waiting for the darkness to clear. "No, no you got it all wrong. She wasn't...I...she only..."

Les walked over to the couch and moved the coffee table aside. "Sure, boss. I know, keep it quiet and all that. But let me show you something that will help in the future." He pushed a button concealed under the arm. The couch began to hum as the cushions fell back and the couch opened into a bed. "There. I'm surprised Laurna didn't show you. It makes things a whole lot more comfortable."

Lonnie tried to gain control of his breathing. His face was flushed and hot. He closed his eyes, and put his hand to his throat. "She disrobed without my asking. I tried to stop her." He inhaled deeply hoping the oxygen would stabilize his vision. Les was wearing a red shirt with little men on surfboards zooming through green foaming waves, but it was flickering, *red, black, red, black, red, black*. Between flashes, Lonnie saw a cheesy grin plastered on Les's face.

The moment of weakness passed. Lonnie walked slowly to the couch, deeply inhaling and exhaling with each step. He got down on one knee and looked under the arm for the button. He pushed it several times. The couch began to hum, but nothing happened. "How do I make this thing work?"

Les put his hands on his knees and leaned down as far as his gut would allow. "Sorry. I forgot about that. The switch is broken. It only goes one way. I guess Harlan never got around to getting it fixed."

Lonnie closed his eyes and slowly shook his head, sighing deeply. His office had just become a bedroom, complete with pillows, sheets and blankets. "Did my brother...I mean did he...you've got to be kidding." Lonnie went around to the end of the bed and tried lifting it, but it wouldn't budge. "*Uggh,* Don't tell me this was how Harlan held auditions?"

"No. Jeremy auditioned the girls, and I had final say. Don't get the wrong idea. This isn't how the industry works. It was just something Harlan did once in a while. He said if a girl couldn't put on an act and convince *him* she enjoyed making love, she wouldn't be able to convince anyone on the screen."

"Well, that's not how it's going to be with me. I want this thing out of here." Lonnie wiped his sleeve across his forehead as he walked to the door. "Where's Nicole?"

"I don't know. I didn't see her. That's why I knocked."

"Just a second." Lonnie stepped out and looked down the hall, just as Nicole turned the corner. She held a folder in her hand, fresh from the photocopy room. She put the file in a drawer and slid it closed.

"Nicole, could I see you for a moment?" Lonnie stopped inside the door. "I just discovered I have a bed in my office. Les was trying to show me how it works, but there's no point because I don't want it in here. Could you call someone and have it removed?"

She tucked in her blouse and shook her head, her ponytail swinging from side to side. "Removed? Where to?"

"Frankly, I don't care. Give it to the Salvation Army. Just get it out of here."

There was a light smile on her lips and her cheeks held a rosy blush. "Yes, sir. I'll do it right away."

Les followed her to the door, but Lonnie called him back. "Just a second, Les. There's something we need to discuss."

Les held up his hand, holding Lonnie off for a moment, and

stepped out of the office just far enough to be discreet. "Don't you dare call the Salvation Army, or anyone else," he hissed at Nicole. "That's fine Moroccan leather, probably cost a fortune. You have them ship that sucker to my house." He spun around and went back inside.

Lonnie gave the bed a wide berth and returned to his desk. Outside, the rain had picked up, spattering on the glass walls. The city beyond looked like a smeared watercolor, the towers bleeding into vertical streaks of gray. He turned and sat in his chair, leaning back with his arm extended and his fingers tapping on the highly polished wood. *Looks like she passed the audition, eh, boss?* Les wouldn't like what he was about to say.

Les found a chair, crossed one leg over the other, and patted his pocket. The cellophane package crinkled, but his hand fell away.

"He must not have used it much," Lonnie said, contemplating the bed in the middle of his office. "Not if he couldn't get it closed."

Les pursed his lips. His shiny head caught the reflection of the lights. "It closes. The motor don't work in reverse, is all, but you can do it manually. Some lever has to be moved and the whole thing collapses back into a couch. There's a trick to it. I just don't know what it is. Never bothered to ask."

Lonnie continued letting his fingers do a tapdance. Les waited, twisting in his seat, trying to get comfortable. When the silence could be felt, Lonnie broke it. "I need you to have Jeremy find us another actress," he said.

Les jerked his head back, narrowing his eyes. He reached into his pocket for a cigarette, but at the last minute realized what he was doing and withdrew his hand. "Come again? I mean, I thought you...She's got what it takes, boss. Don't tell me you didn't like it."

"We had a difference of opinion. I wanted her to accept the changes I was making, and she wanted me to leave things the way they were. She's under the impression people buy tickets just to see her body. I hope that's not true, but if it is, it proves my point, and it's all the more reason I want the film redone. I won't be guilty of producing porn. Anyway, we came to a mutual understanding. She isn't right for the part. You'll have to find someone else."

Les shook his head and folded his arms, resting them on his stomach. "You realize what you're asking? It'll take weeks to do new screen tests, and in the meantime I'll have to keep Lance on a string so he won't take another part. How do you suggest I do that? Kidnap him? Not to mention the fact that you've just doubled the amount of shooting we have to do, and the cost. Where do you figure we'll get the money?"

"No, I don't want you to do any new screen tests. I'm sure Jeremy had others in mind for the part. Just have him pick another actress. Nicole said we're paying a film crew to be on stand-by. I want them back on the lot shooting scenes tomorrow."

"You can't be serious."

"But I am. Tell Jeremy to hire another actress. It's as simple as that."

Les's face turned crimson. He took a deep breath, his lips pinched as though repressing what he wanted to say. "Okay, I'll see what I can do. If there's nothing else, I'd better get going. We don't have a lot of time."

"No, that's all. Let me know what you find."

LONNIE SAT back in his chair staring at the city as it washed down the side of his window. He rubbed his neck and reached into the drawer for a tissue to wipe his eyes. He felt the tension thudding in his temples. *Why me, Lord?* What did it matter? So the people of Posada wouldn't have a hospital. That's the way it had been for hundreds of years, so what? He had three thousand dollars. The money would last a few months, at least long enough to contact the Alliance so he could petition their support. But what about Trudy? The idea struck him as odd. He hadn't thought about her all weekend. Anyway, he couldn't leave her in the lurch. He might be able to leave all this behind, but not her. She and Quentin would be destitute. He turned, swiveling in his chair. A voice, soft but discernible, whispered in his ear. *Looks like you stepped in it again, eh Spud?* Lonnie smacked his hand down flat on the table. *Get thee behind me, Satan!* Then he smiled. The answer was right under his nose. Why hadn't he thought of it before?

"I'm going out for a few minutes," he said as he passed Nicole's desk. "I won't be long, probably less than half an hour." He raced down the hall, driven by some unseen force, through the foyer and into the elevator, down the elevator into the lobby, and across the lobby as fast as he could walk, to the doors of the building. He came to a halt. *Drat. Rain!*

He turned, looking for something, *anything,* to cover his head. He walked back toward the concessions and found an empty donut box sitting on a bench. *Winchel's.* He grabbed the cardboard container and pushed through the doors, running now with the Winchel's donut box over his head to keep from getting soaked. The sidewalk was empty, no street musician or black beret. His strides were long as he crossed the road, his new brown shoes splashing through the puddles. He squeezed between the bumpers of the yellow cabs parked in his way. When he reached the door, he flung it back and entered the building bringing the limp, wet box down as he stood there dripping on the checkered tiles.

She was at a table taking an order. The booth behind her was empty. Lonnie walked over and seated himself, catching her eye as she passed.

"Hi," he said.

She nodded and moved on, holding her pad in the air and writing as she walked. A few minutes later she returned with a glass of water and a rag. She set the glass in front of him and began wiping the table.

"Didn't I just see you in here? What's the matter? Didn't get enough chili?"

Lonnie smiled. *She did notice.* "I'm not here to eat. I overheard you say you have an audition tomorrow. I was wondering if you had time for one tonight."

Her eyes filled with questions. She looked out the window at the black building across the street, and then back at Lonnie. "Nope. Not interested." From a pouch in her apron she removed a napkin and set it on the table, covering it with a fork, knife and spoon.

"It's not what you think. Honest. This is legit. We need an actress. We're in a real bind because we're supposed to start shooting tomorrow. All I'm asking is that you come over and read a few lines. How 'bout it? Please. Nothing ventured, nothing gained."

She didn't answer, but stood looking out the window at the black obelisk, wiping her hands on the rag.

"There will be plenty of people around. No closed doors, I promise."

Her eyes were brown with tiny green flecks that shimmered in the light, but she wasn't smiling. "I don't take my clothes off for anyone," she said.

"Perfect, because this movie is PG. What time do you get off?"

Allison looked at her watch. "My shift ends at six."

"Fine. You know where we are." Lonnie started to get up. He leaned on the table and reached down to retrieve his soggy Winchel's box. "I didn't have an umbrella," he said with a sheepish grin. "Okay, I'll get out of your hair. Six o'clock. I'll see you then."

Allison turned and walked to the next table. Lonnie watched her walk away. He didn't know if she'd come or not, but he'd done his part. The rest was up to her. He took his cardboard hat and dashed across the street, ignoring honking horns as he dodged around taxi bumpers in the rain.

"Mr. Lowen."

"Yes, what is it?"

"We have a problem."

"Yes?"

"Les is going ahead with the final edit. He just spoke with the lab and they assured him the film will be finished on time. I don't trust Les. He's loyal to Quentin. He may just get it done."

"No, the film will not be done on time. I've already seen to that. Things are proceeding right on track, but thanks for your concern. Call me if anything else comes up."

"All right, Mr. Lowen. Good-bye."

AS SOON AS he got back, Lonnie went in search of Les. He checked his office, the boardroom, the screening room, and the halls, but the man was nowhere to be found. He didn't like asking Les to stay after work, but he wanted him there for the audition. Finally, he stopped by Nicole's desk. "You haven't seen Les around, have you?"

"He's left for the day. Is everything okay?"

Lonnie considered the question. *No it's not okay. He's supposed to be here making sure we find someone to take Laurna's place, but...* "Sure, everything's fine."

"Here," Nicole said. She handed Lonnie an envelope. "Carl Monahan from Gladdon's office dropped this by for you."

Lonnie went into his office, tapping the sealed envelope, wondering what it could be. The Striker Films lightning bolt logo was imprinted in gold foil in the upper left corner. His name was typed on the front along with a red stamp that read: "Private and Confidential."

He went to his desk and sat down to look for a letter opener. He found one in the pencil tray of his top drawer. He slid it under the flap, making a smooth cut across the top crease. Inside was a single typed page with no other explanation. He shook it open.

Hey, Spud,

I asked that this letter be delivered one week after the first. I just wanted to know you were still there. See, if you're not, you won't get this letter. I told Barry to destroy it if you weaseled out. Anyway, since you're reading it, congratulations on making it through your first week. I knew you had it in you.

Now I need to get serious for a moment. There are a few things I need to get off my chest, but this is for you only. I need your word you won't share this with anyone, at least until you're sure the time is right. Don't preachers take some kind of vow, like priests or something? If so, I want your vow of silence on this one. What I'm about to say could destroy my family.

I'm trusting you won't use the information wrongly. (I'm not going to tell you everything just yet. First, I have to see what kind of man you are. If you're chomping at the bit to get out of there, then forget it. But if you're still around when the film is released, you'll receive a third letter telling the rest of the story.) Think about it real hard. If you plan to duck and run, stop reading now and throw this letter away.

Where do I begin? My sins are too numerous to mention. I don't have the time or inclination to list them all, so let's just stick to the main one. I'm a carouser, a party animal, couldn't stay at home if you nailed my shoes to the floor, and I like the ladies. I never forced myself on anyone, but on the other hand, I never said no to anyone either. But I never tried to hurt anyone. The girls I fooled around with always got what they wanted. It was Trudy I wronged, and it was you.

You loved her, didn't you? I could see it in those doughy cow eyes you put on every time I brought her home. And I wanted to keep her from you. That was my sin.

Remember the trip to Coahuila? Remember the girl Dad brought along, the one always smoking dope and talking about free love and all that hippie stuff? A real throwback from the sixties, hot to trot. Dad convinced her to give me my first experience, and she was more than willing. You knew what was going on, I could tell. But the way you reacted had me baffled, all that sulking around, it didn't make a lick of sense. I swear, I thought you were gay.

A month later, you and Mom moved out, remember? So that's how we left it. And when you moved back after Mom died, you didn't give me any reason to change that opinion. You were always a wuss. I was just waiting for you to pop out of the closet singing, "I'm gay, let's have a parade." At least, that is, until I caught you with Trudy.

You thought I was mad, didn't you? That's why you ran. I guess you thought I was going to rip your head off, but after I calmed down, I confess that in some kind of sick way, I was proud of you. It took real guts to try and steal my girl right out from under my nose. It wasn't the kind of thing I expected of you.

And now you're probably wondering what all this has to do with life in the big city. Well, stick around, Spud, you'll see. I'm saving the best for last.

Harlan Lloyd Striker

The windows in the station wagon were fogged, but the moon could still be seen on the far side of the glass, as round and soft as an incandescent bulb.

"Ouch!" Lonnie tried to raise himself up on one elbow. The gallon jug of wine had toppled over and worked its way beneath him. He pushed it aside.

"Hey, you're letting in cold air. Give me that blanket." Trudy pulled the cover around her shoulders. The moonlight was diffused, but bright enough to see a faint smile playing across her lips.

"How can you be cold? It's like an oven in here. We need some fresh air." Lonnie crawled forward and cranked the window down a notch.

"Don't you dare! Cut it out!" Trudy tried to swat Lonnie, but he caught her hand. "Oh, no, you don't."

"Hey!"

Lonnie rolled on top of Trudy and brought his lips down to hers. Then he put his arms around her, and embraced her tightly as they kissed.

"That's what I needed," she said. "You're better than a blanket, nice and warm."

Lonnie gave her a hug and then used his elbow to prop himself up. He ran his fingers through her silky auburn hair, so smooth and shiny, as they explored the depths of each other's eyes. "You know, I never thought this day would come," he said.

"You talk too much. Kiss me."

Lonnie slipped his hand under Trudy's neck and raised her head to meet his lips. She pulled him in with a tight embrace, lost in the heat of passion.

"Come away with me, Trudy."

"Away? Where're you going?"

"I don't know. Anywhere but here. We're free now. We can do whatever we want. Besides, you know we can't stay here."

"Why not?"

"Why not? Because Harlan's here, that's why not."

"But I love Harlan. You're not going anywhere, Lonnie. That's your problem. At least Harlan knows where he's going."

The words stung. Lonnie sat up, wrapping his arms around his knees.

"Hey, don't. Let me have the blanket."

"You don't love Harlan. You love me," he insisted.

"I love you both. I'm cold. Come over here and lie down."

A pair of headlights rose over the crest of the hill. Through the frosted glass they looked like two fuzzy balls of cotton. Lonnie was too drunk to consider what they might mean. He was more fascinated with the way they bounced up and down as the car bumped over ruts in the road.

Music, loud with a heavy thudding beat, filtered through the window.

"Wild thing, you make my heart sing, you make everything—groovy."

As the car drew nearer, it began to take shape. It was a low and sleek and growled as it prowled across the field like a powerful white cat. Lonnie could hear voices. A girl was laughing.

Trudy sat up, pulling the blanket around her neck.

Then the headlights hit the side of the station wagon, and the car slid to a stop. It was a convertible—a white Thunderbird with the top down. Harlan was wearing a T-shirt, his muscles flexed and swelling in the moonlight. He leaned on the steering wheel with his arm around a bubble-headed blond. "Well, looky, looky. What do you suppose we have here?"

SIXTEEN

LONNIE WAS thumbing through the script, marking places he wanted Allison to read when the door opened. Nicole stuck her head in, her ponytail hanging over her shoulder. She glanced at the convertible sofa and then back at Lonnie. "I have to leave now, but there's someone here to see you."

Lonnie looked at his watch, 6:05. *That would be Allison. Good.* He started to get up, thinking he'd meet his guest in the lobby and show her to the boardroom, but Nicole let the door swing wide, and there she stood.

Lonnie's eyes went to the bed and back. "Hi, uh, sorry about that," he said, with an apologetic shrug. "It belonged to my brother. It's stuck. I can't get it folded back up."

Allison's brow wrinkled. She waited, seemingly unable to move. She was still in her waitress outfit—pleated blue skirt and white blouse with puffed sleeves—but the apron was gone. Her eyes became furtive, darting around the room. She looked like a mouse staring at a cat, ready to bolt.

Nicole stepped forward, her black slacks rustling as she walked. "I wondered why you left it open. Here, let me help. You have to use the release lever to disengage the motor." Her hand moved a metal bar to the left. "I called a mover, but it'll be next week before he can pick it up. There. See, now it folds up easily." Lonnie watched as Nicole turned the bed into a couch again.

"Thank you, Nicole."

"If there's nothing else, I'll be going now. I have an appointment and I don't want to be late." She turned and went out the door, leaving Allison and Lonnie alone.

"We're going, too. I promised you a public reading," Lonnie said to Allison, hoping to abate her fears.

She appeared to be having trouble deciding whether to stay or go. She had roped her hair in a braid, but it was damp and her blouse was dotted with spots of water. Through the window Lonnie could see the downpour had become a drizzle. He leaned into his desk and grabbed the script before she could change her mind. "Unfortunately, my casting director had to leave, but let's go into the boardroom, shall we? I'm sure someone besides myself will be interested in what you've got."

Allison nodded, but she still wasn't smiling.

They caught up to Nicole as she was slipping her purse over her arm, and walked down the hall as a group until they came to the door exiting to the lobby. Nicole said goodnight, wishing Allison a "break-a-leg" reading.

Lonnie scanned the office, but it looked deserted. "I'll be right back," he said, leaving Allison standing outside the boardroom while he went in search of an audience. After a few minutes, he returned alone. "I don't know what to say. I looked everywhere, but it appears everyone's gone for the day. I don't want you to be uncomfortable. If you'd rather wait, we can do the audition first thing in the morning. Or we can go someplace else. I just need you to read a few lines."

Allison tossed her long braid over her shoulder, took a deep breath, and sighed. "I can take care of myself," she said. "We might as well get it done."

"That would be great." Lonnie opened the door and stepped into the room. It was dark inside. Someone had pulled the drapes. He slid his hand along the wall searching for the light, but came up empty. He leaned back to check the outside wall, but there was nothing there either. "I'm still trying to learn my way around. I'm afraid I don't know where the switch is."

Allison brushed by, her pleated skirt swishing as she passed. She went to the far side of the room where an edge of light spilled along the floor beneath the curtains. She felt around till she found a pull rope and gave it a tug. Light flooded the room. Lonnie shook his head. He turned and saw the switch on the far wall. *Why would they put it over there?* He walked across the room and flipped it on. The room flickered for a moment and then settled into a fluorescent glow. He set the script in front of him on a table big enough to seat sixteen, which made it even more obvious they were alone. He pulled out a chair so he could sit down. Allison walked over and took a seat on the opposite side, facing him.

Lonnie leaned back, trying to appear nonchalant. "I've marked four places from which I'd like you to read." He tapped the script and then slid it across the table. "One shows anger, one a little romance, there's a scene with a bit of sadness, and one where you're asked to laugh out loud. I want to see how well you express emotion."

Allison pulled the script toward herself and began flipping through the pages. She stopped when she found a marked passage, and looked up. "Could I have a few minutes alone to familiarize myself with this?"

"Certainly, no problem." Lonnie stood. "I'll be in my office. How long will you need?"

"Just long enough to go over the lines once or twice. Come back in"—she turned a few more pages—"I'd say about fifteen minutes. I'll be ready."

Lonnie got up, looked at his watch, and went to the door. "See you in fifteen," he said.

LONNIE WANDERED down the hall, passing one empty cubicle after another. Where was everyone? Had they heard the company was going down—*abandon ship, every man for himself*—or was Captain Ahab being so unreasonable his crew was about to mutiny? He had to get out and introduce himself. People couldn't be expected to follow a leader they didn't know.

He wandered into his office and picked up the phone. His heart went into pitter-patter mode. He dialed the number, feeling like a schoolboy calling for a first date. *Rinnnnng...Rinnnnng...Rinnnnng.*

"Hello."

"Hi, Trudy. It's me. Thought I'd better call and let you know I'm back. I didn't want to surprise you by showing up unannounced."

"Well, hello, stranger. Nice to hear from you."

"Sorry, I know I left unexpectedly. I called before leaving, but you weren't home. I left a message. You got it, didn't you?"

"The one that said you were hopping a flight back to never-never-land because you had to see how things were going, but left no other details? Yes, I got it. Not that you cared about how things were going right here. Your sister-in-law, the grieving widow, could use a little consoling, you know. Anyway, I'm glad you're back. What time will you be home?"

What time? It was a loaded question, one Harlan would have avoided—but he wasn't Harlan. He looked at his watch—*Harlan's watch*—the one he couldn't seem to get along without. "I shouldn't be long. I'm doing an audition with a young lady for a part in our movie."

He waited for a response, but none came. The silence was awkward. "She's taking over for Laurna Dove. I mean, if she does well. With the reading, nothing else. It's not *that* kind of audition."

"That's okay, I get the picture. I wasn't born yesterday. You'll be home late, yada, yada, don't bother waiting up. Anything else?"

"No, that's not it. I'll be leaving in half an hour, tops." He winced, wishing he hadn't made a commitment. "All I want her to do is read a few lines so I can see if she's right for the part."

"If I had a dollar for every time I've heard *that.*"

"I mean it. I'll be home by eight."

"Uh huh, we'll see."

"Okay, eight o'clock. See you then."

Lonnie hung up. How could he get Allison out in half an hour and still do her justice? He turned and looked out the window. It was overcast but the clouds were breaking—scattered patches of blue painted on gray gauze. He reached back and rubbed his neck to relieve the tension. *What to do?* A relationship with guarded emotions was not a relationship. He turned and stood looking back into his office.

He could only hope God would soon intervene and show him what to do about...well, take your pick, about Trudy, about Quentin, about the film, the hospital, the mission, about everything—*In all thy ways acknowledge Him and He shall direct thy paths. Right?* He looked at his watch *again*, the jewel-encrusted talisman. He couldn't wait to get rid of it. It was a curse, a constant reminder of what his dear brother was putting him through. It was still too soon to interrupt Allison, but he couldn't stand the wait.

He moved slowly along the corridor, stopping to read the brass plaques on the wall, each one a tribute to the company's success. Some of the awards bore titles of films even he recognized. As he got closer, he could hear Allison's voice coming from the boardroom.

"I really don't care, Kirk. I love you. With all my heart, I do. But I'm dying. Listen to me. This is something I must do alone. You must go on. If you love me, you'll do this one thing I ask. I want to look down from the clouds and see you. I want to know you're happy, and then, from the skies, I'll sing so loud you'll hear me, Kirk. In the whisper of the wind, you'll hear my song."

Lonnie stepped through the door and cleared his throat. Allison glanced at her watch. She had a right to complain; he was early. But he didn't care. He knew what he knew, and he knew she had talent. He'd found his leading lady, and it hadn't taken him half an hour. "I don't need to hear any more," he said. "I didn't mean to eavesdrop, but I couldn't help it. You're perfect. You've got Lisa written all over you."

Allison relaxed. She blushed and brought her roped braid to the front, curling its tip around her finger. "Thank you," she said," but are you saying I've got the part? Don't you need me to read anything else?"

"Are you as good at acting angry?"

Allison furrowed her brows as she flipped back a few pages and then held the script up to the light. "No, I don't accept it," she said. "I won't let you rob me of my life, just because you and some fool machine tell me I'm going to die. I'm *not* going to die. You're wrong. Do you hear me, you're wrong. You..." She kicked a nearby chair so hard it went wheeling across the room, and when she put her face in her hands and started to cry, Lonnie thought she might have injured herself.

"Are you okay?"

Allison looked up with a grin. "Gotcha," she said, her cheeks were dimpled and her eyes full of light.

"Okay, that's it, you've got the part. That is, if you want it. I suggest you go home and spend the evening reading as much of the script as you can. I wasn't kidding when I said we're in a bind. I'll need your decision by morning. If you want to go ahead, you'll have to be on the set first thing tomorrow. But there is something I should tell you before you make up your mind. Since I've taken over, I've found the company's not doing so well—financially, I mean. We owe just about everybody, and I'm told there's no money in the bank. There's a distinct possibility we won't be able to finish what we start. I'm doing what I can to turn things around, but I'm swimming against the tide, so you may quit your job at the restaurant and end up unemployed. I can only promise you'll be paid for whatever time you put in. I'll make sure of that, even if I have to pay you out of my own pocket.

"But there's one other option you may want to consider. If you decide the story has good potential, you can opt to take a percentage of whatever we net. Personally, I think with the combination of your acting and the strength of the story, we stand a good chance of doing really well, so taking a percentage could be the better deal, but you have to decide that for yourself. Any questions?"

Allison brought the document up, evaluating how much she'd have to read. She bit her bottom lip, and then looked at Lonnie. "One does come to mind. Since, as you just mentioned, the success of a film depends a lot on the actors, I'd like to know who's playing the part of Kirk."

"Oh, Kirk. Lance something or other, I think. Lance Able, that's it. Lance Able."

"Come again?"

"I've never met the man. But I'm pretty sure that's his name."

"You don't know who Lance Able is?" Allison pulled a chair over and sat down fanning herself with her hand. "I'm not sure I'm up to this. Lance is *the* number one ticket at the box office. Voted most desirable bachelor three years in a row. How'd you ever get him? Are you sure about the name?"

"Pretty sure. I could be wrong. I don't know one actor from another. We don't watch many movies where I live."

"Who was his co-star before? Who am I replacing?"

"Now *that* I know. Her name's Laurna Dove. I met her earlier today."

Allison began nodding. "That makes sense. I can't believe you want me to star next to Lance Able. Wait till I tell the girls at Splits. What happened to Laurna, if you don't mind my asking?"

Lonnie pulled out a chair and sat down. "I'll tell you," he said, "but what I'm about to say is confidential. That script you're holding was written several years ago by my nephew, Quentin, but for whatever reason, my brother filed it away and never used it. Then last year Harlan dug it out, only he didn't tell Quentin about it. Instead, he spiced it up with so much sex and violence you couldn't recognize the original. Now I come along, only I like what Quentin did better. I decided to redo it the way he intended, but when I talked to Laurna about it, she didn't agree. She refused to accept the changes and walked out. That's why I need a new actress. And that's why you're here."

Allison raised her eyebrows, nodding.

"But until I'm ready, I don't want Quentin knowing what I'm up to. He's had a rough go of it. If you ever get a chance to meet him, you'll see what I mean. He was in an accident that put him in a wheelchair. And he just spent the past few months watching his father die. He's strong, but for the moment I think he's suffered enough. My assistant, Nicole, is the only other person who knows Quentin wrote the script. My management team is out of the loop, and Quentin wrote it so long ago, it would never occur to him we're using it now. I don't want him finding out until the time is right." Lonnie glanced at his watch. "Oh, and one more thing, Quentin isn't to know about our financial troubles either. I don't want him worrying, so please keep all this under your hat."

LONNIE ARRIVED back at the pink mausoleum at eight o'clock sharp. He thanked Frank, his driver, and released him for the evening. Then he entered the foyer and slipped past the two giant portraits of Striker narcissism—B*eauty and the Beast.* He heard TV talk droning in the den and music from the house speakers playing overhead. Suddenly it occurred to him he was still wearing Friday's clothes, the ones he'd worn all weekend. He started through the entry, hoping to sneak upstairs and change into one of his new outfits before dinner, but no such luck. Trudy had radar.

"Hello handsome," she said as she emerged from the sitting room. "Long time, no see." She moved in, tossing her hair from her shoulder. Her lips were softly parted. Lonnie could see a hint of her teeth as she wrapped her arms around his neck and rose up on her tiptoes to kiss his cheek. He was still holding his briefcase so he couldn't return the embrace. Her perfume was light and alluring. Her body, pressed against his own, gave off heat.

Quentin chose just that moment to pump by. His eyes were points of cold fire, his lips flat and white. It looked like he had a piece of cellophane stretched over his mouth. Lonnie heard the elevator motor begin to whine.

"I told you I'd be home," he said.

Trudy brought her hands to rest on Lonnie's shoulders. She played with his collar while exploring the blue of his eyes, and then placed her palms flat on his chest. "A man of his word. I like that. Have you had anything to eat?"

"No. I raced right home."

"I figured as much. The cook put dinner away, but I have a snack prepared in my room. Come on."

"Your room?"

"Relax. I have a wonderful balcony with an awning overhead to keep us dry. Besides, the clouds are breaking and the sun's shining through. Since my room has the best view in the house, I asked

Maria to put together something we could enjoy out there." She took Lonnie by the hand and led him up the stairs, dragging his briefcase behind. He was powerless to resist. He took one soft cushioned step after the other, drawn by Trudy's perfume and the warmth of her fingertips on the palm of his hand. He stopped long enough to set his briefcase down at the top of the stairs.

"New?" she said.

"Uh huh."

QUENTIN WAS working at his computer but looked up when he heard his mother giggle, and watched as they passed by the open door. He smiled a faint smile. Tonight he would prove his uncle's hypocrisy. He'd tested the tiny wireless microphone. He could hear soft bedroom music playing in the background. He'd be able to hear anything whispered within five feet of his mother's bed, or anything spoken within ten. He'd record all their intimate secrets, their pillow talk—every word—and play it back for Lonnie. His uncle would have to leave to protect his reputation. There was more than one way to skin a cat.

LONNIE CAUGHT Quentin's eye—*was he smiling?*—but he continued to follow Trudy, still under her spell. She led him through her room, around the king-sized bed and through the French doors that led onto the balcony. The sheer drapes rustled in the breeze. "Sit down," she said, letting go of his hand as she took a seat. She closed the door behind her and made herself comfortable in one of two white wicker chairs that were covered with cushions of forest green. A long-necked bottle rested in a silver bucket beside two crystal glasses. On a white wicker table were a basket of rolls and a tray with assorted crackers, slices of cheese and cuts of meat.

Lonnie took the other chair and settled in, thankful for the distance between himself and Trudy. "Ahhh, this is nice."

"What did I tell you?"

The clouds had formed into wispy layers of translucence. The sun was partly submerged in the haze with its crest peeking over the top, sending out a fan of rays that struck the bottle-green sea, causing it to shimmer like gold. The air was moist and warm and carried the ocean's musk to Lonnie's nostrils, the most relaxing and peaceful smell on earth. He drank it in, gripping the arms of the chair. "Yes, indeed."

"Well, help yourself to an hors d'oeuvre." She took a glass in hand and reached for the bottle. "I know you don't drink, so I chose a non-alcoholic champagne. The bubbles will tickle your nose, but you won't get tipsy."

Lonnie obliged, and reached for a cracker. He stacked it with a piece of sausage and cheese and took a bite, suddenly realizing he was hungrier than he'd thought.

Trudy filled a glass with the sparkling beverage and passed it to Lonnie. He took a sip. She was right; the fizz did tickle his nose. He was wondering what to say, thankful his mouth was full because it gave him an excuse to avoid the intimacy of conversation. He swallowed and reached for another cracker.

"I'm glad we're alone. There's something we need to discuss," Trudy said, breaking the ice. "I understand you're having trouble at the office."

Lonnie stopped chewing and glanced sharply at Trudy. "Where'd you hear that?"

"If I tell you, I want you to promise you won't say anything. I was told in confidence and I don't want you getting upset at the person who told me." She leaned forward, flicking her hair off her shoulder and then used both hands to steady her glass. Her fingers slid down the long, smooth stem. Her green eyes probed Lonnie for a commitment. "Do I have your word?"

Lonnie finished his beverage. "Of course."

"It was Quentin. He says he was in the office the other day. He heard you scrapped the latest project just because it had Harlan's name on it. He says you've got the whole office in an uproar. He thinks they're about to walk out. He came to me because he wants to help you save face and he needs my support. But he doesn't want you to know about it. That's just the way he is. Anyway, to protect you, he's instructed your staff to go ahead and finish the film the way it was without making changes, at least to the original film."

When Lonnie started to protest, Trudy raised her hand. "Let me finish," she said. "Quentin only wants to provide you with a failsafe in case whatever you're doing doesn't pan out. This way you'll have the original to fall back on. He says no one in the office agrees with what you're doing." She softened her tone. "Now don't be hurt. This is your first try. It takes a long time to figure out what people want, but right now it seems we don't have the luxury of time. I understand we borrowed to finance the film, and we have to be able to pay our creditors. At least this way, if people don't like one film, you can use the other."

Lonnie could think of a million things he wanted to say. *Quentin did...what? He went behind my back and usurped my authority? He has my managers doing what?* He wanted to tell Trudy how the new script was Quentin's own, and how her son was only hurting himself, but it was obvious they shared everything. It was also obvious Trudy couldn't be trusted with a confidence. Still, now he had to wrestle with a new problem, another one he didn't know how to solve. It wasn't just Quentin—it was all of them. They were in on it together, had to be—*ignore the kid brother. Harlan he ain't.* Lonnie felt bile rising in his throat and tried to choke it down.

The sun sank below the horizon, leaving the sky looking washed out and pale, mirroring the way he felt. "Thanks for letting me know," he said. He set his glass on the table and looked at Harlan's watch. "And thanks for sharing the sunset. Well, I'd better be getting to bed. It's already after nine. I flew out of Huatulco at five this morning, so I've had very little sleep. You'll have to excuse me. I need to turn in."

"Already? You sure you won't stay? I was hoping we'd have a chance to talk."

"We will. I promise. But we'll have to do it some other time. I have a long day tomorrow." Lonnie got up, expecting Trudy to follow, but she remained seated, staring out over the blue Pacific, at the open sky and the vast emptiness of space.

When she heard her bedroom door close, she reached into the bag beside her chair and removed a flask. She tried to keep her hands from shaking as she splashed the vodka into her glass.

SEVENTEEN

LONNIE KEPT a grip on the rubber automatic doorstop. The elevator fought back attempting to close by thumping against his hand, *ding, ding, ding.* When Quentin's chair was clear, Lonnie let go and hopped over the threshold to escape. Quentin ignored him and pushed on ahead, with Lonnie trailing behind. Lonnie caught up to the wheelchair and held the door open for his nephew, but by the time he himself entered the office, Quentin was already pumping his way through the interior of the building. He'd managed to make the entire trip without mentioning his reason for being there.

Lonnie had been surprised to find his nephew sitting in the car again. He'd walked out onto the porch shielding his eyes from the bright morning sun only to see the boy's shadow behind the tinted glass of the waiting limo. It didn't take a mind-reader to figure out why. He was there to check the progress of Harlan's original film, the version Lonnie had put the kibosh on but Quentin had secretly revived. Lonnie couldn't say anything about it without compromising Trudy's trust.

Secrets, secrets, secrets. Secrecy and deceit were close cousins. Did Harlan really plan to divulge a secret that could destroy his family? He'd already made him vow not to let Trudy and Quentin know they were in danger of losing their company. Perhaps, in hindsight, that was good. Ben Lowen's takeover was the real issue. If they knew about that, the gloves would come off. They wouldn't let him risk losing their inheritance. Maybe Quentin's meddling was God's way of stepping in to save the company. Lonnie wasn't supposed to know about it, and if he didn't know, there wasn't anything he could do, and if he didn't do anything, the film would be released, the debt would be paid, and Ben would back off. Lonnie would have a clear conscience, knowing he'd neither participated nor given his consent. He would make sure the next Striker film was family entertainment right from the start. The Lord did work in mysterious ways.

Or *was* this the Lord? No! Evil could not be used to bring about good; the end did not justify the means.

Lonnie stopped abruptly. The receptionist hadn't yet arrived, but there, sitting in one of the visitor's chairs, was Allison. Her hair rode in long kinky curls over her shoulders. With her hair braided, Lonnie would have said she was cute, but with it down and flowing, she was downright pretty—*muy bonito*. She had on blue jeans and a white tank top that accentuated her slim waist.

She rose to greet him, holding the script with both hands. "You said you wanted to get an early start."

Lonnie smiled. "Indeed I did. Come on back. We'll discuss it in my office."

Nicole was already at her desk typing. The air around her work space was pungent, as if she'd sprayed her desk with perfume only moments before.

"Morning. You've met Allison, I believe," Lonnie said, stopping to be polite.

Nicole appeared to flinch at the sound of Lonnie's voice. She quickly moved her computer mouse to the screen-saver icon, and clicked before looking up to greet her boss and his guest. "Yes. I see you made it back. "How did it go last night?" she asked, looking at Allison. But Lonnie spoke before Allison could answer. "Fine. We need to have a brief meeting. Could you bring us coffee?"

Nicole stood. "Sure. Do you need me in the meeting?"

"No. That won't be necessary. We'll only be a few minutes."

Lonnie closed the door and went around his desk setting his briefcase on the floor. The city, in the shadow of the morning sun, was gradually waking to the new day as light poured between the buildings and streamed through his office window. He could see cosmic dust floating in its powerful beam. He turned and waved his hand at a chair, inviting Allison to sit down, feeling the sun on his back as he pulled his own chair out from behind the desk. The leather was warm to his touch. "I hope you don't mind my closing the door," he said, "but until we come to an agreement, I'd rather not let the whole office know what we're up to." He scooted his chair in and sat down. "So, did you get a chance to read the script?"

Allison crossed one leg over the other and leaned forward with her hands wrapped around her knee. Her skin was copper, like someone who spent a lot of time at the beach, and she had a faint scattering of freckles over the bridge of her nose. "I think it's a wonderful story," she said. "I only meant to skim through it, but once I got started, I couldn't put it down. The ending almost had me in tears. I can't figure out why your brother wanted to change it."

Lonnie sat back and eyed her speculatively. "And what did you decide? Do you think you're right for the part? I..."

There was a knock at the door. Lonnie raised his finger. "Come in."

Nicole entered, holding two cups of black coffee in the familiar burgundy mugs. She set them on the desk, sliding one toward her boss and the other toward his guest. "Will you be needing me for anything else?"

"No, that's fine for now, Nicole, thank you." Lonnie waited until the door closed behind her.

"I think I agree with what you said last night," Allison began. "This part was written for me. I can do wonders with it."

"So you accept?"

"Absolutely."

Lonnie's face broke into a smile. "Great, that's good news. You had me sold last night, but I prayed just the same, and here you are. That's what I call an answer..."

Lonnie caught himself. He hadn't really prayed—not unless you counted asking that the Lord's will be done in everything, but he hadn't taken time to be specific. Back in Posada, he had boxes of articles on the subject of prayer. It used to puzzle him when he read how busy executives claimed they didn't have time to pray, but he'd only been a businessman for little over a week, and already his prayer life had dwindled from a hour on the beach, to fifteen minutes in his room, to zip this morning when he'd run out without praying at all. And now was when he needed it most.

"So, what did you decide about compensation?" he said, realizing he had to ask the Lord's forgiveness for his oversight. "Do you want to negotiate a contract with my VP of Production, or..."

Allison was shaking her head. "No. I've given it a lot of thought. The way I see it, is this. You said the company was in financial trouble. I'm hoping you'll find the money to do this film, because it has the potential to be big. If so, I want a cut. If it doesn't happen, I wouldn't feel right about taking the money, anyway. I just need to know what percent you had in mind."

Lonnie took a sip of his coffee and set the mug down. He leaned back in his chair, crossed his arms, and snuggled his hands up under his armpits. "I was thinking two percent of net," he said. "We have about fifty million in debt we have to cover first, but if the film grosses a hundred and fifty million, you'll get two percent of a hundred million, and that's two million dollars. And a hundred-fifty million isn't an unreasonable amount to expect from a good picture. In fact, I think we can do better. *Forrest Gump* grossed over three hundred million, but I don't want to be guilty of counting the chickens before they hatch. We could also flop."

Allison's cheeks puffed out round and dimpled, then her face formed an agreeable smile. "That's far more than I expected, and don't worry, we won't flop!" She stood and leaned forward extending her hand across the desk. "You got yourself an actress, Mr. Striker."

Lonnie reached out to seal the deal. Her hand was small, but she had a remarkably firm grip. He let go and picked up the phone. "Les, could you come down to my office for a minute? There's someone here I want you to meet."

LES GLANCED over his shoulder at the so-called "actress" the new boss had hired. She had followed him back to his office so he could go over the details of her contract. He had to do what the new boss-man said, but he didn't have to like it. And he didn't have to make the little priss feel welcome. He decided to park her outside in the hall.

"Wait here a few minutes would you, Sweet Cakes?" he said. He turned and slammed the door so hard the windows rattled.

Allison winced, wondering what his problem was and whether the fat, bald man knew how ridiculous he looked in his oversized tank shorts and that blazing red parrot shirt. Just before the door closed, Allison caught a glimpse of a man in a wheelchair. It had to be Lonnie's nephew. She could see the family resemblance—and they'd come in together. Now she could hear voices, but they were muffled so she couldn't understand what was being said.

"Do you know what your fool uncle has done now?" Les huffed as he dropped into his chair. His face was red, filled with tiny engorged capillaries about to explode. He reached for a cigarette. "He's gone and hired his own actress, some nobody from nowheresville. And he expects her to replace Laurna."

"Relax, Les. I already told you, just play along. Three more days and we'll have *Lost Cause* into distribution. I'll convince my mother it was necessary, and with everybody against him, my uncle will step aside. You just have to be patient."

Les pushed back in his chair, snapping his lighter shut with a brassy *click* as he exhaled a stream of smoke into the room. "That's easy for you to say. I told Lance and the crew to take the day off. Now I have to scramble to get them back. Uncle Lonnie wants to ride down with us. He wants us to begin filming today. I just can't believe it."

He leaned forward, placing his elbows on his desk. "You know what else? I told Jeremy to call Robyn Love, that high-priced hooker your dad gave a couple of bit parts. The one that *thinks* she's an actress. Anyway, I was gonna offer her ten grand to stand in for a few days—just to fake it. Easy money for her. Course, I would have explained that her other services were part of the package, can't fault me for that, but now your uncle's screwed up everything."

"When are we going out to the lot?"

"As soon as I can get the crew together. Hopefully within the hour. But first I have to get little Miss Nowheresville into a contract. She wants a percentage, which of course she'll never see. I'll use the negotiation as an excuse to stall as long as I can, but it won't be too long, your uncle's got a burr under his saddle. He wants us to get moving."

A LINE of palm trees rushed by the window in a blur, looking like pickets in a fence. The limo was quiet and smooth, delivering its ride with air-conditioned comfort. They rode along in silence—Lonnie, Quentin, Les, and Allison—each lost in their own thoughts. Lonnie had no idea where they were going. He only knew they were shooting "on the lot," wherever that was.

They were passing a park now. A large green lawn zoomed by with shade trees and ornamental shrubs, stainless steel drinking fountains, and gray cinder-block washrooms. A large pool swept into view. Public, and crowded. Behind a tall chain link fence, dozens of white towels were laid out on the hot cement, some covered with sun-browned bodies. Mothers watched while kids ran around the aqua blue playground—a white splash here, a long dive there. Lonnie leaned back in his seat, turned his head away from the window, and closed his eyes. A young boy had just bounced off the high dive. Lonnie didn't want to see him land—not even by accident.

The sun was bright that morning, so bright you couldn't look directly into the water for the glare. Lonnie left the locker room first, leaving his brother talking with a former swim coach, a good-looking blond with short cropped hair Lonnie himself had seen and admired from a distance. Harlan had come to practice. He was a diver, regional champ for Largemount's high school team his graduating year. But even though he was no longer in school, he continued to swim for the exercise. Trudy said she enjoyed watching Harlan dive. She compared the arc of his half gainer with the gracefulness of a swan, said it characterized sensitivity and strength. Lonnie figured if Harlan could do it, so could he—what could be so hard?—though in all the years he had lived with his mother, he had rarely, if ever, gone swimming.

He marched straight to the high dive and began to climb. It was only three meters to the springboard. It didn't look that high from the ground, but now each step seemed a mile closer to the moon. Near the top he found himself slowing down. He crawled onto the board but he had to force himself to stand, and even then remained stooped with his hands ready to grab something in case he slipped. What was there to fear? It was just water. He inched forward until he reached the edge. He tried a slight lifting movement just to get a feel for the board's spring, but it responded violently almost throwing him off. His arms flew out as he slowly squatted down reaching for something to hold. He gazed down into the blue abyss. The water looked a million miles away. He should have brought a parachute. The board continued to wobble beneath his feet. It was a bad idea. He began crawling backward, hanging on for dear life. He turned slowly, looking over his shoulder to see if anyone was watching, but the coast was clear. He inched along the board and crawled over the edge, taking one slow step down at a time till he finally felt the deck firmly beneath his feet.

When he turned around, he was staring straight into the face of Harlan. His brother stood there with a slanted grin, hanging onto the ends of a towel draped around his neck. Harlan shook his head and tossed the towel aside. Lonnie made a retreat to the locker room. He hadn't even got his feet wet. He looked back over his shoulder just in time to see Harlan enter the water from a perfectly executed dive.

Lonnie felt the car bounce. He opened his eyes. The limo rolled up the drive and came to a stop inside a chain link fence. At the touch of a button, the window was lowered.

A guard came out of a small sentry station and leaned down to peer into the car. "How you doing this morning folks?" He wore a brown uniform with a chrome badge pinned to his chest. His gun was holstered in black tooled leather.

"Hi, Bob. We're on lot thirty-six today."

"All right, sign here."

Frank took the clipboard and signed his name. It was obvious he'd done it a hundred times.

They drove past row after row of windowless, flat-roofed buildings and made several turns, passing through narrow alleys filled with people. Lonnie felt sorry for those in costume. They had to be hot. As they rode through the back lot, he could see the facade of a full blown city in the distance, but the scenery kept changing. One minute they were in the Old West; the next, in outer space.

They slowed as they approached a circle of five trailers and a tangle of cables and wires. Then the limo rolled to a stop. Les swung the door wide to get out. Quentin, in the seat opposite him, waited till Frank came around with his wheelchair.

Allison seemed anxious to begin, but waited patiently. She was the last to step down as Lonnie held the door and gave her his hand. "Well, I guess this is it. Are you ready?"

"Actually, I'm a little nervous" she confessed. "But I guess I'm as ready as I'll ever be."

Lonnie and Allison followed Quentin and Les as they made their way toward a man with a stubby salt-and-pepper beard who stood beside a forklift. The man wore a baseball cap with a Detroit Tigers logo. He shook hands with Les.

"How you doing, Rusty?" The slices of perspiration under Les's arms caused some of his parrots to look like they'd been through a tropical rainstorm. "You already know Harlan's son, Quentin, and this is Harlan's brother, Lonnie. He's the new boss." Les looked at Lonnie. "Rusty here is our director. It's his responsibility to give life to what we have on paper. That means he calls the shots. Not even *I* tell him what to do. Rusty, this is Allison Young, the girl I spoke to you about..."

But before Les could finish, the door of a trailer on his left banged open. At first Lonnie could only see the arm holding the door open, but then a man stepped out and turned toward the group. "Les, what the freak is going on? I want to know where Laurna is, and don't give me any of this bull about her quitting. Who's this?" He stepped down onto the pavement. He was wearing beige shorts with large outside pockets and white sneakers with no socks. His black T-shirt read, "May The Force Be With You."

"Morning, Lance. This is Allis..."

"I know her name. I mean who *is* she?" He turned to Allison. "Where you from, Sugar? What films have you been in?"

Allison's face lost its color. "I...I haven't been in any films, I..."

"No films. What is it you do?"

"I'm a waitress at present, but I..."

"A waitress! What kind of bull is this? Les, you never said anything about Laurna backing out. You want me to work with a waitress? Get real. *Lost Cause* is in the can. It's fine the way it is. Use it. Don't take it *too* hard, Sugar. I'm sure you're a very nice person, but you'll have to cut your teeth somewhere else. I don't work with rookies." And with that he turned and walked toward his trailer, leaving Allison and Lonnie in wide-eyed shock, and Quentin and Les trying to hide their silly grins.

EIGHTEEN

SECONDS PASSED with the sun beating down on the hot asphalt. The crowd began teetering back and forth, trying to relieve the heat in their shoes, and somehow create a diversion to eliminate the awkward silence. Allison put her hands on her hips and leaned in.

"Just *one* second, Mr. Able." Her unbraided hair splayed out from her shoulders in thick waves. Her brows were knit and her eyes on fire. "You forgot something."

Lance stopped and turned. "And that would be...?"

"Your roots, Mr. Able. You forgot where you're from. You were a cab driver if I'm not mistaken—wheels for hire, right? It's been in all the tabloids: 'From Cabbie To King.' What school did *you* graduate from?"

Lance slipped his hands into his pockets. His baggy shorts hung low on his hips and his black T-shirt rolled loosely over his belt. He leaned back against the side of the trailer, planting his tennis shoe against the aluminum wall. "Beg pardon?" he said.

"I asked what school you graduated from. It's a fair question. You wanted to know where I'm from. I'll tell you. I graduated from Juilliard in New York. Ever heard of it? No, I don't suppose you have. You'd have to be serious about acting for Juilliard to mean anything. Yes, I have experience. It's just that I have it on stage, not in the movies. Before moving out here, I starred in two off-Broadway plays, and I've also had a number of supporting roles. The question is, Where are *you* from, Mr. Able, the school of hard knocks?"

Now it was Lonnie's turn to be stunned. Allison had taken the offensive, and he was too mesmerized by her brashness to intervene.

She forged ahead. "I'll bet you learned how to act while driving a taxi. No, don't tell me, let me guess. It all came naturally? Well I hate to disillusion you, but that's not acting. That's just you playing yourself. Know what? I think you're right. You need someone like Laurna, someone with a great body and no talent. A co-star with talent might push you to excel—heaven forbid! Who cares whether there's a good story or good acting. It's all about looking good. You two deserve each other!"

Sound men and lighting technicians, and people from wardrobe and makeup moved in closer. They formed a loose circle, waiting for Lance to respond—everyone loves a good fight. Allison found herself center stage. It was an awkward moment, standing there all alone, knowing she'd made a scene. She waited for Lance to say something, but he just stood there grinning as though amused by her impertinence. At least he wasn't scowling. Allison flipped her hair off her neck and brought it forward looping a strand around her finger. Someone began clapping, slowly at first, a single loud *clap...clap...clap,* which became faster as the applause caught on. Allison took her cue and bowed, first to one side, then to the other, and like any good actress, made her exit before the applause faded away. People backed up to let her pass, but they continued clapping.

"Wait a minute!" Lance called.

Allison stopped. She took a deep breath, and turned to face him again. He was squinting in the sun's bright light, but his lips wore a wiry smile. You got spunk," he said. "I like that. Okay, Miss Juilliard, I'll give you a shot. Let's set up a scene and do a test. If you're as good as you say, fine, but blow it and you're history. Deal?"

"Sure, no problem. What would you like me to do?"

"I want to see you act, Miss Juilliard."

Allison curtsied and raised her head. "You just did, Mr. Able. You just did."

The gathering began to disperse. The sound men returned to their mixing boards and the lighting technicians to their lights.

Lonnie watched as Allison approached Lance holding her script at her side. They were joined by the director and the three huddled to confer. At first Lonnie had been horrified. Allison's outburst could have scuttled the day, but he couldn't help it, he liked her spirit. She was a feisty little thing—*an off Broadway star, how about that?* He quickly decided if anyone had to go, it would be Lance. He felt a tug on his arm. He turned to see a young man standing at his elbow with a clipboard in his hand.

"Are you Mr. Striker?"

"I am."

"There's a call for you from your wife. You can take it in Monahan's trailer."

Wife??? It took Lonnie a moment but he caught on. Trudy would have introduced herself as, "Mrs. Striker." He nodded and followed the young man through the maze of trailers till they came to one with the word "Director" stenciled on the door. Lonnie mounted the steps and felt the cool air caress his face as he stepped inside. A private air-conditioned suite, tables, chairs, bed...not bad. "Right over there," the young man said.

Lonnie picked up the phone. "This is Mr. Striker."

"Hi. I'm glad I was able to track you down. I wanted to let you know your tux has arrived."

"Tux?"

"For the banquet tonight. Sorry. I meant to tell you earlier, but you disappeared on the weekend and things have been crazy since. It completely slipped my mind. It's for charity. Harlan and I go every year. We need to raise money for the homeless. I've already bought tickets and you're my date."

Lonnie hesitated. He felt his chest flutter. Like a recovering alcoholic, the longer he went without, the easier it was to say no, but the desire never left completely. "I have to wear a tuxedo?"

"Don't worry, it'll fit. It's a rental. I gave them your shirt and pant size. You'll look fine, but you have to be home by four to get ready on time. Cocktails are at six, and we have to fight rush-hour traffic. Can you make it?"

Lonnie looked at his watch—*correction, Harlan's watch*. He began picking at a piece of yellowed tape that was stuck to the table. "Four o'clock, sure. I guess so. I'll try."

There were windows at both ends of the trailer but the light was subdued. Lonnie put the phone down and looked up to see a newspaper clipping tacked to a bulletin board amid a clutter of random notes and business cards. "Striker On Verge Of Collapse," it read.

> According to several independent sources the darling of Tinseltown, Striker Films, is preparing to file for bankruptcy. Once on the fast track, the company fell into trouble earlier this year when it released *Death Ignoble,* its third film to fail at the box office. The recent passing of Harlan Striker, former CEO of the privately held company, has created a leadership vacuum, compounding its problems. Harlan's younger brother, Lonnie, has stepped in to fill the gap but it's uncertain as to whether he'll be able to turn the company around. Meanwhile, Century Films is reported to be preparing a bid to acquire the floundering company from its creditors. The President of Century could not be reached for comment...

No wonder his employees were lethargic about their work. Who could blame them with this kind of tripe floating around? Where did they get this stuff anyway? Ben Lowen alluded to having a source within the company. It was a leak Lonnie wanted to plug—but how? And who was Century Films? Striker wasn't yet a corpse, and the vultures were already beginning to circle.

Lonnie reached for his wallet and retrieved the number of Maniux and Associates. He dialed, and waited for Don to come on the line. He should not have promised to be Trudy's escort tonight. He needed Don's legal advice, now more than ever, but the banquet stood in the way.

"Hi, Don? Listen, I need to apologize. Something's come up. I'm not going to be able to make our afternoon appointment. Can we reschedule? How's tomorrow look?"

"Not good. I'm out all day. Can you come by earlier? How 'bout we meet over lunch. Leave now, and you'll be back by early afternoon."

Lonnie glanced down at his watch, again. "Sure...thanks. See you in an hour."

LONNIE WENT back outside. The late morning sun was causing the asphalt to soften. It smelled like melting tar. Lance and Allison were animated, rehearsing a scene with arms waving. *In this heat?* But it appeared to be going well. He spied Quentin and Les observing the play, but from a distance. Lonnie moved in behind Quentin's wheelchair, taking hold of the grips, grateful for an excuse to get him off the lot before he discovered what script was being used. He leaned forward slightly to get his nephew's attention. "Sorry, Quentin, we have to go. I have another appointment. I'll give you a lift back to the office."

A row of translucent shades were raised over the set to keep harsh shadows off the faces of the actors. A cameraman held his light meter up to take a reading. Piles of cables were coiled at his feet like spaghetti. Lonnie wondered how Quentin would get his chair over, around, and through the mess.

Quentin swiveled his head, looking back over his shoulder. "Relax, Unk. Don't worry about me. You got something to do, go ahead. I can take care of myself."

"But I have the limo."

Quentin rocked the wheels of his chair, swinging it back and forth. His biceps were hard under his sleeves. Lonnie let go of the handles and Quentin wheeled about to face his uncle. "No offense, but I was doing fine before you showed up, and I'll do just fine when you're gone. See you later, Unk." Then he cranked the wheels, again, causing the chair to spin around, turning his back on Lonnie.

Lonnie shifted his attention to Les. "What about you?"

Les rolled back on his heels and fished in his shirt for a cigarette. "I think I'll stick around too," he said, deliberately lighting up and allowing thin wisps of smoke to trail from his nose. He snapped his lighter shut and dropped it into his pocket. "Why don't you stop by after your meeting. I'm sure we'll be ready to go by then."

Lonnie puckered his lips. "Sure. I suppose I could do that."

THE LIMOUSINE was caught behind a bus in bumper-to-bumper traffic. They were lost in the brown haze. It was so thick Lonnie couldn't see the wall of mountains surrounding the L.A. basin, even though they were only a few miles away. *Smog City.* The smell of carbon monoxide was making him nauseous. He rolled down his window, hoping to let in fresh air, but what he got was a raging furnace and a barrage of sound. Cars rolled by, consumed with electronic media: cell phones were glued to ears with words passing through one portal and out the other; radios rambled with news, weather, and sports while *talk-talk-talk* shows filled the psyche with a universe of meaningless opinions, and compact discs rapped out titillating rock-and-roll to a hip-hop beat—*one car even had a TV*—anything and everything to fill the brain-void. *God gave you that mind to contemplate Him, not to spend twenty-four hours a day sponging up useless information. Think, man, think!*

The heat rolled in through the open window adding to Lonnie's stress. Quentin was bound to accuse him of stealing the script. How could he explain why he was doing what he was doing without violating a trust? Or did it even matter? Don had refused to discuss the reason for their meeting, which implied the news was bad. Good news could be shared over the phone; bad news had to be delivered in person.

Lonnie rolled up the window and rubbed the back of his neck. The legal beagles at Gladdon, Vickers and Cox would have made sure he signed the contract if his signature had been required. Don as much as said so. Who cared? Saving the company wouldn't make Quentin any less hostile. At least if Ben won, Lonnie could disappear into the jungle and never be seen or heard from again. He wouldn't have a hospital, and he wouldn't have Trudy, but at least he'd have his sanity—and he wouldn't have to wear a watch!

QUENTIN EYED Allison and Lance as they rehearsed their lines. His fingers gripped the arms of his chair. They might actually pull it off. The director cut in, saying he wanted to rehearse a segment with Lance alone. Allison stepped back for a few minutes and Quentin jockeyed his wheelchair through the gauntlet of cables, rolling up alongside.

"Hi," he said. "Looks like you and Lance have rapport. I think you're good together."

"Thanks."

"Just be careful. This is a cutthroat business."

Allison turned. "Meaning...what?"

"Meaning, I don't want to see you get hurt."

She flicked the hair off her shoulder and smiled. "Thanks for your concern, but I'll do all right."

"Sure. You'll do just fine...as long as they give you a chance."

Allison looked down at Quentin, raising an eyebrow as if to say: *I think you'd better explain.*

"Les thinks my Uncle Lonnie still wants Laurna to do the picture," Quentin continued. "He caught them in the sack together, almost—she was getting dressed. He thinks Lonnie's using you to make Laurna jealous. If that's so, when she comes back, he'll drop you like a rock."

"I don't believe it."

Quentin looked up, squinting into the sun. He used his hand to shield his eyes. "You don't? Well, that's okay. It probably won't happen. I just felt like I should say something in case it does. Food for thought, if you know what I mean. Ah, I think Rusty's trying to get your attention. It's not good to keep the director waiting."

Allison stepped in and took her position, but her response was notably slower, and her voice had lost its bounce. She faltered, missing a cue, and fumbled one of her lines. Quentin sat back and listened, pleased with himself. Anyone could see she wasn't right for the part. She wasn't good under pressure.

Lance was walking in circles, waving his arms in the air. "How dare God let us taste happiness and then take it away."

Allison slipped her arm around his waist and buried her head into his shoulder. "No! I don't want you blaming God. He just wants to end the pain. Don't you see? You can't be angry about that. I don't want you blaming anyone. Things just happen, that's all. There's ..." She hesitated, and then glanced down at her script. "Sorry, I lost my place."

Quentin rocked his chair back and forth. She was blowing it. Too bad. She seemed like a nice girl. *Nothing personal, kiddo, "things just happen."* He smiled recognizing one of her lines. *Well, things do just happen. Wheelchairs happen. That's life.* He tried shrugging it off, but it kept popping into his mind. *Things just happen. Things just happen—so what?* It was a familiar theme—but it was more than that. The whole scene was familiar, not just the line. He began concentrating. He'd seen it before, but where—a movie, a play?

He leaned in, intent on hearing what was being said. An image formed in the back of his mind, like a theater photograph of actors toeing their marks, waiting for their cue. He could see how the scene would play out. He saw hurt on the face of the young man, reassurance in the eyes of his fiancee. Allison wasn't doing it right. She needed to show more compassion, and her timing was off, but that wasn't her fault. She'd been doing fine—until he'd thrown her a curve. He tried to imagine Laurna playing the part. Would she make a good Lisa? No, Allison made a much better Lisa. Laurna was just...Laurna. Wait a minute. *Lisa? Kirk!* Those were his characters. That was *his* story!

LONNIE ARRIVED home late. He rushed into the house, leaving Quentin to manage for himself. Neither had mentioned the day's activities. In fact, after the obligatory greeting, Quentin hopped on his cell phone, leaving Lonnie to pass the time gazing out the window at merging traffic. If Quentin knew what script they were using, he was keeping it to himself, which was fine by Lonnie. He didn't have time to explain. At least not now. He breezed through the foyer nearly bumping into Trudy who had just turned the corner with a martini in hand. She arched back, swaying to keep the drink from spilling.

"Sorry." Lonnie held out his hands. "I know I'm late. I'll try to dress fast." He started to turn but something held him in place. *Trudy!* Queen of the prom. Twenty years flashed by in a second. He could almost see the moonlight and smell the eucalyptus. The hairs of his neck and arms stood on end. *Trudy, Trudy, Trudy.* She was resplendent. Her evening gown was strapless, a dark velvet green with a slit up the side that revealed her shapely legs and a long smooth mid-section that accentuated her tiny waist. Around her neck she wore a silver chain with a diamond pendant. Her hair, swept up and over in a graceful roll, shone like burnished mahogany and was crowned with a small, but elegant, tiara. *Whew!* If he didn't get moving now, he'd buckle at the knees.

"Your tux is laid out on the bed," she called after him as he flew up the stairs. Quentin rolled into the entry. "Hi, Mom." He let out a throaty whistle. "Boy, don't you look nice. What's the occasion?"

Trudy walked over and placed a hand on her son's shoulder. The portrait of Harlan stared down at her—a haughty effigy of the man she once feigned to love. She took a sip of her martini and looked up the stairs. "Just a charity dance. I'm taking Lonnie. We won't be out late. I get the feeling your uncle doesn't like parties."

LONNIE WAS in a room full of penguin-suited men and sequined-gowned ladies all tittering in table conversation. He'd never seen so many pearls and diamonds in one place. The women were daintily coiffured and spoke in hushed tones of the ghastly way everyone else was dressed. "Chartreuse! Really? It's so tacky. This is supposed to be a formal affair." And the men, wearing cummerbunds and tails, made light of the jewels looped through the buttonholes of their shirts. "Of course they're real. I told her diamonds were frivolous, but it was my birthday. What could I do?" Lonnie rubbed his cufflinks, two smooth emeralds set in gold. Had they been

Harlan's? They had to have been. Lonnie had been standing in front of the mirror tucking in his shirt when Trudy marched into the room and placed them in his hand. He didn't want to wear anything of Harlan's, but she'd been clear: The studs supplied by the rental agency were to remain in the drawer.

The soft music played by the orchestra was virtually drowned out by the peals of high-pitched conversation and laughter. There was a hardwood parquet dance floor, but no one was dancing. That would come later, after Lonnie was gone, or so he hoped. Overhead, crystal chandeliers sparkled with prismatic rainbows. The setting was lovely, and the mood romantic. Earlier, on a trip to the men's room, Lonnie had seen two lovers in a dimly lit alcove, locked in a passionate embrace. The man's hands were groping where they shouldn't and Lonnie wondered, if the young woman were to open her eyes, whether she would care that they were being observed.

As for himself, Lonnie felt ignored. He didn't know anyone, and Trudy's attention was being absorbed by the man on her left. Lonnie tinkered with his cutlery while picking up fragments of conversation around the table: "Did you hear another American helicopter was downed in Iraq? Sixteen more dead. We got Sadam. We should get out of there and let the Iraqis alone. They don't want us there, anyway. It's all about oil, know what I mean? Our money-grubbing president stands by and lets innocent children be killed, just so his Texas oil buddies can make a profit. Makes me sick to think about it."

No, it's not about oil, Lonnie thought. *It's about defending the rights and freedoms of an oppressed people...*A server reached in to set a dish of sorbet in front of him. The fragile china, trimmed in gold, was exquisite. Trudy's friend let out a roaring laugh. Lonnie turned and saw Trudy put her hand to her mouth, feigning polite embarrassment. There was no reason to be jealous. The man Trudy was talking to was bald and had a mustache that reminded Lonnie of the Monopoly millionaire. Not someone Trudy would be interested in—unless her interest was in holding Boardwalk and Park Place...

Lonnie brought a glass of water to his lips. He'd asked for water instead of champagne, but he'd received Perrier and, like the champagne everyone else was drinking, it tickled his nose. He wiped his mouth on a linen napkin and watched the woman seated across from him to see which utensil she would use to eat her grapefruit sorbet. (He only knew it was sorbet because he overheard someone say so. It looked like sherbet to him. Why were they serving dessert before dinner anyway?) The setup was boy, girl, boy, girl, around the table, and the seating preassigned. The place card in front of Lonnie read, "Harlan Striker," but Trudy didn't seem to notice, or at least she refrained from saying anything. Lonnie reached out and turned the card face down. The lady seated to his right was returning a tube of lipstick to her purse. She saw what Lonnie did and smiled, her freshly glossed lips shining in the light.

"Hi. I'm Margaret Turner," she said extending her fingers.

"Lonnie Striker," Lonnie said taking her hand and giving it a polite squeeze.

"I know. You're Harlan's brother. We met at the funeral."

Lonnie tried to remember but came up blank. The man to Margaret's right leaned in to join the conversation. "Bill Turner," he said reaching across his wife to shake Lonnie's hand. "Terrible about Harlan. He was a good man. And *so* young. Awful, just plain awful. He'll be missed. But I hear you're stepping in. You've got some big shoes to fill, but we're expecting good things."

"And you'll get them. Just don't expect the same kind of things."

Mr. Turner took his napkin and flipped it open, smoothing it in his lap. His gray hair was cut short except in the front, where it was gelled and spiked. "Of course not. Your films should reflect your own personality."

"Something like that. I'm going to try changing the company's image, tone it down a bit and see if we can't provide entertainment for the whole family, rather than just the adults."

Bill dug into his sorbet, capturing a little yellow slice on his spoon. "Why? Harlan established a nice niche for himself. I'd think you'd want to capitalize on it." He put the bite in his mouth. "Ummm, excellent. Whets the appetite for the entree, don't you think?" His wife turned and nodded leaning forward to take a bite herself, but the action blocked Lonnie's view. Her dark brown hair was pulled back and fastened with a clip that captured dozens of ringlets. A string of diamonds dangled from her ear.

Lonnie waited until she sat back to resume the discussion. "Because we're guilty of fictionalizing life instead of telling it the way it is," he said. "I think our films should reflect the real world, not someone's fantasy."

Bill shook his head. "I'm not sure what you mean."

Lonnie thought about suggesting the man read the book Rolly had loaned him. He took a bite of his own sorbet and let the tart ice melt in his mouth. No, he deserved an answer now. Lonnie wiped his lips with a rose-colored napkin. "I mean almost everything we see in the movies is a distortion of real life. Take murder, for example. There aren't half as many murders in real life as we see on TV, not even a fraction. I'll bet no one here has ever even seen an actual murder. Any takers? How about you, Bill. Have you ever seen a murder? The real thing, I mean."

Bill shook his head and took a sip of bubbly, clearly uncomfortable with the direction the conversation was taking. "In real life? No, I can't say I've had that pleasure." He set his glass down, aware that others around the table were beginning to listen.

"Well, there you go. I doubt anyone in this room has seen a murder firsthand, yet I'll bet everyone in this room has seen a murder on TV. Are we painting a picture of the real world? I don't think so. We should all thank God that the world created by Hollywood doesn't exist."

"But murders *do* happen," Bill shot back.

"Sure they do. But if it weren't for the movies, you'd probably never see one. So why is it a person can watch TV and see about eight murders a day? The perception is that murders happen all around us. We should be afraid to go outside, we could walk into the middle of a shootout. The idea that police cruisers chase bad guys through the streets smashing parked cars and splintering fruit stands, is ridiculous, but that's the picture we paint."

Bill turned his chair to engage Lonnie directly. "Okay. Let's say, for the sake of argument, I agree with you. It's not real, so what? You can show reruns of *Ozzie and Harriet* but that's not real either. Programs like that show families always getting along, but the truth is, kids and their parents fight all the time. Whatever kind of film you do, you'll end up tipping the scales one way or the other. You have to. If you try to show people what they see every day, you'll bore them to death. Now, that's murder!" A few people chuckled. Bill's lips curved down in a smug smile. He began tapping the bowl of his spoon on the table. "The point of film is to show people what they don't ordinarily see so they can better understand the world in which they live. And sometimes that means crawling around in the dirt to expose the dark underbelly of society."

Lonnie took a sip of his water. He leaned forward with his elbow on the table. Bill's wife, Margaret, scooted back, trying to duck out of sight. "See, that's what I mean," he said. "You're talking about showing ugliness. Why would you want to do that? Personally, I like the old movies. They made the world seem like a better place. Ever see that scene in *Swing Time* where Fred Astaire hops a freight train wearing a top hat and tails? Think about it. The movie was made in the thirties at the height of the depression and this guy is traveling around like a hobo, but he's wearing an impeccable suit of clothes. It may not seem like much, but it was a powerful message. It made people believe things weren't as bad as they seemed. They were able to forget about their problems for a few hours, and they left the theater with hope for a better tomorrow."

Lonnie leaned back to see if Trudy was paying attention. He knew these were arguments he might soon have to use with her, but she was still talking to the Monopoly man.

"Contrast that with today," he continued. "Here we are, living in that better tomorrow and, instead of celebrating it, we make films that depress people. We portray American families as dysfunctional. Everyone's either divorced or shacking up with the neighbor, and parents are drunk and abusive. Kids can't wait to run away and hop in bed with the first stranger they meet. That's not the way it is in real life, of course, but we're talking about the movies. The problem is, life imitates art, so the number of teen pregnancies has soared, and along with it every form of social disease. The same is true of the way we exaggerate violence. People in the movies die like ants sprayed with Raid. They're blown up by terrorists, pummeled with meteors, abducted by aliens, and hacked apart by serial killers. Our children see so much death and destruction, the idea of really dying seems unreal. They think it's all make-believe. Then one day some troubled teenager wakes up and realizes he's had enough. He doesn't have to go to school and be ridiculed. He can blow them all away, just like in the movies. And we read about it in the papers and act surprised!"

"Oh, poppycock. No one's goes on a killing spree just because they saw an alien abduction on TV. You make Hollywood sound evil. We're just like everyone else. We respond to market demand. We can't help it if people don't want movies with happy-ever-after endings. It takes vice to get them into the theaters. We have to give them what they want. That's how we make money."

"Boy, I hear that argument a lot. Okay, if everyone wants more sex and violence, why are the big money-makers movies like *Titanic*, *Star Wars*, *Forrest Gump* and *The Lion King*? I was just researching all this stuff. Did you know that of the twenty films that made the most money, only two were rated R? The rest all carried some kind of PG rating. That's eighteen out of the twenty highest-grossing films. And I'm not talking about oldies, I'm talking about today's films. Those are the films people are going to see. So why is it R movies outnumber PG movies three to one? If it was about giving people what they want, we'd make only PG movies. The truth is, we should do it anyway. We have a responsibility to provide the public with clean, wholesome entertainment. Movies have an effect on people. It's like food for the mind. Feed them good stuff and they'll stay healthy. Feed them bad stuff and eventually they'll die."

Bill shook his head and waggled his spoon at Lonnie. "Nonsense! My three kids grew up watching all kinds of movies. They saw their share of sex and violence, but they never went out and killed anyone. You know why? Because they're good kids. They were raised to know the difference between right and wrong. They're smart enough to know the stuff they see on TV is just entertainment. Everything depends on the child's upbringing. If parents would spend more time with their kids, you wouldn't have a problem. If you want to blame something, blame the parents, not the movies."

Lonnie felt Trudy's foot nudging his. He looked over and caught her shaking her head, but he had to respond. "I can't argue with that. Good parenting is extremely important, and I'm glad your kids turned out okay, I really am, but just because your kids were brought up right, doesn't mean everyone's are. Can we afford to ignore the rest? They're watching the same programs, and they're being fed the same junk. And it sticks. Don't think it goes in one ear and out the other. If TV messages weren't able to influence people, companies wouldn't advertise. It's just that we don't all respond in the same way. I'm sure you've seen ads for products you've never bought, but that doesn't mean the ads don't work. There's always someone ready to buy the product. Watching a murder on TV probably wouldn't affect a single person in this room, but that doesn't make it safe for everyone. It's not the ones who aren't affected you have to worry about. It's the ones who are, like kids who don't have the benefit of good parenting. Those are the ones we have to think about."

The man scooted his chair back toward the table, weary of the conversation. "Well, you're entitled to your opinion. I can't say I agree. But even if I did, I don't think not producing those kinds of pictures would change anything. The kind of people who commit murders, are going to commit murders whether they see them on TV or not." He took another sip of his champagne. People around the table began to relax. Loaves of hot bread were being served and Bill's wife, Margaret, asked Lonnie to pass the plate with the tiny balls of butter.

Lonnie handed her the dish. "Then you're going to have to explain why more than sixty university studies tell us prolonged exposure to TV violence leads to a measurable increase in antisocial behavior. Because if what you're saying is true, I'm at a loss."

THEY WERE on the dance floor under the glittering ballroom lights. Lonnie hadn't wanted to dance, but he couldn't bring himself to say no. And now, holding Trudy in his arms, her head resting on his shoulder, enjoying the light fragrance of her hair and the soft music, he was glad he hadn't. His critique of the film industry had come close to spoiling the evening, but fortunately the tension around the table dissolved after he and Bill agreed to disagree. Bill hadn't said much throughout the rest of the dinner, but Trudy had been more attentive. Lonnie preferred talking to her anyway. Maybe she was just trying to keep him out of trouble. She had, it seemed, worked at keeping the conversation light. But at least she'd kept the conversation going.

"Hmmm. I love this, don't you?" she said.

Lonnie pulled his head back, swaying with her body against his own. He could feel the warmth between them. He could feel her heartbeat, and he was sure she could feel his. "Yes, I do," he said, kissing her lightly on the forehead. He would have nestled his cheek against the soft cushion of her hair were it not for the small tiara. He gave her a gentle squeeze. This was *his* night, the night they should have shared twenty years ago. Trudy was his date. It was the night he had longed for—not the one they'd shared in the back of her father's station wagon. There would be no drunken orgy to load him down with guilt—not tonight!—and no Harlan to jump out and steal his girl away.

Trudy, to her credit, was trying to stay sober. Lonnie knew she was trying because she'd placed her hand over the mouth of her glass several times when servers came by to pour. It didn't work. The servers were persistent. As soon as one walked away, she'd turn her back and another would show up to fill her glass. Saying no to a full glass of wine was more than Trudy was able to do, but Lonnie was pleased to see her try. The music stopped. They turned and softly applauded the orchestra. Trudy took his hand and led him from the dance floor. He could feel the pulse of her small fingers resting against his palm. He sensed both excitement and danger—and it felt good.

LONNIE HELPED Trudy into the elevator that night. The effort to stay sober had failed. The more she had to drink, the harder it became to say no. She finally gave up and drank until Lonnie insisted they leave. He held his arm around her waist to give her support. She draped her arms around his neck and licked his ear. The alcohol on her breath was intoxicating, as was the scent of her perfume. Lonnie's chest felt on fire. His fingers trembled where they touched her waist.

"Easy girl," he murmured.

IN THE ROOM across the hall, Quentin pressed the record button and watched the reels of the cassette begin to turn. Everything was set to go. This would be his moment of triumph. He leaned forward, holding the headset to his ear, adjusting the volume till he could hear a hiss of static air. What he was doing now, he was doing for his mother. Whatever her weakness, she didn't deserve to be used. His uncle had to go. Allison had explained why Lonnie, who she claimed was being altruistic, hadn't told him about the script. And while it was difficult to accept, Lance confirmed that *Lost Cause* was an adaptation of his original. Why would his dad do such a thing? It posed no small threat to his plan. He was no longer anxious to see *Lost Cause*—the awful name his father had given the altered version—hit the street, but he didn't need his uncle making things right. He'd find a way to do it himself. He had to.

Les, on seeing Quentin switch sides, had taken a cab back to the office though, in all fairness, Les explained that he understood how Quentin might want to defend a script he himself had written. What did it matter? They'd never finish by Friday, so the point was moot. Quentin elected to spend the rest of the afternoon going over the subtle nuances of the characters with Allison and Lance. Tomorrow morning he would assume his rightful place as head of the company. The recording he was about to make would seal his uncle's fate. He adjusted the volume again. He wanted it as loud as possible in case his mother chose to talk to his uncle outside on the balcony again. He had to capture every word.

"Come're, Lonnie," Trudy said. Her voice was the first sound picked up by the mike, and it caused Quentin to jump and quickly crank down the volume.

TRUDY BEGAN undoing Lonnie's tie. Lonnie was holding Trudy around the waist, trying to walk her to the bed. He felt himself tremble as he reached up to take her hand.

"That's not a good idea," he said.

"Why not? You're in love with me, aren't you? You can't deny it. It's plain as the nose on your face." She giggled and pinched Lonnie's nose.

"Yes, I love you, but it's still not a good idea."

"Party pooper." Trudy turned and kissed Lonnie on the mouth, holding him close as she tugged at his shirttail and tried to loosen his belt. Lonnie gave up trying to resist, but he kept stepping back until they reached the bed. He eased her down and reached for her legs, grabbing her by the ankles so he could remove her shoes one at a time. "That tickles," she giggled. She rolled onto her side and curled into a fetal position, patting the mattress behind her. "Come here," she said.

Lonnie pulled the covers over Trudy's shoulder and wrapped them around her legs. Then he leaned down to kiss her cheek. His desire burned in his chest. "Sweet dreams," he said. He smoothed her hair as her eyes closed and within a minute, she was asleep. He straightened himself and pushed his palm into the small of his back. His face felt flushed and his hands moist. He held his breath—*I am weak, but Thou art strong.* He left Trudy's room with his tie undone, his belt hanging loose, and lipstick on his cheek, but he left *alone. Thank You, Lord.*

QUENTIN WAITED, brooding in the shadows. He pulled his headset down around his neck. He could hear the *swish* of his uncle's feet padding down the hall. He listened for the sound of the guestroom door closing, and then pushed the button to stop the recording.

NINETEEN

LONNIE SAT BEHIND his desk, the same polished desk he'd occupied for the better part of two weeks, wishing he could be somewhere—*anywhere*—else. He pulled his Bible toward him and turned the page to another Psalm. He was glad to be reading again. He missed his Bible the way one would miss an old friend. And why not? To read the book was to know its author, and he and this Author were close friends indeed.

> Thou hast given me the shield of thy salvation; thy right hand hath held me up, and thy gentleness hath made me great...I have pursued mine enemies and overtaken them neither did I turn again until they were consumed...For thou hast girded me with strength unto the battle; thou hast subdued under me those who rose up against me...

Perfect! See, that's what he'd been missing. When God goes before, the battle is won; when God is left behind, all hope is lost. *The Battle is the Lord's.* Yes, he was glad to have his old Friend there to help him once again.

But that wasn't why he'd come in early. He'd come in early to avoid Quentin. He didn't have time to explain things right now; besides, it might prove premature. Tomorrow the issue of who owned the company would be settled. If Ben seized possession, Harlan's mishandling would become obvious without Lonnie having to say a word. Tomorrow, indeed, was the day of battle, the proverbial David against Goliath—only at this point Lonnie didn't even have five smooth stones. He could only pray God was on his side.

He shook his head. He'd tried to reach Don all morning, but the answering service had said he was unavailable. Lonnie had missed the appointment he'd made the day before. The snarl on the freeway turned out to be a jackknifed tractor trailer blocking three lanes of traffic. The police had forced everyone to exit, funneling hundreds of cars into the suburbs, where they clogged dozens of intersections. The backup stretched several miles. By the time they cleared the blockade, it was too late to go on. Frank had used his car phone to let Don know they were turning around, and Don had passed a message through Frank letting Lonnie know that, regretfully, he would not be able to see him until Friday afternoon. *Friday afternoon.* Ben Lowen was supposed to drop in Friday at five-thirty. That didn't leave much time to develop a strategy.

The morning light filled the room—another hot one on the way. Seagulls played against the outline of the city. The buildings in the shadow of the sun looked like stacks of black dominoes. Magnificent creations, all of them, each one a tribute to man's genius. But they were wood, hay and stubble. *Every man's work shall be made manifest: for the day shall declare it, because it shall be revealed by fire; and the fire shall try every man's work of what sort it is.* It was all going to burn—someday. Satan couldn't tempt him with the kingdoms of this world, not when they were destined to become dross. He swiveled his chair around, placing his elbows on the desk as he turned to another Psalm.

The intercom buzzed. He looked at the phone. He didn't want to pick it up. He had arrived before anyone else, and closed his door so they wouldn't know he was in. He didn't want his solitude disturbed. So much for peace—the day had begun. He picked up the phone. It was Nicole.

"Oh, there you are. I've been trying to reach you. Trudy said you'd already left, and I got hold of Frank, but he said he'd already dropped you here. Anyway, we have a situation that needs your attention."

"What's that?"

"Brent asked me not to say. He wants to see you right now. Can I send him in?"

Lonnie rubbed the back of his neck. His skin felt warm from the morning sun, streaming through the window. "Sure, why not."

A few seconds later there was a tap on the door, but it opened before Lonnie could react. Nicole stuck her head in. "Morning, Lonnie. I have Brent."

The door opened wider and Brent squeezed through, shutting the door quickly behind him. He leaned with his back against the wood and his hands still on the knob. He had a harried look about him, like he hadn't been getting much sleep. His eyes were red and his hair frazzled.

"Sorry to bust in on you like this, but it's an emergency."

"That's okay. What's the problem?"

"The problem is, today's payday." Brent let go of the door and rubbed his palms together. He reached up and twiddled the tuft of hair sticking out of his collar.

"So?"

"So, apparently we're broke," he said. "Every Thursday our employees are supposed to have their paychecks deposited into their accounts, but today it didn't happen. I called the bank to see what was going on and was told they've suspended our line of credit. We've been borrowing to cover our payroll, but apparently we've reached our limit."

"Doesn't sound like a big problem. Tell them we're only a few weeks away from releasing a new film. We just need them to extend our credit till then."

"No go, boss. They're not playing ball. Not this time. Normally I think they'd do it, but someone's pulling strings at the top. The loan officer's a friend of mine. He said he received a memo telling him to put a hold on our account until our debt is paid."

"Can you go over his head? Go plead our case to someone in the main office."

"The memo came from the president of the bank!"

"Ouch!"

Brent was still standing. The urgency of the situation demanded he be ready for action. He shifted his weight from one foot to the other. "What I'm hoping is, you said you have money. Can you pull together enough to cover our payroll? I need to assure our employees they'll be paid. Otherwise, there'll probably be a riot."

Lonnie shook his head. All his money was tied up in the hospital, but that was none of Brent's business. "I'm afraid my assets aren't liquid. There must be something we can do. Let's get Michael and Les in here and brainstorm."

Lonnie picked up his phone and punched in Michael's extension, but the line was busy. He tried Les, but there was no answer. "Just a second. I'll have Nicole round them up."

Lonnie went to the door and found Les on the other side. Nicole was away from her desk.

"Oh, good, you're here. I wanted to see you," Lonnie said.

"Brent tell you about our little problem?" Les asked, looking past Lonnie.

"Yes, and we need to talk. Wait in my office. I'll grab Michael and we'll see what we can do."

LONNIE HURRIED down the hall passing cubicles, some empty and some with gatherings of three or more persons. Everyone seemed to be involved in a discussion of some kind, but it couldn't have been about the work they were supposed to be doing because they all stopped talking until Lonnie passed by. They were sharing secrets they didn't want him to hear. That much was obvious. He'd been there almost two weeks and still hadn't found an opportunity to introduce himself. There wasn't much point in doing it now—maybe after the battle—if he survived! The eyes followed him. He could feel their unasked questions piercing his back.

He stopped outside Michael's office. The door was closed all but a crack. He started to knock, but pulled back, inhaling slowly. He placed his hand over his heart, feeling the *thump, thump, thump* as he leaned in closer.

"Yes, sir. We're right on track. How did you get the bank to cancel our credit?...Is that right? Well, it's just as you said. The production house called Les this morning. They've halted work on the final edit. There's no way the film will be finished by tomorrow. Yes, that, too. The employees are ready to walk. When you waltz in offering to save their jobs, you'll be a hero. No, Mr. Striker hasn't come in yet, but he's in for a surprise soon as he arrives. Yes, sir. I had lunch with Barry yesterday. Gladdon, Vickers and Cox are ready to march. They'll deliver notice for Mr. Striker to evict the premises at the close of the business day tomorrow. Oh, I didn't know you planned to be here. Fine, I look forward to seeing you then. Yes. All right. Good-bye, Mr. Lowen."

Lonnie placed his knuckle against the door and eased it open. He was glad to see Michael was sitting. He hated the way he felt with Michael towering over him.

Michael looked up. His face paled for a moment, but the color returned quickly. "Good morning, Mr. Striker. I didn't see you come in."

Lonnie shook his head. "Et tu, Brute?"

"What does that mean?"

"Don't play dumb, Michael. It's beneath you. Just pick up your briefcase and go."

"Are you asking me to leave?"

"Don't worry about the rest of your things. We'll ship them to your home. I'll need your key." Lonnie held out his hand, palm up.

Michael stood and snapped the hasps of his burgundy leather briefcase. He reached into his pocket and removed his keys, slipping one from the ring and tossing it on the desk. "Eavesdropping on a private conversation might be grounds for wrongful dismissal," he said, "but you have bigger things to worry about than that. Please, don't bother shipping anything. Just leave everything where it is. I'll be back tomorrow, and you'll be the one saying good-bye."

Michael squeezed by Lonnie and walked toward the door, but stopped a few feet short. He turned, holding his briefcase in front of him. "Harlan never mentioned having a brother. I've been trying to figure out why. Want to hear my theory? It goes something like this. Everyone knows Buddy liked to fool around. He could have fathered many children. Which leads me to question whether you're a legitimate heir." He stood there, tall and imposing, shaking his head. When Lonnie refused to dignify the comment with a response, Michael reached for the door and made a self-assured, leisurely exit.

LONNIE PLODDED down the hall. His stomach gurgled. He pressed it with his hand. It felt full of acid, like he was wired on caffeine—though he hadn't had his morning coffee. It didn't matter that Michael's theory wasn't true. What mattered was what people thought. If Michael believed he was Harlan's *half* brother, and therefore not entitled to the inheritance, how many others? The same piercing eyes stabbed him as he passed by cubicles and work stations. He feigned not to notice, but he could feel the blows.

Nicole was at her desk. She slipped a sheaf of paper into a folder, closed it, and slid it into her drawer.

Lonnie paused. "I want to apologize."

Nicole looked up. "What for?"

"A few days ago I found out someone was feeding information to Mr. Lowen. I thought it might be you. I know now that it wasn't. I think I hurt your feelings. I'm sorry."

Nicole reached for the vase of yellow daffodils and moved it to the side. She blinked a few times and found a pen. Then she opened her drawer and put the pen away, avoiding eye contact. "Apology accepted," she said, fiddling around for something in the drawer.

Lonnie nodded and stepped back. *Why would she get misty over that?* "Could you join us in my office? You need to hear what I'm about to say."

Nicole removed a tissue. "Darn allergies," she said, dabbing her eyes. She scooted back and got up to follow.

Brent and Les were already seated on the couch. Lonnie took the chairs in front of his desk and turned them so he and Nicole could face the others. They sat down. Lonnie shared what happened in Michael's office, and watched for any telltale signs of collusion. Les fidgeted and squirmed in his seat. Lonnie could see he wanted a cigarette and wanted it bad. Brent gave a light grunt and scratched his fuzzy head. His lips were twisted. He looked like he'd been sipping castor oil.

"The bottom line is, Ben Lowen thinks he's about to come in here and take over the company. I imagine your jobs are secure, all three of you, but I can't say that with certainty. I'm not ready to give up, not just yet, but I want you to know what we're up against. I'm asking each of you to choose which side you're on. I already know where Michael stands, and I've asked him to leave. If you're with him on this, you might as well go, too. Otherwise, you're welcome to stay."

Brent eyed the arm of the couch, idly pinching its smooth leather. "For the record, I didn't know what Michael was up to," he said, looking back at Lonnie. "He's a lawyer so a lot of what he does is confidential. Nonetheless, if I have to choose sides, I'm going with him. Sorry. It's nothing personal, but you haven't got a chance. You're broke, your film isn't finished, and if Michael has gone over, it's because he knows Mr. Lowen's case is iron-clad." He looked at his watch and pulled himself up. "If we leave now, we can catch him in the parking garage. You coming, Les?"

Les just sat there, looking like he was hiding a volleyball beneath his red Hawaiian shirt. He patted his pocket, feeling for his cigarettes, but gave up. "Naw, I think I'll stick around and enjoy the fun."

Lonnie raised an eyebrow, but Les continued to address Brent. "Michael hates my guts. You know that. He'd a got rid of me a long time ago if it weren't for Harlan. Besides, I like Quentin. The kid deserves a break, considering what he's been through and all. I owe it to him and Harlan to try and keep Striker Films alive."

Brent shrugged and reached around to scratch the back of his neck. "Suit yourself, it's your funeral." He made his exit without looking back.

Les waited until Brent was out of earshot, and then turned to Lonnie. "He's right, you know. We haven't got a chance. But if by some miracle you do pull it off, I'm trusting you won't fire me first chance you get."

Lonnie shook his head, mystified. He'd figured Les for the first to leave. "No. Of course not. I won't even be here. I plan to let Quentin run things. As long as you get along with him, you'll do fine." Then he turned his attention to Nicole. "What about you?"

Nicole nodded, her ponytail bobbing up and down. "I'm with you."

Lonnie didn't know what to make of his new downsized team. His faith had been restored in Nicole, but Les? The only important thing was what God thought, and one thing Lonnie knew was that God was not a respecter of persons. While man was busy judging the outside, God was searching the hidden things of the heart.

LONNIE TRUDGED down the hall with a ten-pound weight on his back. His shoulders ached and his head throbbed. He could feel blood surging against the tight skin of his forehead. He'd asked Nicole to assemble the employees so he could explain the situation. She'd put out the word and, though there were fewer than thirty, the boardroom was packed.

Someone had closed the blinds, probably in an effort to block the sun, but it had the effect of making the room seem even smaller. Lonnie paced back and forth, hoping he didn't look as nervous as he felt. He began by introducing himself and sharing a little about his past.

"*Our* mother," (he emphasized the "*our*" to set the record straight), "recognized our differences. She used to say, 'Harlan, you have to remember that your brother Lonnie, well, you know, he's a little different.' " He looped his index finger around his ear and got a few chuckles, a successful attempt at warming up to his audience. " 'And you have to respect that difference.' Well, what was true then, is still true today. Harlan made this company what it is. I give him full credit for that. But I'm not my brother, and since he saw fit to leave the company in my hands, it's reasonable to expect I'll do things differently."

Lonnie went on to share his vision of the new Striker Films. The change of direction was to the benefit of everyone, he assured them, quoting facts and figures to support his case. He gave Rolly credit for supplying the information upon which he'd based his decision and went over the numbers again, showing how R-rated movies generally targeted small niche markets where family films had broader market appeal. The numbers didn't lie. Producing family films would help make the company stronger both morally and financially. Rolly stood in the corner at the back of the room and blushed at the mention of his name, but no one turned to acknowledge him. Les sat in one of the leather chairs toward the front, lighting one cigarette after the other, but remained quiet. Nicole just stood there looking composed and...*what? Intriguing?*

"The problem is I can't afford to pay you, at least not until we're able to arrange additional financing. If you leave now, I'll understand, but the door only swings one way. Once you walk out, you're effectively handing in your resignation. If you change your mind, I won't promise you'll be automatically rehired. We'll interview and select the best person for the position. Conversely, if you stay and I end up losing the company, which is a possibility, I can't promise the new owners will keep you on. The only thing I can promise is that if I win, those of you who stick with me will be rewarded. Not only will you receive any back pay you're owed, but I plan to see that everyone gets a little extra for their effort."

A hand went up in the back.

"Yes."

"How much?"

"That depends on how well the film does. I'm hoping we'll be able to give everyone who sticks around a two thousand dollar bonus. I can't promise it, but I'll do my best. So that you all know where we stand, I'm going to authorize accounting to open our books to all employees. I want you to be able to see for yourselves how well we're doing. And I promise I won't take a dime for myself until the bonus is paid to each of you. Some of you may have heard I'm trying to build a hospital. It's true, so I really need the money, but I'll make sure each of you gets paid first. If we can arrange the financing we need, I'm confident we'll succeed. I believe we have a dynamite script and some terrific actors. And like I said, films that can be seen by the whole family usually do well at the box office. I know we'll do better than we would if we released the current version of the film. I sat down and watched it last week and I can tell you it was pretty bad. I think Michael and Brent would have concurred but, sad to say, they elected to leave. Les, on the other hand, has decided to stay. Les, why don't you share your thoughts with the group? Go ahead and speak freely."

Les shuffled in his seat, scratching his tummy. He took a long slow draw on his cigarette, and stuck out his lower lip to release the smoke into the air. "Look, you all know me," he said. "I've been critical of Mr. Striker since he first walked in here, and I won't go as far as to say I've changed my mind, at least not completely. But I can say we agree on this: *Lost Cause* was a lost cause. Even Brent and Michael thought so. It was destined to end up in the video store alone on the shelf, a one-copy wonder. And we probably would have lost our shirts. At least this way we got ourselves a chance."

Lonnie leaned against the wall. His cheeks puffed as he exhaled, relaxing for the first time since he'd entered the room. "Thanks, Les. Well, that's about it. That's all I have to say. Those of you willing to work with me, please stay behind. The rest of you are excused."

It was a great disappointment to watch as people began filing out, but what did he expect? A bearded man with long hair, standing closest to the door, was first to go. He had the advantage of ducking out without being obtrusive, though Lonnie knew who he was. It was Jeremy Jones, the casting director. He was followed by others. One by one they left until the room was almost empty. Lonnie was pleased to see that Rolly had remained and about a half-dozen others, including two Chinese girls who had worked for Brent in accounting, but clearly two-thirds had decided to abandon the ship before it went down. Les sat smoking like a chimney. His face was red. He clamped his fingers around his cigarette, and pulled it from his mouth. His purple lips broke into a smile. "Hey, we started the company with fewer than this!" he said. It was the most encouraging thing Lonnie had heard all day.

The phone began ringing as the remaining faithful left the room. Nicole picked it up. "Just a second. Lonnie, it's for you. I think you'd better take it."

Lonnie put the receiver to his ear and recognized the voice of Allison.

"We have a bit of a problem over here," she began. "Lance and I have been waiting all morning, but no one has shown up. We thought maybe they were shooting on location and forgot to tell us, but Lance checked around and found out the crew is refusing to work until they get paid what they're already owed. There's a rumor going 'round that we've gone bust."

Lonnie stepped back and sank into a chair, rubbing his forehead. "You're kidding! Man-oh-man. Listen, don't worry. It's not your problem. I'll have Les look into it. You have a number where you can be reached?"

"We're in Rusty's trailer. Have 'em ring it through here. We'll pick up. We're the only ones around."

Lonnie set the phone back in its cradle.

"What's up, Chief?"

"Apparently, Rusty and the rest of the film crew walked off the job. They're refusing to work until they get paid."

Les was out of his seat in a heartbeat. "Whaaaaa? No way?" He reached across the table for the phone and started to dial, but then slammed the phone down again. "We have to go out there. Nobody walks off the job in the middle of a movie. Not if they ever want to work for me again!"

ALLISON PUT the phone down and frowned. Quentin and Lance sat, subdued in the shadows, but no one reached to turn on the lights. The air conditioner hummed in the background.

Quentin leaned forward in his wheelchair. "What did he say?"

"He played it down. Said he'd look into it and call us back. I don't want to be the bearer of bad news, but this may be the end of the project. When I was hired, Mr. Striker warned me they may not have enough money to finish what they started. I just didn't think it would happen so soon."

"Seems a shame," Lance put in. "I went over the script again last night. I think it has real potential. And I was looking forward to working with you, Allison. I mean that."

Allison smiled.

Quentin nodded, affirming his agreement. "What bugs me, is I'm probably the one responsible."

Allison raised her eyebrows. "How's that?"

"Management got together and decided to oppose my uncle. I helped them stall this project in favor of completing my dad's version of the script."

"You did what?"

Quentin started to rock his chair back and forth, but in their confined quarters, there wasn't room. "Well, I didn't know it was my script you were using. My uncle wanted to take over my father's company. I felt I had to stop him. The man's a missionary, for crying out loud! You think he wants to make movies? Think again. He wants to save the world." He raised his hands and waved them in the air like a minstrel. "Hallelujah, brothers, sisters, all God's chillen has got to get religion!" Quentin gripped the arms of his chair. "He doesn't belong here. I'm betting he'd trash the company if he thought he could save us from going to hell!"

Lance shook his head. "I can't believe it. You were working against your own uncle? What happened to blood's thicker than water?"

"Hey. It's not just that. This has always been a family business, handed down from father to son. *I'm* supposed to be running the company, not *him*!"

Allison raised her eyebrows. "I think you and your uncle need to sit down and talk. There seems to be some confusion about what he's doing here, though you're right about one thing; your uncle doesn't want anything to do with this business. He just wants to be a missionary. He hates it here. He can't wait to get back to Mexico."

Quentin rolled his eyes, and tried rocking his chair back and forth, but once again was stymied by the lack of space. "Ohhhh, I'm so glad you cleared that up. I guess that explains why he's still here."

"What *is* your trip? You could be a really nice guy, but sometimes you act like such a jerk! For your information, your father wrote your uncle a letter, *begging* him to get the company out of debt. He's doing what he's doing for you. As soon as the company's back on its feet, he plans to leave it in your hands. He was hoping it would be after the completion of this film, but I guess it's a little late for that now." Allison reached over and yanked the news clipping off the bulletin board. She handed it to Quentin. Striker On Verge Of Collapse, it read. Allison hopped off the counter and stretched. "We might as well pack it in and go home. Can't say it wasn't fun while it lasted."

THE WINDOW was down, letting hot, sultry air into the limousine. Lonnie gritted his teeth and allowed it so Les could smoke. They were en route to the studio. The air conditioner was working overtime, but in spite its efforts to keep the car cool, Les's face was a deeper shade of red than usual. He flicked ashes out the window, examined the butt of his cigarette, pulled another from his pocket, lit the new one off the tip of the old, and flicked the old one into the street. To say he was steaming was an understatement.

Off to his left Lonnie could see the park coming into view—the same park he'd seen yesterday, the same palm trees swaying in the breeze, the same grey cinder-block restroom, and yes, the same aqua-blue pit with the same sun-tanned children running and splashing and diving...He closed his eyes and leaned back into the soft leather cushion, but even with his eyes closed, the unwelcome memory encroached.

Harlan took a bounce and launched himself into the air, bringing his hands down to touch his pointed toes in a perfect jackknife before straightening and entering the water with scarcely more than a ripple. Lonnie sat on the cement with Trudy. She smiled, tossing her auburn tresses, and put her hands together in silent applause.

Lonnie stared at the board. It was still vibrating from Harlan's dive—thuddd twaaaangggg. A week earlier he'd convinced himself to try it, but he'd chickened out. Why? What could possibly be so hard? He knew how to swim. It was only water. Falling into it wouldn't kill him. He watched the person behind Harlan jump off the board. No fancy dive, he just put his arms and legs together and went in feet first, straight as a rod. See? Nothing to it.

Lonnie glanced over at Trudy, who was resting on a towel. Her head was propped up on one arm with her legs curled behind. She had to know. Harlan wouldn't have let it pass. "Ha, ha, ha, big joke. Ha ha, you should have seen him up there, crawling backward, the little sissy."

Lonnie got to his feet. He feared Trudy might say something, but she didn't. She was too busy watching Harlan swim to the side of the pool. Lonnie headed for the high dive. He was going to do it. If he made it to the board and up that first step, there would be no backing out. Someone would be on the ladder behind him, and he wouldn't be able to crawl around them to get down. Besides, Trudy would be watching. Only a baby would chicken out in front of a girl.

He came to within a few feet of the high dive and stopped. The steps were broad, the chrome handles sparkling in the light. He looked over his shoulder. Harlan was hanging on to the edge of the pool, talking to Trudy. It was better that way. He wanted to be able to say he'd done it—that was important—but it wasn't important that they watch. He might not look so graceful on the way down.

He took hold of the chrome rail and paused for a minute closing his eyes. When he opened them, Harlan was hoisting himself out of the pool, dripping water onto the hot, dry cement and all over Trudy! She threw up her hands and twisted away laughing. It was now or never. Lonnie pulled himself up the first rung, and the next, and the next, and the next. So far so good, just another few feet. Come on. Just take a deep breath, and step out onto the board. He looked straight ahead, surprised he'd come this far...but then looked down and felt dizzy. Trembling, he took a step forward, hesitantly, inching out farther and farther, the sandpaper surface scuffing his feet. Suddenly, he was there! He'd made it! All he had to do was jump. He felt the structure begin to shudder with the thud, thud, thud of heavy footsteps. Someone was climbing the ladder behind him. He closed his eyes and took a breath—don't look down! Just open your eyes and jump. Do it! Do it!

It was no use. There were miles and miles between him and that solid blue surface. He would hit the water and splat like a bug on a windshield. He had to get his skinny little body off the board and his feet back on solid ground. He turned to make his retreat, but as he did, Harlan stepped onto the board. For a moment they stood face to face.

"There's only one way down from here, Spud," he heard Harlan say. He looked down again. It was the last thing he remembered before blacking out.

The next thing he knew, he was in the water sinking down, down, down toward the bottom of the dark blue abyss. His eyes were open, but he was paralyzed. He tried to use his arms but they were frozen. He'd had the wind knocked out of him. He'd hit the water on his side—splat—just like a bug! He was starved for air, still sinking, and he couldn't move. He had an unusual thought: At least he wouldn't have to face Trudy. He was going to die.

Then he felt an embrace and a strong sense of comfort enveloped him, like a baby resting in the security of his mother's womb. Lonnie could see the thin veneer of the surface floating above him, smooth and clear as liquid plastic, and then he was breaking through—birthed, into the clear, clean atmosphere of heaven. He opened his mouth but, like an infant unable to draw breath without being spanked, he couldn't take in air. "Someone get the lifeguard!" he heard Harlan scream.

THE LIMOUSINE pulled into a deserted parking lot. Only yesterday this place had bustled with activity. The trailers were still there, but other than that, there was nothing to identify this as the set of a major motion picture. The cameras, the lights, the facade, the people, all were gone—as if they'd vanished into thin air. Les stepped out and stormed off in the direction of Rusty Monahan's trailer. He tried to open it, but found it locked. He took his key, opened the door, and stuck his head inside. "There's no one here," he called over his shoulder to Lonnie. He pounded down the aluminum steps. "You wait here. I'm gonna see what the...I'm gonna see what's going on." Les trundled off, smoking like a steam locomotive.

Lonnie opened the car door and pulled himself out. A thick hazy layer of clouds blanketed the sky and the hot sun soaking through the vapor created intense humidity. It was like being under a wet sponge. He kicked a pebble off the asphalt. And then another. The second hit the side of a trailer with a *ping.* Lonnie stumbled toward an empty set of risers. The moisture under his shirt began to roll down his chest. He sat down and buried his head in his hands. *No actors, no crew, no money, no company, no hospital—and no Trudy! Why, Lord? Why?*

TWENTY

THE SUN was hanging low over the ocean by the time Lonnie arrived back at the house. He climbed out of the limo, his Bible in hand, looking west toward the scarlet horizon. The sun's sultry orb looked tropical, like a slice of pink grapefruit. Though he wouldn't have thought it possible, the mansion, basking in the sun's rosy glow, appeared even pinker. Lonnie stretched, arched his back, and pushed his palm into the soft fleshy spot above his hip where it ached. Now he knew what carrying the weight of the world on his shoulders felt like.

He almost wished he'd never received Trudy's letter calling him home...*almost.*

He'd sat under the oppressive sun for over an hour, waiting for Les to return. The limo was parked nearby with its air conditioner running, but he'd refused to move. He'd stayed outside on the bleachers, soaking in perspiration, as though his self-inflicted discomfort might appease God. He didn't have to hear the news from Les to know it was bad.

Les stomped up, huffing and puffing, and dropped his weight onto the aluminum risers. The redness of his face and the flare of his nostrils told the story. Rusty and the crew had already found other projects to work on. They had no interest in resuming their relationship with Striker Films, whether the company survived or not. Les had threatened to sue for breach of contract, but Rusty brought up several unpaid invoices. A few were more than sixty days overdue. He also reminded Les that his contract called for payment net thirty.

The breach of contract, he said, was Striker's.

Lonnie could see now, that his returning had made no difference at all. Don could find a hole in the Striker/Lowen agreement big enough to fly a plane through, and it wouldn't change a thing. Lonnie didn't have the money or resources needed to get the project done—not now—not *ever!* At least in hindsight he could see where he'd made his mistake. He'd thought it was about doing what was right. He'd stood on principle. But he could see now it wasn't about principle, it was about control. Making the right—or wrong—kind of movie had little to do with it. If he'd tried to complete Harlan's version of the film, he still would have failed. The bank would have cut their line of credit, the production house would have refused to complete the edit on time, and the film crew would have walked. They were doomed to fail from the start.

Mr. Lowen had done an admirable job. He'd made sure everything worked in his favor, and so far as Lonnie could tell, had done it legally, so he had impunity. Obviously Lowen had friends in high places. Well, so did Lonnie. The only problem was, God didn't seem anxious to come to Lonnie's defense. He should have stayed in Posada.

His feet were dragging as he took hold of the wrought-iron handrail and pulled himself up the steps. Too bad he wouldn't be able to finish Quentin's film. It would have been a boost to the boy's self-confidence, and it would have set the company on the right track. Now he faced the dismal prospect of explaining his failure. He reached for the knob and pushed on the thick wood door—*crrrraaaack!* He entered the vestibule with his Bible under his arm, pausing to look into the eyes of the canvas effigy. "Sorry, Harlan, when you make a pact with the devil, there's hell to pay, which I'm sure you've learned by now. But why drag everyone else down with you? At least you could have..."

"Who are you talking to?"

Lonnie flinched, startled by Trudy's voice. He turned, reaching to rub the sore spot at the back of his neck. It had been fun, in a sadistic sort of way. Here he was giving Harlan lip, and he wasn't the least bit afraid—but then, Harlan was dead. The portrait was just an image on the wall. "No one. Well, actually I was letting Harlan know how things are going."

"And how are things?"

Lonnie grimaced, then he straightened himself and began walking with Trudy toward the back of the house. "Not so good."

"I can see you've had a hard day." Trudy took Lonnie's arm. "Don't worry about it. You're home now. Relax. I had the cook save you some dinner. It's in the oven."

Lonnie pulled away long enough to place his Bible on the stairs, and then joined Trudy again.

"Been out preaching?" she asked.

"Nope. It's my security blanket. I like to crawl inside when things get rough. Kind of gives me a warm, cozy feeling, like getting a friendly hug when I need it."

"Ahhh."

Under the warm light of the chandelier, Trudy looked fresh and alluring in her crisp, white blouse. He could almost see the outline of her figure through the smooth fabric. He wanted to bring her in close so he could feel the warmth of her body. Their eyes met for a moment, but broke away quickly. He took her hand as they resumed strolling toward the kitchen.

"I thought maybe after you eat we could sit down and watch a movie together. I have the home theater all set up. We can turn down the lights, make some popcorn, you know, spend an old-fashioned evening at home."

Lonnie felt his stomach tighten. He needed to tell her. He couldn't sit around watching TV pretending life was just hunky-dory, when they were on the verge of losing everything. He should probably tell them both. "Where's Quentin?"

"He called to say he wouldn't be home. We're all alone tonight." Trudy brought her free hand up to squeeze Lonnie's arm. "It's just you and me, kid."

"But how...I mean, how does Quentin get around when I have the car?"

Trudy let go of Lonnie and turned to face him. "We use a

limousine service, silly. He just calls, and they send another driver around to pick him up."

The late evening sun, pouring through the windows, had painted the kitchen a bright magenta. Lonnie felt its warmth erasing his worry-lines, and washing the gray shadows from beneath his eyes. He'd almost blown it. He would have warned Trudy and Quentin about what was coming, just to get a load off his chest, but Harlan had asked him to keep it quiet. It was a request he still wanted to honor. Tomorrow, when the dust settled, they would be able to see for themselves.

Trudy grabbed a potholder, opened the oven, and withdrew some kind of noodly white casserole. She went to the refrigerator and removed a tall carafe. "Water all right with you?"

Lonnie nodded. "Sure, that's fine."

Trudy pulled two glasses from the cupboard and filled them both, but she put the pasta on only one plate.

"You're not eating?"

"I didn't know when you'd be home, so I went ahead and had my dinner. It's after eight, you know."

Lonnie pulled a stool up to the counter. "Don't go to any trouble. Just give me a fork and I'll eat right here."

Trudy passed Lonnie a napkin. She took a sip of water and leaned on the counter to watch.

"And you're not drinking?" Lonnie observed.

"Sure I am." Trudy held up her glass. "What do you think *this* is?"

"You know what I mean."

"Lonnie!"

Lonnie stared at his plate, and then took another cheesy bite. Quite tasty. If the company failed and Trudy had to sell the house, she'd probably lose her cook. "Sorry. I know it's none of my business," he said, "but if you ever *do* think about getting help...you know, if your drinking ever does become a problem, I'd like..."

"Listen, Lonnie, the past few days have been hard on me. You've seen me at my worst. I'm not usually like that. And I don't need help. I drink because I enjoy it, not because I have to. It's just a way to relax."

Lonnie was scraping the dish. "My compliments to the chef. That was delicious." He put down his fork and patted his stomach. "You don't get cookin' like that where I come from. Tell you what..." He eyed Trudy dubiously. "Since you don't have a problem, let's declare tonight an alcohol-free night."

"You missed the point. I said I don't *have* to drink. I didn't say I don't *want* to. I would enjoy a glass of wine right now. I don't like being uptight. Alcohol loosens me up. It helps me unwind. What's the harm in that?" Trudy stepped up to Lonnie's chair. She took his hands and placed them around her waist, pulling him in close, until his head was resting on the starchy crispness of her blouse. He could smell the fragrance of the lilac soap she'd used that afternoon. His blood was surging through his veins. The bell was ringing in his head—*danger, danger, danger.*

"Hummm, nice," he murmured. "I could fall asleep right here. Would you mind terribly if I took a rain check on the movie? I have a headache, and I'm exhausted. I need some rest."

Trudy let go and stood back. "Lonnie Striker! If it's that big a deal, fine, I won't drink, just to prove I don't have to!"

"No, it's not that. It's just tha..."

"What? Me? I swear I don't understand you at all. One minute you're looking at me like...oh, you know, but when I open up, you high-tail it and run. What is it with you?"

"That's the problem. You *don't* understand. It's not about you, Trudy." Lonnie reached for her hand, but she jerked it back. His smile faded. He knew he'd hurt her feelings, but though he'd welcomed her display of affection, he couldn't reciprocate, at least not yet. "There's a time and place for everything, and now's not the time," he said. "Please don't ask me to explain. I can't...I...you'll just have to trust me. Everything will become clear tomorrow. Then, if you still want to, we can talk—about us, about the future, about anything you want—but until then, please don't ask. There's nothing more I can say."

"Now you're being obtuse. Fine. Go to bed. I'll stay down here all alone. But I still won't drink, just to prove my point. I won't touch a drop. Go on now. Get out of here. What are you waiting for? Go!"

Lonnie rose to his feet and stood for a moment. He regretted ending the evening this way. "Good night, Trudy." He leaned forward to kiss her on the cheek, but she pulled away.

She didn't say anything as he made his way up the stairs. She waited until he'd rounded the corner at the top, and then went to the cupboard. She removed a bottle. The glass was smooth and cool in her hand. She unscrewed the cap and brought the bottle to her lips. The liquid was clear as water. She could see right through it, though it distorted what she saw. This was *her* security blanket, something she liked to crawl into. She tipped her head back and began to drink, accepting its warm embrace.

LONNIE LAY awake, staring at the ceiling. He'd slept fitfully for a few hours, right after going to bed, but now he found sleep impossible. He looked at the digital clock. Two fifty-four. Almost three in the morning, and he was still tossing and turning. He brought his arm up to cover his eyes.

He had failed. He'd run out of time, and he'd run out of options. Lowen was about to walk in and jerk the company right out from under him, proving what Harlan had always known—*he was a failure!* And it wasn't even his fault. There was nothing he could do—*nothing!* But that's not how everyone else would see it. They'd pass the buck right on up to the top.

He wasn't worried about losing the company. He didn't care about the company. What he cared about was Trudy, but without the company she'd see him for what he was—*a failure!* She'd pack her bags and walk. No, she wouldn't just *walk,* she'd hate him for the rest of her life. Quentin would accuse him of placing more value on his morals than on his family. He'd try to explain, but the boy, like all human beings, would believe what he *wanted* to believe. The sky outside was overcast, but the moon could be seen shining through a crack in the clouds. He pulled the pillow over his head to block the moon's dismal light.

Lonnie reached over and pulled the chain of the lamp beside his bed. The room flooded with light. He raised his hand, squinting as he reached for his old King James Bible. The leather was worn and had patches where the dye had been rubbed off, and the edges along the spine were split and broken, but it was the Bible he'd been raised on, a gift from his mother, and he refused to let it go. He sank his thumb into the glittering gold pages, pulling the book open. His eyes fell on Ecclesiastes, 9:11.

> I returned, and saw under the sun, that the race is not to the swift, nor the battle to the strong, neither yet bread to the wise, nor yet riches to men of understanding, nor yet favor to men of skill; but time and chance happens to them all. For man also knows not his time: as the fishes that are taken in a net, and as the birds that are caught in a snare; so are the sons of men snared in an evil time, when it falls suddenly upon them.

Great! He tossed the covers aside, dropped the Bible on the bed, and went to the window. The moon looked like chips of white porcelain shimmering on the surface of the pool. Lonnie turned around and went to his closet, flicking on the light. He scooted the hangers back and forth, looking through his clothes. Trudy hadn't left him anything suitable for wearing on the beach. A sport shirt and slacks would have to do.

He got dressed slowly, sitting on the bed to pull his pants on, but it was exhausting, and when he stood to button his shirt, his fingers hurt. He grabbed his Bible and made his way slowly down the half circle staircase. The light from the TV was glowing in the den. Lonnie paused, taking a minute to rest, then went in to turn off the set.

Trudy was sprawled on the couch. An empty bottle of vodka was sitting on the coffee table. His arms were too tired to carry her up the stairs, or even help her to the elevator. He took the bottle into the kitchen, set it on the counter, and continued on to the sunroom. He removed the tablecloth from the table and took it back into the den, spreading it over Trudy. She groaned and moved, snuggling under her newfound blanket, but she didn't wake up. At least *she* could sleep. Lonnie turned off the TV, and the room went black.

He felt his way back to the atrium where he turned left, heading for the patio doors. At the wall he found a light switch. *Good!* The lights used to illuminate the stairs to the beach also lit up the yard. He flicked it on, hoping they were bright enough to read by. He picked his way down the path, his shirt flapping in the ocean's breeze. He stood at the top of the stairs and opened his Bible, but the wind whipped the pages out of control. It wasn't going to work. He started down the steps in hopes of finding shelter. The clouds gathered, covering the moon, and the sky grew dark. He climbed onto the rock shelf that formed a breakwater, and made his way down along the sandy shore. The roar of the waves was ear-splitting. In the far, far distance he could see lightning sparking over the water, and hear the roll of thunder, rumbling like a bass drum. The wind surged around him. He could feel the salty spray stinging his face—or was that rain?

Craaaack! Rummmmble! Boom. The sky overhead exploded like dynamite, and the windows of heaven opened. All at once Lonnie found himself caught in a shower. He tucked his Bible against his chest and ran along the shore, leaping from rock to rock. He wouldn't make it up the stairs without getting soaked. The sky lit up again. *Rummble! Craaack! Boom!* He ducked under an overhanging rock. It wasn't a cave exactly, but it did provide shelter from the downpour. He'd just have to wait out the storm. *Pow! Craaaaack!* Water gushed down the face of the cliff.

Lonnie's hair was soaked. A drop of water rolled down his cheek and dripped off his chin. He crossed his arms over his Bible and shivered.

"The Lord's our rock, in him we hide, a shelter in the time of storm..." His voice was weak, but he would have continued singing if he could have remembered the words. It seemed appropriate. The waves crashed against the wall and pulled away with a *thud-sucking* sound. A salty white spray shot high into the air. The rain continued pelting the rocks. Lonnie pushed back into the shallow crevise to take advantage of the natural umbrella. For the moment he was out of the wind. He held his Bible by its spine and jiggled it open, keeping his wet hands from touching the pages. The words were in shadow, far below the lights at the top of the steps. There was barely enough light reflecting off the paper to read. The passage was from Job.

> Where were you when I laid the foundations of the earth? Declare, if thou hast understanding. Who hath laid the measures thereof, if thou knowest? Or who hath stretched the line upon it? Whereupon are the foundations thereof fastened? Or who laid the cornerstone thereof...Canst thou lift up thy voice to the clouds, that abundance of waters may cover thee? Canst thou send lightnings, that they may go, and say unto thee, here we are?

Lonnie yielded. *Okay, okay. Point made.*

The sky roared with the voice of a thousand lions. *Roooooarrrr Aruuumble Boom!* Lonnie put his hand over his head and ducked. Lights sparked east to west. The waves crashed against the breakwater, sending a fist of wind against the seawall. The pages of Lonnie's Bible began spinning to the right. When the squall stopped, he was looking at Hannah's prayer in First Samuel.

> He will keep the feet of his saints, and the wicked shall be silent in darkness; for by strength shall no man prevail. The adversaries of the Lord shall be broken to pieces; out of heaven shall he thunder upon them. The Lord shall judge the ends of the earth.

Lonnie could feel a drop of water rolling cold and wet down his back. He closed his Bible and shook his head, spraying the rocks behind him. *Rummble! Craaack! Pow!* He'd received the message loud and clear. Perhaps for now he was at the mercy of Ben Lowen, but in God's time, the man would be judged. It was God's job to deal with the wicked, not his. *Trust in the Lord with all thine heart and lean not on thine own understanding. In all thy ways acknowledge him and He shall direct thy paths.* He just had to remember that. God was still in control. If for whatever reason, God wanted Lowen to have the company, then he should have it. And if not, then all Lowen's efforts to wrest the company away, would be in vain.

The rain eased off. The summer storm departed as quickly as it came. Lonnie could see the neon moon breaking through the clouds. Rays fanned across the water, lighting the crests of the waves. It was a scene right out of Melville's *Billy Budd.*

"At that same moment it chanced that the vapory fleece hanging low in the east, was shot through with a soft glory as of the fleece of the Lamb of God..."

And upon seeing that, young Billy was dropped from the main-yard, an innocent man with a noose around his neck—"God bless Captain Vere!"

And the same to you, Mr. Lowen!

TWENTY-ONE

LONNIE HAD to force himself to go into the office on Friday morning, and even then he didn't make it in until eleven. He was exhausted, partly from lack of sleep, and partly from a general malaise. The smiles greeting him were smiles he felt he didn't deserve, which only increased his anxiety. These were his people, the ones who had stayed. They were the ones he should be concerned about. Push come to shove, he could return to Mexico and resume his ministry, but if things didn't work out, these folks would be out of a job. He shared responsibility for that. He tried to look confident; he felt anything *but.*

He had stayed on the beach praying most of the night. By the time he reached the top of the stairs, heartened by the notion of heading back to bed, the hills could already be seen as dark silhouettes against the purple dawn. He had dropped to his knees in the wet sand, and with the waves breaking around him, had repented of his lack of faith, of the sin of despising his brother, of his fear, and of pretending he was strong enough to work everything out on his own. He watched his sins churning in the current, to be carried away on the tide as far as east is from the west. As for the future, he promised he would leave it in God's hands. Faith, he knew, required accepting the fact that God was at work even when he couldn't see the result.

But as he trudged down the hall he also recognized it was one thing to believe God would work everything out in the sweet by-and-by, but quite another to feel like everything was okay in the here-and-now.

He passed through the corridors, making a spontaneous decision. "Morning, Nicole. You look nice this morning." She was wearing a black dress of sheer cotton with a white flower print. Her blond hair was loose and rolled around her shoulders in smooth flowing waves, and she had a silk apple blossom pinned above her ear. Her eyes were blue and bright.

"Morning, Lonnie." Nicole held out two slips of paper. "You have two messages, one from Don Maniux, of Maniux and Associates—I hope I got the spelling right—and another from Ben Lowen."

Lonnie set his briefcase on Nicole's desk and slipped his newspaper under his arm. He shuffled the notes reading them both. "Either of them say what they wanted?"

"Yes. Let's see. The lawyer said he'd be in around two o'clock. He implied you were expecting him. And Mr. Lowen said to make sure you were here at five. He didn't say why. The lawyer also sent a fax. It's on your desk. It was marked 'Confidential,' so I didn't read it."

Lonnie curled his bottom lip. "Nicole, could you assemble everyone in the boardroom. I have something I want to say, and I should probably tell you and everyone else at the same time. Is Les in?"

"He's here. You want me to call him to your office?"

"No. Just make sure he's in the meeting. About five or ten minutes, okay?"

Lonnie went into his office, the office that had once belonged to his brother and would soon belong to Ben Lowen. He tossed his newspaper on the desk. There had been another in a series of articles written by William Best. This one focused on additional reasons for the shooting at West Valley High. Investigators had gone to the boy's house and in his bedroom found a collection of computer games, all of which had one thing in common: the player was one man against the world, whose assignment was to save himself by blowing up everyone else. It was the very kind of violent behavior exhibited by Malcolm Maynard. The authorities were careful not to assert this as the cause for the boy's behavior, but Mr. Best, God bless him, had taken great pains to establish the connection. Lonnie knew such things influenced people, which was why, in spite of all the evidence to the contrary, he couldn't believe God didn't want him to change the direction of Striker Films. He looked for the fax. It was where Nicole said it would be, lying face down on his desk. He picked it up and began to read.

Attn: Lonnie Striker—Private and Confidential.

I have looked into that loophole we discussed. I received a copy of your parent's divorce papers and it was as I thought: neither you nor Harlan were to sell your portion of the company without the consent of the other. However, Gladdon, Vickers and Cox can argue that Harlan's contract with Lowen Enterprises does not constitute a sale but rather a security or collateral upon which they are now forced to foreclose. Our only recourse is to maintain that Harlan should not have put your property at risk without obtaining your signed authorization. But there's a catch. I thought Gladdon, Vickers and Cox (GVC) knew you were Harlan's silent partner and that they'd somehow overlooked getting your signature on the contract. Upon further investigation, I find this was not the case. Apparently your checks were being channeled through my office long before Harlan retained GVC as legal counsel. Since you had given your brother sole signing authority, your name never surfaced in any subsequent legal discussion. In fact, it appears none of the people involved knew of your existence. Gladdon, Vickers and Cox will counter our argument by pointing to the fact that in twenty years Striker Films has never required your signature on a single document. This establishes precedent. They will say their other client, Lowen Enterprises, believed Harlan was the sole owner of Striker Films, and thus acted in good faith. They may even suggest that you and Harlan cooked up the entire scheme to avoid paying a lawful and binding debt. We can go to court but it'll be expensive, and I'm afraid when all is said and done, the ruling will go in their favor. As your acting legal counsel, I have to advise against taking this course of action.

Sorry to be the bearer of bad news. I wish it could be otherwise.

Regards,

Don

P.S. I will be in this afternoon to discuss your options and, should you choose to capitulate, the best way of handling the forthcoming transition.

Lonnie dropped the sheet of paper onto his desk. He closed his eyes and stood facing the window, barely able to breathe. A lump formed in his throat. He squeezed his burning eyes shut, clenching his jaw so hard he could feel the engorged veins of his neck bulging from his skin. *In all thy ways acknowledge Him and He shall direct thy paths—In all thy ways acknowledge Him and He shall direct thy paths—In all thy ways acknowledge Him and He shall direct thy paths.*

He opened his eyes and took a deep breath, gazing out upon the kingdoms of this world. Thousands of windows stared back at him. Ben Lowen probably stood behind one of those windows. Would he be pointing at Lonnie's office, telling his secretary how he planned to be sitting over there in a few hours? Lonnie tried to relax his fist, rolling his fingers open and closed. He rubbed his eyes, blinking several times to clear his vision. One thing was certain, behind those windows sat powerful men, wheelers and dealers, men focused on the accumulation of wealth. *Store not up for yourselves treasures on earth where moth and rust doth corrupt and thieves break through and steal, but store up for yourselves treasures in heaven...*

What was so alluring about this world's goods that men like Barry, Michael and Ben would, at the risk of their very souls, resort to deceit and duplicity to acquire more? Ben already owned a publishing empire, Barry's name was on a law firm, and Michael drove an eighty-thousand dollar Jag. How much was enough? Silly question. There was never enough. That's why wars were fought. He turned away, looking at the watch that circled his wrist like a handcuff. It was time. He didn't want to keep his people waiting.

LONNIE TOOK a side trip to the men's room to wash the redness from his eyes. His throat felt dry. He leaned over the faucet, and brought a cupped hand of water to his mouth. Then he forcefully dragged himself to the boardroom, hoping no one would notice how pale he looked. Everyone was there, but unlike yesterday, the room seemed almost empty. Les sat at the front. It was hard to tell which was rounder, the lump under his polyester shirt or the knob of his bald shiny head. So far he'd refrained from lighting a cigarette—a considerate gesture—but Lonnie doubted it would last. Rolly stood at the back, nervously shifting his weight from one foot to the other. His eyes were tiny dots and his thinning hair curled over his ears. No one was standing beside him, but then he took up enough space for two. Nicole's expression seemed as serene as the petals of her flower, but of course she didn't need to worry. She got along with everyone, including Michael. Whatever the outcome today, she would probably survive. The two Chinese girls looked like identical porcelain dolls.

"*Ahh-hum*, morning. Sorry to pull you away from your work. I'm sure with so few of us, everyone has plenty to do. But I did promise to keep you apprized of our status and, good, bad or otherwise, I owe you a progress report. Besides, I'd rather you hear it from me than through the grapevine."

Lonnie cut a glance around the room. Rolly had stayed because Lonnie promised to change the genre of the films they produced. The man was counting on him. Les looked relaxed, but in a few hours, he'd be out looking for a job. The fact that he'd made an informed decision, didn't make Lonnie feel any less responsible. And the two Chinese girls were smiling. They had high expectations. How was he going to let them down.

"Let me get right to the point. Yesterday I told you it would be hard for us to overcome the obstacles we faced, but that if we stayed together, we had a fighting chance. Well, unfortunately, we've had a few setbacks since then. It looks like our film crew has decided to walk out on us, and our actors seem to have disappeared. I spoke with them early yesterday, but I haven't been able to reach anyone since. And this is the day we're supposed to hand our creditors a completed film, which we don't have, which gives them the right to foreclose. I hired a lawyer to help us find a way out of this mess, but I just received a fax indicating he hasn't had much success, and time is running out. So the thing is, right now the situation looks pretty bleak."

Lonnie made deliberate eye contact with each person in the room. The two Chinese girls were still smiling. They always seemed to be smiling. He'd just said things looked grim. What was there to smile about? Maybe they weren't fluent in English. Maybe they hadn't understood what he'd said. He grabbed the back of an empty chair and pulled it in, leaning on it for support. "I'd like to get an update from you, Les. Have you had any luck finding anyone to replace Rusty?"

Les narrowed his eyes and grimaced. He gave his head a quick shake, as though he questioned the wisdom of discussing the company's problems openly.

"It's okay, Les. We're all in this together. They have a right to know."

Les pulled the unlit cigarette from his lips. He shrugged. "Word's out on the street that we're going under. I haven't found anyone who'll sign with us yet, but I'll keep trying."

Lonnie let out the breath he'd been holding. The air wheezed out like a sigh. His grip on the back of the chair turned his knuckles white. Before the Lord asked Gideon to march against the Midianites, he cut the size of his army down to three hundred men, while the Midianite troops were so many, they covered the surrounding hills. But Israel had won! Lonnie was down to eight. He hoped he had few enough. He let go of the chair and tried to relax. "I guess that pretty much sums it up. I promised to be open with you about where we stood. The way it looks now, it will take a miracle to pull us out of this one. If you want to leave, I'll understand—no hard feelings. I appreciate your staying with me yesterday, but at least then we had a reasonable chance. Now I have to say we're in God's hands. Not that that's a bad place to be. He still works miracles. But it's up to you. If you want to stay—then stay. If you want to go, please do so now."

Lonnie was surprised when no one moved. What were they waiting for, an engraved invitation?

A hand shot up at the back. It was one of the Chinese twins. "Yes?"

"Do not worry, Mr. 'Ronnie. God say everything be okay. You see. Everything be fine."

Lonnie didn't know what to say to that. He only knew her words raised goosebumps on his arms.

LES PUT the soft pack to his mouth, crinkling the cellophane. When he drew it back, a cigarette was in his lips. He looked up, catching Lonnie's frown. "I know. No smoking in your office. I won't light it." He hadn't lit his cigarette in the boardroom either. *He must be dying for a smoke.* He slid the cigarette pack back into the pocket of his shirt. Today's silky, Hawaiian pink print, sported surfboards, waves, and woodies. He crossed his arms over his paunch, his unlit cigarette bouncing as he spoke.

"You really believe all that 'God's on our side' stuff, don't you?" He sucked the cigarette in and clenched it in his yellow teeth. "You got more faith than I do. If they were giving odds, I'd say God favored the other guys. My mother was a Methodist. Did I ever tell you that? Took me to church every Sunday—not that it stuck. 'Course I was usually out back pitching pennies. Couldn't handle all that hellfire and brimstone."

"Look, Les, I'm sorry things haven't worked out the way we'd hoped. I..."

Lonnie looked up at the sound of someone bumping the wall and saw a wheelchair skirting the corner. Quentin rolled back, straightened himself, and then thrust the chair forward. He was followed by Lance and Allison. All three wore smiles as big as Christmas.

Quentin stopped in front of his uncle's desk, his muscles bulging under the sleeves of his white polo shirt. He cranked the wheels of his chair in opposite directions, rocking it back and forth. There was a film box in his lap. "Hey, Unk, come on down the hall, we got something we want to show you. You too, Les." He whirled about so fast one wheel left the ground. For a second Lonnie thought he was going to spill. Allison and Lance parted to let him through and followed him back out the door without a word.

Lonnie looked at Les, but Les just raised his eyebrows and shrugged. He pulled the cigarette from his mouth and leaned on the arm of the chair, struggling to lift his weight. Lonnie rolled back and stood. Quentin went racing down the hall followed by Allison and Lance. By the time Lonnie and Les reached the door, all three were turning into the boardroom.

"What's going on?" Lonnie asked Les as they marched down the hall.

"Beats me." Les said as he parked his cigarette behind his ear.

When they walked into the boardroom they found it empty, but the door that led into the theater was open and they could see Quentin, Lance and Allison moving around inside.

Quentin spun his chair around. "Come on, we haven't got all day. Better hurry if you want good seats."

Lonnie looked at Les and Les at Lonnie, their heads rattling with questions. They entered and took chairs in the same row, but on opposite sides of the aisle. Lance hopped up into the projection booth and Allison killed the lights. Lonnie heard the *whhirrrrrrrrr* of the projector and suddenly, out of the dark, Allison's face appeared on the screen.

"Welcome, gentlemen. Last night while you were home in bed, Lance, Quentin, and yours truly were out making movies. You're about to see three scenes from *An Uncommon Heart,* written and directed by Quentin Striker. So relax and enjoy. I think you're going to like it. Okay, boys, let her roll." The screen faded to black and opened in the reception area of a doctor's office with Lisa breaking the news of her cancer to her fiancee, Kirk.

Lonnie shook his head. This was the real thing. The set, the sound, the lighting, the camera angles, and more than that—the actors—were first-rate. The action was seamless, one scene flowing into the next in a sequenced stream of dialogue and images. He swallowed the lump in his throat realizing he was now faced with telling these kids that all their hard work was probably for nothing. By five-thirty Ben Lowen would own the company. Maybe if Ben saw these clips, he might decide to remake the film, using Quentin's script. At least that would be some consolation. Lonnie saw Les pull a cigarette from his ear and put it in his mouth but he still didn't light it. Quentin sat, leaning forward in his wheelchair. His fingers were laced and he was twiddling his thumbs. His eyes were locked on the screen, critiquing every splice the way a perfectionist examines his work to find the slightest flaw. The third clip was fading to black and was replaced with another extreme close-up of Allison's freckled face. "There you have it. We hope you enjoyed watching our little feature as much as we enjoyed making it. And now, as the lights come back up, please feel free to tell us what you think."

The real Allison reached for the wall and hit the lights. Lance hopped down from the projection booth and Quentin wheeled himself to the front of the room, where he was joined by Allison and Lance. The three stood there, blocking the screen. "Well?" Allison demanded.

Les pulled the unlit cigarette from his mouth. "Un-freaking-believable! How'd you pull it off?"

Allison was giddy and didn't mind letting it show. Her hands floated like butterflies as she spoke. "Lance has friends. He called in a few favors. I mean he knows practically everybody. He just called a crew together, and we started early yesterday and worked through the night. That's all there was to it. None of us has been to sleep yet." She yawned and stretched, as if to emphasize the fact. "It was so cool. There was like this magic. It was two in the morning when we finished the third scene. Lance looked at his watch and we had to laugh. We thought it was around eleven. The cameraman put the film in the can and we rushed it over to a twenty-four-hour lab. Talk about luck, they jumped us to the front of the line. I mean, how many guys doing shift work have an actor like Lance walk in at three in the morning and ask for a personal favor? 'Course it cost Lance a lot of autographs. I think his hand is still sore, but he was a good sport about it. We had to edit it ourselves, but the lab had the equipment and Quentin handled it like a pro. He spent a couple of summers cutting raw footage for his dad. Everything just went ticketity-boo. We made a final print and, voila! There you have it."

Les shook his head. "And Quentin directed, is that what you said? Unbelievable!" He pulled his bent cigarette from his mouth and pointed its filter at the screen. "I know the work of every director in the biz, and what I saw up there matches the best of the best. Way to rock 'n roll, kid."

"What did you expect? I grew up watching films being made," Quentin cut in. "Besides, I wrote the thing. I already knew what angles I wanted to see. And I knew the kind of emotions Lisa and Kirk should be feeling. I just had to communicate it to Allison and Lance. They were perfect by the way, so hats off to you, Les, and you, too, Uncle Lonnie. Good picks on both counts."

Nicole opened the door and stuck her head in. Her flower seemed symbolic. Spring had arrived at Striker Films. "Sorry to interrupt. Lonnie, there are two men in the lobby waiting to see you."

Lonnie looked at his watch, confused. It wasn't even noon, much too early for Don. Besides, Don would likely be alone, and Lowen wasn't due till five. "Did they give their names?"

"A Mr. Ceylon and a Mr. Ramirez."

Lonnie jerked around. "Here? To see me?"

"Yes. They're waiting in the lobby."

He jumped up and smoothed his slacks, and then slipped the flat of his hand into his waistband to tuck in his shirt. "Excuse me. Can we go back into the boardroom? I don't want to make light of what you've accomplished. This is wonderful, it really is, but I have to see these two. You guys need to discuss how we can use this stuff. I'll join you soon as I can."

Lonnie entered the lobby, still wondering if he'd heard Nicole right. *He had.* There in the middle of the lobby stood the priest and the coffee grower, a thousand miles from parish and plantation. He opened his arms and spread them wide. "Paulo, what in the world are you doing here?" He reached out to embrace his old friend. The smell of the priest's musty brown frock took Lonnie back to Posada. He could have been standing in the market with brown-skinned kids chasing squawking chickens, and burros complaining about the weight of the burlap sacks tied to their backs.

Paulo and Lonnie held each other by the forearms, the looping sleeves of Paulo's robe hanging lower than the rope around his waist. "Ah, Lonnie, my son, let me look at you. You look well, my friend, you look well. And look who I've brought with me." Father Ceylon stepped back and waved his arm outward to include the other gentleman.

Enrico was dressed in a blue business suit complete with white shirt and tie. His skin was lighter than Paulo's. He looked more Spanish than Indian. His hair was short and gray and above his lip was a neat gray mustache.

"Yes, of course, Señor Ramirez, cómo estás?

"Bien, gracias, muy bien."

"Well, what can I say. Come on in, let me show you around." Lonnie held the door and Paulo and Enrico entered. "My office is just to the right." More than one head turned as they moved down the hall. People craned their necks to see Father Ceylon's vestments. The man looked like he was in costume, perhaps an actor playing the part of Junipero Serra, founder of the California missions, though it wasn't in their current movie. They stopped at Nicole's desk.

"Father Ceylon, Señor Ramirez, this is my right hand, also known as my executive assistant, Nicole Carter. Nicole this is Father Paulo Ceylon and Señor Enrico Ramirez. Enrico owns a coffee plantation just outside my home town of Posada." Lonnie turned to Enrico and winked. "I should tell you, every time she brings me a cup of coffee, I think of you. American coffee tastes like warm water with coffee flavoring."

Nicole smiled. "I've doubled the strength of his coffee, and he still doesn't think it's strong enough."

Enrico took Nicole's hand and kissed her fingers. "Ah Señorita, you are as lovely as the flower in your hair. I will tell you the secret," he said, letting go of her hand so he could rub his thumb and index finger together. "Mince a few jalapeno peppers in with the grounds and he no more complain."

Nicole started to laugh but choked it back when she saw Enrico looked serious.

The trio went into Lonnie's office. Lonnie offered his guests seats on the couch and turned a chair toward them. "So tell me, to what do I owe the pleasure? Not that I don't welcome your visit, but it can't be because you miss me. I was just home on the weekend."

Father Ceylon smiled and looked at Señor Ramirez. "Yes, but after you left Enrico encountered a little problem." He paused and waited, letting the suspense build.

"Yes, go ahead. Is there something I can help you with?"

"No, on the contrary we came to help you. Our gringo friend is obviously lost. Why don't you explain it to him, Enrico?"

Enrico smiled and began nodding. His mustache turned up and crow's feet gathered at the corners of his eyes. "Si. The problem began Tuesday. The bus from Posada, it came with my workers, just as always, but I saw their faces were long like the horse. Right away I could see something was wrong, but this I decided to ignore. Wednesday production was down and some of my best workers were falling behind their quotas. When I asked what the trouble was, my foreman told me what had happened. He said that you needed money but that the banco had refused you a loan. The people, he said, were sad because the money was for the hospital, and they worried that if you could not finish the hospital, you might not return. 'But why did he not come to me?' I asked. You are a good man, Señor Striker. You have done much for the people of our village. And happy people are good workers. It is largely because of this that I have prospered. They say you need a half million U.S. dollars. If you will permit it, I think I can get my hands on this amount, and I would be honored to help you."

Lonnie was listening, but he wasn't sure he'd heard correctly. At times a thick Spanish accent was hard even for him to understand. "Did I hear you right? You want to loan me a half million dollars?"

"If it will help, si. I have to do something to get my people back to work. What good are coffee beans unless they are picked, eh?"

"Man, oh man, oh man, oh man! Does God do miracles, or what? Yes, I do need the money, and yes, what I'm doing does affect the hospital, and yes...whatever else you said. This is too much. Listen, I was just in a meeting before you came in. Would you come down the hall with me? I have to share this news with the others."

CURIOSITY BROKE from the faces of Les, Lance, Quentin, and Allison when Paulo entered the room. The four were sitting at the boardroom table trying to establish a shooting schedule and pushing Les to put his pessimism aside and accommodate the urgency. Les had finally lit his cigarette. It lay smoldering in an ashtray, filling the room with smoke, but he snuffed it when Lonnie walked in. He'd been walking a fine line. There was a difference between pessimism and making promises he couldn't keep. To his way of thinking, in a few hours they would all be out of work.

Lonnie made the introductions. "I've got some really good news," he said. "You guys did some terrific work last night, I really mean that, but I doubt your friends would be willing to continue without getting paid. And we don't have the money to pay them. Well, the good Lord just took care of that problem. My friend Señor Ramirez has just agreed to loan us half a million dollars."

Les took the news without comment. He sat there unmoved, with a deadpan expression on his face.

"What's the matter, Les?"

"Look, the last thing I want to be is negative, especially when we've seen the work these kids have done. But it's not enough. Brent said it would take a million to do the rest of the film. He wasn't kidding. That's what things cost in this town. And that was based on using Laurna. Now that we're using Allison, we'll have to reshoot every scene Laurna was in. We're practically remaking the entire film. I don't think you'll get anyone to loan you what you need without some pretty heavy collateral, and that's something we don't have. That's why Harlan went to Lowen in the first place."

"How much *will* it cost?"

"I can't say. That was Brent's domain."

"I'm not asking Brent. I'm asking you. You know this business and what things cost. How much?"

Les fished in his pocket for another cigarette. He tapped it out and flicked it between his fingers. "I can cut corners. If Quentin will waive the director's fee, at least temporarily, and our actors can wait until the film is done to get paid, and we all work together to keep the number of retakes down..."

"How much?"

"Two million, but it may be even more."

Lonnie sank into his chair.

"No problem!" All the heads in the room turned toward Lance. He sat there grinning. He was still wearing the same clothes he'd worn in the movie. He pulled his foot up over his knee. With his sandy hair, and in T-shirt and tennis shoes, he looked more like a surfer than Les did in his surfboard-patterned pink polyester.

"What did you say?"

"I said, 'no problem.' Allison told me she's working for a percentage. As I remember, Les offered me the same deal, but I turned it down. Glad I did, too. You wouldn't want a percentage of the revenues from *Lost Cause*, but this film is different. The way it is now, I think my co-star will end up earning more than me, and I can't have that. Les, I want you to rewrite my contract. I insist on getting the same as Allison. I'll return what you've already paid me for doing *Lost Cause*. That's peanuts compared to what I think we're going to make with *An Uncommon Heart*."

Lonnie looked at Les. "Just how much is that?"

Les nodded and slid his cigarette behind his ear, but didn't look up. "A million, five," he said.

"So, that's two million dollars. Just what we need. Whew-eee." Lonnie smacked his flat palm on the table. *Whaaack.* "Thank You, Lord. Where's that little China doll? Let's get her in here. She needs to hear this. In fact, let's get everyone in here. Striker Films is back in business!"

MAN WHAT A RIDE—a regular skyrocket to the moon! *Blast off!* He'd been flat on his back one minute, and exploring the heavens the next. And the change in people? That's what he couldn't understand. Les wasn't cussing and smoking, or at least he wasn't smoking much, and Quentin was treating him like a regular person. And not just him, he was treating everyone that way. Totally inexplicable! Lonnie was as light-headed as a man breathing rarefied air. He had to come down from orbit. He needed to get his feet back on solid ground. He wished Paulo and Enrico could have stayed to share his euphoria, but they were determined to return on the next flight out and, as always, there was one leaving at four. But that was all right. It would take more than that to stop his jubilation. More even than Don walking in and telling him Lowen had won. Lonnie thanked Nicole and asked her to show the lawyer in. He hung up the phone. He had his feet up on his desk with his hands cocked behind his head when the door opened.

"You're looking rather relaxed for a man perched on the edge of a cliff," Don said.

Lonnie swung his feet down and stood to shake Don's hand. "Good to see you, Don. How long has it been? Too long. And you're right. Everything's fine. Haven't a care in the world."

"Then you don't want to hear what I have to say."

"Sure, sure, more doom and gloom, but hey, that's what you get paid for."

Don set his briefcase down, took a seat, and folded his hands, leaning forward with his forearms on his knees. "No, actually, I don't."

Lonnie returned to his chair, still smiling.

"I just spent the past few days looking for a way to solve this problem, but I couldn't find one. I'm sorry about that. I really am. I take no joy in delivering bad news."

Lonnie laced his fingers over his stomach. "Don't give it another thought. I'm sure you did your best, under the circumstances. If Lowen wants the company that bad, he can have it." Lonnie leaned forward placing his elbows on the desk, his hands folded in prayer. He stopped smiling. "But don't let it be said he acted in good faith. Did you know Mr. Lowen, Barry Gladdon, and my own inside counsel, Michael Sugarman, conspired to take this company over? I don't know the exact legal terminology, but to my way of thinking, that constitutes fraud. They were in league together, making sure there was no way Harlan, or anyone else, could fulfill our end of the bargain."

Don was rubbing his hands together, his eyes hardened. "And how do you know that?"

"I overheard a conversation between Michael Sugarman and Mr. Lowen in which it was acknowledged that Mr. Lowen had caused the bank to pull our line of credit. He got our employees so stirred up, two-thirds of them quit. Then he persuaded someone at the production house to stop work on the final edit, which meant the film would not have made the deadline, no matter what I did. My own man, my legal counsel, was feeding him information. And at the same time he was working with our outside law firm, Gladdon, Vickers and Cox, to make sure I was drummed out, and Ben Lowen was ushered in. And you say if we go to court they'll claim Mr. Lowen acted in good faith. That's not what I'd call it."

Don reached for his briefcase and pulled it into his lap. He snapped the locks and took out a pen and a yellow pad and set the briefcase back on the floor. He began writing. "You're making some pretty serious accusations. What do you have to back them up?"

"Nothing. Like I said, I just overheard Michael and Mr. Lowen on the phone."

Don's mouth puckered as he slouched back in his chair, tapping his pen against the pad of paper. "If that's it, you're right. It would be your word against theirs, and they'd both claim the conversation never took place. Too bad."

Lonnie also relaxed. He'd made his point. "Like I said, don't worry about it. It doesn't matter. We've had a very good day. I saw some early clips from the remake of our movie. It's terrific. And we've been able to raise some backing. I hate to lose my father's old business, but if that's the way Mr. Lowen wants it—what can I say? All he'll get is an empty building. We all talked about it, and my employees, what's left of them, have said they'll go with me. We'll just walk down the road and start a new company. We have a dynamite story and some great actors. We'll do okay."

Don sat forward in his chair again. He began shaking his head. "Not necessarily."

"What do you mean?"

"I gather you're talking about using something you already have in house. You can't do that. Your actors are under contract to Striker Films, and the script you're using is company property. When Mr. Lowen takes over at five-thirty today, it will all belong to him."

TWENTY-TWO

LONNIE KEPT his hands in his pockets as he paced back and forth in front of the glass wall at the rear of his office. He looked at his watch—five twenty-five. Would they be on time? It was the threshold of the final showdown, the proverbial shootout at the OK corral. *This town isn't big enough for both of us. I'm calling you out, you mealy-mouthed little coward. Get out here and prove you're a man—draw*! He pulled his hand from his pocket and with thumb raised, pointed his index finger at an imaginary foe. *Bang, bang!* He brought his finger up and blew across its tip, clearing smoke from the barrel. He had to smile at the analogy, but he knew like all mealy-mouthed little cowards, he was ready to sneak out of Tombstone. He wasn't there on his own strength. He was relying on the strength of God.

He looked at his watch—*again*. For some time he had criticized Harlan for owning such an ostentatious piece—the cost of the watch alone could feed dozens of orphans—but he didn't hate the watch. The watch was just a symptom of what was wrong, not the wrong itself. It was the tied-to-time making of the almighty dollar, the concentration on building empires, man pouring wealth on himself, the building of pink mansions, riding around in limos, and the adornment of jewels. It was the sin of vanity, of believing money could buy happiness.

He turned and stared out the window. The skyscrapers stood like blocks of yellow gold in the late-afternoon sun. How appropriate. A great divide separated himself from the other buildings, but across that chasm were men, probably standing in windows just as he was—some good, some bad, but most caught up in the day-to-day accumulation of wealth and power. The kingdoms of this earth were a temptation few could resist. If they could only see that one day it would all be dust, then maybe, just maybe, they would change. *Only one life will soon be past, only what's done for Christ will last.* It was a truth most men waited until too late to acknowledge.

Harlan had waited until it was too late. His once invincible body had been reduced to a pile of ashes. His soul was now in God's hands, and God would reward him, not based on how strong his body had been, or the dollars he had earned, or even the amount of good he had done, but according to whether or not his name was written in the *Lamb's Book of Life.* God required that men give their lives to Christ, as Christ had given His life for men. It was too late for Harlan. Lonnie prayed it would not be too late for Michael, Ben, and Barry.

His watch read five-thirty, and the intercom buzzed. *How punctual.* Lonnie picked up the phone and asked Nicole to show the men in. He also asked that she find Don and have him join them. Lonnie swallowed. He felt his pulse surging and his stomach turning sour. He'd hoped to feel a great swell of relief, as though a burden had been lifted from his shoulders, but it was not to be. He did not like confrontation. He wished he could be anywhere but here. At least after this meeting, it would be over. He was tired of trying to hang on. It was time to let go. It was time to let God have his way.

Lonnie chose to remain standing. He walked around his desk, positioning himself to greet his visitors. The door opened and Ben Lowen, Barry Gladdon, and Michael Sugarman were ushered in. All three wore business suits: Ben in seedy brown, Barry in midnight blue, and Michael in charcoal gray. Lonnie hadn't seen Michael in a suit. It made him appear even more intimidating. The door closed. Nicole would be back in a moment with Don Maniux. Lonnie took a deep breath and extended his hand, forcing himself to be cordial, though his fingers trembled and he couldn't manage a smile. He shook hands with Barry first, then with Ben, and lastly, Michael who stood tall and confident, his dark eyes probing Lonnie as though insinuating it was Lonnie, not himself, who should feel ashamed. Don had cautioned him not to say anything, but Lonnie couldn't help it. He looked up to meet Michael's glare and shook his head. "I can't believe you actually came," he said. "Wouldn't it have been more gracious to wait until all this was over to show your face again?"

Michael started to respond, but Ben raised a puffy red hand, cutting him off. With his brown jacket rolled over his meaty shoulders and his receding hairline, thick black glasses, and heavy jowls, he looked like a cartoon bulldog. When he pushed his bottom lip up, the rest of his face sagged into a frown. His fleshy cheeks jiggled as he began to speak.

"Mr. Striker, I'm aware of a conversation Michael believes you may have overheard," he said. "Let's clear the air on this. Whoever Michael was speaking to, it wasn't me, and since you can't prove otherwise, I think it would be best if we tried to keep the rest of this meeting on a professional level. We are here to present you with a legal demand that you release the holdings of Striker Films to myself. There's no personal agenda here. This is business. Harlan was a bad businessman. That's all there is to it. He shouldn't have allowed the company to become a bad credit risk. He should have been able to raise financing through normal channels. You would do well to remember that I did not approach Harlan. He approached me. In defense of Mr. Sugarman, Michael made an initial attempt to warn Harlan of the contract's considerable downside. Harlan, however, wasn't in the mood to listen. Your brother knew he was dying, Mr. Striker. He knew if he did nothing at all, his wife and son would be left with a bankrupt company. At least with my offer he had a chance. I was his only hope.

"It is unfortunate that neither he, nor yourself, were able to complete the film on time. I suppose if you had, we wouldn't be standing here, though I read the script and knew it would never earn the money needed to pay back the loan, so it's really a moot point. When Michael saw Harlan wasn't listening, he made a business decision. He could stay and go down with the ship, or get on board with me and set a course for the future. He chose the latter. I myself call that prudent."

"Not while he's still on the payroll here," Lonnie shot back. "I call that unethical."

The door opened and Don entered the room. He had on a shirt and tie but no jacket. His casual blue polyester pants were smooth and shiny at the knees, and he carried a scuffed brown leather briefcase. The power suits were on Lowen's side. Don was followed by Nicole, who held a steno notepad in her hand.

"Sorry I'm late, gentlemen. I had to finish a call."

Lonnie took the initiative and began introductions. "Mr. Lowen, this is Don Maniux. He'll be representing Striker Films throughout these proceedings." Lonnie turned to Barry. "Striker Films no longer requires the services of Gladdon, Vickers and Cox, so please regard this as an official termination of any duties you are currently performing on our behalf."

Barry stood there smiling, his jaw jutting out. His silver hair was swept back in smooth waves and his professional blue suit was crisp as starched paper. Three points of a white silk handkerchief sprouted from the pocket of his jacket. By the tilt of his lips, you'd think he'd just been told a joke rather than having just been fired.

Don shook hands with all three men. "All right, let's get down to business."

Barry set his briefcase on Lonnie's desk. The brilliant white cuff of his shirt slid out from the sleeve of his jacket, revealing a diamond-studded cufflink. He withdrew a copy of the signed agreement between Striker Films and Lowen Enterprises and handed it to Don. "Since you're acting as legal counsel, I assume you've already read this. We're here to execute the terms in accordance with section four: "Failure To Comply With Provisions of Repayment." I would like to direct you to item six wherein it states...

"Hold on. Let's not get ahead of ourselves," Don interrupted. "We need to clear the air on a couple of things first. Then we can get into whether you want to *execute* anything. First, let's address the fact that Mr. Lowen inappropriately coerced a principal at the bank into withholding credit from Striker Films, and further manipulated an independent post-production house..."

"I did no such thing!" Ben interjected. "I assume you're referring to a conversation Mr. Striker thinks he overheard. Let's not get off on that tangent. I've already explained that if such a conversation ever took place, Mr. Sugarman must have been speaking with someone other than myself. Now that's the end of the matter. Let's move on to more productive areas."

Don just smiled. He pulled his briefcase into his arms and snapped the locks. "Well, if he was, he used your name when he said good-bye, but that's neither here nor there. I'm sure phone records can verify the call was made to your office, if need be, and we have Mr. Striker's testimony to that effect, along with his description of the ensuing conversation which includes an assertion that you had the bank suspend the company's line of credit and had the production house stop working on the film. I was just on the phone with the district attorney explaining what we have here, and they're very interested. Of course I haven't mentioned any names yet, but what do you think they'll find if they send vice officers to the bank or into the film production house and start asking questions? Any guesses?" Don paused for a reaction, but the room remained silent. "I thought so. Nonetheless, your bigger problem is explaining these." He withdrew a file of memos and notes, some typed and signed, others handwritten. "It would appear Michael took notes on every conversation he ever had with you, giving us the dates as well as content."

Ben shot a look at Michael that would have killed if it could. Michael shook his head but his face was beginning to turn white. It was like someone had pulled a plug and was draining the color from his skin.

"It's a fairly common practice among lawyers. I do it myself. We have to be able to remember what we say to people as well as what was said to us, in case there's ever a challenge. In this file are copies of all your conversations, transcribed for later reference. More important is your offer of employment to Michael, along with a promise that he'll receive five percent of the new company for helping you displace Striker Films' president, Harlan Striker. And it's signed by you. Now here's an interesting one. It promises Barry Gladdon an equal five percent of the new company, not surprisingly, for his assistance in the takeover. I believe you'll note that this one is signed by you as well, Mr. Lowen, with a carbon copy to Michael, who I suppose is acting as Barry's personal attorney. I guess he couldn't trust someone in his own office with it. I doubt his partners know how deeply he's involved in all this. By the way, Michael, I want to thank you for the use of your office this afternoon. You knew Nicole had a spare key to all locked cabinets—didn't you? Of course you did. Harlan insisted on it. You must have thought you'd be back before we had a chance to go through your files."

Color was returning to Michael's cheeks, but he seemed to be having difficulty breathing. Each sip of air came with a little gasp. And Lowen was speechless. His hangdog jowls were crimson, and beads of moisture were swelling on his forehead.

"Here's what it all boils down to. Once this information is handed over to the authorities, they'll probably want to press charges, but whether they do or not, Striker Films is prepared to sue Lowen Enterprises for contravention of contract law and contract manipulation with malicious intent. I believe we can sufficiently prove that through fraud and obstruction, you created an impossibility of performance, so if the criminal court doesn't get you, the civil court will. As for the two of you," Don said looking at Barry and Michael, "you need to be brought before an ethics review board. You're both guilty of inducement and breach of fiduciary duty, not to mention outright fraud. I'd be surprised if either of you were allowed to practice law again."

Michael swallowed hard and cleared his throat, shaking his head. "You'll never make it stick," he said. His words came out raspy and dry. He rubbed his neck, trying to lubricate his vocal cords. "What have you got? A few unsigned memos and a job offer. *Ugggghhhm.* There's nothing there that says I agreed to anything."

"Perhaps you're right, but then, I'm sure a copy with your signature on it can be obtained through a search of Mr. Lowen's files. I'm not concerned about it. Besides, I don't need to make it stick. I won't be prosecuting, the state will. And Mr. Lowen will be the one on trial, not you, but you'll be called as witnesses and should you be caught lying on the stand, I can assure you it will end your career. Perjury is a very serious offense. Anyway, I doubt Gladdon, Vickers and Cox wants the kind of publicity this is bound to bring, nor would it bode well for someone like yourself who will soon be out looking for a job.

"But I have good news. I can make this whole problem go away. As a Christian, Mr. Striker here doesn't believe in taking an eye for an eye. He would rather forgive and forget. He's directed me to propose that you, Mr. Lowen, sign a new contract, one that supersedes and makes null and void the old contract. In a nutshell the new contract says you will get back every penny you loaned Striker Films to the full amount of thirty million dollars. There will, however, be no interest paid on this amount, and Striker Films has up to ten years to repay the debt. Mr. Sugarman, you will sign an official letter of resignation acknowledging that Striker Films owes you no further compensation of any kind including any accumulated vacation time, profit-sharing and accrued retirement benefits. Mr. Gladdon, you will return to Striker Films any amount you have invoiced since the beginning of negotiations with Mr. Lowen so that no money will be paid to Gladdon, Vickers and Cox for services rendered in connection with the drafting or implementation of this contract. That's it. Mr. Lowen gets his money back and you two walk away clean. But I want to emphasize this is a one-shot deal. If any of you choose to leave this room without the new contract being signed, the offer is withdrawn and we'll see you all in court."

FINALLY, LONNIE stood looking out his office window, *alone*, listening to the voice of God. The hubbub and noise of the city, was on the other side of the glass. His eyes scanned the silhouettes of the spiraling structures, now bathed in purple twilight. The windows across the chasm were beginning to blink on. The city never slept.

It had taken several hours for Ben and his lawyers to read through the new contract and come to grips with the terms. They had tried repeatedly to renegotiate this point or that, but each time Don emphasized it was a take-it-or-leave-it deal and ultimately, faced with a long court battle as well as the possibility of criminal charges being laid, Mr. Lowen capitulated. The news had been given to the staff and, even though the hour was late, Lonnie heard the cheers echoing down the hall. The troops were jubilant and ready to party. They had gone on down to Mud Slingers, a local watering hole, to celebrate. Lonnie had promised to join them later, but he really wasn't in the mood. What was there to be joyous about? Three souls had walked away hopelessly lost. He'd tried to share why it was he wanted to be forgiving—Christ, after all, had forgiven *him*, but his words were in vain. Ben had finally said: "Somebody shut this guy up or the deal's off. I'd rather go to prison than listen to this!"

Lonnie looked at the new signed agreement on his desk and then back out the window. In the dimming light he observed the kingdoms of the earth—towering spires festooned with gargoyles and cornices and pinnacles of gilded glass, kingdoms of wealth and power, robed in purple. The color suggested something—didn't it? A purple dusk. Purple was the color of royalty. That's what people missed. They overlooked the fact that God had written the story. All they had to do was take a peek at the end:

> The kingdoms of this earth,
> Have become,
> The kingdoms of our Lord,
> And of His Christ.
> *And He shall reign—forever and ever!*
>
> *Amen!*

TWENTY-THREE

LONNIE SHOWED up at Mud Slingers to take part in the victory celebration, but stayed only long enough to be polite. Quentin was there, but he was unaware of how close they'd come to losing it all. In accordance with Harlan's wishes, Lonnie intended to keep it that way. The same was true of Trudy. No one rushed to tell her the news because, except for the fact that they would now be doing Quentin's film, there was no news to tell. But Lonnie knew something the others didn't. The final barrier to his relationship with Trudy had been removed. He excused himself and went out and bought an arrangement of flowers. He stared out the dark window on the long ride home, cradling the cellophane-wrapped bouquet in his arm. He was thinking about the bumper-to-bumper taillights and about how nice it was not to be in a hurry. He sent Frank and the car back to wait for Quentin and carried his armload of color into the house. Now was the time to celebrate!

He was greeted in the foyer by the life-size portraits, and smiled. "I guess I was premature, Harlan, old man," he said, saluting the ghost on the wall. "Never give up till it's over, isn't that right? You know, this may sound crazy, but I owe you. In some inexplicable way, you had faith in me. I want to thank you for that." The face staring down didn't look any less haughty, but Lonnie couldn't help thinking he saw a twinkle in Harlan's eye.

Lonnie turned, expecting to see Trudy. He thought the sound of his voice would bring her to the door, but it didn't. He crossed the atrium flanked by the two circular staircases and stood beneath the rainbow chandelier, calling her name. When he didn't get an answer, he began to search. He found her passed out on the couch. The radio was tuned to a talk show, the TV to a soap. An empty fifth of Vodka and a glass with melting ice were beside her on the table. Her arm was bent over a magazine. It was cocked in such an awkward way it appeared to be broken. A pool of spittle dotted the pillow under her head. He took the flowers to the garage and tossed them into one of the round aluminum trash cans, the metallic sound echoing off the cement floor. He returned, killing the TV and radio on his way back, before tackling the job of wrestling Tracy into bed. He closed her door and resolved to stop ignoring the problem. He would confront her in the morning—with compassion, not criticism—because whether she knew it or not, she needed his help.

THE NEXT morning he indulged himself in an extra long shower before descending the stairs to look for Trudy. He found her in the breakfast nook, wrapped in a cloak of yellow sun. He entered the room and waited to be recognized, but she leaned over her newspaper pretending not to notice. She was probably worried about what he was going to say, and that in itself provided an opening.

"I had to help you into bed last night."

Trudy looked up from her coffee. "Oh, good morning Lonnie. Did you? Sorry, I guess I must have fallen asleep."

"You weren't asleep. You'd passed out. You were drunk."

Trudy turned the page of her paper, ignoring what he said, as though it was of little importance.

"Trudy, you have a problem. You need help."

"Lonnie, let's not get into this. I already told you, it's not a problem. I've had a few rough weeks, that's all."

Lonnie shook his head. He brought his hand up to rub his neck. "Trudy, you were trying to fight me off. You were screaming at me, calling me 'Harlan.' " He waited for an explanation but she just turned another page. "You don't remember, do you?"

Trudy scooted her chair back, creating a rasping sound as the wood scraped across the tiles. She rose from the table and pulled a pin from her hair, letting it fall as she tossed her head. She walked over to Lonnie. "I was asleep, silly. No one remembers what happens when they're asleep. I must have been doing some kind of sleepwalking. I'm sorry. Did I hurt you? Come're." She took him by the hand and pulled him in close. "The only problem I have is not seeing enough of you." She brought his arms around her back, laying her head on his shoulder.

Lonnie closed his eyes, breathing in her fragrance. He felt his excitement growing. He wanted to nuzzle his cheek against her hair, but he also saw she was creating a diversion. He interlaced his fingers, leaving his arms loose around her waist. "Do you love me?" he asked.

She pulled her head back, forcing him to look into the emerald green of her eyes. "What kind of a question is that?"

"A simple one. Do you love me?" he repeated.

She sighed, and laid her head against his shoulder. "I guess it depends on how you define *love*. I told Harlan I loved him—but I didn't. I was his wife, but I didn't love him. At least not the way a woman should love a man. Some kinds of love aren't worth having."

Lonnie felt her chest heave and tremble against his own and imagined there was moisture building in her eye. He gave her a light squeeze. "Do you love me enough to do me a favor?"

"What's that?" she said, sniffing.

"I want you to go through the entire day without having a drink. I'll stay home so you won't be alone. If you're right about not having a problem, tonight you'll go to bed sober. But if you get to the point where you feel you must have a drink, then I want you to admit you have a problem and agree to get some help."

IT HAD not been easy. Before the day was over, Lonnie had found himself anxious for Sunday to roll around. He got up early and, with the sun still resting behind the hills, headed for the beach, but the wind and waves couldn't console him. He needed to feel the presence of God the way God's presence is felt when He's among His people. Lonnie hired a taxi, and arrived before the church doors opened. But *first* was the last thing he wanted to be. He walked across the street and sat in a small coffee shop, reading his Bible until everyone else was inside. They were singing hymns by the time he entered the chapel and found a seat in the last pew. He had been careful to pick a congregation that supported the Missionary Alliance, but he wanted to keep a low profile. He was drained. He couldn't bear to be called upon to give a mission report, let alone account for his activities of late. He needed to be ministered to by others. Just being surrounded by God's people was lifting his spirits, but he wanted to be left alone. Even Christ needed to withdraw from time to time. He left the church, feeling like God had placed a salve on the wound of his heart.

MONDAY MORNING he was back in the office bright and early, setting the wheels in motion. They had to get the crew shooting again. Les was assigned the task. With money in hand, a select team picked by Lance, and Quentin sitting in the director's chair, they were back on the lot within twenty-four hours.

The ensuing weeks zoomed by like film ripping through a projector, each day a single frame, one picture as independent of the others as any still photograph, and yet each connected to the others as an integral part of the whole. But clear as the image might be to someone watching from a distance, the series of events happened so fast Lonnie could only look back on them as a blur. The weeks became months, closer to the amount of time Les had originally said they'd need, but with the Lowen deadline resolved, it didn't matter. The pressure was off.

Not surprisingly, within a few days of resuming production, the bank mysteriously discovered an error had been made. They apologized and assured Lonnie the credit of Striker Films would be reinstated immediately. That had been a godsend. Costs were escalating rapidly. With good credit, some initial film clips, and a revised script, Lonnie approached several key lenders and was able to increase funding for the project.

While Quentin and Les focused on making the film, Lonnie

developed a strategy for publicity. He hired an in-house marketing manager to replace the one who'd left when things were looking bad. Working with an ad agency, they put together TV trailers, using the clips already completed by Quentin, along with a series of newspaper ads and posters. Film critics were invited to an advance screening, and the reviews began to appear. One actually called it: "A triumphant achievement by the new kid on the block." Almost all were positive. Only one was blatantly negative. "I grow weary of any attempt to squeeze sanctimonious tears from these tired old eyes," the reviewer wrote, but it hadn't hurt. The marketing manager was already negotiating with two fast food chains for the right to distribute souvenir posters.

Just prior to the film's release, Lonnie scheduled a press conference. Rumors about the untimely death of Striker Films were greatly exaggerated, he said. He promised a blockbuster new release soon forthcoming, and then addressed changes he was making to the company. Demographically diverse test groups had been brought in to review not only the new film but also a version known as *Lost Cause.* Twelve percent actually liked the old version better, but that left an overwhelming eighty-eight percent that favored *An Uncommon Heart*. He focused on the film's MPAA rating. The film that won the most votes was rated "G" for General Audience; the other was "R" for restricted. He avoided any mention of the fact that *Lost Cause* was the progeny of his brother. Lonnie stuck to peddling the company's new direction and supported his rationale with the results of his study. No one challenged his findings. How could they? The participants of the focus groups had been asked to select their favorite after watching two versions of the *same* film.

EVERYONE WAS frazzled and fatigued by the time the gala release rolled around, but they were fueled by excitement, and that kept them going. They showed up in formal attire with smiles on and greeted an adoring public that paid up to three hundred dollars a seat (all proceeds going to charity) to be part of the first official screening and attend the cocktail soiree that followed. The theater marquee proclaimed *An Uncommon Heart* in glowing red letters as they pulled up in two jet-black limousines. Frank opened the door and helped Quentin out first, followed by Father Ceylon, Señor Ramirez, and Les. The second car held Lonnie, Trudy, Allison, and Lance. They stood in shimmering gowns and subdued black tie, watching the searchlights stream across the sky until everyone was assembled. Then the entourage—producer, director, actors, and backers—entered the theater together.

Center stage at the front of the theater, Trudy stood by Lonnie's side, cold sober. She had entered a rehab program in the Big Sur redwoods of California's golden coast. It had taken the entire two months, but she was dry as toast. She hadn't seen much of Lonnie—weekend visits were all they were allowed—but with all that was going on, it was for the best. She was flanked by her two favorite men. Lonnie stood to her right in a dashing black tuxedo, holding her arm, waiting to introduce the film. Quentin reached up, taking her hand. He sat in his wheelchair looking every bit as handsome as his father.

Pinned in the glare of a huge white spotlight, it was impossible to see the audience as Lonnie stepped forward and tapped the mike with his finger. He heard a loud *pop, pop, pop*, letting him know they were live. He leaned in. "I am so pleased this day has finally come," he said, his voice echoing through the room.

The theater erupted into shouts, cheers, foot stomps, whistles and applause. The entire staff of Striker Films occupied the first two rows.

"I can see I'm not the only one excited. Some of you have seen this company through good times and bad, and I want to applaud you for that." Lonnie began clapping and the entire theater joined in.

"As most of you know, only a few short weeks ago this company was on the verge of collapse. Today I stand before you as a testimony to the grace of Almighty God, for without His assistance, none of us would be here..."

ALLISON AND LANCE stood in the wings, waiting to be introduced. Allison sparkled. Lance had just been offered a part in another movie and was insisting they give her the female lead. Les stood on the other side of the stage, with a cigarette in hand. Streams of smoke filtered up into the dark red curtains. He took a puff and tried not to inhale, but it was no use. If the patch on his arm was so good, why was he still poking cigarettes into his mouth? He sucked in the smoke and tossed the cigarette to the ground, crushing it with his heel. He, too, had squeezed into a tuxedo for the occasion, but the cummerbund that spanned his portly middle was already stretched out of shape, and the carnation in the buttonhole of his lapel was beginning to wilt. He crossed his arms and shivered. He wasn't cold; he was troubled. He had stayed with Striker for selfish reasons. He never dreamed, not even for a minute, they would succeed. Yet they had. There were probably a million ways to explain how all the pieces had fallen so neatly into place, but the only one that made sense was so utterly impossible it wasn't worth considering. He had to keep reminding himself that there was no God, and without God there was no miracle. The boss man's faith was all in his head. Still, it might be good to keep an open mind...

LONNIE SMILED, his perfect white teeth brilliant in the light. He squeezed Trudy's arm—a sober Trudy. They would not be attending the cocktail hour following the show. They had other plans. Trudy had talked him into taking a vacation. He knew he needed it, and though they'd agreed to separate rooms, just the thought of lying on the beach alone with Trudy—well, it didn't take much convincing. She deserved what she referred to as "her reward." They would be leaving in the morning, right after his final meeting with Gladdon, Vickers and Cox. But nothing could diminish the way he felt tonight—*nothing*! This might just be the greatest moment of his life. He was part of the family, his family—the Striker family—and he was proud!

TWENTY-FOUR

THE LIMOUSINE rolled quietly along the California coast. Lonnie sat looking out the tinted glass at the palm trees. In the distance he could see the white sand beach. Mothers were watching their children play against a backdrop of green translucent waves. Frisbees flew, roller blades whirred and bicycles hummed. It was a perfect day.

Lonnie recalled how good the sun had felt warming his shoulder as he'd held the door for Trudy. He had followed her into the car, imbibing the musty salt of the ocean. He felt the breeze, crisp and cool, caressing his cheek as it swept in from the shore with seagulls caught in the draft like white skiffs sailing across an ever-blue sky. A perfect day in every way—except for the mood of his soul.

Trudy sat on the other side of the car. She wore white web sandals to match her soft cotton blouse and a blue skirt with a Polynesian print that reminded Lonnie of the shirts Les liked to wear. Her head was tilted back so that her hair fanned out across the leather upholstery, her eyes closed against the sun. Climate control kept the temperature in the car at seventy-two degrees. Lonnie could have closed his eyes and gone to sleep the way it appeared Trudy was doing, but there would be plenty of time for that once they were on the plane. They didn't need an excuse to explain their silence. They were both fatigued, and that was reason enough. But though Lonnie needed rest, his mind was perplexed and it kept him on edge. Why was it every time things seemed perfect, something happened to prove they really weren't?

He placed his hand over his stomach and felt it tighten. What was the matter with him? He should be on cloud nine. So much had been accomplished; there was so much to be thankful for. He'd been given an impossible task, one that could not, in human terms, be achieved, yet here he was the conquering hero, riding in the royal coach with his lady fair, ready to right the wrong done to him so many years ago, victorious over his fear and over the sibling abuse that caused him so much pain—and he couldn't even bring himself to enjoy it! He felt cheated—*again!* And this time he couldn't blame Harlan because if anyone was to blame, it was himself. The guilt he'd tried so often to bury, kept coming back to haunt him.

Absalom! Oh Absalom, my son, my son? Lonnie drummed his fingers on the armrest of the car as they merged into highway traffic, heading for LAX. So many cars, so many destinations. Was he destined to bask under a warm Caribbean sun, or would he be swamped by the storms of his conscience?

And why? So much good had been accomplished. The farewells following the launch had been filled with joy, though most expressed sorrow at his leaving. Lonnie hugged them all, even Les, and assured everyone he'd see them again. He'd be in once a month to make sure things were going well. The main thing was to remember they'd done it! They'd produced a winner, at least if comments made by people leaving the theater were any indication. News and entertainment journals had placed cameras and microphones in front of the exiting crowd to capture their initial reaction.

"Terrific movie!"

"Fabulous!"

"I cried all the way through it."

And from the more macho viewers: "Bit of a chick flick, but hey, the old lady liked it. What can I say?"

Those who had stayed with Lonnie were in for a nice surprise. Lonnie told Les he wanted each of his seven loyal employees to receive a five thousand dollar check out of the company's net profits, with Les to receive twenty, if it could be managed. They'd risked it all. They deserved a reward. Since there were only eight in that original group, the total outlay was fifty-five thousand—peanuts in terms of Hollywood dollars. Les didn't see a problem.

Quentin was stepping in to manage the company, but he was a natural. He'd learned from Harlan the way Harlan had learned from Buddy, by growing up in the studio, watching and emulating. Harlan hadn't been much older than Quentin when Buddy's death forced him to assume the same responsibility. Quentin would succeed; Lonnie was certain of it. He had Quentin's promise: Striker Films would only produce entertainment fit for viewing by the entire family. Les, as out of character as it might seem, didn't dissent.

On a sad note, Nicole had tendered her resignation. She wasn't dissatisfied with anything in particular, just her life in general. Lonnie's work with the natives in Mexico had inspired her to do something more important. She had investigated a nursing program and was going back to school. She would, she hoped, see him again. She took his address, saying she would keep in touch. She might even need a reference, especially if she decided to apply for work at *his* hospital. "You never know what the future holds," she said.

The hospital? That was part of the reason he felt uneasy about this vacation. Didn't the people of Posada need him? Father Ceylon assured him everything would be fine. Though not fully utilized, the hospital was open. Contractors were still milling about, and the sounds of hammers, saws and drills could be heard. Things always took longer than they should, but the fact remained that they were open. And more services were being added every day. How could Lonnie reconcile his love of his work, with his love for Trudy? If the time they spent together led to a deeper commitment, as Lonnie secretly hoped it would, what chance was there that she'd join him in Mexico? Face it—slim to none! She'd want him to operate the mission remotely, allowing him one or two trips a year to see his flock.

Maybe it wouldn't be so bad? They could find someone to replace him, especially if he promised financial support. Wasn't money what they really needed anyway? But he'd miss being there. He knew he would feel a great emptiness if he couldn't hold their babies, pray over their sick, and baptize the newly converted. It was part of who he was. He was having trouble determining which would be greater, the hole he'd have in his heart if Trudy wasn't there, or the one he'd feel at the loss of his extended family.

He looked at Trudy. The sun lit her face, erasing the years with a brush of soft light. This was the Trudy he remembered. She was one lovely lady. The prize he'd been denied for so many years was now within his grasp—if he could only get past the guilt. He closed his eyes and tried to ward off the memory.

Headlights screamed through the fogged windows, filling the inside of the station wagon with an eerie glow. The intruder's engine was rumbling, raising alarm—but then came the voice...

"Well, looky, looky. What do you suppose we have here?"

Evil words, Harlan's words, words that caused panic. Lonnie's eyes caught Trudy's. She broke off and began rummaging furiously for her dress, her own fear evident.

"Wait here, toots, I'll be right back."

Lonnie heard the car door slam. There was no time to think; he had to act. He groped for the handle on the far side of the station wagon. He pulled it back, leaning on the door with his weight so that it popped open. The empty space caught him off guard and he spilled butt first onto to the ground, "Ouufffff, ouch!" Now there was a light on in the car, exposing Trudy. He found his legs, slammed the door, and scrambled for the bushes, his bare feet crying out in pain as he stomped over hard clods of dirt. He'd had no time to grab his clothes. Except for his skivvies, he was naked. He dove into the thicket getting cut, poked, and bruised by vines and branches. At least with a full moon, he could see.

He cleared the bush, running as fast as his hurting feet could carry him. He was filled with terror, sure that Harlan was just behind him ready to slam him to the ground. Ready to kill him. He ran, and ran, and ran, and ran, until he had to stop because he could no longer breathe. He leaned over with his hands on his knees gasping for air, waiting to feel Harlan's crunch. He was drooling. He fell into a crawl and tried moving forward again. But he couldn't move. It didn't matter. Let Harlan kill him where he lay. The wages of sin is death—isn't it? He deserved to die. He rolled onto his back. He could feel the cold wet earth against his skin as he stared into space. The moon and stars would be his last sight. They were beautiful beyond belief, seemingly reaching down to comfort him. My God, against you and you only have I have sinned.

He waited for an eternity, panting, his head beginning to pound, waiting for death—but death never came. His breathing slowed and he began to feel a chill. He could hear voices. They were muffled, but loud enough to make out what was being said. Harlan was yelling, accusing Trudy of betraying him, and Trudy responded in kind. How dare he stand her up, and who was the tramp hiding in the car? Lonnie tried to pick himself up. Small clods of dirt were sticking to his back and bits of straw were snagged in his hair. His head was throbbing. He should never have run. Coward! He had left Trudy to face Harlan alone. His sweat was beginning to dry. He no longer felt chilled, he felt cold—freezing cold! He wrapped his arms around himself and stumbled forward. He had to go back. "Ouch!" he said, limping over a rock that pierced the arch of his foot. As he drew near, the voices got louder. He hadn't run as far as he'd thought. He heard a car door slam, the engine cranking over, and the varoommmm as it sprang to life. He stood behind the thicket, shivering, parting the branches with his lacerated arms. He was just in time to see Trudy squeal away, the tires of her station wagon spinning on leaves and mud. Harlan jumped into his T-bird, firing up the engine till it rumbled. The car's white paint seemed to glow effervescent in the light of the moon. With the blond bombshell begging him to stop, Harlan roared off in hot pursuit.

It took Lonnie most of the night to walk home. He didn't know how far it was, only how cold. He couldn't hitchhike. Instead he had to step off the road every time a pair of lights zoomed by. He couldn't bear the thought of being caught running around in his underwear. His numbed blue feet left a trail of blood on the linoleum as he crossed the kitchen, heading for his room. One thing he knew for certain. He could never face either Harlan or Trudy again.

But here she was, as beautiful as ever, and forgiving, for she had never once accused him of the cowardly act he committed in abandoning her. She had made up with Harlan. She'd sacrificed herself to cover his sin. They passed under a sign: "Century Blvd, 1 mile." That was their exit. He tried to swallow the lump in his throat. It was now or never.

"You awake?"

Trudy's eyes opened as she rolled her head in his direction. "Yes. Just resting." She sat up and balled her fists, stretching her arms in front of her. "I've waited so long for this. There's a whole world out there, and I want to see it all. I'm excited. Aren't you?"

"We're almost to the airport," Lonnie said in answer. "There's something we need to discuss, and I don't know how to do it any other way, than to just be direct."

Trudy placed her hands on the seat and pushed down to straighten herself.

"I had a meeting this morning with Gladdon, Vickers and Cox."

"Un huh. Something about another letter from Harlan. How did it go?"

"It was interesting. I thought you might like to read it." Lonnie removed an envelope from his briefcase and handed it to Trudy.

She puffed out her cheeks, her eyebrows raised. The envelope bore the Striker Films logo. Lonnie's name was typed on the front. She bent back the flap and removed several sheets of paper, flicking them open. Her eyes began scanning back and forth across the page. Her free hand fell to the seat and she used it to prop herself up. After a few moments her fingers drew into a knot and her knuckles turned white.

> Well, Spud, I guess congratulations are in order. If you're reading this, you must have somehow managed to save the company, and for that you deserve a

reward. I intend to see you get it.

How's my family doing? If you honored my request, they don't know our little secret so they probably haven't bothered to say thanks. Please allow me: thank you, from the bottom of my heart. Now I have another secret to share, a scandal really. What you do with it is your business, but I'd be careful. The last place you want to read about this is in the tabloids. Ready? Here goes.

Quentin is *your* son, Lonnie.

To answer the question you're about to ask: Yes, I'm absolutely sure. The proof is incontrovertible. I had a DNA test run on some of Quentin's hair. Enclosed is a lab report showing he isn't mine. The results are conclusive. I don't suspect he belongs to anyone else. I'm pretty darn sure the only time Trudy was unfaithful to me was that one time with you. Besides, the family resemblance is there.

No, I have not always known. It took many years of observation to conclude he had more of you in him than me, though I turned him into an athlete in spite of himself. What could I do? I didn't want him growing up to be pansy like you. I think you should applaud me for that.

One time, one stupid time, you had to be with my girl and you didn't have the sense to use protection. I was always careful about that. Buddy would have killed me otherwise. I knew it didn't make sense, but I never thought to question Trudy. When she told me we had to get married, I assumed I'd screwed up. Accidents happen. I figured it was the price I had to pay for messing around.

But it was you! You're the one who should have got married. You always wanted Trudy; you should have had her in the first place. I just hope it's not too late. I bequeath her to you, and the son you share. Take good care of them, Spud. And promise you'll do your best to see Quentin doesn't get hurt. In spite of what you think of me, I love him as my own, and personally, I think he's suffered enough.

No more messages from the grave. If you have the heart, please pray I rest in peace.

Your now deceased brother,

Harlan Lloyd Striker

Trudy lowered the pages into her lap. Her lip was quivering and her eyes turning red. "I was going to tell you," she mumbled in a voice so soft it was barely audible. She shook her head slowly. "I was going to tell you, but...I was afraid you wouldn't understand."

"So you knew, then?"

Trudy nodded. A tear rolled down her cheek and spilled onto the piece of paper in her lap. "I knew. I kept it to myself as long as I could. I thought you might come back, but when you didn't, I...I had to do something. You understand? I had to protect Quentin. He needed a father, and I didn't know where you were."

Lonnie reached out to comfort her, but she pulled away. Her eyes grew hard as she threw off his hand. "I'm not some kind of trophy you can pass around. What's this, 'I bequeath you to Lonnie?' Harlan can't give me away! I don't belong to him, or to you, or to anyone!"

The limo pulled into the lane for unloading, and stopped at the curb. Lonnie sat back and bit his lip. He took a breath and let it out with a long slow sigh, allowing his head to fall back till it bounced off the cushion. It *was* too late. He had broken God's law, and there was a price to pay.

He looked over his shoulder. Frank was hefting pieces of luggage from the trunk onto the sidewalk. How would Quentin feel about his mother? She'd lied to him all these years. Did he even have to know? It was a question Lonnie didn't have to answer just now. He had time, lots of time. And from here on in, time was on his side.

He stretched the flexible band of Harlan's Rolex and slipped it from his wrist, setting it on the seat next to Trudy. "Thanks for the loan," he said. He stepped out of the car, closed the door, picked up his new green garment bag—and walked away.

EPILOGUE

FROM THE AIR the bush is so thick the ground is invisible to the naked eye. The rustling vegetation is a blanket that hides everything. Pushed by winds channeling up the valley, the jungle looks like sheets of green cotton flapping in a breeze. From the air, you can't see the village, but the birds know where it is. They sail down to where the sky touches earth at a mountain wall known as "The Inn."

Lonnie stands at the edge of the cliff, his body naked except for his briefs. He turns scratching his beard, his eyes following the slope upward until it disappears into the heavens. He can feel his hair resting on the back of his neck. He shades his eyes. From his vantage point, he cannot see Posada, though it is directly above him. He is much lower on the mountain, only a dozen feet above the ocean itself. He has come to bury the past. He has come to purge his soul and find release.

Harlan had grown up like his father: big and boisterous, and right about everything. He had good looks, money, and a white T-Bird with bucket seats. He had everything a young man could want—including Trudy! But what did it gain him in the end? Like everyone else, he was made of dust. *The Lord giveth and the Lord taketh away—blessed be the name of the Lord!*

Lonnie sips in his breath, half-wishing Trudy were there to see him. She's living the life—now in Spain—and still sober. Her postcards wish him well. She will return for their monthly board meeting, and see him then. It's better this way. You can't change the past—or blame others for its making.

Lonnie spreads his arms wide to the north and south, embracing the world. The sun sparkles on the surface of the blue-green water below. Today is a perfect day. On a day like this, he can do anything. He looks down and sees the white foam breaking on the rocks. A small rowboat sways back and forth on the tide. Paulo's hands work the oars, keeping it in position. The padre's upturned face beams like the sun, egging him on.

Lonnie smiles, and picks a spot where he knows the water runs deep. He sucks in his breath, closes his eyes, and leaps forward. For a second he is suspended in air. Then he feels the wind whipping his hair. He is aloft, arms spread like wings, graceful as a swan. He opens his eyes and sees the water rushing toward him, the vaulted blue of heaven mirrored in the sea.

Look For
Other Exciting Titles
By The Same Author

IF I SHOULD DIE

R.I.P.

KEITH CLEMONS

Deep in the secluded, pastoral green of Oregon's Emerald Valley, something strange is happening. People are beginning to disappear. Some claim their friends are being euthanized. Journalist, Laurie Best, called upon to secretly investigate allegations made against the suspect retirement home, isn't so sure. She's pro-choice. In her view, self-determination is a right, but the old folk's claim they're being put down without being asked, and that constitutes murder. Their stories seem credible, but they lack proof. It looks like Laurie will have to argue with the angel of death to determine if God alone has the right to decide who's to live—and who's to die.